NATURAL FATHER

Andy Knaggs

AN M-Y BOOKS PAPERBACK

© Copyright 2016
Andy Knaggs

The right of **Andy Knaggs** to be identified as the author of
This work has been asserted by him in accordance with the
Copyright, Designs and Patents Act 1988

A CIP catalogue record for this title is
available from the British Library

ISBN–978-1-911124-16-0

PROLOGUE

Well, well, well… would you look at that? It really was beautiful: beautiful enough to live for, beautiful enough to fight for; to die for even, if necessary. A butterfly, purple-winged and perfect, had landed just six or seven feet away from the man. He watched it, transfixed. It was a Purple Emperor. He knew that, and he knew exactly how unusual it was to see one up close. As he watched, the butterfly's wings fluttered briefly; they had white smudges on them, brilliant in the sunshine. The creature was busy feeding on something in the undergrowth. Oh, it was glorious… beautiful. He smiled.

Noiselessly, he turned his head to catch the eye of a companion behind him, wanting to share the moment. Nancy was closest to him, and he could tell by the expression of reverence on her face that she too had seen the Emperor. Sensing his gaze, Nancy reluctantly raised her eyes from the butterfly to acknowledge the wonder that had landed in their midst. She shook her head at him, mouthing a silent "Wow". Behind her, Liam grinned uncertainly. The man smiled and turned back to the butterfly.

Jesus, it was warm here. Shafts of sunlight burst through the canopy of beech leaves, casting dappled patterns of alternate dark and light on the woodland floor around the man. In his hand he held a saltshaker's worth of soil that he had scrabbled up from the ground. He crouched there and rolled the dirt between his fingers: sifting it; enjoying the contrast of dry, crusty surface grains with the darker, cooler stuff he'd prised from just below the surface. Tiny flecks of white betrayed the presence of chalk.

He listened to the sounds around him. It seemed so peaceful, so tranquil here, away from humans, but in reality he was surrounded by noise. Birds were having a riot high up in the branches, apparently competing in song. There was that special buzz all around that told of thousands of different insects, almost all unseen, going about their endless business: fetching, carrying, fussing in the heat. He fancied that if he were to click his fingers they would all cease their droning and he would hear the minute vibrations of the Purple Emperor's membrane-thin wings.

The butterfly shimmered in the barely discernible breeze. He watched for a few more seconds, hardly daring to breathe, before reluctantly deciding it must be time to get a move on. He heard whispers and low sniggers behind him, and then Nancy shushing whoever it was to silence. It was time to get his mind on the job. He let the handful of soil trickle back to refill the hole where he had scraped it up, but odd grains stuck to his palms, clammy with sweat. He brushed them off, and checked his watch. Any second now…

He glanced behind him, to left and right, and saw that everyone was there; everyone was watching him, crouching down and waiting for his signal to move. No one was sniggering now, not even Liam. Vince's face was grave, ashen, he observed; like a man who had gone for a pleasant walk in the woods and discovered a concentration camp. The analogy worked well, he thought. Vince would soon lighten up. Well, maybe.

The man squinted up to where, far above the forest floor, branches and leaves swayed gently in the breeze. He closed his eyes and composed himself; forced himself to breathe evenly and deeply. This was it. He raised his right arm so that everyone could see his signal. This was what it had come to. It was a beautiful day, and it felt good to be alive and free. As free as a butterfly… the perfect omen. The arm came down.

Then he was on his feet and running, heading for the treeline in front of him, and out of the corner of his eye he saw the Purple Emperor take sudden flight in a blur of frantic, panicked motion, the beginning of it all. Behind him the stamping, rustling footsteps, lots of them, told him that he was not alone. Sprinting fast and closing on the treeline… almost there… and no sooner had he thought that than he was bursting from cover into the glare of sunlight and destiny.

CHAPTER ONE

The dark-haired woman folded her arms and scowled across the desk at her managing director. "If that's the way it is, Richard," she said, more loudly than was necessary, "if you're not prepared to back me on this, then there's no point in me working here. I'll resign."

Richard Cambridge sat back in his chair, linked his hands behind his head and cleared his throat before he replied. The woman facing him was seething with anger. "Come on now, Kay, let's not get too dramatic about all this. You've only been here three weeks, for a start. You can't resign. I won't let you."

"But, Richard, you're not *letting* me do the job you asked me to do! That particular meeting is a key part of the whole campaign I'm putting together. We've got to reach out. Isn't that the point of the initiative?"

Kay Campbell, recently appointed Head of Public Affairs, challenged the head man at contract research company Maier Science, her new boss, with a defiant glare. He couldn't hide his amusement. He started chuckling, and that made Kay even angrier.

"Richard, don't just laugh at me! I'm trying my bloody best here to help you. I'm trying to do the job you employed me to do, and you're giggling like a silly bloody teenager. Stop it!"

Richard's mirth intensified. He hid his face in his hands as he laughed. Kay sat back and waited, counting quickly to ten but finding she needed to keep counting up to and beyond twenty, before Richard's red face finally emerged from behind his hands. She called him a bunch of names in her mind, but outwardly just bit her lip and stewed in her own indignation.

"Oh, Kay, you are priceless," he told her, still shaking with mirth. 'Listen, I'm sorry for laughing. I know you're doing a great job, and I understand that you want to prove yourself. I can assure you, you have my total respect and confidence, and this document is exactly what we need. Exactly what we need apart from one thing: I'm not going to meet with SMAC. Those parasites are not interested in finding out the truth. They've got their own agenda, and I'm not going to give them the satisfaction of acknowledging them."

"Well, I disagree with that strategy," Kay said pointedly. "I think you've got to meet them. If we're ever going to change the public perception of Maier's activities, then SMAC is where we need to start."

Richard smiled at her again, this time encouragingly. "Okay, then we'll have to agree to disagree on this, and you can view it as your personal challenge to try and change my mind. This will be fun! A clash of the Titans. But I'm willing to bet you won't have succeeded by Christmas. Shall we put a fiver on it?"

Kay sighed and fiddled with her pen, feeling up against it. Then she put down the pen, very deliberately on the desk, and looked up at her boss, poker-faced. "Make it a tenner and I'm in." She reached out her hand to shake on the arrangement, which he accepted with another laugh.

"No letter of resignation then?"

"No," she replied. "Not this time. But don't mess with me, Cambridge. I'm going to keep banging this drum, so you might as well get used to the noise. I'm a highly experienced professional, and I'm used to getting my own way."

"Kay, you are brilliant, but sometimes I do wonder whether you're even aware that I'm the boss here and you're not."

She pulled a face at that pointed comment, but acknowledged that he had pulled rank with tact and humour, which had to count for something. "Now let's wrap this up," Richard went on. "I've got to get away this evening to take Muriel out for dinner, and I have a mountain of work to shift before that."

Kay looked at her watch and reacted with surprise. "No way - it's gone four! Another nanny is coming round for an interview this evening, so I need to get away early."

They continued talking for ten minutes more, discussing various aspects of the campaign Kay had devised. Then she walked out to her car, drove through the security gate and set off for home.

As she drove, she thought over the meeting and the campaign that was her brainchild. It was a series of actions and initiatives designed with one purpose in mind: to improve the public perception of Maier Science, a company that ran a laboratory licensed to test potential new consumer products on animals.

Within Kay's campaign were outreach projects to bolster mutual communication and understanding with local civic heads, particularly in the nearby city of Salisbury: police chiefs, local media from TV, radio and newspapers, and public interest groups; there was also political lobbying, PR programmes, and plans to approach potential investors. The company website needed sprucing up too. In fact, Kay had argued, it needed hauling down and starting again from scratch.

There should be openness and engagement on all fronts and with all interested parties, even with SMAC – a four-letter acronym that stood for Stop Maier Animal Cruelty: a group of animal rights activists that had latched on to the company and its business activities, and now dogged its every move. The group maintained a semi-permanent picket in the woods across the road from Maier's facility, which, Kay had been shocked to discover, looked rather more like a prisoner-of-war compound than the clean, modern office complex she had been expecting. Fifteen-foot-high wire fences were topped with rolls of barbed wire all the way around the three-acre site. Access for staff and suppliers was through a security gate, manned by guards whose receding hairlines and expanding waistlines suggested their glory days were etched in history. The "gate" consisted of a solid iron bar that the security men raised and lowered by the press of a button in their small control hut. Stalag Luft 3, Nick had called it when they had first driven past Kay's new place of work. There were no machine gun towers visible, but it had been hard to disagree with him.

Thank God it was down a quiet country lane where most people would never see it, Kay had thought. Barbed-wire fences faced by huge banners proclaiming Maier Science to be animal-killing scum was not a promising image to work with, and had quickly brought the enormity of the task home to her. Still, that was why they were paying her so much money and, after all, her financial cut from her old partnership with Wilf at Palmerston PR would not last forever.

The banners and shouted insults of the protesters as Kay drove into and out of work most days were still unsettling, but she had only taken the job after receiving assurances that the SMAC allegations of animal cruelty were baseless. The challenge had energised her professionally, and she was enjoying being back at work after almost two years spent looking after her new pride and joy: Davy, the little boy she and Nick had brought into the world.

Motherhood, she found, had consumed her while at the same time nourishing her soul. She loved every moment of it. The first stumbling steps; the magic of the first word to cross Davy's lips; the feel and smell of his soft hair and skin; the giggles and the screams; the sleeping and the not sleeping.

When she'd found out that she was pregnant, back in the days when she'd lived in Hertford with her husband Lee and Nick was just a man she'd met in unusual circumstances, who had to be too good to be true, she had been terrified, for reasons she kept to herself. For years, she had fought Lee about parenthood. He had wanted children, she had wanted only her career, and it had driven a fatal wedge between them. But then Nick had come along, and in the sudden glowing turmoil of their lives being turned upside down, Kay had made a mistake with her contraceptive pills, and Davy was conceived. Somehow, knowing that the baby was Nick's, and not Lee's, had made all the difference.

Things had not been straightforward for Kay and Nick even so. As soon as she discovered she was pregnant, she had left the house in Hertford that she'd shared with her husband Lee – left it for good, she had decided right then. She had loaded her car with the clothes she wanted and driven to Nick's flat in Camden to break the joyous news to him. It was a drizzle-swept Tuesday evening and he had been out as it happened, following Lee and a friend of his all the way to Luton where he observed all that they did in the shadowy night-time streets.

Nick was acting at Kay's request. She had become suspicious of her husband's moods and behaviour so Nick had agreed to follow him, to find out what was going on. That turned out to be shocking. Poor Nick was a shoeshine man at Liverpool Street Station at the time, with no training whatsoever in undercover work. He found himself hiding in the dark recesses of a dingy alleyway as Lee and his companion, a young man named Billy, had tried to launch an attack on a Muslim man who was passing by. It all seemed to be carefully planned in advance but had gone horribly wrong when Nick's mobile phone had rung at the vital moment, just as Billy was about to strike their unwitting target. Confused by the ringtone coming from the shadows behind him, he had hesitated and the intended victim had taken his chance to counter-attack with a knife, leaving Billy stricken on the floor. No doubt hardly believing his luck, the Muslim man had taken flight, leaving a cowering Lee behind him.

Nick had run off too but in the opposite direction. He fled back to the station and got on the next train to London. He had told Kay everything when he returned to his flat later that evening to find her waiting, wet and windswept, by the front door, even though she might have sat in her car and kept dry. She hadn't been able to keep still, she was so keyed up. Nor could Nick – he was in bits and pieces about what he had just witnessed. What Lee had been involved in was a big surprise to Kay. He had no background in race hate, that she knew of.

They had talked long into that night. Nick had been so upset by what he had seen that he had even thrown his mobile phone away in disgust – hurled it without ceremony into the River Thames. But after all that drama, the news of Kay's pregnancy made him glow with delight.

She stayed at his, and the next day things quickly moved forward. Kay had taken time off from work so that she could find herself a new flat. Nick's was actually owned by his girlfriend, an Australian called Justine, who had been away in Melbourne visiting her hospitalised dad. Nick and Kay really needed to talk more, to spend time together and work things out, but there had been little opportunity for this so far. And then Justine had turned up the following night, hotfoot from Heathrow.

Kay and Nick were out at the time, viewing a property for Kay to move into. They drove back to the flat to discover the lights were on, which could only mean that Nick's girlfriend had come home. His shock at the discovery turned to blind panic when Kay reminded him that some of her possessions had been left lying around the flat – clothes, make-up, toiletries. Given that, and the obvious conclusion that Justine would come to, it was a surprise that Nick's clothes and possessions weren't already in a pile outside the front door. They drove around the corner, parked the car, and debated what their best course of action was. Should Nick go in now? Should he come back the next day? What was certain was that Kay would need somewhere else to sleep. She got on her phone to arrange a hotel room, and once that was booked they decided that Nick should go into the flat. Kay would wait for him in the car for two hours, after which she would go to the hotel where he would be able to find her once he had the chance.

Feeling sick with nerves, Nick summoned up the courage to let himself in. It was an understatement to say that Justine was angry. There were no pleasantries. She did virtually all the talking, in a very loud voice, hurt and anger etched into her face. She said she had been calling Nick repeatedly on his mobile, first before she had boarded the plane in Melbourne, then time after time upon reaching London. The first call had rung and rung before going to voicemail. That was the one that had reached Nick while he hid in the alleyway observing Lee and his friend, and had caused Billy to hesitate – and suffer the consequences. The later calls Justine had tried to make had not even got through to voicemail. It was as if the mobile had been destroyed, she said angrily. True enough, Nick acknowledged to himself – it was at the bottom of the Thames by then, and would remain there.

And then she had got home and had found another woman's clothes, another woman's moisturiser, another woman's bloody Veet, for Christ's sake, littering her flat! Unless Nick had turned into a tranny while she was away, she'd draw the inevitable conclusion. Nick was by then too shame-faced, too beaten down, to argue. The pain he saw in her eyes was only matched by his own guilt.

"You've got ten minutes to pack what you want to take, including all of that bitch's stuff, and then you can get the fuck out of here, and get the fuck out of my life!" Justine bawled at him. Then she had slumped down on the sofa and hidden her face as she wept. When Nick tried to touch her, to soothe her, to explain things to her, she rounded on him viciously and pushed him away. There was nothing to be done anyway; Kay was waiting for him outside. He packed some things and left, closing the door behind him with a heavy heart. He was appalled at himself and his own actions. He had never hurt anyone this much, he was certain of that.

Kay was waiting in the car, where she'd said she would be. They drove to the hotel in almost complete silence, both of them thinking about the enormity of this latest development: now they really were together, but what did they even know about each other? At the hotel they checked in, had a drink in the bar, and shared a few feelings and fears. Nick had been on the verge of tears since leaving Justine's, and Kay could see how badly shaken he was. It was no surprise when, after a couple of drinks, he had wanted to go upstairs and sleep.

That was exactly what they did until the morning light woke them hours later. Then they smiled at each other, heads close together on the pillows, and it felt like the first moment of the rest of their lives.

It still felt good now, more than two and a half years later, thought Kay, as she guided her Audi confidently around the winding country lanes between work and home. It had been the happiest time of her life. They had both needed to escape in some way, and so, later that day, they had jumped into Kay's car and driven away from London, having tied up some loose ends with their jobs. They had headed west from the M25, with Nick holding the roadmap and calling out suggestions for where they could stay.

Eventually, and for no particular reason other than the fact that neither of them had been there before, they decided they wanted to see Stonehenge. They took the A303 and Kay's car ate up the miles, leaving London and all it represented far behind. After the silence of the night before, laughter came easily to them – more and more easily, in fact, the farther they drove.

By the time they had reached the tourist attraction, the daylight was already starting to fade. There wasn't going to be much time to see Stonehenge and they were in the middle of Wiltshire, with nowhere to stay for the night. They drove slowly past the eerie stone circle, seeing knots of people standing and gazing at the powerful sarsens and lintels that rose out of the creeping gloom.

"Mmm... a pile of rocks," Nick muttered under his breath.

Kay giggled and slapped his arm playfully. "Don't be such a bloody philistine."

They headed for Salisbury to find a hotel, and ended up staying there for a week – sightseeing, walking the old streets of the city, marvelling at its cathedral, and falling in love with the nearby countryside, the rolling hills and valleys, the copses and hedgerows.

Halfway through the week, while enjoying the weak October sunshine outside a pub in the sleepy little village of Hindon – some twenty miles from Salisbury – after another day of peace and happiness, they decided to stay in Wiltshire for good. If possible in this village, with its two pubs, its church set halfway up the hill, and its air of complete seclusion from the rest of the world.

They went for a stroll down the hill, past cottages bearing quaint, sweet names such as Honeysuckle, Rose and Azalea; yellowing lime trees lined the pavement all the way down, and at the bottom they found a lane leading to a small school, with just beyond that a handful of bungalows set in a cul-de-sac. It was a picture of England in repose that Kay could only have dreamed of back in the hustle and bustle of London commuting. She wanted it for herself. She wanted to share her life with Nick and bring their child up here. They had nowhere else to go, and could put down roots wherever they chose. Nick hadn't needed much persuading. They were both enchanted and excited by the prospect.

It hadn't all been sweetness and light, though. The first night that they stayed in Salisbury, Kay had turned on her mobile phone. She had deliberately left it off for a couple of days, partly so that work queries wouldn't disturb them, and partly because the dark shadow of her husband Lee still hung over them.

She found many missed calls, voicemail and text messages waiting for her, mostly from Lee, but also from her old business partner Wilf, warning her that her husband had been calling the office continually. It was a sobering reminder of the world they had left behind and from which they were not yet free, wherever they ran to hoping to start a new life. Kay shared a mortgage and a joint bank account with Lee, although she had her own money as well. She was more than happy for him to keep the house, since she had no intention of returning to it anyway. She didn't want anything from Lee, in fact.

She decided on the spur of the moment to call him and tell him this. It would be the last time she would use the mobile phone. It was on a contract from the office anyway, but she would switch it off again immediately after speaking to Lee and then return it to Wilf. She took some time to write down a bunch of important phone numbers from the Contacts list, then jotted down a few thoughts as she composed herself. She called her husband's number while Nick watched. Lee answered very quickly.

"Kay, thank God..."

"Lee, listen: I'm not coming back. It's over. I've met someone else, and I won't be on this number again. You can keep the house and everything else. I don't really care. Goodbye."

And that was it. She had hung up, switched the mobile off, and tossed it onto the bed by Nick's feet.

"Done and dusted, babe," she'd said, bending down to kiss her new man. Nick was slightly perturbed by what had just happened, and over the next few days it ate away at him. Kay seemed to imagine that uttering that brusque farewell, getting rid of her mobile phone and job, and setting up home with him in Wiltshire, was all that was required; that they would both live happily ever after with their baby. Nick saw it slightly differently, though: wasn't she going to divorce Lee? It wasn't a clean break if she was still married to him. Kay was uncertain about the technicalities, and didn't want to enter into any sort of negotiations that would let Lee know where they were. She was running away from it all, Nick told her. She was vehement about her decision, however.

"I never want to see him again, and I don't want him to know where I am. The only thing that matters now is us," she said.

For the time being, they had agreed to let that situation lie. There was enough to do anyway: finding a flat to rent in or around Salisbury while they looked for something more permanent; contacting various financial organisations of which Kay was a client, either to cancel payment arrangements or to get communications placed on hold until they had a new address; and finding employment for them both.

That all seemed a long time ago now. They had got lucky with the house-hunting and snared a big dormer bungalow they had seen in Hindon almost as soon as it came onto the market early in 2008, just three months before Davy was born. By that time, Kay had come to an arrangement with Wilf back at Palmerston PR. She had received a substantial lump sum that represented half of her stake in their business. The rest he would pay her over a period of two years in the form of a monthly retainer. Kay became, in effect, Palmerston PR's office in the West Country. She even picked up some new clients to add to the firm's portfolio.

As for Nick, they had decided that he should be free to start afresh in whatever job took his fancy. There was no pressure. It was an opportunity to do something interesting or different, something that made him happy – even if the money wasn't amazing. In his past working life he'd been in banking and then, after some hard times, had started getting himself back on his feet as a shoeshiner. That was how Kay had met him, when Nick had cleaned her husband's shoes for him while the warring couple argued at Liverpool Street Station one morning in 2007.

Nick wasn't going back to either of those jobs, that much he knew. The fire of ambition did not burn bright within him; he was unclear what he wanted to do next. The answer came unexpectedly. He had joined a temping agency, and for a few months did spells of office work. He hated it. He hated being in an office, and he hated most of the people he had to work with. To his way of thinking they took themselves far too seriously.

He also did some bar work in Salisbury, and it was while pulling pints one evening, with Kay sitting at the bar to keep him company, that the pair of them got talking to a friendly older couple who had frequented the pub several times before while Nick was working. The man's name was Jerry, his wife's Lorna. He had a smiling, weather-beaten, craggy face, making him look older than his alleged age of forty-eight. She was a petite blonde, laughing often and mostly deferring to Jerry, whom she obviously adored. They seemed a sweet and contented couple.

It turned out that Jerry worked as a landscape gardener. He had been doing it for years, and ran his own business. But he wasn't getting any younger, and it was getting more and more tiring doing the heavy lifting and the digging that was part of the job. Nick happened to mention that he was trying to decide on a new line of work, and quite fancied something outdoors.

This was in February 2008, not long before Kay and Nick moved from their rented flat into the bungalow in Hindon. Outside the pub, the rain was pouring down. They had been talking for only half an hour or so, but Kay had been intrigued to see how well Nick and Jerry were getting along. Already they were taking the mickey out of each other.

"Outdoors, eh, fella? You reckon you could you work in that sort of outdoors?" Jerry gestured with his thumb towards the window, where rivulets of rainwater were streaming down to run off the windowsill and drip onto the cobbled stones of the marketplace outside. Jerry was chuckling as he said it and he looked Nick squarely in the eye, awaiting the answer.

Nick didn't back down. "Yeah, that wouldn't bother me at all. Why don't I come and help you out tomorrow, old fella? I can push your wheelbarrow for you."

Jerry pretended to be taken aback. Turning to his wife, he muttered, "How about that then, bloody Cockneys, eh?" Then he smiled back at Nick. "Okay, young man. I'll take you up on that. I'll show you what a proper day's bloody work is."

Much laughter and verbal jousting later, Jerry and Lorna prepared to head out into the continuing downpour, and it was settled: Jerry would pick Nick up at 6 a.m. the following morning, and take him out working for the day.

"And six o'clock is a bloody lie-in for me, boy, I tell you," was Jerry's parting shot.

"I've had worse, Jerry. I'll be ready," Nick had promised.

And it turned out that he loved it. The weather was filthy that first day, but the work was honest and fulfilling, and he and Jerry got on famously. They laughed a lot and made good progress with their work. Nick showed some aptitude for the job and soon it became a regular thing, three days a week at first. Then Jerry calculated that, with Nick's help, he could take on more work, and actually give Nick full-time employment. For his part, Nick enrolled in a local college to study for a BTEC qualification in horticulture as soon as he was able. Soon after that, Nick and Kay moved into their dream house, and soon after *that* Davy was born, before Nick's disbelieving eyes, in the Maternity Unit of Salisbury District Hospital.

Whenever she thought of it, Kay would still beam at the joy and wince at the pain of that day, and she did so again as the car swept around the last corner and entered the village of Hindon. She would be home within a minute. So much for slowing down the pace of life here in Wiltshire, Kay thought: she needed to pop over to old Mrs O'Neill's to pick up Davy, then drive Nick over to Salisbury, where he was going to a snooker hall with Jerry and a couple of other men; then back home in time for 6.30 p.m. when there was a new girl coming round to be interviewed for the position of part-time nanny to Davy. Jemima, her name was. Jemima Bond. It was a good name, and Nick and Kay had laughed about it when Jemima had first responded to the advert, Nick going into one of his flights of fancy about her being the sister of secret agent James Bond, and cracking a bunch of corny jokes to that effect. I mean, Double-O Three and a Half? Please...

Someone had to be called Jemima Bond, Kay had supposed out loud, trying to stop herself from laughing and drag the conversation back into the grown-up sphere; Bond was a fairly common surname, she said, and Jemima was a pretty name, kind of doll-like. Kay wondered what this Jemima Bond looked like, and whether she would live up to Nick's expectations for a beautiful but deadly secret agent.

Well, she thought, turning left past the pub, on to the High Street, and heading downhill past the pollarded lime trees and chocolate-box cottages towards School Lane and their home, soon enough she would find out.

***

A little boy sat playing with his toys on the living-room floor; his mother, sat on the sofa, watching him with proud and adoring eyes.

Moments like this were wonderful for Kay; moments when she felt truly blessed. There were others that she and Nick shared, such as their eyes meeting and expressing, without words, exactly how lucky they knew they were. Her work was done for the day, but with Nick out for the evening, it was just Kay and her son tonight, having quality time together.

She sipped her red wine and smiled to see Davy's serious expression. He got so caught up in things; in his endless curiosity he wanted to know everything, touch everything... and break most things. Sometimes, when he needed help with whatever had grabbed his attention, he would look up at her with imploring brown eyes, forehead furrowed. Usually he would utter just two plaintive words – "Mummy, come" – and Kay's heart would melt all over again.

He was happy at the moment, though, wearing his favourite outfit – Woody the cowboy from the *Toy Story* movies – and singing a nonsensical little ditty of half-formed or made up words to himself as he scribbled in a drawing pad. Toys and crayons and bits of colourful bric-a-brac littered the carpet around Kay's feet, and had been spread around every corner of the room in Davy's pursuit of fun. He was doubly excited tonight as well, because Kay had told him that a woman was coming to meet him – a woman who would look after him when Mummy went out to work during the day. Only if Davy and Mummy liked her though, Kay had assured him.

Jemima Bond was due to arrive at any minute now. She would not be the first nanny Nick and Kay had tried, and that caused Kay to feel a little nervous.

The last one, Chantelle, had not worked out well. She was a young girl who lived in the village, the daughter of a couple Nick and Kay had met in their local. She had just left school after taking her A-levels and was looking to earn a little money before going to university. She proved to be apathetic about her duties, however, and her conversational range didn't seem to extend far beyond what had happened on *The X Factor.*

Then one day Chantelle turned up late, causing Kay to be late for work. Worse, Kay could smell alcohol on the girl's breath. That was the end of that. So Nick and Kay had decided to advertise for a new nanny, and it had taken a few weeks before a CV turned up from the soon-to-arrive Jemima Bond. She seemed to have relevant qualifications and experience, which was more than could be said for Chantelle, and nobody else had applied, so Kay had called her and fixed up a meeting.

It was another fine day in late June and the patio doors were open, allowing a welcome breeze into the house. Outside, hardly a voice or a car engine interrupted the quiet in this secluded corner of the village. Given Nick's developing fondness for horticulture, the back garden was too small really, as was the bungalow itself. They would need more space as Davy grew up.

Kay heard a car pull up outside and went to look out of the kitchen window, taking her glass with her. A yellow convertible VW Beetle had stopped immediately behind her black Audi. The hood of the Beetle had been down but was now sliding back into place over the top of the car. Kay couldn't see anyone in the driving seat at first but then a couple of seconds later a figure popped up into view – she must have been reaching down to pick something up off the floor of the car, Kay thought. All she could see at this point, though, was long, dark hair tied neatly in plaits and topped by a jaunty brown suede cap. The Beetle driver then pressed a mobile phone to her right ear and spent a few moments speaking. After finishing the call, she swung the door of the VW open.

A slim young lady wearing black-rimmed glasses was revealed. She was dressed in a light blue denim shirt hanging loose over black leggings and white plimsolls. She swung a patchwork corduroy bag onto her right shoulder, then looked around briefly before appraising the door of Kay's house and starting to walk up the path, past Nick's red Alfa Romeo on the drive. Kay watched her for another second, taking in a few more details: a narrow, plain, serious face that was still girlish – as if there remained some living to be done yet, a hardening of her skin and muscles, a little definition. This wasn't yet the face of the woman she would be – though Jemima was twenty-five, according to the CV she had emailed. The expression she wore was impassive, regarding Nick's car with an air of cool detachment as she passed it. There was just a flicker of acknowledgement towards the face watching her from the kitchen window as she approached the front door.

"Guess what, Davy darling – your new friend Jemima is here," Kay called, rushing back through to the living room.

Davy looked up, beaming his gap-toothed grin. He clambered to his feet and was off towards the front door at a trot, his toys forgotten. Kay put her glass of wine down on the table next to the sofa, and hurried after him. They reached the door at the same moment, just a second after the girl outside had rang the doorbell. Kay helped her little boy to pull the door open.

The smile that greeted them both was striking. The young lady Kay had watched get out of the VW Beetle and walk up the garden path had looked a little apprehensive perhaps, but this new girl was someone that Kay wouldn't have hesitated to put in front of clients back in her London PR days. They would have been eating out of the palm of her hand in minutes. Jemima had a face full of freckles, Kay saw; a face that now brimmed with energy and enthusiasm as she fixed her grey-blue eyes first on Davy and then on Kay.

"Hello, Mrs Campbell, I'm Jemima. Pleased to meet you."

She extended a hand to Kay. The handshake did not match the smile for dynamism or conviction, Kay noted, the fingers hanging limply in her hand. Jemima rapidly broke contact and fixed her attention back on Davy.

"He's going to be a heart-breaker, isn't he?" she enthused. "Hello, Davy!"

"He certainly is," Kay responded, trying to match her smile. "Davy, say hello to Jemima." He had gone shy, and was hugging Kay's left leg.

"Hello, Yemima," he said in a small, bashful voice.

The two women laughed. "Please come in, Jemima – if I can just prise this kid off my leg," Kay said with obvious effort. It was hard, with Davy gripping her leg, for her to open the door fully so that Jemima could step inside. They laughed again as Kay, with difficulty, dragged away her leg, little boy attached, to make room. The door swung fully open and Jemima stepped forward as Kay scooped Davy up in her arms and walked towards the living room, calling over her shoulder for Jemima to come through.

As she entered the living room, Jemima exclaimed, "Oh, such a beautiful house." Kay beckoned her to sit down and they took seats, Kay on the sofa and Jemima in the armchair by the living-room door. Now each could size up the other properly for the first time. Davy seemed struck dumb and was standing behind his mum's legs, just in case a barrier was necessary between himself and this newcomer. Probably the smile had dazzled him too, Kay thought. For now, the boy sucked his thumb and looked at Jemima with a mixture of fascination and uncertainty.

"Can I get you a drink of something? Tea? Coffee? Wine?" Kay asked brightly.

"No, I'm fine Mrs Campbell, thanks..."

"Call me Kay – please." A pause then: "Actually, I'm not really a Mrs Campbell. That's my maiden name. I used to be a Talbot... long story..." Kay raised her eyebrows as if to establish it would be ill advised to make her tell that story. Jemima just smiled and showed no sign of wanting her to do so. She waited.

"Well, anyway..." said Kay. She turned and grabbed some sheets of A4 paper that had been next to her glass of wine on the dining table. "So, I've read your CV. You're twenty-five and you live in Salisbury; you've got an NVQ in Children's Care, Learning and Development, and your driving licence is full and clean. There's obviously much more to Jemima Bond than two sheets of paper, though, isn't there? Tell me how you got into child care."

Jemima's grey-blue eyes had been restless, darting around the room a little tentatively, taking in her new surroundings. Now she turned her attention back to Kay and her son. Her face really was quite freckly, Kay thought, and the black-rimmed glasses made her look... bookish. Was that the word?

"Yes, I've been looking after toddlers since I was ten," said Jemima. She didn't speak with the local West

Country burr to her voice, Kay noticed. A glance down at the CV reminded her that Jemima was an Oxfordshire girl. "My parents had a car accident the year after my brother Josh came along. We lost Daddy, and Mummy was confined to a wheelchair."

"Oh, I'm sorry. That must have been terrible for you."

"Well, yes… it was really hard, but you get used to these things. Anyway, because of that I had to look after Josh from an early age, and I found that I loved it. It's such a magical thing, watching babies grow and learn."

Kay was touched by Jemima's story, and part of the reason was that she had not seen her own father for years – since around the time she had settled down with Lee, in fact. He was, so far as Kay knew, still living on the same rough housing estate in South London where she had grown up, and still frittering away his days on booze, fags and horses, she supposed. She felt an ache of guilt that she didn't even know that much.

Jemima was still speaking. "When I got the chance I studied child care at college, and since then I've worked with a few different families – agency work mainly. But I'm looking for something a bit longer term."

"Yes, the agency – is that where you know this person Sarah Sykes from? The one you put down as a referee. I wondered about that. Couldn't find the agency on a Google search and the number on the form was unobtainable for some reason when I tried it."

"Oh, really? That's odd. Well, I know that Sarah left them soon after I signed off. We kept in touch, though, and she knows me really well."

"Okay, well, I haven't got round to writing to her yet – been so busy with work that I keep forgetting. I hope you don't mind, but I jotted down a few questions to ask you. I've never really interviewed for a nanny before, so if it's okay…"

"No problem Mrs Cam… sorry, Kay. That's what we're here for, I guess." Jemima smiled reassuringly.

Kay had flipped over one of the sheets of paper to reveal some handwritten notes. She drank some of her wine, put the glass back on the dining table, and then smoothed Davy's brown hair affectionately with the now-free hand. He remained by his mother's knees, still looking at Jemima with awed interest.

"I think he likes you," Kay said. Jemima unleashed that smile again. "I've never seen him so quiet," Kay went on. "Maybe you should move in full-time!"

Both women laughed, and Davy, aware of being the centre of attention again, blushed like mad. "You gone all shy, darling," Kay cooed.

"He's gorgeous – you're so lucky," said Jemima. Kay told the boy to go and shake their new friend's hand and say hello. He did so at the second time of urging, reluctantly at first, but when he reached Jemima he threw his hands round her neck and kissed her, wetly and clumsily, on the cheek. Then he mumbled "hello", and settled against her arm, resting his head there, cheeky and possessive now while his mum looked on fondly. As for Jemima, she looked enraptured by the match-winning approval she had apparently already pulled off.

"Well, I'm wondering whether I even need to ask you all these questions," said Kay waving her notes, "since the boss has clearly made his decision already. Congratulations!"

She reached over to shake Jemima's hand, laughing as she did so, but though she didn't refer back to her list of questions, the interview wasn't quite over. Kay wanted to get to know this young lady a little better, to cement the favourable impression left on her so far.

"So what made you move to Salisbury, Jemima?"

"My boyfriend – well, he didn't make me, but I wanted to be with Stuart."

"Oh, right – so you live together?"

"Yes. He studied at Oxford – that's how I met him – and then he got a job here, so I moved to be with him."

"Ooh, sounds serious. Do I hear wedding bells?" Kay drained the rest of her wine. She looked up again, smiling, only to see that Jemima seemed suddenly hesitant.

After a second or two of visibly wrestling with the words, she replied wistfully: "Well, I hope so – but you know: men." Almost instinctively she gave Davy a little squeeze on the shoulder, as if to mark him out as a future exception.

Kay could sympathise. She said: "Yeah, not half. My husband Lee was a git, but I'm very happy with Nick now. You must meet him sometime – well, of course you will, when you start. He's out playing snooker at the moment."

"You're not married, though, are you?" asked Jemima, happier not to be talking about herself.

"No, not yet; I'm still married to Lee even though I left him more than two and a half years ago." Kay hesitated before confiding: "He doesn't know where I am."

"Oh my God! That's amazing." Jemima raised her fingertips to cover her mouth in a show of disbelief.

"I'll sort it out one day," Kay laughed. "Anyway, I must just get a quick refill." She took her empty wine glass from the table, rose from the sofa and walked through to the kitchen. Jemima turned to smile at Davy, who was still standing by her side. It was the first time that she and the boy had been alone together.

"I must say, I do like your cowboy outfit, Davy. Are you the sheriff?"

"I'm Woody! Snake in my boot!"

The two of them giggled as Kay re-entered the living room carrying her glass and the bottle of wine, half-full. Davy reached up and pulled Jemima's cap from her head, cramming it on his own in place of his cowboy hat. It covered his face, causing more giggling. "So," Kay said brightly, intent on a fresh start, and remembering a key question from the hand-written list that she had put aside some minutes before, "what sort of food will you prepare for Davy?" It struck her that she had said the word *will*, rather than *would*, as if it had become a fait accompli that Jemima had the job already.

The girl quickly had her business head back on too. "I love cooking actually, so I could do lots of things. I could make a nice little Shepherd's Pie with fresh vegetables. And I remember Josh always used to love the sausage casserole I did for him. I assume you would want a balance of meat and veg, really?"

Kay had sat back down on the sofa, and was pouring herself some more wine. "Yes, that sounds very good," she said, placing the bottle on a coaster on the dining table. "And how well do you know this area? My little boy needs to be entertained, not to mention worn out, during the day!"

"I've thought about that," replied Jemima. "I mean, I'm still getting to know it really, but I did some research on the internet. I wondered if Davy likes animals? There are a few places like Longleat, and a farm near Swindon where you can get close to the animals and learn about them. If the weather is nice that could be fun. Also there's a wildlife rescue centre in Salisbury, and lots of parks and playgrounds. We could even have a picnic by the cathedral. I made a list of ideas anyway."

At this, Jemima took a folded piece of paper from her bag and handed it over to Kay. There was a good list of places to go to and things to do typed upon it – enough to reach on to the other side of the sheet. Kay was impressed. There was too much information on it for her to study in detail right now, so she folded it back up and put it on the sofa beside her, voicing her thanks.

Kay continued to pick out questions from her own list, enquiring about Jemima's disciplinary views, what she most enjoyed about looking after young children, what skills she had learned on her NVQ course, and the ticklish matter of salary. Everything was talked through satisfactorily and Kay felt herself relaxing a little. This was an intense young lady – Kay felt she was constantly being scrutinised – but Jemima seemed nice enough and she certainly seemed to know her stuff. Davy was quite attached to her already, which was the most important thing. Nick would be pleased.

"It's Davy's second birthday in the middle of July. We're hoping to do a little party and get some of the local toddlers to come over. It would be great if you could help me with getting that together in the run up to it," said Kay.

Jemima nodded and said that she would love to. She had a query of her own too. "Can I ask, does Davy have any grandparents?"

Kay grimaced slightly. "Not really," she began, before pausing to gather herself. "Neither of Nick's parents is around now, and I lost my mum years ago as well. Dad is up in London somewhere as far as I know, but we fell out when I got married to Lee and we haven't spoken since."

"Oh, I see. Well, that's a shame. I always think it's a lovely thing for children to have elderly people in their lives to look up to. But if they're not around, they're not around."

Kay could only shrug. Thinking about her dad made her feel guilty. She looked at Davy, who was entertaining himself by spinning Jemima's cap around on his head. It really was too complicated to explain the story about her dad, the hurt he had caused, and the things he had said. Kay felt her eyes welling up and glanced away, out of the patio doors, to conceal it. Looking out at the garden, it suddenly struck her as an excellent change of subject. "Come and see our garden, Jemima," she insisted with a smile. "Do you like to be called Jemima by the way, or do you prefer something shorter?"

"Jemima is good."

"Okay. Come and see out here. It's Nick's pride and joy."

Kay took up her glass of wine and led the way through the open patio doors. The early-evening warmth hit them as they reached the threshold and halted there. A sweet, heady scent filled their nostrils. Nearest to the house, the garden had a curved border full of yellow and red flowers, leading to dark pinks, then pale blues, purples and lighter pinks furthest away. In the far left corner was a weeping crab apple tree, its purplish foliage drooping earthwards, and in the far right corner a rocky water feature gurgled down to a pond. Small piles of rocks, the same as those in the rock cascade, were dotted around the flower beds.

At the door Davy stood by Kay's side and started pulling at her jeans, saying, "Mummy, play." Kay stroked his hair, but said, "Not now, darling, Mummy's talking to Jemima. We'll play in a minute." He was obviously feeling a bit neglected. Jemima stood next to Kay, scanning the garden from crab apple tree to water feature.

"It's a bit small for what Nick wants to do with it," Kay went on enthusiastically. "I think he'd quite like a football pitch so he can kick a ball around with Davy without smashing the flowers to bits – but it's just beautiful, don't you think? I can never remember all the names, but over there we've got some foxgloves… Digitalis something or other; here there are hollyhocks and poppies; those blue ones there are forget-me-nots, the pink ones are called Candytuft… can't remember what those purple ones are. There are some lovely red roses there. The tree is called Royal Beauty – I chose that – isn't it just gorgeous? We'll get some amazing dark red apples from that in the autumn, but they'll be too sour to eat, I think.

"Nick made the rock feature and the pond all by himself, would you believe? Mind you, it took him weeks to get it done! We've really taken to pottering about at weekends – spend hours out here with Davy. I try to help Nick, but I've never really done any gardening before. We haven't finished yet, though. He wants to put in some decking and we want..."

There was a sudden flurry of movement to Kay's right and a cry of: "Davy, no!"

She was startled from her horticultural exposition to discover that Jemima was no longer beside her. She had dashed the two or three yards back inside the front room to the dining table, and Kay now saw what had happened. Jemima had Davy in one arm, and the bottle of wine in the other; Davy, looking both guilty and confused, had both hands full of tablecloth. Only the timely arrival of Jemima had stopped him from accidentally pulling the wine bottle down onto either him or the carpet.

"Oh my God," Kay exclaimed, rushing over to grab hold of her son, who was close to tears.

"I'm sorry, Mrs Campbell, I saw Davy tugging the cloth and the bottle was about to fall, but luckily I just got here in time," said Jemima, now relinquishing her hold on Davy as his mother took control. Kay picked him up and held him close as tears started falling.

"No, please, don't apologise. I should be thanking you for acting so quickly. I can't believe I was rabbiting away about the bloody garden and not paying attention to what Davy was up to. Now, now, baby. It's okay. No harm done. Now, now."

Kay paced the room from side to side, comforting the boy, watched by Jemima who, having performed her good deed, now didn't seem to know what to do with herself. Somewhat gingerly, she put the wine bottle back onto its coaster on the table and stood there awkwardly, a slightly uneasy expression on her face. Kay thought she knew why.

"I want you to know that I don't make a habit of leaving bottles of wine around for Davy to grab hold of. I usually just have one glass when I get home from work, and the bottle stays in the kitchen out of his reach.

"It's okay, Mrs Campbell. Accidents happen. No harm done."

"Well, accidents like this shouldn't happen. I guess I just got carried away and wasn't thinking. It won't happen again. You must think I'm a terrible mum."

"Not at all, no. Really... don't worry about it."

The boy was still grizzling. "He'll be all right," said Kay, patting his back. "He likes a little cuddle from time to time, you'll find – don't you, Davy darling?"

They sat down again and chatted while Davy recovered from his misadventure. Soon he was sufficiently recovered to detach himself from his mother, and within minutes he and Jemima were giggling together as they played with his toys on the floor. Kay smiled with relief and took the offending wine bottle back to the kitchen.

"Davy, my favourite little cowboy," she called, walking back into the front room, "you can play for another twenty minutes with Jemima and then it's bath time and beddy-byes."

CHAPTER TWO

Gorgeous oranges and golds marked the evening sun's final slide towards the horizon as Jemima Bond pulled up outside the second house she needed to visit that night. The text message had arrived from Stuart just before she had left Kay and Davy at about 7.45: *Meet round Nancy's place at 9, urgent stuff.* Yeah, right, Jemima thought, whatever. She had some interesting news of her own to deliver about the woman she had spent the last hour or so with.

After a quick bite to eat back at the flat, she set off for Nancy's house in Coombe Bissett, along the A354 from Salisbury. It was just after 9 p.m. when she knocked on Nancy's front door. Nancy Jennings herself opened it a few seconds later. She had greying shoulder-length hair and laughing eyes, and a brisk, busybody nature that quickly switched to stoic determination when it suited her.

"Ah, the latecomer graces us with her presence," said Nancy airily, before turning away and leaving Jemima to close the door behind her. She felt a familiar tightening in her stomach. Nervous, anxious, inferior – that was how Nancy usually made her feel. There were other voices coming from further inside the house, and Jemima walked through to a front room that was crowded with seven other people.

"At last! How did it go? Get the job?" asked the bearded man reclining in an armchair by the door. He spoke with an understated Scottish accent, and though his blue eyes appeared amused, his tone of voice gave every indication of serious interest.

"Yes, I did. I start next week," replied Jemima from the doorway. "I laid it on thick and the bitch believed every word of it. I just about stopped myself from scratching her eyes out. Aren't I a good girl?"

"Bravo," said Nancy from the sofa, where she had resumed her previous seat. There was a general murmur of approval from the other people present, four men apart from the bearded Scot, and one other woman besides Nancy.

"Awesome! Bloody awesome," the bearded man continued. His beard was insubstantial: a thin strip of brown hair tracing his jawline and a wispy moustache over his top lip. The hair on his head was only a little longer and receding above each temple. "Now grab a seat, we want to get cracking."

There was nowhere to sit, apart from on the floor. Jemima moved uncertainly towards the window opposite the bearded man, hoping that one of the men would do the gentlemanly thing and vacate a seat. No such luck. It wasn't surprising, though, bearing in mind that Pippa Babcock, the third woman present, was also sitting on the floor, leaning back against her husband Vince's legs. He was blissfully comfortable, the ignorant bugger, sitting on the sofa next to Nancy. Jemima flung herself down and sat with her back uncomfortably against a wall. She looked back at the man with the beard.

"I've found some stuff out already, Stu. We could really screw with this woman's head," Jemima said.

"Yeah, later, Jemmy," said Stuart McCormack, somewhat dismissively. Most people called him Mac; Jemima was one of the very few who still used his first name.

"No, listen to me, guys," she protested. "I've got her husband's name – she lives with another man that she had the baby with – and her husband doesn't…"

"Jemima, later! This is more important. Now, everyone – this here is Barry. He's got something to show us that we will all be very interested in," said Mac.

Jemima noticed for the first time a scruffy looking man with narrow eyes and greasy black hair sitting close to Stuart. She also noticed Nancy looking at her reprovingly. She had been shouted down and it gave Jemima a familiar sinking feeling. Naughty Jemima, silly Jemima, shut up, Jemima, later, later, later. Fuck, fuck, fuck, why would no one listen to her? It was infuriating. She bit her lip as the man called Barry started to speak.

"Shall I just go straight into it, Mac, or…?"

"Yeah go for it, pal. The floor is all yours." Mac waved a hand casually.

"Okay. Well, Mac got in touch with me through ALF about six months ago," Barry said. His voice was deadpan, the accent from the north-west of England, Manchester kind of way. "My background is in science, you see, and that was important. What we wanted to do was get someone into Maier, to see exactly what was happening in there and get some film of it so you guys can nail these fuckers for good. So, to cut a long story short, I've been working in the lab there with a concealed camera, and what you're about to see is the result of that."

Barry had been looking around at the other occupants in the room – all strangers to him – as he spoke. Now he turned back to Stuart McCormack: "Shall I run it, Mac?"

"Be my guest, pal."

Barry pointed a remote control towards the widescreen TV and DVD player that was in the corner next to Jemima, and the screen flickered on. There were a few seconds of black screen with a digital countdown in the top left-hand corner, 5, 4, 3, 2, 1... then the pictures began.

Within seconds the footage drew outcry from around the room. They saw a row of beagles, half a dozen small dogs, each trussed up in some kind of harness, each with its snout covered by a conical mask with tubes protruding from the end. The doleful-eyed dogs were in various stages of distressed collapse, a couple wilting alarmingly. A low voice spoke over the pictures – recognisably the voice of Barry – explaining that the dogs were being tested with a perfume that was to be used in a cleaning product. He added that there should have been technicians comforting the dogs throughout this ordeal, but the manager and the other technician were in an adjacent room playing cards.

The camera then went with its operator through to that room, where two men wearing blue overalls were sitting at a table, doing just as Barry had said: one studying a hand of cards, the other looking up at Barry as he entered. Again Barry's voice could be heard as he stopped in the doorway. In a louder voice than his previous commentary, he addressed the man who had looked up. The words rang out around Nancy's front room: "What's going on, George? Shouldn't we be looking after these little guys out here?"

There was the sound of laughter from the table, and "George" smiled towards the camera that he didn't know was there: "Chill out, Bazza. How many more times, mate? They'll be over and done with soon." After a pause he added: "Anyway, I'm busy fleecing knob head here. Why don't you go and stroke the little fuckers for me?" Another burst of laughter from the second character at the table, and the camera turned back towards the row of dogs as Barry exited the room, leaving the card-playing technicians to their game. He uttered a low-pitched expletive.

There was then an obvious edit in the footage as the picture cut to another view of the dogs, two of which seemed to have passed out or maybe worse. Jemima felt tears welling in her eyes. Mac, sitting forward in his chair, stroking his beard, gave vent to a few expletives of his own.

Another scene showed a different technician roughly disciplining a dog. From the sofa, Barry provided a comment: "This guy is called Lewis Leathbridge – complete scumbag. He does this kind of shit all the time."

There were further scenes showing animals such as rats, mice and rabbits being subjected to inhalation toxicology treatment. The footage was all over in six or seven minutes of what was at times poorly focused and barely audible video. The point it illustrated was crystal clear though: this company, Maier Science, was testing a range of chemicals on innocent animals, and doing so in ways that went against the most basic tenets of civilised behaviour towards animals, not to mention defined codes of professional ethics.

Jemima felt sick. She looked around at her companions. Pippa had tears rolling down her cheeks, while the face of her husband Vince was working with fury. Mac looked glum; Nancy, grim and tight-lipped. Barry used the remote control to switch the TV off. Silence fell for a few seconds as everyone reflected on what they had just seen.

Vince Babcock broke the silence. "This is just what we need. Stick that on the telly and their arses will be toast. Banks, insurance companies, clients, shareholders – you name it, they'll drop Maier like a hot potato. We've got the bastards."

He smiled triumphantly around the room. It was a rare thing to see, Jemima mused silently – Vince actually grinning from ear to ear. He was usually carping on about something, either a decision that Stuart had made or at poor, oppressed Pippa, just because she was there. Jemima disliked Vince with some intensity, for both those reasons. Still sulking at the way that Stu had batted her revelation about Kay aside without even hearing it, Jemima waited for him to respond now to what Vince had said. He would disagree for some reason, and Nancy would side with Stuart. That was how SMAC meetings generally unfolded.

"Aye, it's useful stuff, Vince, but we can't take this to the media," said Mac, leaning forward in a thoughtful pose. "They would want to know how we did it and why we didn't get their journalists involved so they could shoot the footage themselves. This isn't the smoking gun they would want. But there's an opportunity to change things with this, and we should do it ourselves."

"That's bollocks, Mac, we've..."

"Vincent, how many more times do I have to tell you? Watch your language in my house," Nancy rebuked him sharply. Vince made a face at her.

"We're all grown-ups, Nance. Anyway, it doesn't change the fact that this is our chance to bury these filth bags for good. We mustn't waste this opportunity," Vince insisted.

"You haven't even listened to my bloody suggestion yet, Vince," Mac countered evenly. "Give me a chance, for Pete's sake."

"Perhaps that's because I know it's going to be a load of naïve, idealistic bullshit," Vince answered, looking pointedly at Nancy after speaking the final word. Now Pippa spoke up.

"Vince, please… why can't we just talk about this reasonably? Why does it always have to be you and Mac arguing?"

Vince gave his wife an unmistakably displeased look. Then another of the men present, an Indian in his late thirties called Bhupathi, spoke calmly into the silence. "Well, let's hear it, Mac. We all want the same thing, and that's to bring these Maier criminals down." After a pause he added: "We're all getting tired of pussy-footing around."

Mac turned his hands, palms upward, towards his audience. "It's simple: we keep the TV option up our sleeve. We take this evidence in to show Maier and hit them with it; we get the police involved, maybe start talking to the local press, and we try to achieve this for ourselves…"

"You must be joking, Mac," Vince interrupted.

"Let me finish."

"You want to *talk* to these scumbags? That's unbelievable. That really does take the fucking biscuit!"

Mac sighed. "All I'm saying is that we can really make this happen: our little group here, taking on the animal-torturing corporate bastards of Maier Science and shaming them into submitting to our demands. Don't you see? We use the threat of TV exposure to get exactly what we want."

"You think we can shame them into doing what we want? You live in a dream world, Mac." Vince didn't try to disguise his disdain.

"Don't be so ruddy negative, Vince." This time it was Nancy who had got involved.

"I'm being the opposite of negative, Nancy," he insisted. "Look, the only thing these people understand is direct action. As Bhup said, we've done enough pussy-footing around, enough fact-finding, enough talking. It's time to hit them where it hurts: national profile and targeted campaigns against everyone who has anything to do with Maier Science. We expose the malpractice, undermine the support infrastructure, scare away their clients, and eventually get these bastards to go out of business. They will understand that all right."

"Yeah, like that's worked elsewhere before, you fucking dipstick!" Mac countered. For the first time it seemed his temper had frayed. Jemima saw the blaze of anger in his eyes. No longer was Stuart leaning forward engagingly, stroking his beard in that thoughtful way he did. He still leaned forward, but now the tautness of his limbs, the bark in his voice and the withering look in his eyes, all channelled towards Vince, were clear signals that boiling point was close at hand.

Barry, the man who had presented the video evidence and who was a relative newcomer to the group, tried to defuse the charged atmosphere in Nancy's front room. "Come on, guys – let's not get too het up, eh? Everyone can have an opinion, everything can be discussed."

Vince ignored the new man. The few hairs on the top of his bald head seemed to stand erect in umbrage. "Remind me how you come to be leader of this group, Mac. We never seem to actually *do* anything. Endless fucking research, planning, talking – it's like a cosy little parish council committee. There are animals being killed and tortured out there in the name of research and we just sit here talking shit, month after month."

"Vince, we will do plenty, don't you worry about that," Mac fired back. "Everything we've done so far is the background work on these bastards. The action starts now, with this film. And in answer to your question: I'm the leader of SMAC because we had a fucking vote on it, and I got more votes than you. So don't make this about my leadership, because you've already lost that one once, pal."

"Fine, let's have a vote on this then," Vince replied with equal heat.

"Fine."

Mac looked at Nancy, who appeared to be irritated by the macho squabble being played out in her front room. "Okay," she said, "hands up if you agree with Mac's plan to confront Maier directly with the video and not go straight to the media."

Mac raised his hand, as did Nancy, and Jemima, and a young man who had barely spoken, Anthony; after initial hesitation Bhupathi, who was sitting next to Anthony, also raised his hand. The mathematics was already obvious, but even so Nancy went on: "And those who agree with Vince?" Only Vince and Pippa raised their hands, though Jemima wondered whether Pippa did so mostly in the interests of marital harmony. Barry had abstained.

"Barry?" enquired Mac.

"I'm going back to London, Mac. It's not for me to get involved. Anyway, it doesn't look like my vote would make much difference."

Vince stood up. "Come on, Pippa, we're out of here. These idiots wouldn't know what to do with a gift horse if it galloped through their bloody living room. Let's go and find some real activists to work with."

He strode out of the room and towards the front door. Pippa jumped to her feet, her cheeks crimson, her eyes cast down. "I'll talk him round, Mac, you know what he's like," she said quietly. Vince was already out of the house, and Pippa, with her blonde bobbed head bowed, rushed out after him.

Mac looked around at the faces that were left. They watched him and waited, all so serious, holding back until they knew how best to react. He burst into hooting laughter. "Can you believe that guy? Jesus H..." he said to Nancy. Jemima smiled, now that smiling was allowed again. "What a performance! Can you believe that, Nance?" Mac said again. "Unbelievable!"

Everyone was nodding agreement. Soon Mac's mirth levelled off, and he relaxed back in his armchair. Jemima took her chance.

"Right, can you all listen to me now?"

***

It was 10.15 that same evening and Kay was curled up on the sofa again, with the TV on low, and the baby monitor by her side emitting only peaceful, contented, steady breathing sounds from a sleeping Davy upstairs. Nick didn't seem to be far behind his son. He was sitting on the floor, leaning back against the sofa, letting his muscles relax after a long day. He had got home from the snooker club in high spirits about an hour earlier. They had munched through the steak and chips that Kay had prepared, and the dirty plates remained where they had left them on the dining table.

Nick knew that this was their time of day to chat, but his eyelids were starting to droop – not helped by Kay's soothing fingers working through the hair on the back of his head. Man, this was what life should be about, he thought: a good day's work, a bit of sport and a laugh with some other guys, a good square meal and a great woman to come home to. He listened with renewed intensity to Davy's monitor, hoping that concentrating on that would keep his eyes open. His son, his boy, the apple of his eye – words couldn't describe the feeling it gave him to hear confirmation of Davy's wellbeing, seemingly carried over the airwaves from far away, but in fact from that little bedroom on the left, just up the stairs.

Maybe he would pop his head round the bedroom door again, as he'd done briefly when he got back from snooker earlier. It was enough just to watch the boy at times. Both of them were still full of wonder: Davy at his new world; Nick at the bundle of perfection that chance had delivered to him, and the new meaning it had given his life. To be a dad... he still pinched himself every day in wonder. Maybe he would go and see Davy again; just to look at him and feel the tingle it gave him in his finger-tips. Yes, that would be good.

"You asleep, babe?"

Nick heard Kay's voice behind him, softly teasing but sudden enough to make him jump at the intrusion into his reverie. Kay started laughing at the jerk his shoulders had made. He turned his face towards hers, close by on the sofa, and smiled back.

"No. Never. You must be mistaken. I'm wide awake."

She gave him a look – part sceptical, part amused. The heavy pressure on his eyelids couldn't really be resisted, though, and she saw them falter even as he smiled at her. Dead giveaway! She laughed again, and he knew he'd been rumbled.

"Bless," she said, and stretched forward to kiss him. "Poor tiredy boy."

"Yeah, busted!" said Nick. "Tell you what: shall we do that washing up now before I float off into la-la land for good?"

They collected the dishes and went through to the kitchen together, adding the plates to the pile of pots and pans and mugs and utensils that needed cleaning. Kay ran the water, Nick went back and collected the baby monitor from the front room, and then hunted out a clean tea towel so he could dry up.

"What time is Jerry picking you up tomorrow?" Kay asked while the water rose to a frothy peak in the sink.

"Six o'clock again."

"I'll sort your lunch out after we've done this then. 'Weapon of Choice'?"

"Oh yeah, go for it, bad girl."

Kay fiddled with a small MP3 player that was docked on the window ledge, and then started to wash the first dish in the pile next to her. A few seconds later, as Nick stood beside her ready with the tea towel, music began – the chugging beat of a Fatboy Slim tune – and Nick, hamming it up to the full, adopted a pose borrowed from the video that had accompanied the song, in which the actor Christopher Walken did a solo dance, using tables, escalators and other props to accentuate his dance routine.

Nick, imitating Walken, held his hands like a dog holding its front paws up, and then as the tune kicked off he moved through parts of the routine, sashaying across the kitchen while Kay, working her hips into the groove, with her hands in the suds, giggled. Soon they were both pulling off moves, some copied from the original; some very much their own artistic interpretation, often with a foamy dish in hand. Throughout, their laughter accompanied the tune. It was a common diversion they used to make the chore of washing up more enjoyable. Nick was putting a bit too much into it, though, and a backlog of items ready for drying was starting to fill up the draining board.

"Come on, slow coach – a bit less silliness and a bit more productivity from you," Kay chuckled. "I thought you were tired?"

"Sure thing, boss, I'll snap to it," he said with a final shimmy. He took up an oven tray to dry, and listened closely for a few seconds to the baby monitor. The tune ended and another track came on. Kay turned the volume down on the MP3 player, and picked up some dirty cutlery to wash.

"So... this Jemima girl seems nice," she said. Evidently she wanted to talk, not dance.

"Yeah, you said. Davy was okay with her?"

"Oh, he loves her. He took to her straight away. She's got eyes in the back of her head as well. I was showing her the garden, going on about all the work you'd done on it, and little did I know that meanwhile our monster was trying to pull everything off the dining table! Luckily Jemima got there just in time to stop him from doing any mischief."

"Well, that's good then. She'll need to keep her wits about her," Nick chuckled. Something about the way Kay had her head down, concentrating on a fork she was cleaning, struck him though. Her mood had darkened after the hilarity of the last few minutes.

"What's up? You okay, honey pie?" Nick ventured lightly. Kay shrugged, as if that passed for an answer. Nick put down the tea towel and took her in his arms. He watched her closely.

"I'm fine," she said, resolutely avoiding meeting his eyes.

"Hey, come on. You know you can't pretend with me. What's up?"

She sagged against him. "Oh, it's nothing really. Just me being silly. It's nothing."

"Being silly about what? There's no such thing as silly – we're talking about our little boy, Kay."

She looked up at Nick and now he could see tears in her eyes. "It's just... oh, I don't know, I'm such a silly cow. Talking to Jemima today got me thinking about Dad. She asked about Davy's grandparents, so I told her that none were around. And it made me feel really sad. And then there's Davy's birthday coming up, and a part of me would so love for Dad to meet our little man and see how good everything is for me now. I know Dad's a drunken old waster, but I suppose I just hoped things could be a bit different – for Davy's sake, you know? It would have been so cool for him to have had a granddad, wouldn't it?"

Her eyes shone but behind the tears Nick could at first see only regret. The subject of Kay and her dad was one that only occasionally came to the surface. Nick knew enough to realise that Kay believed the distance between them, emotional rather than physical, was unbridgeable. The scars were still raw, and usually she reacted with anger to any talk of her father. This occasion felt different, though. There was not just regret in Kay's eyes, but also, Nick thought, actual yearning. He decided to explore that.

"Well, babe, let's go find your dad then. Put everything right. Why the hell not?"

"Because, Nick..."

"Because what?"

"You don't know.... You don't know what happened between us in the past. He was really hurtful to me. I swore I would never forgive him. And now I'm confused about the whole thing and the way I feel about it."

"Jesus, Kay, the only reason I don't know is because you won't tell me."

She looked downcast. "Look, why don't we try and find him and see what happens? Maybe things will be different now," Nick reasoned.

"I wouldn't know what to say to him," said Kay, pouting a little. "I'm scared of it, Nick. I know I'm stupid and silly and everything, but I don't want him to hurt me again, and now today has got me thinking about it all over again."

"I'll talk to him."

"How will you..."

"I'll talk to him. Tell me where he lived last time you saw him and I'll find him and talk to him."

Her voice wavered: "Why would you do that, babe?"

He gave her a mildly outraged look. "Because it's about you, and I want you to be happy, and because I agree it would be great for Davy to have a granddad in his life. Just write down your dad's name and his address – or the last one you know of. Do you have his phone number?"

"No, not one that works. I remember the address where he used to live, 'cos I lived there for years too. He never moved and I don't suppose he ever will, the stubborn git. Are you sure, Nick? If you find him and he's horrible to you, then don't tell me about it. We'll just forget about it. I won't ask you about him, I won't even think about him."

The self-delusion in that statement was obvious. They both knew that, but Nick answered soothingly. "No problem. Leave it to me. We don't have to speak about it again."

She searched his face for a couple of seconds and seemed to find the reassurance she sought there. "Better finish these dishes before the suds all go," Kay said, sounding drained, diminished. She turned back to the sink, but Nick held on to her waist and squeezed her closer once more. "Thank you, babe… thank you," was all he heard from behind the long, dark locks of hair that obscured her face.

***

Dear Diary,

I always thought that keeping a diary was a load of old bollocks. Think I did it for about two months when I was 12 years old, but I got bored with it and just stopped one day and never started again. It was crap anyway: "3rd January 1987, too cold to go out and play, stayed in and played Pacman instead; 4th January 1987, still freezing cold, listened to U2 albums all day while playing Pacman." See what I mean? Total bollocks.

So I always reckoned diaries were kept by kids, or man-hating women, or by people with no mates. No one to go to the pub with, to shag with, to watch the football with, etc. But here I am, writing one now, which says a lot about my circumstances, I suppose. I've got time on my hands now, and I reckon that if I use it constructively (which this diary is supposed to do), then maybe I will be better able to understand how it is that I've got this time on my hands, and some of the anger might go away. Bloody hell – therapy – I must be turning into a Yank! Anyway, to be honest, it's not so much a diary, more a look back at stuff that happened.

Where to start, though? I've thought about this for a while, and decided that the best place to start is when the missus left me. The bitch! So much for anger management, eh? All I got was a phone call from her, saying she'd met another bloke and she was fucking off with him. Don't try and call her or find her or anything. That was getting on for three years ago now. I should mention her name, I suppose, since she's kind of a major fucking player in this unfolding drama. Anyway, it's Kay. Kay Talbot, as she was when we were married. Thinking about it, we're still legally married, though it certainly hasn't felt that way for a long time now. A long time.

We were married for ten years before she left me with the flat in Hertford where we'd lived together. I had no idea where she'd gone. Tried ringing her, emailing her, tried her boss (she was a PR tart) but he wouldn't spill the beans, the jumped-up poof. She just disappeared off the face of Planet Earth. The mobile-phone contract was cancelled, so she must have had a new number that I wasn't intended to know. I couldn't get information about where she was from anyone. Nobody – banks, mobile phone, work, etc. – would tell me, for security reasons. When I said I was just trying to track down the wife, people got even more suspicious for some reason. I spoke to a solicitor, and she just said that if Kay hadn't shown up in a couple of years, I would have grounds for divorce.

The thing was, though, I didn't want to get divorced by then. I wanted to get things going again, let bygones be bygones. I'd just had a bit of a shocking experience that I would rather not go into here, but let's just say I lost a close mate. He was killed; murdered in fact. I saw it with my own eyes, and that kind of shit makes you think about stuff; reassess where you're going in your life. I came away from that wanting to start again with Kay, to rekindle the old magic. I'd even convinced myself that I was prepared to accept the way she felt about having kids. This was the big problem, you see: I wanted kids, she didn't. There was a lot of shit and bad stuff said by both of us on that one. I'm not proud of it, but fuck it, she was wrong, and it still makes me angry. Jesus, I look around at my situation and it still makes me fucking angry, and I should know better by now. For fuck's sake, Lee boy, stop doing this to your-self. I'll have to stop writing for a bit. Sorry.

Anyway, so my mate got stabbed up, I legged it and laid low for a couple of days, then I went back to make it up with the wife, and that's when the old gin-soaked tart rang me up and said she'd left me and gone off with some tosser. I had wondered, 'cos I'd got home and found that half her clothes were gone from the wardrobe. I didn't take it too well, oh, no. I mean, fuck, talk about kicking a man when he's down. What she'd left in the wardrobe went up in smoke after that. Hell of a bonfire!!!

There were some pretty bad times after that, I won't deny it. I was messed up bad. Thinking about Kay and what we'd had when things were good; thinking about the mistakes I'd made and the ones she'd made; just realising really that I still bloody loved the woman, even after all that. I mean, Kay is beautiful. She's stunning, amazing, drop-dead gorgeous. I'd been a proud man to walk into many a room with her on my arm, let me tell you. And I wanted that feeling back, I really wanted it back. Well, I know now that I never will get that feeling again. Blotted my copybook a few too many times for that, old chum. God, I hope this ink don't run with all the water that's falling out of my eyes and onto the page!

Ah, get a grip, Lee. Keep going son. Just got to get through this bit. Deep breaths. Yeah, so, I knew I wanted Kay back in my life, another chance, but in the meantime I just had to get on with it. Went back to work and kept my head down. There was some stuff in the papers about Billy, and that freaked the shit out of me. I reckoned they'd get round to me sooner or later. I mean, we must have been on dozens of CCTV cameras together, at various places in London, the night he was killed. Fortunately, the mobile phone I'd used for all that stuff was a pay-as-you-go job, and I'd ditched that. Eventually, though, I couldn't handle that type of aggro any longer, and I went to see the Old Bill and told them the lot – or as much as I knew anyway, which wasn't a great deal. It felt fucking good to get it off my chest and help them with their enquiries, and they were good enough to thank me and offer me some protection if I needed it. I was a bit worried that Billy's old mates would come for me, but it never happened.

Well, would you believe, two years went by? More than two years, in fact, about two and a half. Still no word from Kay. Still no divorce papers. I was still looking for her, if you know what I mean, but the world's a big fucking place and she could have been anywhere. There are a lot of Kay Talbots out there, although there was only ever one for me, and there are also a lot of Kay Campbells (that was her maiden name). I'd searched the internet for hours and hours, fucking months of my life probably. Now I can look back and admit I was obsessed with it, but who wouldn't be? She was my wife and I loved her and I had this faith – is that the right word? Faith? Yeah, I'd say it was as it goes – this faith that she could love me again. I am a dreadfully deluded prick sometimes.

I knocked around with a few birds during that period, looking for something to fill the hole, this fucking gargantuan Kay-shaped hole that kicked me in the nuts every day when I woke up; but my heart weren't in it, that's the truth of it. I didn't care about them. I mean really care, in the same way that thinking about Kay made me feel. They were just bits of fluff, bits of fun. I used them, abused them, and then got rid of them when I was bored. Is this something else for me to confront? Am I also a womanising bastard who treats birds like pieces of shit? Add that to the charge list as well? Ah, bollocks to it, guilty as charged, your honour. I wasn't happy. I didn't know where I was, who I was or what I was doing – how could I treat them right? It wasn't possible for me to love them, or even like them particularly. Honestly, I don't know how I look at myself in the mirror, but somehow I do. The world's a shit place, and I can't be wracking myself with remorse, raising my hands to the Lord in supplication, for everything shit I've ever done. Everyone fucks up at some time.

Then an amazing thing happened. Two and half years (all right, I admit, I happen to know that it was 958 days since she'd left, okay?) after Billy died and everything rubbish that followed that, there I was at work – in fact, I'd just got back from lunch with Dave Ramsbottom, sat back down at my desk and there were some emails sitting in my junk mail folder. Nothing unusual about that, we have a strict spam filter on our work emails. And usually I probably wouldn't even have bothered looking at them, just deleted them whenever I could be bothered. But this particular day, for some reason, I had a look and among the crap about Viagra and Rolex watches and tarts from Russia, who promised to show me a good time, was one email with a title that couldn't have been more calculated to grab my attention. It said: Kay Talbot.

Just those two words.

I had to open it, didn't I? It was impossible to know who it was actually from. The email address it had come from was a Hotmail one, called jb4sm2010@hotmail.com. All very cryptic, but the message inside was pretty short and to the point. It said:

Your wife is working for Maier Science, near Salisbury in Wiltshire. From A Friend.

And that was it. I can remember feeling a bit hot under the collar at that point. There was a whole rush of emotions unleashed by that message. I must have read it twenty times, probably more, God knows, before I could even get up from the desk. I felt sick and yet just stupidly happy all at the same time. You've got to remember I'd become almost resigned never to see my wife's beautiful face ever again. This kind of desperate sadness that I'd carried around with me for more than two years – well, suddenly there seemed to be some kind of hope. I knew that whatever happened – whether Kay spoke to me or not – I would see her face again. I would get the chance to try and explain that I had changed, that we could make a fresh start.

I suddenly felt alive again.

Well, the first thing I did was compose a reply. It took me fucking ages and then I deleted the whole thing and just typed: Thanks. Who is this? *And I sent that email back. I don't know whether I actually expected an answer really or not, but the following day I got an undelivered message back from the computer system. So that was that. I guessed that whoever it was, this guardian angel of mine, had set up an email account just to send that one message, and then closed it down again.*

Anyway, at that point I didn't really care. My mind was on fire with the prospect of seeing Kay again. Even though I had some urgent work to do, I couldn't resist getting on the internet and Googling this company, Maier Science. It threw up a whole load of stuff. Not just their own website but all kinds of articles and mentions. They do animal testing (yeah, tossers, I know), and they'd obviously had some heat from pressure groups. There was one in particular that was mentioned quite a lot – they called themselves SMAC, which I quickly learned stands for Stop Maier Animal Cruelty. These guys were having a right pop at the Maier people. There was so much stuff online, though, that I decided I needed to get on with my job for the afternoon, and have a proper read that evening when I got home from work, so that's what I did.

I learned shit loads of stuff. I read everything on Maier Science's website, and I read everything on the SMAC website, and then I read some local newspaper articles where this guy Stuart McCormack, who is the leader of the SMAC group, was ranting about cruelty to bunny rabbits and all that. I spent bloody hours reading this stuff, and it gave me a stiff neck, sitting there looking at a computer screen until 2 a.m. There was no mention of Kay in any of this, but she's a professional PR woman so it wasn't rocket science working out what her role would be in the whole caboodle.

That night, when I finally decided to go to bed, I remember feeling like it had been one of the best days of my life. I knew what I was going to do now, and I knew I would see my Kay again. I felt so happy. Next day, I went into work (it was a Friday) and booked the next two weeks off for holiday. I had shit loads of my holiday entitlement left cos I didn't take much time off. Whenever I did, I would just end up sitting around thinking about Kay and the mess I'd got myself into, so I used to throw myself into work instead. When I spoke to my boss Lukas and asked for some, he seemed almost relieved. He said he thought it was a great idea, that I'd been working too hard for too long (and I did feel pretty shagged out, to be honest) and a holiday was long overdue. Fucking hell, it was all he could do to stop himself from pushing me out of the door! I was a bit taken aback by his reaction, to be honest, because we've had some ructions over the years, me and old Lukas Baptiste.

With that sorted out, I got on the internet again, found some B&Bs in Salisbury, phoned one up, that was full up, phoned a second one, spoke to a middle-aged bird called Margaret. She had a vacancy so I was in. I was on such a high at that point that I even rang the number for Maier Science. A woman answered and I asked for Kay. She said did I mean Kay Beckett or Kay Campbell? I thought quickly. Ah-ha! Campbell is Kay's maiden name! So that's what she'd done... Kay Campbell, I replied, and she put me through. Oh, my heart was beating like fucking Keithy Moon let loose on a new drum kit, I tell you. Then Kay's voice came on, sounding all professional and polished and eager to serve.

"Hello, Kay Campbell here," she said. And I just listened to it – the voice of my wife, the woman I love. I could

have screamed with happiness, but Emma across the desk from me would have thought I was an even bigger weirdo than she already did. So I listened to Kay talking, saying: "Hello? Hello? Anyone there? Hello?" She sounded that little bit more exasperated each time. It was magic. Then she put the phone down and I looked at the receiver as if I'd just been cut off. Then I put it back on the handset. Emma gave me a funny little smile, though why I didn't know or care. It was just a perfect, beautiful moment, hearing Kay's voice again.

Saturday morning, I packed the car, and then I set off for the West Country. The sun was beating down on my convertible Beamer as I cruised down the M4 doing a smooth 90, and with rolling green fields and hills replacing the suburbs of London, and Kay getting closer by the second, not even slow-coach wankers blocking up the outside lane on the motorway could take the grin off my face. Hold on to your hat, Kay girl – I'm coming to town!

CHAPTER THREE

Another day, another panic… why was it always like that? Kay thought to herself as she bad- temperedly searched through a pile of documents on her desk. Around her, colleagues in the open-plan office were quietly going about their business. Not her though, no. She was in a mad rush to respond to Richard Cambridge's request to see a letter that had been sent to Maier Science by the contract cleaning supplier it used, airing several grievances.

The boys and girls at SMAC, so it seemed, had been hassling members of the cleaning staff at home, engaging in some sort of psychological warfare by making frequent silent phone calls in the evenings, verbally abusing people as they got in their vans to go to work, and finally daubing the managing director's car in the middle of the night with spray-painted insults such as 'Animal Murderer', 'Nazi Scum', and other baseless accusations. Things seemed to be escalating towards confrontation, and the cleaning company was concerned for the safety of its employees.

Kay had showed the letter to Richard two days earlier when it had first arrived. He had been preoccupied with other matters at the time, but now he wanted to speak directly to the cleaning company's managing director, and he wanted to re-read the letter before he did so. Kay knew she had it on her desk somewhere, but she needed to find it and deliver it to Richard before she could leave the office for a lunch appointment with someone she hoped would become a useful contact. She was running behind schedule already.

She had arranged to meet a local newspaper reporter – the intriguingly named Ted Chillingworth. When she had first seen his by-line in the paper she had amused herself by wondering whether he was perhaps a crazed axe murderer in waiting. At the moment, though, he was merely the senior reporter on the *Salisbury Journal*, and Kay wanted to foster a relationship there in the hope of getting some positive coverage for Maier Science in the near future.

First, however, bloody Richard had asked to see the bloody letter, and it was currently buried in this bloody mountain of stuff. Kay had only been at the company for a month, and already her desk was a tip – printed off emails, newspaper cuttings, printed research off the internet, internal documents. Some bloody idiot had predicted the paperless office years before. She had enough of it here in these random piles, she reckoned, to wallpaper the inside of Buckingham Palace four times over.

She continued flicking through the first pile, looking out for the distinctive green and blue logo of the cleaning company. Why didn't she develop a system? Have special folders for different types of documents? Actually file things away properly? Yes, all good ideas. Her phone rang and she huffed at it: the last thing she needed was another interruption.

She grabbed it hurriedly and stated her name: no sound from the other end. Was she getting the silent treatment from SMAC now as well? She didn't have time for this crap anyway. "Hello? Hello? Anyone there? Hello?" she repeated, her hackles rising quickly. Still nothing.

Oh, for God's sake. She threw the receiver back into its cradle carelessly, and went back to her piles.

Eventually she found the offending letter in the second pile. "Hallelujah," she muttered sourly. She ran through to Richard's office and left the letter in front of him; he was on the phone again, and gave just the briefest nod of acknowledgement. Minutes later Kay was in her car and exiting the Maier Science compound, through gates that were today being operated by cheery Brian, and driving out onto the narrow country lane outside.

There were a couple of protesters across the road, a man and a woman dressed in t-shirts and jeans, standing at the treeline, next to banners and placards bearing insults and calls to action. They jeered at Kay as she turned right out of the gates but she ignored them with studied concentration and started off down the road to Salisbury, driving a little faster than she felt comfortable with, given the narrowness of the road and the close proximity on both sides of high hedgerows.

Her mind was at last able to turn to her forthcoming meeting with Mr Ted Chillingworth, senior reporter. When she had spoken to him on the phone this morning to confirm that the meeting was still on, he had been what you might call uncommunicative – loath to appear even remotely enthusiastic about meeting her, or probably any PR, for lunch. Typical bloody journalist, she thought, miserable bastard. Maybe he would lighten up a bit after a drink. Kay went through in her mind again the things she wanted to say. She had even scribbled a few notes down on a piece of paper that was now in her handbag. At some point she would excuse herself to go and powder her nose, a tactical retreat that would allow her to remind herself of anything she had forgotten.

Fifteen minutes later she was turning into the Pay & Display car park next to The Pheasant Inn, old Tudor premises with the typical half-timbered external appearance. Kay had seen a picture of it on the internet; it looked very "olde worlde", she thought. Inside it was bright and airy with wooden tables and chairs and dark brown laminate wood flooring. She checked her watch – it was 12.30 almost on the dot. After all that, she was on time.

Where was Ted though? She had a number for his office, which was just around the corner, but he had declined to tell her his mobile number, saying instead that the office would put her through. She had spent some time looking him up on social media in advance, finding a LinkedIn profile with a picture. She walked around the entire pub but saw no one who looked like the man in the profile picture. Kay ordered a gin and tonic at the bar and then wandered off with her drink to sit at a table next to a window.

There was a menu on the table and Kay started browsing through it. Mostly it was standard pub food, but there was a specials board next to the bar with some other alternatives on it. Kay busied herself reading about burgers and chips, sausage and mash, and lasagne. The jacket potato with tuna mayo took her fancy. She would order that and then call Ted's office.

"You Kay Campbell?"

She looked up to see a man standing beside the table looking at her. He was in his mid-forties, unshaven, his hair shoulder-length and dark, with a few grey hairs sprinkled through it. He wore a blue denim shirt with the sleeves rolled up, and blue jeans. He was wiry and athletic-looking, with alert blue eyes.

She stood up. "Yes, hi – you're Ted?"

He nodded and they shook hands. "It's great to meet you," said Kay. Ted simply nodded again. "Can I get you a drink?" she asked, moving out from behind the table.

"Yeah, I'll have a Boondoggle," he replied, and watched her walk up to the bar. He stood by the table for a few moments, seemingly unsure whether to join her or not; eventually he sat down in the seat opposite the one Kay had been occupying, and waited for her to return. She watched him from the bar; he was staring at the wall. The only part of his body that moved was his right foot, which tapped an insistent beat on the wooden floor. Kay noticed for the first time that he had a small, black leather document case of some kind, which he had placed on the floor by his feet. Presumably that was where he kept his notebook.

Soon she returned to the table with his pint of ale, which she left in front of him as she sat down again. She smiled at Ted. "Thanks for agreeing to meet up anyway. Are you guys busy at the moment?"

"I'm always busy keeping up with the exciting go-ings-on in Salisbury," Ted answered. His voice was heavy with sarcasm. Kay laughed, although there was little humour to be found in Ted's deadpan expression. She reached for the menu again.

"Are you peckish? The food is on me," she said. "Feel free to order what you want."

"I haven't got time," he replied. "I've got a story I've got to work on, so you've got about twenty minutes."

That was disappointing. It meant that Kay would have to wait a bit longer for her lunch since she didn't want to be the only one eating at the table.

"Okay, right, I'd better get on with it then," she said with a smile that she hoped would help him remember his manners. "Here's my business card. Can I take one of yours?"

"Haven't got any with me," Ted replied, taking Kay's card and putting it in the breast pocket of his shirt without even looking at it. He seemed to be going out of his way to try as little as possible. Well, if he wasn't going to say much, Kay decided, then she would have to fill in the empty spaces herself.

"So, I've been with Maier for about a month now. The company is keen to work with local stakeholders like the newspapers, TV and radio, the local authority, civic groups, you name it, to clear up a lot of the misunderstanding there is about what we do."

"Misunderstanding?"

"Yes, absolutely. There's a lot of misunderstanding about what Maier does and the methods we use."

"You mean that people think you torture fluffy rabbits to make sure a deodorant is safe?"

"Exactly. That's exactly what I mean. People assume that. But the procedures and safeguards adhered to in the lab all conform to international standards and are regularly monitored. Look, I've brought some information for you to take away and read."

Kay produced a printed brochure from her bag and handed it across the table. It was a glossy, colourful piece of corporate literature that Maier Science used as part of its marketing to potential clients, boasting of the company's expertise and experience in contract research. "It's a bit out of date, but informative all the same. I'm working on developing some new marketing collateral," Kay continued.

Ted took it from her and scanned his eyes across the first page. Kay felt certain this apparent sudden interest was a sham. Nothing about this meeting was particularly surprising to her. She had met with frostier reporters who wrote for national newspapers, so Ted's attitude didn't bother her. It was just the way it was with some journalists – they would keep their distance, and guard their morally superior objectivity, usually until you got them drunk on your expenses.

There wasn't time for that now, but there were other ways to get closer to an uncooperative journalist. Kay decided to dangle a little carrot.

"Of course, I'd be happy to arrange for you to come and have a look inside the site; meet with Richard Cambridge, my boss; see what we do, speak to the lab technicians. You'll soon find that Maier Science is actually a very high-tech organisation operating at the leading edge of science and research, as well as providing employment for dozens of local people. It's actually a great success story. I can arrange that for you, no problem."

"People don't want success stories, they want scandal," Ted responded carelessly. "They don't want good news, they want disaster or sex or depravity. Or they want to see pictures of their own little kiddies and babies looking all sweet and cuddly in the newspaper."

Cynical as well – he was a real charmer this one. "I disagree, Ted. I think that right now, in the middle of a recession, more than at any other time, people want to read about success, about something positive; more than anything, about a local company that's giving local people jobs rather than putting them on the dole queue. Of course, if you're not interested in that kind of story, I could always give it to Eliza Drummond at the *Gazette* as an exclusive instead."

The *Western Gazette* was the big competitor to the *Salisbury Journal* for local news. Ted leaned towards Kay.

"Hang on. You know Eliza, do you?"

"I know everyone, Ted," Kay lied.

He was resting his left arm on the window ledge next to the table. He drummed his fingers on the wooden surface as he thought for a few seconds. Suddenly he laughed – a reaction that was out of keeping with his manner up to that point. He actually has teeth, Kay thought to herself. It was the first remotely pleasant thing he had said or done since they had met.

"You're very good, Kay, I'll give you that. Very good. You know what buttons to press."

"I've been doing this for a while. I don't know what the other PRs are like that you talk to, but I do know what I'm doing."

"I'd want it as an exclusive: full access, one-to-one with Robert Cambridge, our own photographer, et cetera. Don't bother with Eliza; she doesn't know her arse from her elbow anyway. She'd probably prefer a deadly dull council meeting, since they put plates of chocolate biscuits out. But if it's an exclusive, then I'll take it to the editor."

Ted took a swig of his beer and smiled. Kay smiled back. "That's great, Ted. It's Richard, by the way; not Robert. Richard Cambridge. There is one other thing. We would need to see the copy before it's published."

"Why the hell would I let you do that?" Ted snapped, the smile fading. "Buy a fucking advert, Kay if you want control over what goes in the paper. It's quite simple."

"It's a deal-breaker, I'm afraid. Richard won't agree to it otherwise. I'll mention to him about taking out an advert, but as I'm sure you can imagine, we don't advertise too much because people always kick up a stink. Look, it's for factual checks only. I'm not going to change your copy – I can't write as well as you do, Ted. But there might be some quite technical information involved in this story, and correct me if I'm wrong, but you're not a technical writer, are you? The last front-page story I saw with your byline was about some traffic lights on the A30."

Ted drank more of his beer. "Ouch!" he muttered, turning his eyes away to look out of the window. No journalist liked to be reminded of their more pedestrian moments. He seemed to be weighing things up in his mind. Eventually he looked back at Kay and said decisively: "I'll take it to the editor and see what he says. But this can't end up being just powder puff nonsense. Your boss has to know that he's speaking on the record and that I might ask him a bit more than just how much the turnover was this year. You'd better get all his media training up to date, Kay."

Now it was her turn to laugh. That really was quite funny in a macho kind of way. Jeremy Paxman had a lot to answer for, she reflected. "Yeah, of course, Ted. I told you, I've been doing this for years – and doing it at national level as well. I know what the game is. He'll be ready for a rumble, don't you worry about that."

Kay continued laughing and saw Ted join in, but with less gusto, as if suspecting (correctly, as it happened) that he was being mocked a little. "I'll get you a good story, don't worry about that," she said, by way of pacifying him.

They discussed possible dates for Ted to come and visit, and after a few minutes a date was agreed upon in late June. Ted took a small diary from his black document case and made an entry on the relevant page. They engaged in a couple more minutes of small talk while Kay sipped at her gin and tonic. Ted was into music and guitars it turned out. He played in a pub band, he said, and had a voluminous record collection of old rock 'n' roll vinyl, which was his pride and joy, next to the custom 1972 Fender Telecaster electric guitar hanging from his living-room wall.

By the time she had gleaned this information from him, Kay was feeling ravenously hungry. It was time to make a move, find a sandwich shop and then head back to the office to report to Richard on his upcoming interview. He would be pleased, she knew. It was one part of her plan coming together. She finished the last of her G&T.

"Well, I'm going to make a move then, Ted. Thanks for your time," she said, gathering her things together and rising from the chair. "I'll send you an email to confirm everything we've talked about, and perhaps we can have a chat on the phone nearer the time – just to run over a few things, if that's okay?"

Ted nodded a brief assent, and reached for his pint of beer, which was still half full. He remained seated. Kay offered him her hand, which he shook.

"Nice to meet you, Ted."

"And you, Kay."

Their eyes met one last time over the handshake. Kay hoped to look positive and gratified by the outcome to the meeting. She saw that Ted's eyes maintained the generally impassive expression that he had maintained throughout the meeting, but there was a little glint there, if she wasn't mistaken; a little suggestion of some other emotion that she would have to guess at. She released her grip on his hand, turned and walked out of the pub.

***

Ted remained at the table for a couple of minutes, contemplating his pint and then watching Kay through the window. She got into her car and quickly drove away. There was a call he needed to make now, but he didn't feel inclined to rush himself. What the hell? His boss wasn't looking at him; he could take a while to finish his drink before heading back to the office and the prospect of a stuffy, stultifying afternoon reading amateurish press releases and bickering fruitlessly with an overheated editor.

God, it was boring. It didn't do to think too deeply about his career progress or, more accurately, the lack of it compared to all those reporter friends of his who had long ago graduated from local newspapers to the nationals. Somehow, for reasons that Ted was all too capable of bitterly blowing out of proportion, the chance had never come his way, and maybe now it never would. He was stuck in this rut, with Malcolm Coward, a fussy, untrusting, unspectacular editor ahead of him, who showed absolutely no inclination to vacate the seat, in spite of his advancing years.

Still, going into the Maier Sciences facility promised to be a more interesting diversion; not a bad sort, that PR bird, as well. Ted took his phone out of his pocket, but instead of using it to make a call, he found his favourite game on it, took a swig out of his drink, and started tipping his phone this way and that in order to guide a cartoon monkey character around a colourful assault course, collecting bananas along the way. Insanely jolly arcade music provided the soundtrack. At one point, Ted lost control of his rampaging ape, and the icon careered off track and tumbled head over heels into an abyss. Ted tutted with self-reproof, finished his pint, and started the game again with a new life.

Presently, one of the bar staff came by and collected the empty glass.

"Another one, Ted?" the woman asked.

He didn't take his eyes off the game. "No, got to get going, Cath. The old bastard'll be wondering where I am."

The woman stopped to talk, which was irritating since Ted was clearly focused on other things. "Anything happening then?" she asked. He paused the game.

"No, love. The usual load of old tripe, you know. Read all about it Thursday."

Cath persisted: "What about the new bypass? That going to go ahead, do you reckon?"

"Oh, er, there's a meeting about that next week, I think. Gary T's been working on that one; he knows more than me."

"Right you are, Ted. See you soon then."

The woman continued her round of the pub, tidying up tables as she went, and Ted resumed his monkey mania. His concentration was broken, though, and soon the monkey was falling to its inevitable demise again. He finally got up and left the pub; hot sunshine outside. He found the phone number he needed on his mobile phone, and called it as he walked. The voice that answered had a Scottish accent.

"Ted, how you doing?"

"Very well, Mac, very well. Got an interesting piece of news for you: just met with a PR woman from Maier Science. I've been invited to go inside and see the place… interview your mate Richard Cambridge too. We should meet up beforehand. You can give me a few pointers."

"Fucking ace, pal. When are you going in then?"

"Friday the twenty-fifth."

"Right, right… how about we get together on the Wednesday of that week then – that okay?"

"Should be – I'll have to get back to you. I'm just walking to the office, but I'll drop you a text later on. Hey, Mac, I told you I was the only reporter you needed to know, didn't I, eh?" The two men laughed at the observation.

"Aye, you sure did, pal, and you will be rewarded. Outstanding fucking work! Okay, let me know about that Wednesday then, Ted."

"I will, Mac, I will."

Ted pocketed the phone and walked on briskly towards the newspaper offices with the sun on his back.

***

Night had fallen after a hot day and there was a sense of oppression lifting as the air cooled under a clear, dark sky. In the village of Beechingstoke in Wiltshire, Brian Ames, fifty-eight-year-old manager of an office stationery company, helped himself to a chocolate from his wife Pat's post-dinner treat, a box of Milk Tray that, to help save money, she made last for a week these days, instead of just two nights.

From the kitchen came the sounds of Pat doing the washing up. All was well. Brian stretched out on the sofa and concentrated on the television. There was nothing much on – Pat liked to watch cookery programmes, and Brian was happy enough to go along with that, since he was very much the beneficiary of his wife's culinary prowess. On the TV, they were making some kind of Thai-style steamed fish meal, with three teams competing against each other. Brian listened to talk of ginger, jasmine rice and pak choi with only passing interest; he was happy to take their word for it, and it was better than thinking about reams of paper and paperclips, staplers and sticky notes. He had been doing that all day at work.

Presently, the clatter of plates and cutlery in the kitchen ceased, and soon Pat came back into the front room to sit by Brian's stockinged feet at one end of the sofa.

"How many of my chocolates did you pinch?" she asked lightly, taking one from the box for herself.

"No more than four, dear," he replied, returning the smile. Pat tutted but focused on the TV cookery show, and from his end of the sofa Brian saw her face in profile; she grimaced slightly, unconsciously it seemed, as she listened to the commentary.

"Uh...trout..." she commented, with evident distaste. Brian supposed therefore that a Thai-style trout wouldn't be coming in his direction in the near future. Still, tonight's chicken teriyaki had been superb, as the taste of soy sauce on his tongue reminded him. Pat's cooking had got better and better since the kids had left home. She was quite proud of her creations, and Brian was a willing consumer.

He was still lying prone on the sofa a few minutes later, struggling to keep his eyes open, when there was a ring of the doorbell. He and Pat looked at each other quizzically.

"Oh, go and answer it, love, please. I've just sat down," said Pat. She had got her excuse in first, and the fact that she was closer to the door wouldn't, he knew, make any difference. He drew his legs up and swung them off the sofa.

"Who the hell can it be – it's gone bloody nine o'clock," Brian mumbled, removing his spectacles as he sat up. He rubbed his eyes and reluctantly rose from the settee, then pulled his trousers up around his protruding belly and walked in front of Pat, causing her to tilt her head to one side for a second to see the TV screen.

As he walked through the hall Pat called something about showing the buggers the door if it turned out to be someone selling something. He thought that was what she had said anyway, and that was exactly what he planned to do if it was a salesman or someone collecting for an obscure charity.

Brian opened the front door to find himself confronted by two people wearing black balaclavas and dark clothing. There was no time even to question in his mind what this was all about before one of the strangers spoke.

"Are you Brian Ames of Image Stationery?" the person said. The voice was female. Brian was still too foggy of mind from being almost asleep on the sofa half a minute before to wonder why he was being asked this. Why were these people dressed all in black, though?

"Er, yes. Yes, I am, why..."

He got no further. From behind their backs the two people suddenly revealed small polythene bags filled with what looked like white powder; the woman who had spoken drew her arm back and then released her bag at Brian's head with some power, yelling the word "SMACK!" as she did so. The second person did likewise an instant later: "SMACK!" – this time a male voice.

Brian was knocked backwards, not by any force of impact particularly, because the objects turned out to be quite soft, but by surprise and alarm. Then he found that he couldn't see anything because his stinging eyes were filled with clouds of white powder. He cried out in panic more than real pain. Behind him he heard the consternation in his wife's voice as she shouted to him. Was he okay? she was asking. He really didn't know the answer to that. His fingers clawed at his eyes and he started to sob: "Oh, God, I can't see. Pat, help me, I can't see!"

He was being shouted at again as he staggered blindly in his own doorway. The female voice was addressing him harshly.

"That's for working with Maier Science, Brian. Murderers! Image Stationery – murderers! Don't make us come back again, Brian. Filthy murderers! Murderers!"

The male voice was joining in on the word "murderers", giving it added emphasis. Somewhere in Brian's mind, this was all starting to fall into place, but the smarting in his eyes was making him cry and then it was even harder for him to see. He had sunk to his knees, hands still to his eyes, and he heard Pat's voice amongst the clamour of the attackers' and his own yells. It was hard to breathe. Then he felt his wife's hands on his shoulders and the other voices were suddenly more distant, whooping and laughing it seemed, still punctuating their yells with shouts of "Murderers! Murderers!" Brian heard his wife shriek in a most untypical way.

"You bastards! What have you done to my husband? You cowards! I'll scratch your eyes out if I ever get my hands on you!"

Brian was coughing uncontrollably now, still surrounded by the dry cloud of floating powder. It was flour, he reckoned, which at least calmed his panic a little. Pat was kneeling down in front of him, her hands on his shoulders, talking to him. She raised him to his feet, forced him to turn around and then pushed him into the bathroom, sitting him down on the toilet seat. He could hear running water from the taps.

"It's only flour, I think, Pat love. It's in my eyes though," Brian gasped.

"Yes, I know," she said. "Cheap flour at that, I'll bet. I'll soon get you sorted, love. Oh, what a dreadful mess..." She spoke in such an unflustered way, and worked so quickly to soothe his eyes with water, that it made his heart tug with pride. This was why he loved her, why he had married her. "You do look a bit like a snowman," she informed him as she worked.

Some minutes later they emerged from the bathroom, Brian's eyes red raw from the trauma of what they'd been through, his hair and clothes still caked in dusty white powder like an overused blackboard. They went back to the open front door, but their assailants had long since fled. Much of the flour had settled now, dusting the carpet, curtains and doormat in what looked like streaks of unseasonal snow. Outside, they saw their next-door neighbour Gary standing with his back to them, wearing a baseball cap and seemingly regarding their Volvo car with interest.

Brian stepped outside, and called out: "Gary, did you see them?"

Gary turned around quickly and did a double-take when he saw the state of his neighbour. He grimaced. "No, Brian, I didn't. More to the point, have you seen this?"

And now Brian did see. The silver car was covered in spray-painted slogans and insults. It was ruined. Brian felt helpless shame at the sight of it, the slanderous lies it brought to his door and to his road.

In that dry way that Brian was so familiar with, Gary observed what didn't need to be said out loud. "Apparently you're a murderer and a pig, my old mate. Should I be taking you in to the coppers and getting my reward, or making a bacon sandwich out of you?"

CHAPTER FOUR

When Stuart McCormack was a boy, he found entertainment in the normal ways that little boys of his age did. He pulled the legs off crane flies out of sadistic interest; he used a stick to stir up ants' nests, to relieve his own boredom; he threw worms at unsuspecting little girls for a giggle. Something had changed him, though, and he remembered quite vividly what it was.

Growing up in rural Perthshire, he was used to rolling green fields, sparkling clear lochs and plentiful livestock, to which he paid little heed as he walked to school every morning with his sisters, Mary and Hannah. The cows and sheep were just part of the scenery of his youth.

But when he was eleven years old, the McCormack family – Major Murdo McCormack of the Scots Guards, his wife Elspeth and their three children, Mary (15), Hannah (13) and Stuart – went on holiday to Mexico. They spent their time travelling and sightseeing, or relaxing around the hotel swimming pool, playing silly games. Stuart remembered it as a happy time, mostly.

Then, one evening towards the end of their two weeks in Mexico, they went to watch bullfighting at the colossal Plaza México, the world's largest bullring, in Mexico City.

Stuart could still recall the imposing steel and concrete of the outside of the structure, climbing steeply, seemingly to the heavens, almost beyond the imagination of a small Scottish boy. The evening was clear and blue and warm, like every other evening had been for two weeks. Thousands of people milled around outside, drinking from beer bottles and skins of wine, and munching on snacks of tacos and enchiladas.

Inside, the Plaza was even more impressive. They walked through a long, white-walled tunnel that brought them back out into the glaring sunshine, banks of seats rising and descending on all sides of them. Stuart had felt uneasy at the height of their seats and the steepness of the terracing that dropped down towards the distant central ring. The crowd started to gather as the minutes ticked by towards the 4 p.m. start.

He had asked his dad about bullfighting earlier in the day, because he didn't really have any concept of what actually happened in it. His dad had explained that men with red capes and brightly coloured suits would encourage the bull to run at them, and would then step smartly and skilfully aside as the bull bore down on them. He told his son – erroneously, as Stuart later learned – that the cape was red because the colour provoked the bull. It was a contest of honour and courage his father had said. He didn't mention the spears that would be plunged into the bull's thick hide, that would gradually sap the strength and the life from it. He didn't mention the final dramatic thrust of the sword that would despatch the tortured creature from its ordeal, in a puddle of its own gore.

When it got to 4 p.m. a fanfare sounded and the crowd acclaimed the arrival of a succession of men – the *toreros* – in sequined uniforms of gold and red, silver and white, silver and blue, gorgeous sparkling creations, all of them wearing strange bicorne hats; they walked out into the centre of the ring accompanied by two men on horseback, the *picadores*. A trumpet sounded and a vast clamour of "Olé!" rose from the crowd. Stuart looked around, startled by the noise. There were 40,000 people in the Plaza México – he had never been in such a vast, uproarious gathering.

A bull, dark and agitated, trotted into the ring and was met by the *torero* in gold and red, the matador. He drew the bull on towards him with graceful sweeps of a red cape, the elegance and drama of the arm movements matched only by the flashing feet of the matador's sidestep, his mesmerising choreography. The bull came on, and came on, thrusting its horns forward at its tormentor with bloody-minded insistence. From the far end of the ring, one of the men on horseback came forward and – Stuart watched him – drove a lance into the bull's back. The crowd yelled another ecstatic "Olé". Stuart felt suddenly shocked and repelled.

He saw his own anger reflected in the bull, which turned indignantly towards the *picador* on horseback, and made to gore man and horse, whatever was in his furious path. The horse had padding around its flanks for protection, but there were uncomfortable moments as the *picador* attempted to extricate himself from the bull's onslaught. When he did so, and wheeled away across the ring, the bull turned to face more men, this time on foot, three of them dressed in silver-brocaded finery – the *banderilleros*.

Over the next few minutes they each performed their own macabre dance with the bull, which now held its head and horns lower following the encounter with the *picador*. The bull charged, increasingly incensed and maddened as the *banderilleros* swayed and shuffled and lanced the bull again and again with short spears decorated with what looked like strips of fluttering tinsel; six of the spears were soon flapping and hanging from the bull's back and neck, which were now shiny black with blood. The bull looked demoralised and overwhelmed but was still standing, though its proud trot had been reduced mostly to a shuffling, faltering gait as it wheeled to face one threat after another.

The people all around Stuart were cheering and waving, greeting each strike by the *banderilleros* with applause and cheers and exultant calls. Stuart's cheeks were wet with tears, as wet as the bull's neck. He suddenly became aware that he was tightly gripping the hand of his sister Mary, who was sitting bolt upright to his left, her own face stonily set against what was happening in front of her.

The matador was striding back out to the centre of the ring as the rest of the *toreros* retreated, having done their work. He carried a small red cape and a sword. Stuart knew instinctively that this was to be the coup de grâce. He didn't want to watch, and sank his head behind his sister's arm; but he heard the cries of the crowd, felt the warmth of the sun and the electricity of excitement around him. Down in the ring, a series of graceful manoeuvres caused the bull to charge sluggishly at the cape, and at times it seemed that the matador was doomed to disaster, so close upon him did the bull come, but always the man's dexterous feet spirited him out of danger.

Forty thousand people cried multiple Olés as the matador toyed with his fast-fading foe. A wave of anticipation seemed to pass through the multitudes, and Stuart made the mistake of peering from behind his sister's arm at just that moment. He saw the bull stagger forward, nostrils flaring, eyes sinking, saw the flurry of red cape and the gold-clad matador performing a smart step to the right; then the sword was raised and the matador leaped and drove the blade down with expert precision between the bull's shoulder blades. Another charged shout of "Olé!" crashed around the precipitous terraces and the bull staggered and then fell to its knees, blood streaming, so it seemed, from its mouth and nostrils, staining the sandy ground red.

The matador took the adoring applause with a theatrical flourish. Little Stuart McCormack, heedless of the long traditions of bullfighting, uncaring about the skill and nerve of the smiling matador, but feeling distressed and nauseous and confused by the murder that had been committed in front of him, and more so by the fact that people were celebrating it, escaped the clutch of his sister Mary and pushed past anyone in his way; he reached the steps in the aisle and ran up them, closely followed by Mary and his mother. The noise of the baying crowd soon receded as he ran headlong back into the long, white-walled tunnel leading away from the bullring, Stuart's only escape route from the horror he had just witnessed. He ran quickly but Mary ran quicker, and soon he was enveloped in his mother's and eldest sister's arms.

The world was a different place for Stuart after the experience of his first and only bullfight. It wasn't all instant change for the schoolboy, but over the years that followed, as he thought through the issues related to humans and animals and made his own mind up, the regular pattern was one of disgust with the way animals were treated. It went beyond sports (not that Stuart saw them as sports) such as bullfighting, horseracing and fox hunting; these were just the obvious examples of human barbarity; very soon after Mexico he decided that his conscience would no longer allow him to eat meat of any kind. Before he had left school, his reading had taught him much about the extent of animal testing around the world and he was even then thinking deeply about what he could do to change opinions and end such experiments. He contacted animal rights organisations and became a member. Often his mother, Elspeth, paid his subscriptions. She had been shocked by the bullfighting and its impact on her son, and though she was far too conservative to encourage activism, she saw that he was passionate about animal rights and that it gave him a path to follow.

Major McCormack wasn't quite so understanding: he had seen action in the Falklands as a young lieutenant, and had served in Northern Ireland, and later as a peacekeeper in the Balkans. He wasn't at all squeamish about a few dense bovines being put to a long-drawn out death in the name of entertainment. He didn't mince his words either, telling Elspeth in the taxi home that sultry Mexican evening, and loudly enough for all the kids to hear, that: "They're just bloody animals, Elsie. They breed the big buggers to go into the ring."

He had been miffed that his night out was cut short by his son's over-reaction. Why was the boy being such a bloody sissy? It was the start of a schism between Stuart and his dad that only grew wider when the boy turned into a young man and started getting involved in animal rights activities. It was all too weird and silly for Murdo McCormack. He had hoped that his boy would follow him into the regiment, but Stuart showed no desire for it. His mind was too caught up in fanciful ideas of changing the world.

It was a shame, because the lad had something about him – a stillness and confidence, a self-assuredness – that Major McCormack believed to be the ingredients of natural leadership. The boy had something special inside of him, but he was determined to waste it, it seemed. He was intelligent and a great listener – he had to be, growing up in a family with three older females – but he wouldn't listen to his dad's prompting for him to consider a military career. It was a bitter disappointment to Murdo.

The only compromise that Stuart made was to agree to go to university. What his dad didn't know was that Stuart saw it as both a way to escape the constant tension at home, and to get closer to the action he really wanted. Down south in England there were some big animal testing firms, and groups of activists were operating against them. He felt he had grown out of the Perthshire countryside.

Proving his sharp intellect and academic prowess, Stuart won a place at Oxford, reading Law. By the time he started his studies in 2003, Mary had fled the nest and married, while Hannah was travelling around the world with two of her friends. Without the girls there, things weren't good at home. Murdo had left the army and wasn't sure what to do with himself next. Elspeth wasn't used to him being under her feet. Stuart was pleased to get away to Oxford, from where he was able to make more solid contacts with different groups of activists, and to start taking part in operations.

After six months of studying law, however, he had had enough. He was not enthused by the subject, partly because his mind was elsewhere. He was close to quitting the university, but a place opened for him on a different degree course, Archaeology and Anthropology. He applied, was accepted, and switched subject. On the first day of his new course he met Jemima Bond, a quiet, studious, dark-haired girl who was sitting in front of him. She was instantly drawn to him, and Stuart, whether he liked it or not, had a new friend.

In fact, a small clique of students gathered around Stuart. Murdo McCormack had been right about his son's personal magnetism. The group would meet in the pubs of Oxford, or stretch out on the grass outside the colleges and libraries, and there they would discuss everything in the world. More often than not, it was Stuart who spoke the most, and the most forcefully too. He found that people listened to him, attached weight to his opinions, even some of the bright young things at Oxford. It was quite a revelation.

Four of them in particular became very close: Stuart, Jemima, Mario Corrini, a flamboyant Scotsman of Italian descent, and Amanda du Plessis, blonde, South African and beautiful. Stuart and Jemima had already become occasional lovers. Stuart indulged her affections whenever it suited him, or when the beer intake had weakened his resistance. Secretly he was enraptured by Amanda's charms, though. She was the one he really wanted. She was available too, and during his second year on the "Arch and Anth" course he finally won her. Stuart assumed that Jemima was hurt deeply by this new development, but she kept her own counsel and waited for the circle to turn again. It was as if she knew it would.

The four friends studied on into their last year at Oxford, and readied themselves for exams. There was less partying, less debating and putting the world to rights. Even animal rights issues took a back seat for Stuart as he and the other students crammed for their exams. In the interim between sitting the exams and receiving their results, though, there was a shock for him. Amanda failed to turn up for a date, and only by speaking to other students did he find out that she had actually flown up to Scotland with Mario. They had been secretly seeing each other for months it turned out. Jemima was waiting for Stuart at his digs when he got back there after discovering all of this. His reaction, at first, was one of anger: anger at Amanda and Mario for being lying bastards; anger at Jemima, who it turned out had known plenty about what was happening, but hadn't told him. What kind of fucking friends were they all? he had demanded to know.

Jemima kept her nerve and told Stuart that he'd been an idiot; had been wilfully blind to the signs, and that he wouldn't have believed her even if she had told him Amanda and Mario were lovers. Stuart got drunk, vented more anger, drank some more, and then took Jemima to his bed.

It wasn't the beginning of a proper relationship between them. Stuart went back home to Perthshire for a couple of weeks, and had a series of blazing rows with his dad about what was to happen next in his life. Murdo McCormack demanded to know how his son was finally going to contribute. Stuart's mind was blank on that point. He had lost his girlfriend and his best male friend, Mario. He had no idea what he wanted emotionally, and nothing appealed to him professionally, especially not the military.

The inferno that had ignited in his heart on that long-ago day at the Plaza México still burned strongly. It was all he cared about, and all he could see himself doing was protesting against and trying to change mankind's shameful treatment of animals. He knew lots of people back in England who agreed with him. That was where he now belonged.

One morning the confrontation between Stuart and his dad escalated into a physical shoving match, which only ended when Murdo raised a fist to strike. He managed to stop himself, but that was all the prompting Stuart needed to up sticks once more and head south, back to Oxford. Jemima was still around, living in a village near Witney. Stuart took digs in Oxford and through an agency started taking temporary office work to support himself. In the meantime, he was quickly back in touch with his animal rights contacts and was soon gaining experience in carrying out operations that targeted research laboratories and the individuals and companies who worked with or for them. There was direct action, such as demonstrations and nuisance calls, and indirect action, including research and surveillance. Stuart viewed this very much as his apprenticeship.

It went on for about a year, during which time Jemima had moved into her own flat in Oxford. The two of them mixed almost exclusively with other rights activists, and therefore had few other friends to speak of, apart from a few colleagues from the various menial jobs they did to pay for their upkeep.

In the meantime, there had been upheaval in the McCormack household. One week early in 2008 Elspeth McCormack's Lottery numbers came up, and she found herself better off to the tune of £8 million. It was a staggering piece of news for Stuart to receive – a surreal thought. It still seemed unreal as he travelled up to Perth on the train to attend a party arranged to celebrate his mother's good fortune. A further shock awaited him: Mum had a new, younger, man. Stuart was introduced to Fraser at the party – he was tall and slim, disarmingly friendly, and only about ten years older than Stuart. Nothing was explicitly said, but it was obvious from the interaction between his mother and this man that something was going on.

Standing morosely in one corner of the room was Murdo McCormack, watching with shifty, suspicious eyes as the man who seemed to be taking his place talked to what he considered to be his errant son. It was all too bizarre. When Stuart spoke to his dad, he found that Murdo already had plans to leave. He had signed up to work for a security contractor in Iraq, and would be departing from Scotland in a matter of days. He had the defiant yet bitter tone of voice of a man who was deeply hurt but was too proud to admit it.

Not for the first time, Stuart was glad to get away and return to Oxford. He wasn't upset or even surprised by what had happened to his parents. He felt largely indifferent to the fate of his family now. Dad was off to Iraq, Mum was looking after herself, Mary was already on her second marriage, and Hannah was in New Zealand and not really talking to anyone. What was the point of it all?

The most important fallout from the whole situation, though, was that Stuart's mum had cash to burn. She had always supported his animal rights aspirations, helping him to make his financial contributions while at university. Having come into such a windfall, it didn't take long for Elspeth McCormack to enquire of her son as to how she could help him out. Since she had money, there was one obvious way: if Stuart didn't have to work part-time to pay his rent and food bills, then he would have more time to devote to the work he wanted to do – campaigning against cruelty to animals in all of its guises. Stuart wasn't greedy; he didn't need to live in palatial splendour. They quickly came to an agreement, which ensured that an allowance gave him all the time he needed for animal rights. Thanks to the Bank of Mum, it turned out that there was value in family ties after all.

Once that situation was sorted out, Stuart's career quickly went into overdrive. Within the hierarchy of the various animal rights units that came under the umbrella of the Animal Liberation Front, "Mac" was swiftly identified as a star in the making. He was committed, passionate, intelligent, charismatic and daring. The young man would go far.

Early in 2009 it became known that a German company was to set up a UK operation in the countryside outside Salisbury. It erected research laboratories, storage blocks and office buildings, and surrounded them with a range of security measures designed to keep out prying eyes and unwanted visitors. Maier Science had arrived, and Stuart, watching undercover of the wood opposite as the builders completed their work, found that the sight instantly raised his hackles.

With him, crouching in the undergrowth that day, were Nancy Jennings and Vince Babcock – two activists he had met through his ALF activity. Vince, who was prematurely bald and not given to patience, was even more militant than Stuart. Given free rein, he would have happily stormed across the road and set about the building workers with their own tools. Nancy was a former air stewardess in her late forties, whose husband, a top-class tennis umpire, had run off with a player half his age nearly a decade before. Her motivation came from a pure love of wildlife of all kinds, and she was a voracious reader on any subject related to the natural world.

Eventually, the three activists headed back through the woods to where Nancy had left her car, and drove back to her house in nearby Coombe Bissett. Even before they reached the village an agreement had been reached: they needed to set up a group to target Maier Science, to make it see that the UK was no place for its monstrous experiments. All the experience they had gained so far as activists had led to this point – it was time to break away from ALF and focus on this new threat. They would seek approval from the leadership, but whether they received it or not, this was their new path. And so Stop Maier Animal Cruelty, or SMAC, was born. Mac moved to Salisbury and Jemima soon followed, still waiting for Mac to realise the good thing they should be sharing.

***

The formation of SMAC was more than a year ago now, and it had been fifteen years since the awakening of Mac's purpose in life, that tumultuous evening in blood-spattered Plaza México. He felt that his desire to prevent or at least disrupt the activities of organisations such as Maier Science was undiminished, whatever Vince might think about his strategy. There had been discussions over who should lead SMAC back at the start, and at times they were heated. Nancy hadn't wanted to take charge, and it was left to Mac and Vince to contest the issue. In true democratic fashion, a vote had been held and Vince had only secured the support of his wife. Nancy, Jemima and the other volunteers voted for Mac. Grouchy at the best of times, Vince had taken his defeat badly, but Pippa had talked him round, and he had grudgingly accepted the situation.

Even Vince was in high spirits this evening, though. They sat in a circle around the campfire, a metal brazier from which the flames leaped and crackled and lit their happy faces with a flickering glow.

Vince and Pippa had just arrived back at the SMAC camp, which was in the woods across the road from the Maier facility. They were the last of the group to return from the evening's activity. Over at the treeline their banners faced towards Maier, proclaiming their strident opposition. Fifty yards deeper into the woods, there was a small clearing amongst the beech trees, with the brazier in the middle and four tents scattered in the trees nearby. Only occasionally would any of them actually sleep in the camp. The tents were used more for shelter in inclement weather. It was their camp, though, helping to strengthen the feeling of togetherness in their cause, and they would meet there sometimes when there were things to discuss. Such as now.

It was just before 10 p.m. and everyone was excited. It had been a fun evening. There was nothing like a bit of "direct action" to get the blood pumping again. They had divided a list of targets up between them – two calls for each group of two people. Mac and Nancy had visited Brian Ames and Lucy Schwarzman; Vince and Pippa

Babcock had been to see Janis Swann and Elena Cristofides; Bhupathi and Anthony had dropped by at the houses of Steve Womack and Martin Cawte. What all of these people had in common was that they were suppliers of products or services to Maier Science.

There was a second thing they all had in common now: they had all been pelted with flour bombs on their own doorstep.

Vince and Pippa had taken their seats around the campfire now and, judging by the story that Vince was telling with rarely heard gusto, Pippa Babcock's accuracy with a flour bomb left something to be desired. Mac did the rounds handing out bottles of beer as Vince held court.

The couple's first call that evening had been to Janis Swann, who ran a cleaning business that Maier Science used. When the unsuspecting Ms Swann answered her front door, she found two balaclava-wearing figures outside, each of whom proceeded to throw something at her. Suddenly she couldn't see through a swirling cloud of tiny white particles. But it could have been much worse for her, because Pippa Babcock's throwing arm had caught her husband's shoulder as it was about to deliver its powdery package. The bomb burst on Vince's shoulder, some of it skewing off to hit the wall, while the rest of the flour showered the married couple just as they were yelling the war cry: "SMACK!"

Fortunately, not too much flour had got into their eyes, but they were laughing and coughing so much that they couldn't deliver the rest of their message, and had to dash back to the car to make their getaway before Janis herself could recover. After cleaning themselves up, they paid their visit to the second target, Elena Cristofides, and this time Pippa stood on the other side of her husband, so that her throwing arm couldn't interfere with the success of the operation a second time.

"That's what you get when you let a bloody woman try and throw things," Vince said, by way of a punchline. The men laughed in agreement, while Nancy, who was sitting next to Vince and also laughing, gave him a semi-playful whack on the arm; Jemima poked her tongue out disdainfully; Pippa made a yeah-whatever face at her husband, and contented herself with telling everyone that Vince had stalled the car as they had tried to make a swift exit. Whether it was true or not, Vince suddenly, even in the midst of his own laughter, had to defend himself amidst hoots of derision from around the fire.

Mac smiled to himself and sat back down in his chair. Above the curl of the dancing flames he saw Jemima looking at him. He winked at her and they both smiled, but he knew that she was annoyed with him. She had wanted to take part in the flour-bombing as well, but they had split into pairs, and since there were seven of them, one person had to be left out. Added to that, there had been a possibility that Jemima would need to stay late with the little boy she looked after for Kay Campbell, the public relations woman at Maier Science, who had alerted Jemima a few days before that she might be going away on business this same evening. The trip hadn't even happened in the end, but when they were planning the attacks it had made Mac's decision that much easier. He had promised Jemima that she could be involved next time. She would be okay about it, eventually.

Bhupathi was relating the abuse that had been shouted at him and Anthony by Steve Womack, who had come lurching out of his house, completely blinded by flour, in the ludicrous hope that he might catch his assailants. The language had been colourful enough to make a squaddie blush.

"How close did he get to snagging one of you?" asked Nancy.

"Nowhere near – the damned fool ran into the bloody bird bath in the front garden," answered Bhupathi, his dark eyes shining at the memory of the moment. Laughter rang out. "Oh, man, you had to be there! I was laughing so bloody much I couldn't get the key in the bloody ignition," Bhups continued between his own chuckles. Anthony, who certainly had been there, was bent double with mirth.

Just then, surrounded by general merriment, Mac noticed over Jemima's shoulder that someone was walking towards them through the trees, about fifty metres away. It was a man with short dark hair, wearing a tracksuit top and jeans. He didn't seem to know that he had been spotted. He just came on, picking his way carefully but steadily between the tree trunks, swatting the odd clawing branch away from his face.

There was something about the way the man moved that told Mac this wasn't just a member of the public having an innocent stroll in the woods. This guy looked like he had a direction and a purpose in mind, and right now that direction was straight towards the SMAC camp.

He was getting closer. Mac felt suddenly alert, but no one else around the campfire showed any sign of having spotted the trespasser. And that was exactly what he was, to Mac's mind – he was trespassing on SMAC property. After a successful night of action, Mac's thought processes were sharp and decisive. He was not worried about the prospect of confrontation. He was instantly up on his feet and walking around the circle of chairs and then straight at the oncoming figure. The laughter and the crackle of burning wood were now behind him, the air cooler.

The man had stopped as soon as he had noticed Mac walking towards him, and now stood waiting amongst the trees about thirty metres short of the camp. Surprising, thought Mac. He hadn't expected the guy just to stop. From behind he heard Nancy call out to him.

"Everything okay, Mac?" He glanced round to see her, Jemima and Anthony standing and watching him; the others remained seated, but even those in shadow had turned their heads to watch. He waved a hand towards them to demonstrate he was unconcerned and continued walking. Very soon he and the trespasser were face to face.

Mac spoke sullenly. "Can I help you, pal? Looking for anything in particular?"

The other man didn't seem at all perturbed. He replied in a clear, even voice, with a London accent.

"Maybe... I'm looking for the leader of SMAC. That's you, isn't it..." he paused, as if wanting to savour the taste of the next word all on its own "... Mac?"

A glimmer of a smile played around the newcomer's lips. Mac wasn't amused. He didn't beat about the bush.

"Who the fuck are *you* then? Are you a cop? A journalist?"

He laughed lightly. "Steady on, Mac, I'm not that ugly, am I? I'm neither of those. I'm a supporter of what you guys do. Quite fancy a bit of that for myself, as it happens. I've come to join."

"Why?"

"Why not? I agree with what you do. Is it so unusual for someone to want to join up with the famous SMAC?"

Mac ignored the question. "We're not recruiting, pal," he said, after no apparent consideration.

"Come off it, mate. There's not many of you in the group, is there?" The newcomer looked past Mac towards the camp. "I'm not asking for a fucking signing-on fee. I just want to help out, do my bit."

Mac stared at him for a few seconds before saying: "I don't know you from Adam. We get..."

The other man had stepped forward and offered his hand. "Name's Liam. Pleased to meet you."

Mac looked at the hand. "Yeah, whatever, pal. As I was about to say – we get our people sent to us from the big boys. I've only got your word for it that you're not a copper or a fucking reporter. You're from London, not from round here."

He made it sound like an accusation.

"What's that got to do with anything?" Liam demanded, sounding surprised. "From your accent, you're hardly local yourself."

Standing there in the dark, face to face with this stranger, with just the green-clad branches for back-up and the campfire chatter lost behind the trees, Mac couldn't help but feel slightly exposed. Maybe he should have told Bhups or Vince or Anthony to come with him when he had walked away from the fire, just in case any trouble started. For the first time, he took the opportunity to study the man in front of him. Liam was a bit bigger and heavier than the slightly built Mac. He had short, dark hair and a ruddy complexion. He stood with his hands pushed into the pockets of his tracksuit top. He didn't seem bothered by Mac's distrust of him.

Mac paced a few steps to his left and then back to his right, thinking. Finally, he stopped moving, now appreciably closer to Liam than he had been before. They were close enough to smell each other's breath. "How the fuck did you know we were here anyway?"

"I drove past the Maier place and saw your banners out the front there. I was just getting familiar with the area really, driving round the back of the woods, when the car in front of me pulled up behind a couple of others. I pulled over and saw a man and a woman get out and disappear into the woods. Seemed obvious that this was where you guys hung out, so I sat there for a while, trying to decide whether to come in and introduce myself. Finally plucked up the courage. I suppose, being totally honest, it's fair to say that I followed you in here. Sorry about that, pal."

At this appropriation of his own habitual form of address, Mac looked up sharply. He studied the other man's face closely. Was that a piss-take? Liam's expression gave nothing away. He seemed friendly, patient, composed. Mac needed time to think, and decided to buy it by lighting a cigarette. That should test this guy's patience.

He stared at Liam as he took a packet of cigarettes and a lighter out of his jeans pocket, and then he sparked one up. Mac blew out a cloud of smoke that hung between the two men, floating lazily on the still night air. Liam waited, serenely it seemed.

Mac thought: was this stranger trustworthy? It was uncommon – unheard of, in fact – for someone just to come up and offer their services like this. The original members of the group had been operating for the main Animal Liberation Front organisation before SMAC was formed. Those who had joined since had been sent to Mac by the ALF, either because of their geographical proximity to Maier Science, or because Mac had requested more manpower. He hadn't been advised of a new man coming along to join, so this clearly had nothing to do with the ALF. Even if this guy Liam was telling the truth, Mac wondered whether he really had any idea what he was asking to get involved with.

"What experience of animal rights activism have you got?" Mac demanded.

Liam shrugged as if it didn't matter. "None yet. I've been living up in London, stuck in the middle of the rat race – wife, mortgage, working hard, playing hard. I didn't have the time or opportunity to do anything like this, anything that was actually worthwhile. But I made a few bob, rang the changes, and now's my chance."

Mac continued to eye the newcomer closely. "What did you do in London?"

"Banking. Nowadays I'm a self-employed financial adviser, though." At this he offered Mac a business card. The paper felt thin and cheap; it was probably from one of those machines you saw in shopping centres and such like, thought Mac, reading the details. Liam was still talking. "I've never known anyone who was into this kind of activism before; just never moved in those sorts of circles, I suppose. But that doesn't mean I haven't been interested in the issues. You guys shouldn't think it's only you who care about these things."

Liam Walcott, financial adviser, the card said. There was a mobile phone number and an email address underneath – just a Googlemail one; well, anyone could set that up, reckoned Mac.

"All I'm doing is offering to help," Liam continued. "I can understand why you would be suspicious – some bloke turning up out of the blue. It does sound a bit unlikely. But if I was being planted by the Old Bill, or if I was an undercover journalist, don't you think whoever wanted me here would give me a better cover story? I'd be dazzling you with my supposed knowledge and experience, wouldn't I? As it is, there is no cover story. I'm just offering to help."

Mac looked up from the business card and scrutinised Liam's face again. It was a fair point of sorts, he supposed. The same half-smile was still visible on Liam's face. Mac found himself being swayed by the apparent sincerity behind the explanation. Still, he had another question to ask.

"What made you leave London then?"

Liam nodded at him. "Good question, Mac. Well now, let's just say that matters of the heart were making it difficult for me to stay." They looked at each other, then Liam shrugged and held his hands out, palms held upward as if he were pleading. "I came to get away from the ex-wife."

Mac allowed himself a small smile. "Expensive?"

"Could have been worse, fella. Could have been worse."

"Any kids involved?"

"Nah, managed to escape from that one, thank fuck. Otherwise it really would have been expensive."

Liam laughed, and Mac smirked and nodded his head in man-to-man empathy. A gust of wind set the leaves in the canopy above whispering. Mac puffed on the cigarette and blew the smoke back out again; he flicked some ash from the end, aiming to appear as coolly nonchalant as a French movie star. He carried it off pretty well, he thought.

Liam tried again, this time with just a slight edge of impatience to his voice. "Listen, Mac, I'm not trying to find out all your secrets. I just want to do something… to contribute, you know? I don't need to be involved in planning anything, mate, so you don't have to reveal any of your secrets to me. I'll do exactly what you order, like a good foot soldier or a solid citizen. What do you say?"

Mac drew on the cigarette again, and shrugged. "I might be able to use you, I suppose," he said. "Tell me what you know about Maier Science then."

"Not as much as you guys," laughed Liam. "You know, I just read stuff – news reports, your website, their website – but since they're a pack of lying bastards anyway, I probably shouldn't believe anything they say."

As Liam was speaking, Mac heard lightly rustling footsteps approaching from behind him. A couple of seconds later Jemima was at his side.

"Everything okay, Stu?" she asked. "Who's this?"

Though her words referred to Liam, she didn't look at him. She looked at Mac, and he turned towards her. He was mildly irked by the interruption, feeling suddenly hurried into making a decision.

"Jemmy… yeah, everything's fine. This is, ah, this is Liam. He wants to help us. That's what he says."

Jemima turned towards the other man, whom she hadn't acknowledged up to that moment. He smiled and thrust out a hand to take hers.

"Liam Walcott. Good to meet you."

"Likewise," Jemima replied, and shook his hand briefly. She turned back to Mac. "Everyone's wondering what's happening. Vince wants to get away."

"Jesus Christ, Jemima," Mac muttered, looking down at the ground.

Liam shifted his weight from one leg to the other and looked like he was about to say something, but then he seemed to think better of it and kept shtum instead. Jemima regarded him coldly all the same. Mac finally looked up and rolled his eyes. He had come to a decision.

"Okay, Liam, let's take you over to meet the other guys, and we'll see how you get on. I can't say any fairer than that, pal."

Liam looked delighted. "Excellent! Perfect. Thanks for the opportunity." The three of them turned and began to pick their way through the trees, Jemima in the lead, back to the gaggle of people gathered around the fire. "I should warn you, Vince is getting insufferable over there," she said over her shoulder to Mac.

"Huh, tell me something new, eh?" he snorted, then more loudly said to the man walking ahead of him: "We've had a busy night, Liam. You'll hear all about it in a minute." The faces of his troops, the SMAC members, looked at the approaching threesome with interest, and they instantly began to size up the stranger who was about to be set in their midst.

CHAPTER FIVE

Dear Diary

I still felt like the master of the universe when I got down to Salisbury. I was singing along to the CD player all the way down, and I felt happier than I had been since... well, let's think about that now... probably since about two years after Kay and I got married. That feels like another life, and it was really. Feels like that guy was murdered at some point.

Okay, Lee – deep breaths now, let's get started on a happy vibe, shall we?! Right, so, I parked up the Beamer outside the Easy B&B and sat on the bonnet of the car for a few minutes, just breathing in the fresh air, listening to the street sounds, enjoying the sunshine and feeling a kind of tingle of anticipation about the future. This really was a new way for me to be thinking, after the past few years. It was a new dawn. Then I grabbed one of my bags from the car and rang the crusty old doorbell.

Margaret, who runs the Easy B&B, turned out to be a bit crusty too. Mid-fifties, I guessed; bit puffy around the eyes, too much make-up, tarty clothes, bit of a fading, desperate, filthy look in her eyes. Easy, indeed. She looked me up and down in a way that suggested it had been a while. I fancied her not. She gave me my key and laid down the house rules. I was fucking relieved that they didn't include servicing the landlady. She asked if I wanted a welcoming cup of tea, but I declined, fairly politely, I think, and headed up the stairs to room 12 – that was a nice touch, Kay's birthday being the 12th February.

Anyway, you don't need to know about me unpacking my clothes and trying out the bog for the first time, do you, so I'll cut out the next hour of that day. Suffice to say, it was a bit of a shit-hole of a B&B, and what with the stained 1970s wallpaper, the busted toilet seat, and the old brass downstairs on reception chain-smoking like her lungs were made of graphene, I rather wanted to get out and explore the town. I did that, found a boozer, and sat down with a beer to think about my next moves.

High on the agenda, of course, was finding the Maier place. I haven't explained the plan yet, have I? Well, at that stage it still needed a bit more fine-tuning on the specifics, but basically I reckoned that just leaping out of a doorway with a bunch of flowers as Kay walked along the road would probably get me arrested. I thought I'd stand more chance of getting her back, or at least of her talking to me, if I showed that I'd put a bit of effort in to finding her; effort and some creativity. She's big on that kind of shit – she sees it as being part of her job requirement and therefore it's in her DNA. (I think that's what she once said years ago when I was half listening, anyway.) So I wanted to find the SMAC people, and see if I could ingratiate myself with them. I reckoned that they would probably come into contact with Kay, given her job.

So, find Maier Science, find SMAC. All this activism sounded a bit of a lark, and I thought it might be good fun too. First, though, I needed a cover story and, would you believe it, a new identity? Yeah, fucking James Bond, man! When I say new identity, though, I don't mean the whole fake passport and plastic surgery thing. No, I just wanted some basic stuff like business cards, a website under construction, Twitter and LinkedIn profiles. I had decided to pass myself off as a self-employed financial adviser, just moved into the area and getting my business off the ground. I thought that the SMAC people might look to do some research on me before they would let me get too close, but if I was new to the freelance game that might explain the lack of a trail on the internet. I also, as it happens, know enough about financial matters to give anyone advice, so I didn't mind if they tested me on it.

I sat in the boozer and thought about all of these things. I wanted a different name too. I didn't want them to know I was Lee Talbot, in case they had looked into Kay's background before and put two and two together. So during pint number two, I flipped over to a fresh new page in my notepad and jotted down some possibles. Oh, I came up with some fucking corkers, I was pissing myself laughing! I had fun for half an hour, and then decided none of them would be any use so I came up with something normal instead. It wasn't very scientific in the end: Liam because it was quite close to Lee; and Walcott after my favourite Gunner. I realised that I could have sat there for hours and come up with hundreds of names, but why bother? I just needed a temporary identity, and Liam Walcott of Liam Walcott Financial Services would be as good as any.

It had a kind of style to it anyway, I thought. I nipped into the pub toilets and looked at myself in the mirror for a few minutes, getting used to the idea of being Liam and not Lee. Practising how my new alter ego would hold himself, how he would react when spoken to. That was the advantage of Liam being so close to Lee, you see – it would be easy to get used to answering to the name. So I posed in front of the mirror for a bit, and studied this new guy.

Maybe he should have a little goatee beard, I thought at one point. That might look cool. Had to ditch that idea, though, since it takes me weeks just to grow a few wispy bits of facial hair!

After that I had a wander around Salisbury city centre for a while, which was full of shoppers enjoying the nice weather. There was a busy open-air market on the go, although by this time it was late afternoon and things were starting to slow down. Then I found a shopping centre called the Maltings, also open-air, and with a beautiful shiny river flowing by. There were ducks out on the water and people were throwing bread for them to peck at. I even bought a small loaf myself and ripped up a few slices that I tossed out for the little fellas. All perfectly charming in a very English way, if you know what I mean. Anyway, I saved the rest of the bread for another day and put it back in the bag with some tins of beer and a big packet of Doritos that I'd bought at the same time.

Outside one of the shops I found what I was really looking for: one of those vending machines that you can get business cards printed from while you stand there. As I was doing it, though, I realised that I would need to put a website address on there, and I didn't even have a domain name, having only just decided what I was going to be called. I thought quickly and came up with www. lw-financial.co.uk and hoped that when I got back to the hotel room and fired the laptop up, I'd find that the domain name was still available. I chose a nice little design for the business card, and printed off twenty, and that was that job done.

I went straight back to the Easy B&B and got the domain name sorted out, by which time evening was approaching. I still had a big itch to go and see the Maier place, though, so instead of chilling out, having a shower and thinking about getting some eats, I headed back down to the car, set the Satnav and off I went again.

It was about a twenty-minute drive through some winding country lanes to get there, since it's situated kind of in the middle of nowhere, amongst the woods. One second you're driving along, surrounded by hedgerows and trees on both sides, then you come round a bend to the right and suddenly it all opens up in front of you: wire fencing topped with barbed wire, security guards on the entrance, hanging around one of those huts where the controls are to raise and lower the barrier that lets cars through. Beyond that were some buildings, and then as I kept driving more wire fencing that quickly gave way to more trees and hedges; and then it was behind me – gone already. There was nowhere to stop and get a better look, or even to turn around – not without blocking the road and risking getting rammed by some fuckwit with his foot to the floor, anyway.

So I carried on, and after several minutes there was a T-junction, where I turned left. A mile or two later there was another left turning that I took. I sped along another lane for quite a few minutes, woods on every side. At one point I drove past a small concreted area, a layby cut into the woods and separated from the road by a low metal barrier. I guessed it was somewhere to park up, but I went past too quickly to stop. A little later, as the trees started to thin out, there was another T-junction, and I realised that this was the road I'd been on some time before, from which the Satnav had told me to take a left, to get onto the road that led past the Maier Science facility. I'd come round in a circle, or maybe a rectangle.

Minutes later I was driving past Maier again, slower this time, and noticing two other things for the first time: firstly, the small corporate sign that hung next to the security control room, with Maier's blue logo on it – so small it was as if they were embarrassed; and secondly, the half a dozen or so banners that had been put up amongst the trees facing the site, proclaiming, shall we say, the odious nature of what happened inside this place? So I had found the first signs of SMAC.

It was then that I had an idea, or perhaps it was a re-alisation. Maybe these SMAC guys hung out in the woods there – you know what these tree-hugging types are like – at one with nature, and all that bollocks. And that small layby round the other side of the woods – maybe that was ideally placed to provide access to their camp.

I was back there a few minutes later, pulled the Beamer into the little slip road and switched the engine off. By now it was starting to get a bit dark, and I sat there for a min-ute thinking about it. I wasn't really worried about get-ting lost in the woods in the dark, but was I ready to meet these SMAC people yet? There were no other cars parked there, though, and I wondered how they got to and from the place, since we were in the middle of nowhere – miles from any villages, bus stops or train stations, as far as I knew. It didn't seem possible that they spent all their time here. I mean, everyone has to eat. Either someone brought food in, or they lived on fucking twigs and berries, and no one, not even soap-dodging animal rights weirdos, will do that for long.

I got out of the car and started off through the woods. Having driven along both ends a few times already, I had a good idea of the distance I'd have to walk before reaching the opposite treeline – the one that faced Maier – but it took longer than I expected, picking my way between the trees and the undergrowth. Soon enough, though, I saw some tents up ahead. As I got closer it became pretty obvious that no one was at home. The tents were all zipped up, nobody was moving around or talking. I got to the little clearing where the tents were and stopped. All was quiet.

I counted four tents, and there was also a collection of chairs scattered around a big, round metal can-type thing that was blackened in parts by fire. It was all surprisingly tidy. I'd half expected there to be litter everywhere – empty bottles, food packaging, newspapers, etc. I remember thinking: I guess these SMAC people aren't messy bastards like I am! At that point I didn't know anything about two particular busybodies called Nancy and Jemima, who kept everything just so, and scoured the camp for litter like proud mums picking bits of fluff off their little boys' school uniforms.

It felt a bit weird really, standing there in the camp used by these people that I'd read about. I felt like a gunslinger wandering around a ghost town in the Wild West. Being a nosy fucker, though, it didn't stop me from unzipping one of the tents and having a look inside! There wasn't much in there – a sleeping bag and a pillow that didn't look much used, a small torch for seeing in the dark, a Harry Potter paperback, and some headache tablets.

I wandered around for a minute, and then I heard a sudden noise from among the dark trees. It made me freeze where I stood. It had sounded like a twig breaking beneath the weight of a foot. I listened for a few seconds more. There was nothing, except a bit of breeze blowing through the branches, rustling in the leaves. I looked around, searching the trees all around, but could see nothing in the shadows.

It had spooked me a bit, to be honest, so I decided to get out of the place. There wasn't really much to see anyway.

First, though, I wanted to see the Maier place from the woods, so I jogged over to where the trees bordered the road. I hid from view there, by the treeline, and looked out across the road to Maier. Although it was a Saturday night, there were a few lights on in the various buildings, and one fella was sitting in the control room at the gate, talking on a telephone. I lurked behind a tree so that I wasn't seen. Strangely enough, it took a few seconds before the thought even came to me that this was where my Kay worked. In one of those buildings, over there beyond Stan the Security Man, was her desk, where she'd been sitting when I'd called and heard her voice. This place, with its perimeter fence, barbed wire and security guards, was where Kay had come to start all over again.

To get away from me.

I didn't have that specific thought right there and then – I was too wrapped up in believing that I would, could, get her back – but sitting here now, it seems unavoidable.

Well, there I was – just me, and the trees, and the wind, and thoughts of Kay. I turned around and walked quickly back to the car without even looking at the tents in the clearing. I'd done everything I needed to for now. Drove back to the B&B, had a shower and got dressed, and walked back into the city centre. Had a bite to eat, and then visited a few drinking establishments. Even got chatting to a couple of birds, who invited me out to another bar that was open till late. They're very friendly people down there in the West Country. But you don't need to know about that bit. Mind your own business!

Anyway, I've just noticed how much I've written! Here I am, prattling on, and you're still waiting to find out what happened! Patience, friend. Funnily enough, I'm finding this writing lark to be quite therapeutic somehow. I do get angry sometimes, but I spare you from the worst of that, dear reader, by the simple expedient of putting the pen down and retreating to the other side of the room, until the nasty clouds in my head clear.

So, to continue, I went back and drove past the woods twice the next day, and again on the Monday, but there was no one there. On Tuesday night I hit the jackpot, though. As I approached the little slip road where I'd parked on the Saturday evening, the car driving in front of me slowed to a stop and two people, a man and a woman, jumped out and quickly disappeared into the woods. The car then pulled away but I saw that there were two cars already parked in the layby. I went round the block again to think about it – suddenly I was feeling nervous – but when I got back round to the parking area I pulled slowly in there, stopped behind the two other motors and cut the engine.

I sat thinking for another few minutes. Was I ready for this? I might only get one chance to be accepted. In fact, they would probably be a tight-knit bunch, and suspicious of outsiders, so I would definitely only get one chance. I had my cover story, such as it was, and my new business cards, but no other ID – I mean, my passport and driving licence, bank cards, etc., were in my real name of course. I didn't want them to make a connection between Kay and me because then my motive would be thrown into question. Weighing it up, my plan was almost to play on my lack of preparedness as proof that I was genuine.

With a gulp of nervous anticipation, I got out of the car and headed off through the trees. It was pretty dark again, and not the nicest time to have unseen branches flick across your face like an insult, but I could soon see the glow of their campfire ahead. Some acting was going to be required. I discovered a newfound talent within myself that night, though, because they let me in!

The leader, Mac, came and met me halfway through the woods and asked what I wanted. We had a chat and I was working on convincing him when this bird came over. Not bad- looking, but she gave me a sour look as we shook hands. This, it turned out, was Jemima, and she had a thing for Mac. That took about five and a half seconds for me to work out. After a couple of awkward moments, I was invited over to meet everyone else. There was a bunch of questions obviously, but I blagged it, and after a while I found myself getting on better and better with Mac, an older bird called Nancy and two guys, Anthony and an Indian fella they called either Boops or Booper. I guess we just clicked. There was one bloke who was a bit of a miserable bastard, by the name of Vince – I got the impression then, and it turned out to be true, that he was always like that. Still, he kept asking about me producing proper ID, and I promised him I'd "bring some next time", though he had no concept of how bad my memory can be!

He was the only one really who seemed uncertain about me, so I guess that makes him the sharpest tool out of the lot of them, since he was actually right.

It turned out that they had been having fun that evening, calling on people who worked as suppliers to Maier and throwing flour bombs at the poor fuckers on their own doorsteps. Can you believe that?! As if it was going to make any difference! As if it's going to help some poor fucking monkey they're doing experiments on in that place. Anyway, I kept that under my hat and turned to Mac to ask if there was any chance I could do something similar. There *was general discussion about the merits of that idea, which ended with Mac and Anthony agreeing to pick me up the next evening to go and do some "calls". Vince didn't want to go anywhere near the idea, until he'd seen proper ID, but Mac made the decision. That seemed to be the way of things: Mac and Vince would disagree, and Mac would get his way.*

No phone numbers were swapped or anything – I hadn't been totally accepted yet – but we just arranged that the two guys would collect me from a particular street corner in Salisbury at 7 p.m. and off we would go. After that, Mac asked me to leave as they had some things to discuss, which I did. Next evening at 7, I was there waiting and the guys turned up in a nice Audi, which was one of the motors I'd seen parked up the night before. Off we went. There wasn't much conversation; mostly we just listened to the radio, though Mac asked what I'd been up to, and I said I'd been putting the bits and pieces for my business together, like the website. I didn't know where we were going or who we were going to see, and I didn't ask either.

We drove for a good hour or so before pulling up in a residential street somewhere the other side of Swindon. Mac and Anthony got out and left me in the car to watch. They approached a door, dressed all in black and wearing balaclavas, rang the bell, and when it was opened, pelted the guy with flour. It was proper crazy shit. Then they legged it back to the car and we sped away, pissing ourselves laughing. I had no idea whether this kind of crap was even legal or not – I guessed not really – but fuck me, it was a hoot.

We drove back towards Salisbury for another twenty minutes, crossing the M4 again, and eventually we stopped in a little village called Axford. On the way, Mac told me that he and I would do the next job. I have to admit I was well up for it after watching the first one. It was quite a thrill to walk up to the door, knowing that we were about to inflict mayhem on the poor bugger inside.

Mac knocked loudly and a youthful-looking man opened the door, with a little girl standing in front of him. Mac said: "Adam Barnes?" The guy nodded, and then Mac threw his flour bombs and yelled: "Smack!" I did the same a second later. I must admit, the little girl being there almost stopped me in my tracks, but I had to do the job. It would have been fatal to my chances if I'd blown out. So I threw my little bombs, and they exploded really quite satisfyingly on the target, one straight in his reeling mush, and one in the chest. We ran off, but I can still remember now how the little girl cried out "Daddy, Daddy" in the doorway. There wasn't any time for guilt, though. We scrambled back into the car, Anthony gunned the engine and off we went.

We had a good laugh on the way back, and by 9.30 they had dropped me off back at the same street corner in Salisbury where they'd picked me up more than two hours earlier. I'd done my first job for SMAC. I walked home via a couple of pubs, feeling pretty fucking pleased with myself. Not that pleased that I fancied having a go on Easy Margaret at the B&B when I got in though. I mean, come on…

CHAPTER SIX

Nick had grown accustomed to the tranquillity of Wiltshire: of village life, long days spent labouring in gardens and parks, and listening to birdsong. Driving through the South London suburbs that morning had served only to remind him of how much he enjoyed his current idyllic lifestyle. The London traffic had been angry and impatient, with snarling motorbikes cutting him up, and ignorant bus and lorry drivers crowding him out.

Once inside the M25 ring, he had driven up the A3 past Wimbledon Common and Richmond Park to Wandsworth. Then there had been a bewildering succession of smaller A-roads around Clapham, Brixton and Tulse Hill. Eventually, after getting completely lost twice and nearly crashing once, he had got to the A215 – Denmark Hill. A few back roads later and he had found his destination – a road called Champion Hill.

It had not been a fun journey up from the countryside, but now at least Nick had parked the car and could think about his task. Denmark Hill, in the South London borough of Southwark, was unfamiliar territory, and he looked at the maisonettes to his left with some nervousness. He and Jerry had finished off Mr and Mrs Shepherd's borders the day before, and they were to take a short break now before starting on a new floral feature in a local park in Salisbury. Nick had taken advantage of the day off to drive up to London, armed only with the piece of paper on which Kay had written the address where she hoped her dad still lived.

She had not seen him for more than ten years, and Nick's task was to see if Les Campbell did indeed still live at number two, Birdsall House on the Champion Hill Estate. If he did, then Nick hoped to speak to him and tell him about his daughter's life now. It was clear that Kay wanted to reach out to her father again, but was too scared of something – rejection, Nick guessed – to do it herself. Well, for the love of Kay…

A brief shower of summer rain was just beating itself out on the windscreen, and Nick waited for that to finish. Already the sun was out again, and it would just be a few seconds more before the rain stopped completely. He rehearsed his opening lines again, and saw in his mind's eye the face of Kay's dad, which he remembered from the twenty-year-old photograph she had of Les – her only keepsake. The whole thing was a bit scary, in fact. Kay had never said much about her childhood in this place, nor about her dad, but the impression Nick had got was that these were pretty mean streets, and Les Campbell had been quite of piece of work: a hard-drinker and a womaniser. He had also always despised Kay's choice of husband, Lee, which seemed to be the main reason for the estrangement from his daughter for all these years. At least that was one thing Nick would have in common with Mr Campbell.

The rain had stopped and Nick got out of the car, filling his lungs with the freshness left behind in the air. It was a nice day now and everything here seemed quiet. There was a map of the Champion Hill Estate mounted on a board in front of the maisonettes. Nick sauntered over to it and saw that behind the first set of flats, which were called Appleshaw House, were another three buildings, and Birdsall House was on the left of the three. A driveway wound down from Champion Hill and round behind Appleshaw, and Nick took this path on foot. Birdsall House quickly came into view. Each of the buildings was five storeys high, he saw, with something like eight or nine flats to a floor.

It didn't take much thought for him to deduce that the red door that was second from the left on the ground floor might be Les's flat, number two. Nick couldn't help but feel a sense of wonder at these moments, as he stepped ever closer to that door. He was thinking of Kay now, not her dad. This was where she had grown up. It was hard to believe he was here. It was like treading upon hallowed ground – to be walking these streets where she had run and played as a girl. In his mind's eye he saw the red door open as he approached, and young Kay, a girl of ten but unmistakably her, came running out, looking excited and mischievous, shouting and giggling as she ran past Nick to go and play with her friends, leaving the door open behind her.

He paused, transfixed by this vision of a phantom Kay as she ran by; then with a smile on his face he carried on, perhaps ten metres short of the red door now. To his right, the door to a stairwell suddenly swung open, and tearing out of it ran a dog, heading straight at him, giving every impression it was not intending to stop until it had knocked him off his feet. Nick was alarmed and took a step back. The dog, squat and muscular, its fur half white, half brindle, and with a dramatic black patch of fur around its right eye, mercifully came to a halt before it reached him, but its eyes flared at him and its whole body bristled with aggression. It barked and snarled. Nick took another step backwards.

"What the…" he said out loud, voicing real fear. He did not dare take his eyes off the dog. Suddenly there was another sound.

"Drogba! Come on, boy. Drogba!"

Nick looked up from the white, snapping teeth that had held his attention for the past two seconds and saw a man standing in the background, smirking. He was quite young but looked unkempt – dressed in an old pair of trainers, tracksuit bottoms and a scruffy t-shirt; his blond hair plastered flat to his head with too much hair gel.

That smirk was annoying. Surely the bloke could see Nick was terrified. Why didn't he put a lead on his belligerent mutt and let everyone go about their business peacefully?

"Don't worry, mate – he won't hurt ya," the man called over to Nick. The dog was still snarling at him though; there was no easing up in its ferocious aspect. "Come on, Drogba!" the man called again.

Nick spoke angrily: "Are you having a fucking laugh, pal? Why don't you put it on a lead? It's a fucking menace." He had even turned side-on to the dog, subconsciously, as if to protect softer parts of his anatomy.

The man jutted his chin towards Nick. "Who are you ordering around, chief? I'll do what I want with my dog, you follow? Come on, boy, leave the Big Chief Man alone."

The man started walking away. He had no dog lead in his hands, Nick could now see. This was how he always took his pet, if you could call it that, for exercise. The man stopped again after a few paces. "Bruv, you're scaring the shit out of him, innit! Chill bruv, fuck's sake."

"*I'm* scaring the shit out of *him*? I'm just standing here. It's down to you to control the bloody thing. He could kill someone."

The man glared at Nick with severe dislike. He glared back, from owner to dog, and back again. Finally, the man walked reluctantly towards the scene of the stand-off. Nick, not being sure whether he was about to be attacked by man, dog, or both, took another step backwards.

"You proper fucking moist, man," the man laughed derisively. "Scared shitless of a little dog, innit? Come with, Drog." He reached down and grabbed the dog by its collar. The dog didn't much like that; it seemed to have been mesmerised by Nick until that point, though despite its threatening stance it had never got closer than perhaps two paces from him. When its owner pulled its collar from behind, it instinctively snapped at this new threat. Its fangs didn't catch the man's hand but they came close, and he reacted by giving the dog an almighty whack on the flank, which sent it sprawling and whimpering to the ground in front of Nick.

"Don't fuck with me, you little shit!" the man shouted, wagging his finger in the startled dog's face. Again he grabbed its collar, black leather with heavy metal studs, and dragged the dog off with him, without saying another word. Nick watched them depart towards the main road. He breathed deeply a few times. Peace had descended. Once again he was left with bright, late-morning sunshine, raindrops glistening on the concrete and the blades of grass. Did that actually just happen? He watched, bemused, as Drogba now trotted happily alongside his owner. They soon disappeared round the far side of Appleshaw House.

Nick wondered if he was being watched by nosy parkers from behind every window in the flats, after all the commotion the dog had caused. Looking around, he couldn't see anyone watching him, though. It took a few seconds for him to remember why he was there, and then self-consciously he walked the final few metres to the door of number two, Birdsall House. He rang the bell, but heard no corresponding chimes from inside the flat. He rang it again; still no sound. He rapped on the door with his knuckles and waited. After a number of seconds, he knocked again. Nothing seemed to be stirring. There was a small window to one side of the door, and Nick peered through. It was impossible. The window looked like it hadn't been cleaned for years, or perhaps ever. There was a grimy net curtain on the inside, and beyond that darkness.

Nick stepped a pace back and tried to think what his next move should be. There were a few possible scenarios. It could easily be that Les Campbell no longer lived here; maybe no one did. Or perhaps Kay's dad did still live here, but was out somewhere. Or he could be lying in the bath, or listening to music with headphones on. Jesus, the guy could be deaf for all Kay realised after not seeing him for years. Who knew if the man was even still alive? Nick had accepted all along that this entire journey might prove to be a complete waste of time. It was an unpalatable thought to have, standing here at Kay's old door.

He wasn't going to give up easily, though. One way or another he would find this man. Nick stepped forward again and rapped harder upon the wooden door. More futile seconds passed by. Nothing. Not a sound. Maybe he should hammer on the door with his fist. He was about to mutter some bitter and unworthy words beneath his breath when, from the flat to his left, he heard the sound of a chain being rattled, and bolts being worked. The door was protected by iron bars. He had noticed this with interest when he had first been walking towards the flat – before Drogba the Dog had invaded his sense of calm purpose. It was, quite obviously, an inverse of penal theory: the bars were designed to keep people (and trouble) out. Nick reflected that he had never seen any houses where the owner had felt the need for such precautions in the picturesque Wiltshire village he now called home.

Then the white-painted door opened, just enough for him to see that a black woman was standing there looking at him with curiosity mixed with trepidation. She spoke brusquely.

"Who you looking for, mister?"

Nick walked a little closer to her. "Hello. I'm looking for Les. Les Campbell. Does he still live here?"

"Who wants to know? You his friend?"

"My name's Nick. I'm actually his son-in-law."

It was a little white lie but he reckoned it had the definite advantage of keeping things simple.

"Oh…"

The woman seemed to have to think about that for a moment. Nick could only see part of her face in the narrow slit of doorway she had left open. He guessed that she was middle-aged and somewhat plump.

"Do you know where I might find Mr Campbell?" Nick persisted.

"He never said anything about a daughter before," the woman responded, sounding disappointed, but Nick's heart leaped at the words. Les Campbell lived here still, or at least he was known to this woman. This was progress.

"Oh, he and his daughter fell out quite a few years ago," Nick explained. "I expect that's why he didn't mention her." It was time for his ace card. "We've got a little boy together, Kay and me. That's why I wanted to find Mr Campbell. He doesn't know that he's a grandfather, you see, and he should."

His message seemed to land in sympathetic ears. The woman opened the door another few inches, and poked her head round.

"You gonna finish the old fool off telling him them things," she said, and laughed a big, happy laugh. "You put him back on the sauce with that one!"

Nick thought it best to laugh with her, and as he did so he moved closer. "So he still lives here then?" he ventured. "Is he about? There's not been any answer."

"Mr Campbell not here. He's out. You find him at the hospital, mister."

"Oh… which hospital is that? Is it near?"

"Yeah, mister. You not from these streets? King's College – just up the road here. He been in there for a few months now. He got a bad, bad liver. What's the boy called?"

"I see. Our son is called Davy." Nick took out his wallet and showed the woman his favourite picture of Kay and their son. She beamed at the heart-warming image.

"Beautiful… that's beautiful," she said softly. "That Mr Campbell's daughter? And he never said nothing 'bout her. Too busy getting blotto, drinking himself into the grave. You go and see Mr Campbell. You make his day."

"I hope so, Mrs… sorry… what's your…"

"Gladys. Gladys Odembe." They shook hands formally through the bars on her front door. "Very pleased to make your acquaintance, Mr…"

"Nick," he helped her.

"Mr Nick." She held on to his hand. She seemed enchanted by it.

"Mrs Odembe, can you tell me if Mr Campbell is in a particular ward at the hospital? I'd like to go and visit him."

"Oh… well, they took him to the one for sick people with bad liver. He not well, but he in good hands there, praise to God; good hands there. You find it over Denmark Hill, past the park."

She gestured with her head in the direction behind Nick. She still had hold of his hand. Nick was thinking that she had taken a bit of a shine to him. It was time to thank her for her help and move along.

"Okay, that's great, really fantastic," he said, and relaxed his grip, hoping to get his hand back. "Thank you very much Mrs Odembe, you've been very helpful. I'll drive over to the hospital now."

"Davy – that's a nice name, lovely name," she said. She still had hold of his now limp hand. It appeared that she wanted to keep the conversation going. Nick pulled his hand back and started to turn away, further suggesting to her, he hoped, his readiness to leave.

"Thank you, yes, we like it. He's a special little boy."

"Oh, he's an angel, a little angel," said Mrs Odembe. She finally took the hint and let go of Nick's hand.

"He certainly is. Thank you again. I must leave now. Thanks, Mrs Odembe, I really appreciate it."

Nick started walking away, silently thrilled by the news the woman had shared with him, and hoping that

Les Campbell would be well enough to see him. The last thing he heard before he was out of earshot was Mrs Odembe calling: "Give my regards to Mr Campbell. Tell him I cancelled his milk."

With a wave but not a look back, Nick hurried on and seconds later was back in his car. He was tingling with excitement. It seemed his detective work had paid off. Nothing, except perhaps for a bossy hospital matron, was now going to stop him making contact with Kay's long-lost dad.

***

Communication had never been Les Campbell's strong suit, and he really was at a loss for the right words to say to the young man standing nervously at the foot of his hospital bed. He had never been a great talker and from his teens onwards it had been clear that he was more at home horsing around with the lads from the football team than engaging in intelligent conversation. As he got older, the same macho bravado characterised Les's approach to other drinkers in the pub as well as to the bookmaker. To women he seemed the strong and silent type, with an air of mystery that intrigued them. Many girls imagined there must be deep waters running beneath his brooding exterior – but they quickly found out they were wrong. The young Les Campbell felt impatient and inadequate in any conversation where he was expected to give a serious opinion on anything other than sport, and was uncomfortable in most scenarios that didn't involve drinking and fooling about with his mates. It was all so much easier than having to be attentive and considerate towards a girl.

His football skills earned him trials at Leyton Orient, and a brief spell as a youth player on the club's books. Drink put paid to it, though, and before he was twenty years old, that avenue was pretty much closed down to him. Les fell back into, for him, an easy life of beering it up with the boys most nights a week, park football at the weekend, and endless hours in front of the screens at the local bookies. For work, he helped out friends in the building trade mostly, never really settling, never really skilled, and certainly never embarking on anything that might be construed as a "career".

Things changed after Elizabeth Hennessey, known to all as Betty, came into his life early in 1976. She was tall, dark-haired and glamorous, and always had plenty to say for herself. She started working behind the counter at the bookmaker's, and Les was captivated. He wondered how he could get to be with a girl like that. After his initial advances were met with little enthusiasm, he took to splitting his time between two different bookies – not to avoid her, but to try and give the impression that he wasn't a complete waster who spent most of his time gambling. Unfortunately for Les, Betty's friend Fiona happened to work at the other bookmaker, so the ruse failed. Betty held out for a month before finally agreeing to go on a date with Les. They were married within a year, and a baby girl arrived a few months later: Kay Elizabeth Campbell.

It wouldn't be true to say that Les cut down appreciably on his drinking throughout this period, though. In fact, the session with which he welcomed little Kay into the world – while mother and baby were at the hospital still – was one that he fondly recalled as a classic night. Some difficult, tempestuous years followed the arrival of the baby. Of course, like all fathers he doted on his child, but in a practical sense he needed to be both at home and sober to do that, and those circumstances were rarely in conjunction. An inevitable spiral of events then took place: whenever he was at home in the flat they shared in Denmark Hill, Betty took him to task about his gallivanting, they argued bitterly, and Les would storm out and invariably find someone to drink with.

It was no one's idea of love's young dream but somehow Betty stuck it out and devoted herself to bringing up her little girl, with or without the help of her husband. She could only hope that at some point, if she was lucky and if she waited for long enough, Les might grow up and accept his responsibilities. He did at least put some money on the table every Friday, though if she left it there too long it could easily disappear with him to the pub again.

As Kay grew into a toddler, though, there seemed to be a softening in Les's attitude. He started to buck his ideas up when Kay was about five years old. It was hard for Betty to take it seriously at first, to believe that things really were getting better; but he started to go out with his mates less, and instead came home from work in the evenings and spent time with his young family. He said he wanted to change, and most of the time he backed up his words with actions. It took several months for Betty to feel satisfied that a corner had been turned, but where there had once been a scowling, perpetually angry drunkard prowling the flat whenever he came home, she was starting to see again the man she had married – reserved, but funny and cheeky at his best. Their family life started to flourish as little Kay discovered a dad she hadn't really known before.

It seemed that their happiness was sealed when Les and Betty decided to try for a second baby. Kay had started school at Dog Kennel Hill School, close to the flat on the Champion Hill Estate; Les had full-time work with a friend who was a plasterer. There was money coming in, and life was good.

Then tragedy struck. One morning, having walked Kay to school, Betty went for a coffee with some of the mums, before heading off to the shops to get the week's food in. While in Sainsbury's she began to feel pains down one side of her body. She finished the shopping and walked back home, with the pain getting worse. Soon the next-door neighbour, an elderly man by the name of Mr Preston, heard Betty crying out in agony. When he heard this for the third time, he went to investigate and knocked on the door, calling out to her. Her cries seemed to come from deep within the flat and it was hard to make out clearly any of the words.

Mr Preston quickly found a young man passing by, and together they broke the door open. They found Betty Campbell lying on the living-room floor in a pool of dark blood. She had no wounds that they could see. They called for an ambulance but the situation was way beyond either man's comprehension. All they could do was hold her hand and try to comfort the stricken woman as they waited.

The ambulance from King's College Hospital, just down the road, arrived in a matter of minutes but it turned out that nothing could be done to save Betty. She died soon afterwards at the hospital from what turned out to be an ectopic pregnancy. She hadn't even known that she was pregnant, but it was reckoned she was six weeks gone. Betty Campbell was just twenty-nine years old.

It was a shattering blow, both to the little girl that she left behind without a mother, and to the husband who had finally started to straighten himself out. As a supposedly temporary arrangement, Kay was installed in Les's parents' house in nearby Camberwell. They would ensure that the little girl was taken to and picked up from school, and that she had food and company in the evenings, while Les was often out early in the morning and returned late because of work. It was left as an open-ended arrangement and that was how it stayed – Kay grew up between the ages of six and thirteen seeing her dad only at weekends and on some evenings if he wasn't on a job, or, as increasingly became the case, out propping up a bar again.

Even the weekends were at the mercy of Les's hangover. It wasn't that he wasn't interested in his daughter's life or her progress at school. He took great pride when she showed up well in her academic lessons. Young Kay particularly excelled at English – she was a capable and enthusiastic reader at an early age, and showed an ability to write engaging stories.

But it seemed that Les was unable to help himself when it came to taking responsibility for his drinking, and he was no longer just a social drinker either. The grief of losing a beloved wife would knock any man backwards, and Les was certainly not the first to find solace at the bottom of a pint glass. But if none of his mates were around – and more and more of the old crowd had settled down or moved away – then Les would very often head down to his favourite haunt, the Joiners Arms on Denmark Hill, by himself, in the hope of finding company, something to sustain or divert him while he drank himself into the ground again.

Now in his early thirties, Les still had his looks, and there were numerous women over the years, but none who could replace Betty; no angel to drag him back from the brink he continually took himself to. Nor, as he got older, was he able to work consistently after a heavy one the night before. He had done well for a number of years, working as a plasterer with his friend Pete Watkiss. Pete had a business to run, though, and customers to satisfy, and he couldn't afford to have one of his guys frequently turning up late on important jobs. Not surprisingly, Pete's patience started to wear thin.

Over the course of several years, Les's drinking tested that patience severely. There were mornings when he turned up late, too inebriated to be trusted with the job in hand; there were some mornings when he didn't turn up at all, only to call Pete hours later and try to explain his absence with some feeble excuse. It was only their lengthy friendship, dating back to their teenage years, which kept Les in his job. Twice during this time Pete snapped and sacked his friend, only to back down under Les's pleas for another chance.

Despite this, little changed in Les Campbell's behaviour and matters would almost certainly have come to a head finally, resulting in Pete's letting him go for good, had Les not injured his back on a job one day. Helping some other men on a site, he tried to lift a heavy pile of bricks but did so carelessly. As he stood up, a sudden severe pain shot across his lower back. He froze, dropping the bricks in alarm. In agony, he was taken to hospital. The diagnosis was bad: an extreme herniated or "slipped" disc. Les couldn't know it at the time, but he would never work in construction again.

Kay, who was then aged thirteen, a strong-willed, clever girl with dreams to be a famous, powerful journalist who went to witness wars around the world and wrote about what really happened, moved back into the flat in Denmark Hill to look after her bed-ridden dad. As soon as he was back on his feet, though, Les repaid the care that had been shown to him by heading to the pub to quench his thirst. Mixing alcohol with the painkillers he took for his damaged back turned out to be a very bad idea. After three pints he fell off his bar stool and landed on his backside, causing still more damage to his spine.

If Kay felt any anger at the way he had added to his incapacity, she hid it well. It was a lot for a girl of her age to cope with, but with the help of her grandparents she kept going. Over a period of a few years, Les's back slowly improved thanks to some surgery and a considerable degree of physiotherapy. However, he was told that it would never fully recover, and that working in the building trade or any other occupation that involved heavy lifting was out of the question.

So the two of them settled into a routine of sorts: Kay completing her schooling; Les drawing disability benefit and doing odd jobs – delivering leaflets, minding the counter at a local newsagent's, driving a van and delivering flowers for a florist – to supplement the cash a bit further. For a period of time, Kay's pleas to her dad even succeeded in tempering his incessant drinking. It was as if he had suddenly realised the importance of his daughter in his life, with Betty gone and his back in pieces. Some good years came and went. Kay left school and studied media at college for a year, but it was obvious that there was no way the family could afford a university education for her.

Instead she got a job working at a public relations agency in central London. It wasn't the daredevil war reporting that she'd once hoped to do, but it was media-related and she soon found that she was a natural at it. With her money coming in, life became a little more comfortable for the Campbell family. In 1996, Kay had enough spare to go on holiday to Benidorm with some girlfriends, and when she came home two weeks later she had a new boyfriend. One night late in the first week a boy called Lee had walked up to her in a night club and asked if she wanted to dance. They laughed together for the rest of the night and by the time he left to fly home five nights after that, they were giggling together about their marriage plans.

As it happened, their wedding took a little longer to bring about. Lee lived in Hertford – right around the other side of London and then a few miles north – but since they both worked in the city the relationship stayed strong. After two years and considerable cajoling from Lee, they found a place to live in Hertford, and Kay, at the age of twenty-one, left home. Shortly thereafter she and Lee tied the knot.

Kay should have been at her happiest, but there was a cloud hanging over her life. Her dad had refused to attend the wedding. He had never taken to Lee, and right from the start had made no secret of his disappointment in his daughter's choice of partner. He was on the booze again, and that didn't help Kay's attempts to reason with him.

During the course of the two years that she and Lee were dating before they moved in together, there were only two occasions on which he came to stay over at the flat in Denmark Hill. The first time was in the early days of the relationship. Les had reluctantly agreed to let his daughter's boyfriend sleep in the flat. Kay met Lee after work in town on a Friday evening, had a couple of drinks with him to calm her nerves, and then they got on the train to Denmark Hill, to have a few more drinks around Kay's neighbourhood. When they popped into the flat early in the evening, however, so that Lee could meet Kay's dad, Les was nowhere to be seen. He had already headed out for his Friday evening's entertainment. Kay had told him that they planned to stick their heads around the door to say hello, and her dad's absence seemed spiteful.

They came back home again in the early hours of the morning, giggling tipsily, and their noisy high jinks and laughter woke up Les, who was slumbering on the sofa in the living room. Not surprisingly, he grumpily told them to "piss off to bed", and then fell asleep again, surrounded by his empty beer cans. He was woken some hours later by the sound of running water. All was dark, but he could hear liquid splashing out in the hallway. Les staggered to his feet and lurched across the room to pull the door open, only to find his daughter's boyfriend, dishevelled and disorientated, urinating blindly into the airing cupboard. Les didn't hesitate; he threw the near-naked Lee out of the front door, sending him sprawling onto the grass outside, and slammed the door shut, locking him out in the 4 a.m. chill. Les then went to bed, ignoring Lee's plaintive pleas and timid knocks on the door. Kay, who had been asleep through it all, found her boyfriend sitting sheepishly on the doorstep, shivering in his underpants, more than three hours later, after she had woken and puzzled for a time over his possible whereabouts.

Les stayed in bed that day, sleeping off his own hangover, until after Kay and Lee had left the flat, so there was no face to face apology from either of them. Instead, Kay left a handwritten note apologising on Lee's behalf, which Les barely acknowledged when he next saw her. All in all, it was an inauspicious start to the relationship between Kay's dad and the man she was growing increasingly serious about

Several months after Lee's first disastrous visit to Denmark Hill, they tried again. Kay didn't even mention to her dad that Lee was coming back with her, calculating that Les would either kick up a stink and simply refuse permission, or else ensure that he was not in the flat all weekend. Les was therefore sitting in the kitchen poring over the football pools in the newspaper when his daughter came in with her man in tow.

"Hi, Dad – you remember Lee, don't you?" she said, smiling apprehensively. "We're going out for a curry and a couple of drinks, nothing too boozy, if you want to come and join us?"

In response, Les had merely stared at the two of them for several uncomfortable seconds, before muttering, "Fat chance, pissy pants," and then turning his attention back to his choice of score draws for the weekend. Unfortunately, Lee bit on the provocation instantly and made a move towards Les, who reacted with surprising speed to grab Lee's arm, jump to his feet, and quickly pin him by the throat up against the kitchen wall. Instantly they were shouting abuse in each other's face while Kay yelled at them both to stop and tugged in vain at her dad's arms.

As the two men screamed furiously at each other, inches apart, it was hardly surprising that a quantity of saliva escaped accidentally from Lee's mouth – Lee maintained that it was accidental, in any case –and hit Les in the face. Les believed, in fact he was certain, that this upstart City boy who was screwing his little girl had deliberately spat in his face. In a flash, the palm of his left hand made stinging contact with Lee's right cheek, not once but twice; Lee, now under assault, found extra strength out of his desperation and managed to push the older man a yard back – far enough for him to extricate himself from Les's grasp and duck swiftly out of the kitchen door, closely followed by a tearful Kay, who put herself between her retreating boyfriend and rampaging dad.

They made for the front door as Les came after them, bellowing in outrage about the insult dealt to him. He landed another blow on the back of Lee's shoulder, reaching over the protective figure of his daughter to do so. Then Lee had the front door open and the two lovebirds fled outside, assuming that Les would end his pursuit at the threshold.

They were wrong though – Les kept coming, despite being shoeless. His stockinged feet thudded on the concrete and grass outside, close behind them. At this point, Lee truly took to his heels in terror. Les seemed like a madman to him. Lee ran, and Kay followed quickly behind.

Finally, Les stopped running after them and shouted a few more choice obscenities at the fast-retreating back of his adversary. Then he tramped furiously back to his flat, slammed the door behind himself, wiped his face clean, changed his socks, and resumed his study of the football fixtures.

It would be an understatement to say that thereafter the atmosphere in the flat was frosty. Les refused even to consider discussing what had happened and why. Kay tried but her dad was too obstinate, too uncaring it seemed, and certainly too wasted most of the time, to talk about things in an adult way. It was a pretty hellish time for her and was a big factor in her decision to set up house with Lee, near his parents in Hertford. At the time, her father's attitude was mystifying and upsetting for Kay. Her upbringing had been difficult, even before the loss of her mother, but father and daughter had always shared a bond of affection up until this point. Then suddenly – apparently because he didn't like her boyfriend – her dad just cut her off; he didn't seem to care anymore.

A matter of months after leaving home Kay married Lee, but her dad refused to attend, passing up the opportunity to give her away at the altar. Instead, Betty's brother performed that duty. For Kay, the split was now frighteningly real. She went off to live her life without a parent to talk to, although she had always hoped that one day things might change. She kept Les's address and phone number for that reason. Within a year of getting married, she discovered that the only thing that had changed was her dad's phone number. Had he done it deliberately? Had he done it to hurt her? She did not know, but all that she had left of him now, save for a few memories of varying degrees of fondness, was a scrap of paper with an address written on it.

But what of Les – what was going through his mind during all these events and their aftermath? The problem could be summed up in two words: jealousy and miscommunication. He was unable to find the words to express how jealous he was; unable – sober or not – even to articulate the fact of his jealousy to his confused daughter. It would only encourage more questions that he couldn't answer.

This was new territory for Les. Lee was Kay's first serious boyfriend, and was certainly the first she had ever brought home. But things went much deeper than that. Seeing his daughter, his only child, growing up and starting to live her own life, meeting the man she wanted to spend that life with, had provoked deeply unsettling emotions in Les. Whether it was really true or not, he couldn't avoid feeling that his own life was as good as over; that there wouldn't be any good times ahead for him.

The fear of that had been there in the background for some time, dimly registered; in a rare moment of clarity, he realised that it had been building since the death of his wife. Horrible things were happening in his head and in his heart. It shouldn't have been this way, with him taking it out on his only child, but a cocktail of negative feelings – grief, blame, insecurity, panic, depression, self-doubt, self-loathing – combined to bury what he should have felt: the hopefulness and pride of the father of the bride.

There was an added factor. He felt an instinctive dislike for the man she had decided to marry. Les was a man who had spent his working life grafting and building. It was rough, rugged work – you were on your feet, or sometimes your knees, all day. Your hands became hard and calloused, covered in nicks and grazes. At lunchtime you read the *Sun*, took the piss out of your mates and wolf whistled at any passing women. Lee's world, as Les imagined it, was completely different. He was a suit, a City boy, the antithesis of everything Les knew about. It wasn't proper work, to Les's mind. Deeper down than that, though, if only Les had been able to acknowledge it, it made him feel inferior and inadequate. It didn't make him feel better, as it ought to have done, that Lee having a well-paid job at the bank meant Kay should be well provided for throughout her married life.

These had been his feelings even before the flashpoints with Lee. Those events only sealed Les's distaste for his future son-in-law, and when it came to the wedding, he was too proud, too stubborn, to back down. He disappeared back down to the bottom of a pint glass instead. It was far easier than talking it through, even if that meant estranging himself from his own daughter. It hurt, but he found ways to numb that pain.

The decade that followed the wedding of Kay and Lee passed in an alcoholic haze for Les. He kept taking the destructive medicine that was supposed to make him feel better but which continued to blight his life. He took jobs here and there – menial stuff that didn't put his back under strain. Housing and disability benefits bolstered his meagre income, and a long line of credit in the local pubs, based on years of building up goodwill, kept him in beer. His waistline expanded. He became something of a local celebrity, if you could call it that, often to be seen hunched against the cold, shuffling to the pub, and then staggering around the streets again hours later.

In his mid-fifties, however, things changed forever. There would have been numerous signs that problems were being stored up for the future, if only Les, like many men, had not ignored them. He became accustomed to a feeling of weariness, but assumed it was a natural consequence of his lifestyle. Sickness, itchy skin and a particular tenderness of the abdomen were also early danger signs, but he spoke to no one about it. It would go away.

Months went by. At first the comments of a few people in the pub about a yellowish tinge to his face were voiced as leg-pulling accusations of Les getting underneath a sunbed, chasing his youth, going through a mid-life crisis. But then someone noticed that actually the whites of his eyes had that yellowish tinge too. Another of the regulars knew the word for what it looked like: jaundice.

Even then, of course, he needed some convincing to go and see a doctor. He carried on drinking for another few weeks. His hair was thinning, and his beer belly growing fast; he had spells of dizziness that he couldn't explain; his ankles and feet seemed swollen – something else he couldn't explain.

Then one night, lying in bed feeling sad and broken about his life and the way it made his body feel, he had to visit the toilet, and there he was unable to stop himself vomiting, choking with pain. When he'd stopped retching, he looked down and saw his vomit was red-coloured. A cold feeling seemed to pass across his shoulders, a chill that sank into his bones and made his stomach quail with panic and fear. He was left drained, both shivering and sweating at the same time. He needed help, he knew. He remained squatting there for a few minutes, weighing it up, fighting away tears. He even considered ignoring all these things; just lying down and giving up, accepting his defeat, feeling too pained and aggrieved to carry on.

But the pain was actually too great for that. His body felt broken, sore all over. He couldn't live like this any longer, and he couldn't die like it either. He staggered to his feet, wiped his mouth, and called a taxi. Twenty minutes later he was at King's College Hospital, further down Denmark Hill. It was almost the first time in his life that he had done something to help himself.

It didn't take the world-class experts there very long to diagnose Les with acute cirrhosis of the liver. Blood tests and biopsies proved them right. The blood in his vomit had been caused by swollen veins in his oesophagus, which required immediate attention. Les was hospitalised. He endured an endoscopy, followed by an injection into the swollen area to make the blood clot. The problems with his ankles and feet, and with his expanding stomach, were caused by a build-up of fluid in his body. This was another common indicator of advanced cirrhosis. He was given some tablets and later tubes were used to drain this fluid away – a treatment that was repeated every few weeks.

Most importantly, in his hospital bed he had no access to alcohol. It was a measure of how sick he was that he found he didn't even want any. He was frightened by everything that was happening to him – his own mortality staring him squarely in the eyes. Even so, he wondered what his self-control would be like, should he ever get out of hospital and find himself at the mercy of temptation. Would he really want to live enough to make the right choices?

Les's treatment continued for weeks, which turned into months. And he was still there, resting in his hospital bed in Dawson Ward at King's College Hospital on a Tuesday afternoon, when his first visitor in all that time arrived. A nurse had turned up at Les's bedside and told him that a man was waiting outside to see him; he claimed to be Kay's partner, but his name, he said, was Nick. Not Lee? Not Lee.

Les gave no outward sign of the earthquake that had rocked his heart at the mention of his daughter's name. It had been some years since he had heard it spoken aloud, rather than just resounding in his own head. Though his mind was a jumble, he had told the nurse to show the man in. There was a tingle of something that felt like excitement in his fingertips. It was a strange, unfamiliar feeling. Instantly it made him fearful of losing something.

The man who walked through the door a few seconds later was a skinny fella, quite tall and lean. He was suntanned, with sun-bleached brown hair that covered his collar. He was in his early to middle thirties, Les guessed, and he looked a little tense. The nurse pointed towards Les's bed and the man looked over, nodded, and started walking. Had something happened to Kay? Was she in trouble? Les was filled with apprehension.

***

Nothing could have prepared Nick for the shock of coming face to face with Kay's dad for the first time. Of course he'd expected to find a man in poor health – he was, after all, visiting him in hospital, and Mrs Odembe had told him that Les Campbell had been very sick. Nick knew little about liver disease, though, so hadn't really been able to prepare himself mentally for the sight of the exhausted, yellow-skinned man lying before him.

However, it wasn't Les Campbell's appearance that really struck Nick, even though this man looked to be a good deal older than his late-fifties, which he knew Kay's dad to be. It was Les's eyes that Nick would always remember. He tried to read them, to understand what lay behind their dull stare. They reacted not one jot to the presence of the new person before them, but they were watching him very carefully, that much was evident. It was disconcerting. Nick was there for a good reason, however, and he wasn't going to be put off. He had had enough time to think about this moment in advance; he knew what he was going to say, and had rehearsed it carefully. Now he began in a respectful and business-like way.

"Mr Campbell, my name is Nick Newman. I live with your daughter Kay. We have a baby boy together. I know there have been disagreements between you in the past, but we both thought you should know about this."

Saying the words gave Nick another moment to remember, or in this instance to savour, all that had happened to bring Kay and him together. With his announcement, something changed instantly in the wan-looking man in the hospital bed. There was new animation in his eyes and expression, but disbelief too in the way his mouth had dropped open. Nick felt a rush of pride and excitement to see the effect his words had had.

It took a couple of seconds but Les Campbell was finally able to speak.

"I'm a granddad?

"Yes, Mr Campbell, you are. Your grandson Davy is nearly two years old."

"Well, I'll be... Davy... do you hear that, Jonno? I've a grandson... Davy."

This seemed to be directed to the man in the bed to Nick's left. He hadn't even looked at the occupant until now, but saw that "Jonno", who he reckoned wasn't much older than himself, was watching them with interest.

"I hear you, Les," Jonno replied, "that's a bloody turn up for the books, mate." He smiled ingratiatingly at Nick, who looked back at Les Campbell, prone in bed, his head and shoulders propped up by several big pillows. He looked completely stunned – staring at Nick as if he had just introduced himself as a Martian.

"Is my little girl okay? Is she happy… healthy?" asked Les, in a stronger voice.

"Yes, she's great, Mr Campbell. I do everything I can to try and make Kay happy."

"Where is she? Is she here?"

"No, she's working. We live in a little village down in Wiltshire. To be honest, Kay felt a bit… I don't know if scared is the word, but… it will mean a lot to her that I've been able to find you. She would love to see you again. And she'd love you to meet Davy."

At this, Les cast his eyes up to the ceiling, blinking away tears. Instinctively Nick moved around the side of Les's bed. He felt a need to be closer to this man who meant so much to Kay. He stopped halfway along the length of the bed.

"Is it okay for me to sit?"

Les patted the bedclothes at the side of the bed in reply, and Nick perched himself there. Everything about this moment made it feel like one of the most important of his life so far. "Are you okay, Mr Campbell?" he asked quietly.

"I'm… I don't know. I don't know what I am. My head don't know whether I'm coming or going. I can't believe it…"

These were all the words that Les could coax his tongue to form before he was overcome by the weight of the moment, and the tears started to fall in earnest. Nick waited as Les sobbed in front of him, weighing up his next words, certain of the gravity of this scene, awe-struck by the impact of his announcement on the ailing man. Jonno felt no such emotional constraints.

"He's happy really, fella. Don't be fooled by his blubbing. He's happy really."

Jonno laughed at his wisecrack, and Nick smiled kindly back at him, though he would have been quite happy for this onlooker just to roll over and go to sleep.

"Take your time, Mr Campbell," said Nick, turning his attention back to Kay's dad. Les was rocking and shaking, hands clasped to his face to hide the tears, and Nick wasn't completely sure whether he was still crying or if he was now laughing at his friend's mickey-taking – or both. Soon enough it became clear.

"Bugger off, Jonno," croaked Les, taking his hands away from his face again – a tear-streaked, yellowed face; a tired, happy face that bore such a big smile Nick would have bet it was the biggest it had carried for many a year. Then Les repeated his earlier words: "I can't believe it. I can't believe it. A grandson..."

"Congratulations, Les," someone called from across the ward. Nick turned and saw that several of the patients were ear-wigging the conversation. They all seemed happy for their mate. An emaciated old fella in the corner gave Nick the thumbs-up.

"Cheers, Mal, I'm made up," Les said, responding to the call of congratulations. "Cheers, everyone."

He was getting his emotions under control again now. He looked once more at Nick, his eyes brimming with hope. "Will you bring them to visit me? That would be... I'd be..."

Les's voice tailed off. He didn't seem to have the right words at his command and settled into a slightly embarrassed silence instead, perhaps hoping the sentiment was already clear.

"Yes, Mr Campbell. Well, actually, what I was going to suggest, before I discovered that you were here in the hospital, was that you come along to Davy's second birthday party in a month or so. I was going to pick you up and drive you down to Wiltshire. It's not going to be a big party, but… well, anyway, you know what? I haven't even asked how you are, and how the treatment is going. That's probably the most important thing really."

"What date is my grandson's birthday?" Les asked. He put extra emphasis on the word "grandson", as if it was his new favourite word; as if he had never said it before in his life.

"It's the sixteenth of July," Nick replied.

Les reached over to a switch on the unit next to his bed, and pressed it. "We'll soon see," he replied. A few seconds later a nurse Nick had met at the ward desk earlier came walking in and made for Les's bed.

"What's up now Mr Campbell? Are you okay?" she asked as she approached, using that tone of voice nurses use – weary and put-upon – when they are ribbing a favoured patient.

"Miss Peters, I want you to make sure I'm well enough to walk out of here on July the sixteenth. Can you do that for me?"

"Good God, I hope so, Mr Campbell. I don't think I could stand much more of your constant moaning about our cordon bleu food. Why – where are you thinking of sneaking off to?"

"I've got a grandson, Miss Peters. It's going to be his birthday that day."

"A grandson, eh? Well, good for you. Anyway, I don't know, I'll have to talk to Dr Sandhu about how you're doing. We'll see."

"Yeah, speak to the doc for me then, would you, love?"

"Only because it's you, Mr Campbell. Now, is everything else okay here?"

Les nodded that it was, and the nurse walked off smiling. Nick had been waiting patiently; now that he had Les's attention again he said, "Got something to show you, Mr Campbell," taking his wallet out. He opened it and retrieved the photograph of Kay and Davy that he had shown to Mrs Odembe earlier, outside the flats. He handed it over to Les, whose face lit up. He held the photograph delicately, almost reverently, like the most precious jewel. For several seconds he was lost in his own thoughts. Nick saw emotion working in his face.

Eventually he was able to drag his eyes away from the picture and towards Nick. Les spoke haltingly. "You see, you've got to understand, Nick, I didn't think... I was sure... I was never going to see Kay again... the way things were. And that muppet she got married to... well, there was no way back... no way to... it seemed to be all over for me."

He looked from Nick to the photograph and back again. "Oh, God, I've missed my little girl. I didn't even know how much... I was too busy killing myself. Ah, God, what was I thinking?"

At this, he had to stop speaking. Once more tears streamed down his face – a fatigued face, lined by life and loss. He held the picture of Kay and Davy in one hand, and sobbed helplessly into the upturned palm of the other. The room around Les's bed was hushed. Nick kept his eyes cast down, slightly awed by the depth of emotion being shown by the man in front of him. He wanted to reach out to Les Campbell and tell him everything was going to be fine: things could be mended; he would finally see his long-estranged daughter, and meet the new addition to his once-splintered family. Nick wanted to reach out but there was still a gulf between them that had yet to be filled by the closeness of familiarity. And, after all, they were men, with men's natural reluctance to show emotion, and they had only just met.

Fortunately, Jonno broke the silence for them. "You're a good man, Les. You deserve this. Give the lad a hug, eh? He seems a good sort. Thank you, Nick, for doing this."

There was a murmur of assent around the ward. Les struggled to rearrange his pillows so that he could sit up better, and sniffed noisily, unattractively, as he battled to contain his tears. It took a few seconds but then, still sniffing, he was able to wipe the sleeve of his pyjama top across his face. He looked up at Nick at last, and laughed self-consciously.

"I'd better not hug you just now, son – you'll get covered in snot and God knows what else." He put out the hand that was not holding the picture of his daughter and grandson towards Nick. "Give me your hand, son, while I look a bit longer at these two. Just spend a bit of time with me while I look at them."

Nick took Kay's dad's hand and moved further along the bed towards him. Les Campbell was calling him "son". Nick felt sure that he had great news to take back to Kay; news that would thrill her. When he spoke, the words came out so naturally he didn't even have to think about them.

"Take your time, Dad, take your time. I'm not going anywhere just yet."

CHAPTER SEVEN

Jemima Bond felt accepted and she felt trusted. It was a startling realisation, and not exactly what she had expected to happen when she had taken the job of looking after Davy Newman. At SMAC meetings she was usually ignored or belittled; virtually patted on the head and told not to trouble herself with important matters, whenever she opened her mouth to contribute. Mac, her long-time friend and SMAC leader, was one of the worst culprits for this.

But sitting here now, her head swimming as she squinted up at the soaring cathedral spire, four hundred feet up in a perfect blue sky, all of Mac's beard-stroking theorising, Vince's bolshie indifference and Nancy's prim propriety, seemed like a lot of self-important hot air.

A magnificent greensward stretched out from her feet in every direction. In front of her, laid out on a wide tartan blanket, were a variety of plastic tubs with different-coloured lids, containing sandwiches, cakes, and a variety of other savoury and sweet snacks. There were bottles of fizzy drinks, a bag-in-a-box wine pack with a small plastic tap, and plastic cups. Beyond the drinks and containers and foodstuffs, Kay reclined on her elbows, eyes half-closed, smiling in the lazy warmth. And next to her was Davy – making two toy vehicles, one held in either hand, collide with each other while he provided a constant nonsensical commentary. From time to time,

Kay's hand would sneak out and give the lad a tickle, and he would gurgle with pleasure, even if it did interrupt his game.

Jemima looked around her and wondered at the idyllic scene: a beautiful day, a nice picnic, a mother and her little boy enjoying quality time together; and close by, a majestic old cathedral, its hushed power and serene grace adding a timeless quality to an otherwise everyday event.

It all gave Jemima mixed feelings. In the weeks since she had started looking after Davy she had come to love the little boy. She had been worried about that happening before she'd started, and sure enough it had. Still, her feelings for him did make the job so much easier than it might have been. What really surprised her was how well she got on with the parents. Nick was thoroughly nice, and Kay could hardly have been friendlier, always seeking to include Jemima in family activities and constantly remarking gladly upon the spark there was between her own mischievous cherub and the nanny.

Several times Jemima had turned down these invitations to take part in family events, not wanting to get too close to Kay. She was supposed to hate her employer because of her role at Maier Science, and things had certainly started off that way, but in the process of becoming smitten with Kay's twenty-three-month-old son, Jemima had found herself warming to his mother too. She had to keep telling herself what her real task was: to use Kay as a means of discovering information about the goings on at Maier. So far, Jemima had discovered nothing of significance. There had been no papers or computer files in Nick and Kay's house that implicated the company in possible malpractice; no ill-judged revelations from Kay whenever Jemima asked her how her day had been. She didn't seem to bring her work home with her – either literally or figuratively.

Today Kay had taken the day off work, wanting to take advantage of the weather and to spend time with Davy. It had been a sudden decision, and there was no time for Jemima to think of an excuse not to come over to Salisbury with them. She was, after all, supposed to be looking after Davy all day, and she got the impression that Kay wasn't going to take no for an answer to this picnic invitation.

Jemima pressed a button on the mobile phone on the blanket in front of her. It lit up and showed her the time. It was nearly 2 p.m. They were expecting Nick to come and join them any minute. He had said he would be able to knock off work early, and would drive into Salisbury and find them on the lawn of the cathedral, where they now were. Jemima looked up from the phone and saw Davy staring inquisitively at her with his earnest, trusting eyes that were so like his dad's. Jemima poked her tongue out and won a giggle from the boy. He went back to smashing his toys together.

Not for long, though. Jemima was just sitting back again and contemplating reaching for another sandwich when suddenly Davy shouted out: "Daddy! Daddy! Ball!" He pointed too, and Jemima looked behind her to see that Nick was jogging towards them across the grass, dribbling a football as he did so, though with no great natural aptitude, judging by the way he was concentrating on the ball at his feet. Kay opened her eyes and started laughing.

"My God, what is that man of mine doing? He'll bloody kill himself if he's not careful," she exclaimed. Davy had dropped his toys and starting running towards his dad, his little legs pumping recklessly in his excitement. Jemima joined in with Kay's laughter and watched Nick and Davy converge upon each other. Nick saw the boy coming and slowed down. They were still twenty metres or so away from the women when Davy reached the ball. Nick tried to drop a shoulder and do a little trick with the ball to sidestep his son, but was surprised to find that Davy's kick was aimed true and hit the ball full on, causing Nick to stumble and leave it behind at his son's feet. Realising that he was about to be embarrassed, Nick continued the stumble deliberately, clownishly, and then fell flat on his face, causing Davy to yelp in delight. There was laughter all around, even from strangers sitting nearby enjoying the sunshine, as Nick remained prone on the ground, covering his head with his hands in mock shame.

After a couple of seconds he got up sheepishly and smiled over at the women. Davy was running around frenetically, keeping the ball near his feet. "Daddy, play ball!" he kept shouting.

"Daddy will play ball in a minute, Davy. Stay there while I say hello to Mummy," Nick called back. Then he jogged over to the picnic blanket, passing Jemima with a cheery hello, and bent down to give Kay a kiss.

"You just got tackled by a little boy who's not even two years old yet," Kay informed him. "I'm surprised you've got the nerve even to come over here – honestly!"

"I let him win," Nick protested, slumping down on his knees.

"Yeah, whatever. Have some sandwiches, babe. Are you hungry?"

"No, not really. I had something with Jerry earlier."

Kay tutted and winked at Jemima. "Darling, you knew we were having a picnic. You should have left some space for these lovely sarnies we made earlier. There're cakes and things too."

"Yeah, so I see. It's a lovely spread. Actually I will have one of those cakes there," Nick said, reaching over to pick up a container with some Bakewell slices in it. He removed the lid and took one out.

"Nick, we're on the savouries and you jump straight to the flipping cakes. And you're still as skinny as a rake," Kay complained.

"Fast metabolism, dear," he said, grinning through a mouthful of Bakewell slice. He leaned across and kissed Kay on the cheek. "You girls having a nice day?"

"Oh, it's beautiful… so relaxing. I've hardly thought about work. We're having a lovely time, aren't we, Jemmy?"

"Perfect," she confirmed. In the background, Davy was still shouting and running around with the ball, calling for his dad to join in. Jemima nodded towards the boy, and said to Nick: "I think Davy wants to play Match of the Day, Nick. Do you want me to have a go while you eat something?"

"Ha-ha – how are your dribbling skills, Jemima?" he asked, biting into the cake again.

"That depends on how much I've had to drink," she deadpanned.

"No, it's okay," Nick said, smiling, "I'll go and do what dads do. Anyway, I'm out for revenge after he just hacked me down."

"Oi, big man, don't you go kicking my little man," Kay warned him. "God, talk about bloody Competitive Dad Syndrome!"

Nick finished off the last of his cake. Then he leaned over again, gave Kay another peck on the cheek, and said,

"As if I would." He jogged off to play football with his son. "Save me one more of those cakes, ladies," he called behind him. Then: "Davy! Come back here with that ball!"

Behind him the two women laughed again, and Kay rolled her eyes. They watched as Davy attempted to kick the football to his dad, only to kick the ground and fall over. He looked up at his approaching father and his face broke into a massive beam, followed by a mischievous giggle. Soon they were kicking the ball between the two of them, or trying to at least; little Davy's technique and leg strength still had a lot of developing to do.

"David Beckham and his boys had better watch out," Kay said, raising a doubtful eyebrow.

Jemima let out a wistful, "Aaah, David Beckham…" and Kay smiled knowingly back. "Yeah, he's not bad, is he?"

The sun burned down on them still, and grabbing a handful of crisps, Kay settled back on the blanket, face upturned to catch the rays. Jemima watched for a few seconds from behind her sunglasses, mulling over an idea in her mind. She wanted to get the conversation back to something Kay had said earlier, when she had told Nick that it had been such a lovely day she had hardly thought about work. It seemed to be an opportunity to get her talking about her job, and that, after all, was the real reason why Jemima was here.

She needed the question to come across innocently, though, and quickly realised that the best thing would be just to say it straight out, so that it would seem a natural continuation of their previous conversation, rather than something that was weighing on her mind.

"Do you find it easy to switch off from work, Kay?" she began. "It must be difficult with such an important job."

Was that natural enough? Was it the right side of the dividing line between interest and intrusion?

"Oh, well..." said Kay languidly. There was evidently no offence taken, as she stretched her arms out above her prone body. Then she turned on to her side to face Jemima. "You know what? I love my job," she said matter-of-factly. "I love working... always have done. Yeah, it can be a bitch sometimes – in fact, there's plenty of rubbish stuff going on at the moment – but I actually quite enjoy it when the shit hits the fan. It's better than having nothing to do."

After saying this she smiled, and Jemima could tell, even though both she and Kay were wearing sunglasses, that Kay was now looking beyond her, to where Nick and Davy were playing. Nick's calls of encouragement to the boy and Davy's screams of delight at Daddy's tricks were a constant background clamour.

"Those boys are very funny," cooed Kay.

"You do very well not to bring all those problems home with you," remarked Jemima. "I've worked for people before – professional people like you – who were... well, let's say you soon learned to keep your head down when they'd had a bad day at work."

"Look behind you," Kay replied, pointing to Nick and Davy. "They're the reason why I'm not like that anymore – my boys. I can't come home from work, hug my baby boy and my Nick, and still feel angry or upset about something outside our life together. I look at Nick, and I look at Davy, and I know what's really important to me.

"Even the other day," said Kay, sitting upright now as she got into the subject, "when Richard told us that security was going to be going down on Davy's birthday and they wanted everyone to do extra hours. I'd already told

Richard I wanted to take that day off, to get Davy's party ready, and then he springs that on me! I mean, why not pay for some big security blokes to walk around for a few hours – as if I could do anything if someone broke in any way! I was bloody furious when I left work, but it all kind of melts away the minute I walk through the front door at home. How can you be angry when you've got Davy's little face to look at?"

Jemima had listened to all of this with great interest but with a blank expression on her face. Only her fluttering heart would have betrayed her mounting excitement. She had done it! She had vital information for SMAC, information they would never have found out, or at least not until too late, without her.

"Security?" she ventured, hardly daring to believe her luck.

"Yeah, cameras and stuff… you know, alarm systems. They've got to do maintenance or something. I meant to tell you, of course, because I was hoping we could arrange everything for the party together, but Richard is being such an arse. Don't worry, I'll keep working on him and eventually he'll do what I want, because he always does. He knows what's good for him! Actually, thinking about it, your handwriting is nicer than mine. I could do with you writing out the party invitations to the other mums. You don't mind, do you?"

Jemima was thinking: Davy's birthday, the sixteenth of July, it was still a few weeks away. There might be time to plan something big to take advantage of the security blind spot. Stuart would have some ideas, she knew. He would be very pleased with her when she got the news to him.

"Jemmy, are you okay?" Kay said. "You seem miles away."

Jemima snapped out of her thoughts and looked at Kay, whose sunglasses were now in her hand. A single cloud had moved across to block out the sunlight for a few seconds. Kay was looking inquisitively at her. "I was just saying that I'd like you to write the invitations for the mums. You know, for Davy's party. Your handwriting is a lot smarter than mine."

"Of course," Jemima smiled. "Yes, sorry, Kay – I suddenly remembered something I needed to talk to Stuart about. Have you bought the invitations yet or are we making some? I can do it whenever you want me to."

Jemima's desire to reach for her mobile phone and text Stuart at once was strong. Kay continued rabbiting on in the background – going on about party games, which children they should or shouldn't invite, food and drink… all the things Jemima really had no interest in right then. She wanted to speak to Stuart right away, but Kay was still talking at her. Jemima decided to keep agreeing.

A couple of minutes later Davy came scooting over and asked his mummy for his baseball cap, which was in one of the bags. Kay rummaged around for it and took the opportunity to wipe a few grass stains from his shorts and his knees. It was an opportunity for Jemima. She quickly sent a text message to Stuart: *Call me asap.*

Then Davy was running off again to carry on kicking the ball with his dad and Kay resumed her exciting breakdown of the party plans. Mercifully for Jemima, two minutes later her mobile phone started chirping, and she saw that it was Stuart.

"Sorry, Kay, you don't mind if I…" she said, rising to her feet and gesturing with the phone to indicate that she needed to walk a few yards away to take the call. "It's my boyfriend. I won't be a minute."

Kay waved her away and selected a cake to eat. Jemima answered the phone while she was walking.

"Hi, are you okay?"

"Hey, Jemmy, yeah, tip-top. What's up?"

Jemima deemed that she was now at a safe enough distance from Kay to speak, though she still kept her voice low.

"I've got some news for you. I think you're going to be very interested in this."

"Go on then."

"On the sixteenth of July, Maier's cameras and security system are going down for a few hours while they're being serviced. They've asked staff to work late, to cover while it's being done. Kay just told me. If we ever wanted to get in there, this could be our chance."

"Oh, really… that is very bloody interesting indeed. Well, this means I need to get the video meeting sorted out bloody fast. Good work, Jemmy!"

"We should call everyone together and come up with a plan," she suggested.

"We'll see about that. We need some more info first – like times for a start. Find out as much as you possibly can, girl."

Jemima half turned to look over at Kay on the picnic blanket. She wasn't there, though. Instead she had run over to Nick and Davey in her bare feet and was joining in the game. The three of them were laughing and dashing around. Then Kay and Nick tussled for the ball, which ended with Nick hitting the deck again. There was more laughter. Jemima watched them with bitter-sweet thoughts in her mind, knowing and despising the organisation that Kay represented, and yet seeing this perfect happiness in her personal life with this man and their little boy. It was hard to stay angry with her; that much Jemima was discovering to her chagrin, time and time again.

"I'll see what I can do, Stu," she replied. "What's happening about the meeting with Maier to discuss the video footage? Kay hasn't said anything about it to me."

"We're waiting for confirmation," Mac said. "The police are involved as well. I don't think that bastard Richard Cambridge wants to do it, but by the sound of it your friend Kay is persuading him to engage with us. Any day now, Jemmy, any day now. Obviously Vince thinks we should go straight to Plan B."

Davy was now lying on top of his prone dad, having a wrestle, while Kay had Nick pinned down by the legs. She had removed his trainers and was tickling his feet, eliciting shrieks of helpless mirth from the victim. Everyone around was enjoying the free show, and the volume of hilarity had gone up several notches further. Jemima had to smile. It was a funny scene. Then Davy saw her across the field and waved to her, although in doing so he found himself suddenly tickled by his dad, and collapsed in fits of giggles. Amongst the giggles was a just-recognisable call of "Yemima" from the little boy. He wanted her to play too, it seemed.

"Okay, I've got to go, Stu. I'll come round later and let you know what else I've found out."

❋❋❋

With a thud and a heave Nick turned the earth over, putting his back into it. Dark soil cascaded from the prongs of the garden fork like a mini-avalanche onto the exposed flower bed. Nick took a pace to the right and slanted the fork into the earth again, his bare arms and shoulders – glistening with sweat – tensing, his lower back taking the strain. He had about another ten metres of this to go – turning over the crusty, white-flecked, chalky top soil in readiness for the removal of debris and weeds, and then the application of manure and bone-meal into the newly exposed, damper soil.

Another thud and a heave and then Nick straightened, took a deep breath and drew a sticky arm across his dripping forehead. It was early July, another warm day, and this was thirsty work. He thrust the fork back into the soil, and wandered off to pick up a big bottle of water that he took a swig from. Wiping his mouth with the back of his hand, he looked over at Jerry and sniggered. His boss was working a few metres away, digging over another patch of soil while singing loudly to the Lady Gaga song *Bad Romance*, which was playing on a radio placed on the ground between them. Nick joined in as he walked back to grab the fork handle.

Their voices were not notably tuneful. Nick chuckled to himself as Jerry continued singing, mimicking the delivery of the flamboyant American singer. Fork in his hands, he got stuck into working over the bed in front of him for a few minutes. Nick knew what it meant to have tired limbs these days, but he could say for certain that he was fitter than he had ever been. Many men of his age – mid-thirties – needed to keep in trim by visiting the gym a few times a week, to pump iron and pound the treadmill.

Not so Nick. He worked out every day in the middle of a field or a garden, digging and lifting for Jerry. It had been hard at first. He had worked in office jobs and then for a few years as a shoeshine at Liverpool Street Station. Neither occupation had been useful preparation for the rigours of life as a landscape gardener. There had been some really trying months to begin with, but over time Nick found that his body adapted, long unused muscles found definition, his stamina steadily improved, and his fingers became calloused and stopped cramping after hours gripping a shovel.

Even when his muscles were tired, it was actually a pleasant feeling; he had the satisfaction of knowing he had done a good day's shift, and invariably, especially if the weather was good, it had been fun too. His skin had been baked by the sun; both he and Jerry had the kind of tan that other people spent thousands of pounds trying to cultivate. These days Nick looked in the mirror and saw a healthy and happy man.

It took ten more minutes of hard work before he'd finished turning over what was be a new flower bed. Then he spent another few minutes collecting bits of debris such as stones and weeds that he had yanked out. He was still doing this when his mobile phone, underneath his shirt on the grass next to the radio, started ringing.

"Nick, your phone," called Jerry, who was working closer to it.

"Can you get it for me mate? I've got my hands full of rubbish," Nick replied.

"It's an 020 number... someone in London," Jerry mumbled, before pressing the button to answer the call. "Nick's phone," he stated.

Nick was picking his way out of the flower bed, his hands full of stones and weeds, which he then deposited into a bucket.

"No, this isn't Nick, but he's right here. Hang about, my old fruit," said Jerry. He held the mobile phone out. Nick was brushing his hands clean.

"Who you calling an old fruit, you old goat?" he scoffed, taking the handset.

"Buggered if I know. Some bloke disrupting my boy when I've just got him bloody working, that's all I know."

Nick ignored the jest and wandered a few yards away before speaking into the handset.

"Hello."

"Oh, hello, is that Nick?"

"Yes…" He recognised the voice, he realised. It took him only a second. "Mr Campbell – so good to hear from you."

There was a chuckle at the other end. "Less of that 'Mr Campbell' nonsense, son. Last time I saw you, you were calling me Dad, and we should stick to that."

"Right you are, Dad. Where are you calling from? Are you okay?"

"I'm still at the hospital, son. But Doctor Sandhu came round earlier, and he said I'll be good to go soon. They've given me some tablets and drained all my beer belly away. I look like a bloody movie star now."

They laughed. Les certainly sounded better than when Nick had visited him before. If the hospital was satisfied enough with his condition to discharge him, then that would be great news. Nick still hadn't told Kay he had found and spoken to her father. Ideally it would be a surprise that he sprang on her on Davy's second birthday – hopefully by walking through the door with her long-lost dad after picking Les up from London that morning.

The look Nick hoped to see on Kay's face when she found herself face to face with her dad again, after all these years… it was going to be one very special moment.

"So, you're going to be okay for the sixteenth then, Dad?"

"Yes, Nick. They're chucking me out of here in a few days' time. Poxy NHS probably need the bed for someone else now. I ain't been decent enough to croak on them, so they've had to fix me up. I've got no car or nothing, so you'll have to let me know where to get the train to."

"Train? No, no, no. I'll come and pick you up and drive you down here. We'll put you up for a week, if you like. Your daughter would bloody kill me if I let you get a train all the way here."

Les hesitated briefly at the mention of his daughter. Then he said: "How is Kay? Is she okay about all this?"

"She doesn't know about it, Dad," Nick admitted, feeling a pang of guilt. Perhaps he should have told her. What if something happened between now and the party? Who could guarantee that none of them would go under a bus before then? He tried to explain. "I want it to be a surprise for her. I promise you, it will make her year to see you again. She asked me to try and find you, and she wouldn't have said that if she didn't want you back in her life, would she?"

Who was he trying to convince – Les Campbell or himself? The older man was silent for a moment. Then he said: "You know best, Nick. You're calling the shots. You've already made my year just by coming to see me. I've been hurting for so long, in so many ways, I didn't know which way to turn next. I'm very grateful that you found me in the hospital, that's all I can say."

His voice was wavering with emotion once more by the end of this speech. Nick could hear it, and sense the depth of feeling behind the simple words. He wasn't sure how to respond. "It's okay, Dad. It's okay," he said finally. From somewhere he found further inspiration. "This is one of the most important things I've ever done, Dad. It will make Kay so happy, and there's nothing more important to me than that. It's going to be a fantastic day, I promise you."

He didn't expect a joke to come back, but then he didn't yet know Les Campbell very well. "I would say I'll drink to that, son," the older man said, "but I'm not allowed to do that anymore. Doc Sandhu would bloody kill me, if the booze didn't!"

***

Dear Diary

I found out a few things over the days that followed my first SMAC flour-bombing mission. The name Ted Chillingworth, for instance came into my world. Good name eh? He was a reporter on the local paper, and it turned out that through Kay he had arranged to go and interview the Big Boss Man at Maier Science. Mac was on pretty friendly terms with Ted, and I imagine he saw Ted as a way of getting negative stuff written about Maier. I suppose the idea was that it was another way of putting pressure on them. He was "my journalist", as Mac put it.

Anyway, Ted went to do this interview with Kay's boss – Richard Cambridge, his name was – in late-June, just a few days after I'd been on the mission with Mac and Anthony. We all found out exactly what Cambridge had said before any of Ted's readers did, because when he left the research site after the interview, he drove directly round to the parking area at the back of the SMAC camp and walked through the trees to find Mac, just like I had. This had all been arranged. Ted did the Maier interview and then the SMAC one, telling Mac as he did so exactly what this bloke Cambridge had said, and getting Mac's official reaction. He said he intended running the two interviews alongside each other in the paper.

I was there at the camp when Ted came through the trees. He was a scruffy bastard – unshaven, and with an air of complete indifference towards pretty much everyone at the camp apart from Mac. I was introduced and he clearly didn't give a toss what my name was or if I lived or died. I wasn't important. Mac was. We sat in the clearing there and listened in to the conversation as Ted set a little recording device going between himself and Mac, and consulted a notepad to check on various quotes from Cambridge that he had made a point of scribbling down. It turned out that, according to Ted, this Cambridge bloke had said some pretty derogatory stuff about SMAC. He called them "pesky little rich kids making trouble" and "Tuesday terrorists living off Daddy's credit card". I can imagine Kay was tearing her luscious dark hair out of her pretty head, listening to her boss saying stuff like that to a reporter. She would have known how it would look in print.

Anyway, Mac heard these quotes and reacted calmly (ha! Vince certainly fucking didn't!). He reiterated the points that he had already made about animal testing, said that SMAC had certain evidence about malpractice at Maier, and challenged Mr Cambridge, through the pages of the local rag, to meet with SMAC and discuss these is-

sues. When it came out in the newspaper a few days later, I had to agree with Nancy that it reflected very badly on Richard Cambridge and Maier – the way that the lab director came across as being arrogant and dismissive of the rationally argued points Mac put forward. Ted had written it that way, you see. It was a bit of a hatchet job really. In the newspaper the following week there were several letters from locals slating Cambridge's attitude, demanding that dialogue was opened between the two groups, and commending the newspaper on its journalistic standards. I must admit, I did wonder whether those letters were actually written by Mac and his mates! I expect Mrs Chillingworth, wife or mother, penned a little note in praise of Ted too. But I bet Kay was fucking furious! There she was, trying to improve the image of her company, and this had happened. Earn yer bread, Kay my darling!

Anyway, quite soon after the newspaper came out an email arrived in the SMAC inbox, and, lo and behold, it was from a certain Kay Campbell. It invited us all to a meeting to be held at the Maier facility, with Mr Cambridge, other Maier directors, Kay herself, and Chief Superintendent Usher of the Wiltshire Constabulary.

There followed the usual argument between Mac and Vince (maybe I should call them Tom and Jerry, since they fought like cats and dogs over everything), with Mac feeling triumphant at this new development, which was all part of his "plan of engagement", and Vince saying "fuck that, let's blow the fucking doors down in the media". I think Mac wanted the glory himself really. I always felt that. Well, he won as usual. They had a slanging match (as usual) and Vince stormed off with meek little Pippa in tow (as usual), but not before Mac had shouted in Vince's face that since he (Vince) didn't agree with this course of *action, then I would represent SMAC at the meeting instead of him.*

Can you imagine how my heart leaped on hearing that? I would be meeting Kay again. It was everything I'd wanted. I can still remember now, as I write this, that I sat back in the B&B that night and wondered how the fuck I'd pulled it off. My plan was working better than I could have dreamed. It was a delicious thought.

Of course, I had to disguise my excitement when Mac said that, and I also had to put up with glares from a few of the others at my rapid promotion through the ranks. It was Mac, Nancy and I who would go. After some to-ing and fro-ing a date was arranged: 6 July. I put a red circle around that day on my Kelly Brook calendar on the wall in the B&B.

Around that time, I got a chance to see the video they had secretly filmed inside the Maier place too. Bastards! How can you treat animals like that? All right, I admit, I forgot myself for a moment and laughed at one bit when a bloke was swinging this monkey around (literally swinging it round in a circle at arm's length, like he was about to throw the hammer in an athletics competition) and I was reprimanded in stern, schoolmistress fashion by the redoubtable Ms Jennings, or Nancy to me and you.

I managed to get myself out of trouble by spluttering some old rubbish about it being just incredible that anyone could be such a total piece of shit as even to think about it, let alone actually doing it. Probably a good job that Vince wasn't there at the time, 'cos he would never have swallowed that bullshit, but these schmucks did. I managed to get sufficiently het up about the rest of the video to cause everyone to settle down again anyway. I suppose it was pretty sick stuff. Basically just idiots bored at work, entertaining themselves.

Okay, this is about to get hard to write down, but another thing I discovered during this time was, for me, a bombshell of nuclear strength. Mac's bird, this little piece called Jemima – well, it turned out that she was doing a bit of spying on my Kay. I said this Jemima's surname was Bond, didn't I? Turns out she was a regular little 007! She worked as Kay's nanny. Yes, you read that right – her nanny. Kay had had a baby. After all the shit we went through about kids, and her not wanting one, her mum having died of complications, and Kay's career instead coming first and everything, she went and had a fucking baby anyway, with this bloke she had run off with. Nick his name is. They had a little boy called Davy and he was nearly two years old at that point.

I heard this piece of news when Jemima reported to the group that she had learned from speaking to Kay that Maier Science's security system was going to be down for maintenance on 16 July. At the time Mac took that information and put it in his back pocket, keeping it for Plan B he said, depending on how the meeting and the video went. Vince was adamant that we should stuff the meeting (well, he would say that – he wasn't going to be in on it after his previous outburst) and take advantage of the maintenance thing to break in and let all the animals out. It seemed a stupid idea to me. I mean, can you imagine it? What would a load of fucking monkeys do with themselves, wandering around the country lanes of Wiltshire?! Everybody else seemed pretty enthusiastic about it, though, so I went along with it. After my previous ill-advised outburst of laughter, I had to be careful to say and do all the right things.

I don't think I was able to stop my jaw from hitting the floor, though, when Jemima told us about this picnic at Salisbury Cathedral with Kay and Nick and the little boy, where Kay had said too much about security at the Maier lab. I was reeling inside, absolutely fucking gutted. It's not too much of an exaggeration to say that it was a life-changing moment. The idea that Kay had had a baby was, to be truthful, sickening. I had always wanted one with her and she had refused, and now, after everything I'd been through, the fucking bitch had gone and had a fucking baby anyway! I think I need to stop. I cannot describe the temptation, or maybe it's a need, that I have to write the word FUCK over and over – a hundred times, a million times – in GREAT BIG FUCKING CAPITAL LETTERS right now, just to get it OUT of my system. I want to throw this stupid fucking diary at the wall and bash my head to smithereens on the desk.

I can't do this now. I'm sorry. No, I'm not. I'm not sorry at all. Just fuck off and leave me alone.

✱✱✱

It's been more than a week since I last wrote anything. Not that I've been busy or anything. I've eaten, slept, and sat on the khazi – that's about it. I suppose I had to spend some time thinking things through again before writing any more of this. Coming to terms with the way my life and Kay's have diverged is a process I'm still not at the end of. Not by a long way. So I apologise for the way my last entry ended. I apologise about a lot of things really. I'll try not to tell you to fuck off again, but I'm not going to sit here and promise anything. Sometimes this shit just takes me over.

Anyway, Kay and this Nick geezer have a little boy. Hearing this news hurt me more than I could ever describe. People talk about feeling like they've been knifed in the heart by stuff.

That's exactly how it was for me. After Jemima Bond said those words I had to leave the room. First of all, I headed into the loo at Nancy's house, thinking that a few minutes on my own would sort me out. I couldn't stop fucking crying though. After a few minutes I realised I couldn't walk back into the room where the SMAC bunch were still sitting around talking about this meeting at Maier and what they wanted to achieve from it. I looked at myself in the mirror and saw I was in a right state, all red-eyed and fucking pathetic. So I just left. I sneaked out by the front door and closed it as quietly as I could behind me, then walked to my car and drove back to the B&B.

Thinking about it now, I kept pretty good control of myself really. I didn't slam Nancy's door behind me and kick the crap out of any passing strangers, put it that way. It was a bit hard driving with the waterworks gushing uncontrollably, but I got back to Salisbury all right. I texted Mac and said that I'd been sick all down myself so that was why I'd left pronto. The sun was just going down on a balmy old June evening and I felt so sorry for myself, I reckoned that I deserved a pint. So I went out for a bite to eat in the town, then cruised a few bars, tried to chat up some birds, and got fucking nowhere for a while. Then I got talking to this pisshead called Tony – Tiger Tony, he introduced himself as. We started taking the piss out of each other at the bar – well, he was clearly wearing a syrup and a fucking dodgy one at that. After I ripped the piss out of him about that, he started having a pop at the "bum fluff" on my chin, asking if I was old enough to drink in pubs. We ended up best mates for the evening, and off we went gallivanting.

Some of it is a bit hazy now, but we ended up talking to a couple of Dorises in a club, and would you believe it, I scored! Unbelievable! Her name was Millie or Billie or something similarly silly! (How's that for fucking poetry eh?! Getting into this writing lark now...) What I remember best was that she was quite tall with long dark hair – dark as Kay's. She did tell me what she did for a job but I can't remember that now, and I wasn't much interested even then. It was hard enough to concentrate on keeping my eyes open and securing the blag without making a dick of myself.

To cut a long one short, I woke up in her bed next morning. I was laying there and she was asleep, and all I could see of her was her hair. I didn't want to think this but it was kind of unavoidable. It reminded me of all the years spent waking up next to Kay, knowing she was there in the bed with me, knowing she was mine, that the woman beneath that mass of dark hair was my wife. Even with a bastard of a hangover my mind quickly went back to the day before's shitty news about this baby of hers. I suppose I was half-expecting to get angry again, or, worse, more waterworks. Although if I'd woken up Millie/Billie by crying, I guess I could have turned it to my advantage with the right story, and got a sympathy bunk-up out of it.

But no – much more important than any of that, I had a different thought. It's going to sound shit now, of course. You're going to say: "Lee son, get a grip. Let it fucking go." And you'd be right, but that wasn't my frame of mind right then. I still wanted Kay back, as I've now said lots of times. I was looking at the back of Millie/Billie's head, thinking about Kay, and it suddenly struck me that the only thing that had come between me and the missus was the kids thing – her not wanting any. Well, clearly that had all changed now. It turned out that the old mare did have some maternal bones in her heavenly body. So there was now nothing, no emotional shit like that, standing between me and her any longer.

I expect you can see where I'm going with this, and it's now obvious to you exactly how big a complete fucking dickhead I really am. Right there and then, lying under Millie/Billie's turquoise-patterned sheets, I convinced myself (because I wanted to) that this meant for sure Kay and me could and would get back together again. All I had to do was speak to her, tell her that everything was forgiven, and off we would ride into the sunset, together forever.

I was too cock-a-hoop to consider the many barriers to this – like the fact that she might hate me and actually be in love with this other bloke. We were still married. I had never been sent any documents about a divorce or anything. She had just left it. In my mind, that meant the door was not closed.

I even convinced myself there was a chance that I was the father of this little boy. I worked it all out – the kid must have been conceived when Kay and I were still together. So why not? Anyway, what was more important was that if she already had one kid, then she might well have another, so why not with me, the original love of her life, the one she'd made all those vows to?

It made perfect sense to me at that moment, and for the next few weeks. Nobody could have talked me out of it, and no one even tried to, of course, because I didn't mention it to anyone. I kept it in my heart, just between me and Kay, and when a couple of days later the meeting at Maier Science was arranged for 6 July, my path was laid out before me: when we next came face to face, Kay would learn all about the rest of her life with me.

CHAPTER EIGHT

Monday 5 July 2010, 8.52 a.m.

Kay waited patiently, fourth in the line of cars outside the Maier Science facility, engines grumbling as if in solidarity with their drivers' Monday morning temper. A big white lorry had pulled up at the single metal barrier at the entrance to the site. The driver was leaning out of his open window from time to time, to exchange words with Terry, the middle-aged security man who was on duty this morning. Early on in their exchange, Kay had watched the lorry driver produce some paperwork that he had handed over, and now she could see Terry sitting in his little control cabin, speaking on the telephone.

This was all well and good, and for sure Terry was only doing his job, but Kay had been sitting here for several minutes now, backed up on the country lane that passed outside the front of the facility with another three cars in front of her, presumably all also employees of Maier, turning up for work on Monday morning. All well and good, but Kay was supposed to be sitting down for a very important meeting about the upcoming SMAC visit with the managing director Richard Cambridge at nine, in just a few minutes' time, and he had another meeting at ten before leaving for London for the day. There was another car in the queue behind her now too. Everyone was waiting for Terry and white lorry man to get the latter's credentials established before he could enter the site. Chris Moyles was holding court on Radio 1 on her car stereo, and his breakfast show team were tittering at him ranting about something or other. Kay looked blankly at the wire fence to her right. She was bored now.

8.54. She turned the radio off and sat in silence, stewing with irritation. There was a gate for entering the site, and a gate for exiting: why didn't they just let employees in through the "Out" gate at times like this? Nobody was leaving the place right now – it was Monday morning.

It had been a nice weekend; idyllic really. Decent weather, a barbecue round at Jerry and Lorna's on Saturday night, a bit too much wine; her two men, Nick and Davy, all day Sunday, mucking about in the garden as she tried to recover from Saturday's excesses. Kay thought about the laughter and the love that had filled the weekend. In fact, she never lost sight of it. She remembered her life before coming to Wiltshire with Nick. It had been mean, angry, debilitating, dispiriting. It was hard to believe sometimes that all that shit had happened with her husband. She didn't often think about Lee. She liked to believe that she had moved on in every way, although there was still a piece of paper that said she and Lee were married, and one day she would organise for another piece of paper that would say they were not; and then she would tie a golden knot with Nick.

Kay was gazing vacantly out of the window, noticing nothing, thinking about Sunday afternoon: fizzy drinks and sandwiches on the patio; helping Davy work out a jigsaw puzzle... when sudden movement by the white lorry up ahead intruded into her daydream. At bloody last! Terry had obviously got the confirmation he needed that the lorry driver and his load were legit and had opened the barrier. In front of Kay the cars began rolling forward, and within half a minute she herself was beside Terry, waving her ID at him, although she scarcely needed to.

"What was that all about?" she called out of the open window.

"What? The lorry? Oh, some pillock. I'm surrounded by them. Nobody tells me a sodding thing. Change the delivery dates, and don't pass the information down to Security. Bloody useless, those bastards in there, I tell you."

"Oh, well… I'll make sure to pass that on to them," Kay joked as the barrier started rising in front of the car. "Have a good day, Terry, I'm sure it will get better."

"Fat chance…" she heard him reply as a parting shot.

The Audi sailed on towards the car park at the rear of the office block. By the time she had parked it was 8.57. 'Effing 9 o'clock meetings – why Richard, why?

She ran up the stairs to her office and grabbed a yellow foolscap folder from the desk. Richard hated being kept waiting – there was no time even to make herself a coffee before going in for the meeting. Arriving at a run outside Richard's closed door, she stopped and took a couple of seconds to gather her wits. She knew that Richard Cambridge liked to indulge what he saw as her slightly maverick personality for the sake of a bit of light entertainment, but he also didn't appreciate having his time wasted.

Kay needed to be certain of what she was going to say. She had spent plenty of time thinking about it, examining all the angles, reading and re-reading the coverage of the interview with Ted Chillingworth in the local newspaper. Even though she didn't have all of the information that Richard would want, she knew what she wanted him to say. This was, after all, the centrepiece of her entire work for Maier Science – to help it engage better with the community, with its stakeholders, even with its detractors. A charm offensive against SMAC was needed. It was just that – and this was the nagging fear – Richard Cambridge wasn't exactly the ideal man for it. Yes, he was somewhat smooth, but he was also liable to fits of temper and/or sulkiness when someone begged to differ. Ho-hum... Kay took a deep breath and then rapped twice with her knuckles on his door. She heard a ringing "Come in, Kay" and went in.

Richard was standing by the window, looking down doubtfully at the unknotted tie draped around his neck, adjusting the length of the silk to each side for optimum effect. His aftershave assailed her instantly.

"Sorry I'm a bit late, Richard. There was a traffic jam outside the gates caused by some sloppy admin work. Terry wants us all to know that we're useless bastards." She sat down on the chair across the desk from Richard's own.

"I'm sure he does. I saw the cars waiting, and in fact I saw you sitting there with steam coming out of your ears. Rather good fun to watch, as it happens. There! How do I look?"

He turned, smiling, away from the window to face her, with the tie now completed.

"Perfect, Richard. I'm pleased you're feeling so relaxed..."

"Oh, I'm not, Kay. Don't mistake my apparent suave insouciance for the real thing. Quite frankly, I'd rather gouge my eyes out with a spoon than sit round a table with that load of work-shy parasites." He had moved round behind his desk now, but was still standing, looking at her with a half-smile on his lips.

Kay felt her eyes roll momentarily. After all the presentation coaching and pep talking she had done with him. She stared at him and said nothing until he shifted uncomfortably and said, "Shall I sit down?" He did so without her assent.

"It's good that you've sat down, Richard," Kay finally said, nicely, like an air stewardess. "Because now you will be more comfortable after I've broken your legs."

"Ooooh!" he winced, shaking his head. "So soon? It usually takes a few minutes before we get to that point, Kay. Good joke though, wouldn't you say?" He flashed her a smile, one calculated to annoy, she knew. This was the usual way with their verbal jousting, but she looked at him crossly even so: this matter was too serious for him to act like a schoolboy.

"Yeah, except that it's not really a joke, is it, Richard? You do actually feel like that."

He shrugged and waved this away. "Shall we get started?" he said. "I've got to get this out of the way before I can focus on meeting Carvill and Kai later."

This was the chairman of the Maier Science board, Lord Jeremy Carvill, and Kai Maier, son of the company's founder, and himself now its young, in-over-his-head global chief executive since the death of Andreas Maier the year before. Kai was making a flying visit to London from his head office near Hanover, on the way to further business meetings in the United States. Richard Cambridge was only in charge of the UK operation. He was required to present on the state of the UK business to his two superiors in a meeting at the Institute of

Directors this afternoon. He would have to be serious and play that one straight, thought Kay.

"What time does the train leave?"

"Quarter to eleven. I'm going to finish my presentation on the journey."

Kay nodded. "Right, so I emailed you the list of people attending the meeting tomorrow. Any questions about that?"

"Yes. I thought there was meant to be a police officer coming. Usher, wasn't it? The Chief Super – Top Brass."

"He can't make it now. I'm waiting to get the new name through from their PR woman."

"God... probably some useless minion. If they can't come up with someone impressive, I'll cancel the bloody thing. So, three of these SMAC buggers... where is it now?" Richard was searching on his computer screen for the email. "Yes, here we go: Stuart McCormack, Nancy Jennings and Liam Walcott. A rum bunch, I'll bet. What do we know about them?"

Kay pulled a sheet of paper from her folder, and placed it in front of Richard on the desk. She summarised what she could remember as he picked the sheet up.

"Stuart – from a military family, his dad fought in the Falklands War plus various other places, after that worked in security in Iraq; two sisters (so he's probably hen-pecked); read archaeology and something else beginning with 'A' at Oxford..."

"Anthropology, it says here."

"Fell in with the animal rights crowd there, and joined ALF sometime early in the noughties; established SMAC two years ago. Nancy Jennings – née Lawrence; co-founder of SMAC; daughter of a butler, would you believe; went to acting school, not much success there;

was an air stewardess with Monarch Airlines, now runs a haberdashery business. She was married to a tennis umpire – a proper professional one – but he ran off with a younger model."

Richard was reading the notes in front of him, rubbing his chin thoughtfully. A few seconds later he looked up.

"And Liam Walcott? There's nothing here about him."

"That's just it. We've not been able to pinpoint exactly who this Liam Walcott is. There are several Liam Walcotts around, but none of them seem to have any prior links to ALF or any other activist groups. We came up with a blank on him."

Richard looked vacantly at Kay for a few seconds. He sat back in his chair and blew out his cheeks. "Is that a concern?"

"It's not ideal, Richard, no. Stuart is the leader, though, and Nancy is a co-founder, along with another man…" Kay checked her notes briefly "…Vince Babcock. He's not coming, though. Maybe he's ill or something, and this Liam is being groomed for promotion. Anyway, as I say, Stuart is the leader, so I don't think we need to worry about Liam too much."

"Hmm. Okay, if you say so, Kay. And Mr Chillingworth – our erstwhile friend – promise me he's not going to be within ten miles of this place tomorrow?"

Kay laughed. "I can't promise exactly that, but he's not coming to the meeting. It's you, me, Phil, the police officer – whoever that turns out to be, and the three SMAC representatives. It's going to be lovely, we're all going to get along nicely, and you're going to behave with perfect charm and grace."

"Naturally. Why isn't Phil here now? Has he been briefed already?"

He was referring to Phillip Blundell, Maier Science's head of laboratory services. "Well, you've seen the emails. Hopefully you looked at the presentation slides I sent you both as well. I've had a few sessions with Phil to lay the groundwork for this, and we're meeting again later today in the lab to go through things one last time."

Richard nodded in acceptance, though it had taken some persuasion on Kay's part to get him to agree to a guided tour of the laboratories and research facility for their visitors. His attitude veered continuously between the desire to engage SMAC head on, as he had in effect hired Kay to do, or to cut off all contact with them and pretend they didn't exist. He still had lingering doubts over the worth of the upcoming meeting, and that didn't make Kay's job any easier.

"We've never got to the bottom of this alleged 'malpractice' that Stuart McCormack mentioned in the newspaper," Richard stated, intending it as an invitation for Kay to tell him otherwise. He rubbed his chin again and looked at her expectantly.

"I did ask for clarification."

"And?"

"They didn't reply."

"Oh, that's good of them," snapped Richard. This was the kind of thing that made him nervous: that he and the Maier organisation were reaching out to a group of people who were implacably against everything the company stood for; that it didn't matter what Maier said or did, it could never win them over. "So we're going in completely fucking blind. That's just fabulous," he said. He looked suddenly terrified. Kay had been dreading this bit.

"I've spoken to Phil about it…"

"And I'm sure he said that we do everything by the book. But what if we haven't? What do I say then?"

"It's probably just bluster, Richard."

He laughed sourly. "Please tell me, Kay… please, for the sake of all that's holy… tell me that isn't the best we've come up with."

"Richard, you know exactly what to say. I've told you before, we practised it together, and I put just this scenario in the recommended answers document I spent all that time putting together for you." She was exasperated. He was making another mountain out of last week's mountains – the ones she'd believed she had already helped him theoretically to scale.

To avoid the awkwardness of them bristling at each other across the desk, Kay flicked through her papers and found the printed copy of the recommended answers document. She slid it across the desk towards him.

"If you find yourself blind-sided by anything like this, you say: 'I can't comment on this until we have had a chance to examine the evidence and conduct an internal investigation, but it is our policy and commitment to adhere to all the provisions and the code of practice contained within the Animals (Scientific Procedures) Act 1986.' That's all you need to say."

"Yes, yes. I remember all that. Should I say any wrongdoing will be severely punished?"

"If you really feel the need, but I'd rather you just say that we and the competent authorities will investigate it and publish our findings, and not mention anything to do with discovering wrongdoing. Let's not even hint that it's possible."

"I see. Will they accept that? I don't see why they would."

"They will have to. We can't be expected to comment any further when they haven't even given us a chance to assess this so-called evidence of malpractice. So in a sense, the fact that they have refused to respond to our advance request gives us firmer ground to stand upon. We're quite within our rights to take this approach. Of course, if they don't like it, the copper will be there to make sure they don't breach the peace in any way."

Richard gave her a look: part amused, part apprehensive. He took the "recommended answers" document, waved it at Kay and muttered "A bit of light reading for the train", as he slipped it into his briefcase.

Then he turned back to her, forcing from himself a nervous sort of smile: "So, let me get this straight," he began. "We don't really know much about who is coming from SMAC; we don't know exactly who is coming from the police; and we don't know anything about what these bastards are going to put in front of us when they get here. What on earth could possibly go wrong?"

***

Evening: sometimes the circumstances of her life were all too much for Kay, and tears would roll from her eyes and flow down her face with slow, steady grace, like the Thames she had left behind her, only hinting at the turbulence of the emotions below the surface.

This was one of those times. It was Monday night, just before ten o'clock. Outside the open patio doors the summer sky was still blue, but a forbidding shade with a blanket of cloud moving across it, hastening the change to slate grey and the darkness to follow. The air felt heavy, as if the heavens were aching to release the tension. Kay had thought to herself five minutes before that a deluge was on the way, maybe even a thunderstorm. That would clear the air of this oppressiveness. She hoped the thunderclaps would not wake Davy, snuggled under his sheets.

She looked down at Nick through her tears: his dozing head was resting upon her lap, the rest of his body stretched out along the sofa. He looked as free from care as his son did – both of them breathing evenly and happily; Nick now with just the beginning of a low whistle in his steady breathing that could quickly turn into a snore if unchecked. Perhaps the thunder would wake him up too. Perhaps that would be no bad thing, Kay thought, especially as her leg was starting to feel numb beneath the weight of his head.

She continued to weep silently, looking at the face of the man she shared her life with, and thinking about the child asleep in his bed. Just three years before, she could never have imagined this life. She wouldn't even have wanted it, remembering her own mother's fate. She was living with Lee in Hertford then, casting around, sometimes desperately, for just a little emotional support and finding hardly any. But Nick had changed everything for her and here they both were: happy and fulfilled with their son; counting their lucky stars every day and night. Although she hadn't spoken of it to him, Kay's mind had even turned towards the idea of another baby. She would get round to mentioning that at some stage, when the time was right. Perhaps finding her dad would be the right moment. Her mother's face – smiling in an old holiday snap – swam into view in Kay's mind's eye and out again.

For a few moments she studied Nick's tranquil face, as if there could be clues about his progress with her dad there. There was nothing in his crumpled, relaxed features to suggest it, though. Well, why would there be? He was sleeping! The ten o'clock news was just starting, and Kay rubbed her tears away and focused on the TV. Soon enough her thoughts had turned to work and tomorrow morning's meeting with SMAC. It wasn't something she was looking forward to. It was impossible to feel anything but trepidation about an event where Richard Cambridge was expected to speak and act the right way. She had learned that lesson the hard way, as she'd listened with dismay to her boss answering Ted Chillingworth's questions several weeks before. When she had seen the interview in print, it looked every bit as bad as she had feared it would.

Nevertheless, she had pressed on with the job that they had employed her to do: the wide-ranging public relations campaign aimed at improving the image of Maier Science in the eyes of its detractors. There had been some successes here and there – the local mayor and councillors had proved easy enough to win round, and various local business groups had been happy enough to engage with Kay. But the media and the pressure group were a different thing altogether. She was going to be judged on her success in bringing these people into the fold, yet achieving that success depended on Richard playing ball and acting like a professional managing director. It was an uncomfortable thought.

Even if Richard did perform as she hoped, she had serious misgivings about SMAC, and the likelihood of them being pacified by anything that Maier said or did. They had made it their mission to snipe at the company in any way they could, and the more she thought about it, the less likely it seemed that a presentation and a tour would nullify their purpose. Based on everything that had happened since she had taken this job, Kay now knew one thing for certain: she had no respect for or pride in her own company, in the way that she had felt once before with the PR agency she had set up with Wilf; and she suspected that she had been very naïve in thinking this battle with SMAC was something she could ever win.

Well, all would be revealed when Stuart, Nancy and Liam turned up in the morning. Kay's leg had gone to sleep now and she tried to flex it slightly, to get some blood flowing, without disturbing poor, tired Nick. It didn't work, though. He gave a weary groan and shook himself awake, looking up at her questioningly.

"Sorry, darling. My leg has gone stiff. I didn't mean to wake you up," she explained, stroking his hair.

"Ha. I shouldn't use you as a pillow really, should I? Are you okay? What time is it?"

"Five-past ten."

"Huh... what's that been... thirty or forty minutes then?"

"Something like that, yes." She kissed him, smiling brightly. "I think it's going to rain soon: thunder and lightning, the works."

Nick was silent for a few seconds as he looked through the open patio doors, his brain processing this prediction. Eventually he conceded: "Do you know, I think you might be right. Feels like some heavy shit in the air. Anything on the news?"

"Generous George Osborne and Andy Murray, the happy-go-lucky Scotsman, so far. Are you tired, babe? Go to bed if you want to."

Nick roused himself to swing his feet down and sit upright next to Kay. He was getting himself together gradually. "No, I'm okay. I wouldn't sleep without you being there anyway. I'll sit up with you. My turn to be the pillow."

Kay accepted the invitation to snuggle up against him, surrendering to her own weariness, but her mind was still preoccupied with work. Nick sensed her distraction, and guessed the cause.

"Thinking about tomorrow?" he asked, and kissed the top of her head.

"Yeah, a bit… and other things. You know – like I do."

Nick tilted her face up towards his, and saw for the first time that she was teary-eyed. "Hey," he said softly, "you've been crying. Not about work, I hope? Or me for that matter."

She laughed just as softly. "Cry about work? They can all piss off as far as I'm concerned, babe. I don't like any of them – Richard, Phil, Kai, Ted bloody Chillingworth, Stuart bloody McCormack, Nancy flipping Jennings, Liam whoever. I'm dreading this meeting tomorrow, but I think I'm going to be gone within six months: find something better for the soul."

"Ha-ha – will that pay as much?"

"Probably not. It doesn't matter, I'll find something. We'll be okay."

"But tears on a Monday night…"

She looked up at him. "No, they were good tears. They were Nick and Davy tears. You know I get a bit like that sometimes, if I think too much. It was just…" Now she looked away, out into the dark blue night. "I suppose I was thinking about my dad a bit as well," she ventured.

"Your dad? Let me worry about your dad, Kay," Nick said. He sounded quite assertive. Kay gave him a sad little look and then rested her head in his lap. She was silent for several seconds.

"Are you worried about my dad?" she finally said. It was scarcely more than a whisper, as if she was scared to say it out loud.

Nick breathed deeply. Did she really want to know this now? He had thought she had contented herself with just leaving it all to him, but actually it probably wasn't such a surprise that she should sound him out like this. It was natural to want to know, he told himself.

"Honestly?" he asked, raising an eyebrow at her.

"What other way is there between us?"

"No, I'm not worried. Do you want me to tell you everything? I can do. There are things to tell."

Kay sat up to study Nick's face. She rested a hand lightly on his shoulder. "You've found him? You've spoken to him? That would be enough to know."

"I've found him, Kay, and I've spoken to him."

"Was he happy? To hear about me… about us, I mean?"

"He was as happy as a father finding his daughter after a very long time apart should be. He was as happy as any man would be to discover that he is a granddad. In fact, he was happier than that, because it was so unexpected. He didn't believe that it would ever happen in his lifetime."

Kay's eyes shone as she looked at Nick. She muttered an "oh my God" as she wrapped her arms around his neck and pressed herself against him. She whispered repeated thank yous. There didn't need to be any further words spoken. He had made her happy again. He had given her another important moment in her life. They both knew that.

Nick knew that Kay would not ask him for any more details. They both understood what was to happen: that he would bring Les along to Davy's birthday party in just eleven days' time. Nick wondered briefly if he should mention Les's cirrhosis. He decided not to spoil the moment. Another opportunity, less fraught with relief and joy, would present itself.

From outside, a sudden hissing noise began, instantly strong and urgent. The rain had arrived, and immediately behind it came the first rumble of thunder. Kay ignored it and kissed her man. Then she sat back and looked at him. Work was forgotten.

"We should close the back door," Nick commented. "The rain's getting in. Might be cats and dogs in a minute, looking at it."

"Yeah, thank God. I can breathe again now."

Kay got up and closed and locked the patio doors. She walked over to the television and switched it off. She went back to the sofa and took Nick's hand.

"Come on, babe. Bedtime."

CHAPTER NINE

The SMAC delegation was late the following morning. At five-past ten, when they were five minutes overdue, Kay phoned from the boardroom, where she, Richard, Phil and a WPC Emma Stanhope from the Wiltshire Constabulary were waiting, down to the security control room on the front gate: had the SMAC people come through yet? The answer was no. Not a sign yet.

Ten minutes later, the call finally came through. They were on their way up, being accompanied by security man Brian, who would escort them to the boardroom. By that time, the four people assembled there had been reduced to bored, desultory conversation, like strangers in a waiting room. WPC Stanhope had already apologised several times to counter Richard's griping about her lack of seniority compared to the originally promised Chief Superintendent Usher. Stanhope stood her ground nicely against Richard's anger, Kay thought. She would do fine.

Fairly predictably, some of Richard's wrath was aimed at Kay too, it obviously being her fault that the senior police officer in the area had better things to do than officiate in a dispute between a local company and some private individuals. Kay and the police officer exchanged eyebrow raises as Richard pontificated. He was clearly very nervous and agitated. Phillip Blundell ignored it all and sat quietly at the table, reading through his notes again – no help for the two women from that quarter. The SMAC people couldn't walk in the door soon enough, Kay had time to reflect, so this bloody meeting could get underway.

When the delegation was eventually ushered into the large meeting room, Kay was quickly struck dumb. First of all, a short-haired young man with a carefully sculpted beard, wearing a camouflage jacket and a confident, superior smile, came in; he was followed by an older woman with greying hair, who was dressed in what seemed to be golfing apparel: chequered trousers and a purple polo top with a logo on the left breast. Behind her was Lee Talbot, the man Kay had married more than a dozen years before. The man she had walked away from one tear-filled evening two years before when she had discovered herself to be pregnant with Davy. The man she had fervently hoped never to see again was now in a meeting room, standing opposite her.

The Maier people had risen from their seats and stood in line to greet their visitors. At the head of the two lines of people, the man in the camouflage jacket – obviously this was Stuart McCormack – was shaking hands with Richard Cambridge and announcing in his mild Scottish accent that they were sorry for being late, they were "not used to being up this early". His apology sounded as sincere as a man saying he was sorry for eloping with Miss World might do.

Kay, third in line behind Richard and Phillip, only dimly registered this wind-up, though. She was paralysed by the apparition standing in line behind Nancy Jennings. Their eyes met and held, until Lee moved forward to accept Richard Cambridge's proffered hand. Then Kay's attention was diverted as Stuart McCormack stepped in front of her, demanding eye contact and a personal greeting. She managed to recover enough to shake his hand, state her name, and mumble a welcome; his gaze lingered on her momentarily before he moved on to WPC Stanhope at the end of the line. Then came Nancy, with a weak, single shake of the hand; in fact, more like a shake of the fingers than the hand, so little warmth was conveyed through it; and then, in front of Kay for the first time in more than two years, was Lee. He was smiling and obviously enjoying this moment, seeing the shock and literal horror in her face.

He put out his hand and started with a lie: "Hi, I'm Liam Walcott."

She could feel panic rising in her throat, gripping it, choking off any possibility of finding words to handle this situation. She needed to do something. Richard was watching, so was Phillip. She was sure of it, even though Lee filled the entire scope of her vision.

"You must be Kay," he prompted her, relishing his joke even more no doubt, his hand still on offer.

Kay looked away and bit back words of anger, bitter insults. Some kind of professional PR executive autopilot needed to kick in, to prevent disaster from unfolding, give her time to think about what was happening. She heard herself say, yes, she was Kay. Her skin crawling, she took his hand, and shook it even more feebly than Nancy had hers just seconds before. Both of these things she did without wanting to and without being conscious of initiating them in any way. But they happened, and Lee then had to move along the line to the WPC and introduce himself as Liam once more. Kay started breathing again, having stopped the moment she caught sight of her husband.

They all sat down and SMAC faced Maier Science across the table for the first time. Stuart McCormack chose a seat directly opposite Kay and stared at her while everyone settled. This was slightly disconcerting but really only a minor discomfort after the shock she had already suffered.

What was now supposed to happen was that Kay was to make a very short introductory statement, outlining what the agenda would be. She had prepared what she had to say in her mind and had practised it several times. The entire thing had been completely erased by the sight of Lee. Nevertheless, Kay rose to her feet. She would have to ad lib.

She gathered herself, cleared her throat and began. "So, thank you for joining us today at Maier Science. On behalf of Richard I would like to welcome you to our facility – one of Europe's most sophisticated research sites. Also present are Phillip Blundell, our head of laboratory work, who can answer all your technical questions, and WPC Emma Stanhope from Wiltshire Constabulary, who is here to oversee our discussions today. And I'm Kay, head of public affairs at Maier Science."

Something had stopped her from stating her surname as Campbell. Was it that she felt uncomfortable confirming in front of Lee what she called herself these days, even though her cover was already obviously blown? Or was it just that she was worried he would pipe up and say, Actually, Kay darling, your surname is Talbot?

There wasn't time to think about that: everyone was looking at her, including a still amused Lee. "We are conscious here at Maier that there is some concern concerning (concern concerning? Uh, horrible! She felt her cheeks burn with professional humiliation, but had to plough onwards) … well, concerning some of the research practices that we undertake here at the facility. These have of course led to some adverse comments in the media, most recently in the case of Ted Chillingworth's piece in the *Salisbury Journal* – an interview that was sanctioned here at Maier, giving Mr Chillingworth unprecedented access to our executives, but which then misrepresented a number of comments made by the company, to the detriment, we feel, of objective reporting.

"We understand that our work can sometimes arouse strong emotions, and we believe that through a higher level of engagement, both with supporters and with our detractors, such as the members of Stop Maier Animal Cruelty, we can tackle these emotive issues head on, and hopefully reassure you that here at Maier we take the welfare of the animals we work with very seriously. As Richard and Phillip will soon outline, we meet and in fact usually exceed the requirements of the national and international standards bodies that regulate our practices."

Kay had a quick look around at her audience. Stuart McCormack was listening intently; Nancy Jennings looked bored; so-called Liam Walcott was smirking. That look hadn't left his face since he had walked into the room a few minutes ago. Kay was finding her confusion quickly shifting gear into anger every time she saw his loathsome face.

Picking up a sheet of paper, she went on: "Before I hand over to Richard and then Phillip, I just wanted to quickly run through the agenda, which you can see on the table in front of you. Obviously we are running a little late now, but both Richard and Phillip will speak for around fifteen minutes each. We've got some sandwiches and biscuits and things ready on the side there, and after the presentations and some refreshments, we'd be delighted to show you around the laboratory and answer any questions you might…"

"We don't need a tour of your bloody facility," Stuart suddenly butted in. He glared at Kay. She stared back in surprise for a second.

"I'm sorry? You…"

"We don't need a tour; we don't need an agenda; and we certainly don't need any of the lies and corporate fucking claptrap you think you're going to win us over with."

"Now look here…" began Richard, taking offence at Stuart's bad language and his tone.

"Because we've already had the tour, and what we found is going to be of interest to far more important and influential people than the *Salisbury* bloody *Chronicle*."

Stuart McCormack paused for effect. The Maier people just looked at him across the table, clearly baffled.

"We seem to have their attention, Mac." It was Nancy who spoke next, in a precise, Middle England accent.

Richard Cambridge's face was alive with indignation. "What on earth do you mean by this? Explain yourselves."

Stuart smiled calmly. Looking from Richard to Kay and back again, he said: "Liam, if you wouldn't mind…"

At once, Lee picked up a small laptop case that he had put down by his feet under the table and stood up. He quickly went about taking the computer from the case, flipping it open and switching it on. "It's okay, I don't need a power socket – this won't take long," he said. "Thanks for the offer, though."

"I don't suppose there's any chance of some coffee?" Stuart piped up, the sarcasm heavy in his voice.

Kay expected Richard to explode now. This meeting was unravelling before their eyes, and she knew who would be getting the blame for that. Richard, it turned out, was still cool, though, in spite of the fury behind his eyes.

"You suppose correctly, Mr McCormack. The last thing you people need is refreshment at our expense."

"'You people'? What do you mean exactly by 'you people', Richard? Oh, yes, of course, here it is..." Mac looked towards Nancy, who was handing him a cutting from a newspaper – everyone knew it was going to be from the *Salisbury Journal* – and he began to read aloud:

"'Cambridge made no attempt to conceal his low regard for the people behind the SMAC movement, describing them as "pesky little rich kids making trouble" when we first discussed them. Further into the discussion he got his teeth more poetically into his theme, calling them the "un-great unwashed", and "Tuesday terrorists living off Daddy's credit card". Is it not a valid position to take, the *Journal* asked him, to be concerned about the welfare of animals that are being kept from their natural environment and experimented upon, for the sake of producing more effective washing detergent?'"

"Mr McCormack, I know what the article says," Richard interjected. "That excuse for a journalist won't be darkening these doors ever again. I expect he's a friend of yours, isn't he? Of course he is – more than likely a fully paid up member of your 'gang'."

"Ted Chillingworth has no connection with SMAC whatsoever," Stuart stated firmly.

"Ready to go, Mac," came from Lee/Liam.

The SMAC leader scarcely missed a beat, suddenly turning a big smile on his hosts. Kay realised that she had not been breathing for several seconds now. If she wasn't mistaken, things were about to get worse.

"Richard, Phillip, Kay, WPC Stanhope," Mac began. "Two months ago a member of the ALF secured a position working in the laboratory at Maier Science, here at this facility. While working here he was a witness to some truly appalling scenes of abuse and wilful neglect of the animals under this company's care. He was able to capture some of these incidents on camera. The quality, I admit, isn't Hollywood, and the behaviour is most definitely not human. I hope this video makes you people feel as sick as we did when we saw it. If it doesn't, then you really are beyond any hope of redemption. Liam, please."

Lee pressed a button on the laptop computer and swivelled it round so that the screen was facing the Maier executives. He then sat back with his arms folded against his chest. Kay thought again how good it would be to wipe the smirk off his face, either with her fists or some blunt implement. Stuart and Nancy also sat back, exchanging smug looks.

The video began to play and there was silence in the room for the next several minutes, apart from the poor quality audio emanating from the computer. It was harrowing enough for Kay to watch; it must have felt like the end of his professional career to Phillip Blundell. More than twenty years of working his way up through the company, learning the basics, advancing through the grades, taking on more responsibility, writing and implementing policy, working through the endless paperwork of international standards, getting the top job, stamping his personality and professional ethos on his team, enjoying the accolades of industry recognition plus the financial rewards that came with it, anticipating the big job in the US that was almost certainly the next step on his career ladder... it was all being torn down and trampled upon, right before his eyes on that computer screen.

Before the video had reached its conclusion, Richard Cambridge had turned away from the table, sullen and silent, and sat looking out of the window. Kay, noticing this, assumed he was deep in thought about the company's next move. Her eyes went back to the video. She had never liked the laboratory, but this was scandalous, heart-breaking stuff, indefensible: the laughter of the men; the squeals of the animals; their black eyes, startled and terrified. Kay felt that her role in this meeting was now redundant, and expected that a different kind of redundancy would quickly follow. The public relations campaign she had been brought in to undertake wouldn't survive this. It would be full-on crisis mode from now on and they would want a new face to lead it. WPC Stanhope, mute throughout the entire meeting so far, had spent some time jotting a few notes down in her little rectangular pad. Kay, her own notebook being open in front of her on the table, considered scribbling a resignation letter there and then. Instead she put down her pen and forced herself to watch.

Finally, the nightmare was over. Lee turned the computer back towards himself and pressed a few buttons to switch it off. He looked up at Stuart and nodded. The SMAC trio treated themselves to a very public, private smile. Richard stood up and stalked over to the window, straightening his tie, fiddling with his cufflinks. Stuart McCormack waited. The others waited. This was the most important moment of the meeting. Maier must acknowledge its faults and do the right thing.

Richard turned to look at WPC Stanhope. "Officer, I believe this footage has been obtained illegally. There are laws against industrial espionage that I think must come into play here."

"Oh, you've got to be fucking kidding me!" shouted Mac.

Richard rounded on him. "Don't use that kind of language in my boardroom, boy."

Nancy burst into an offended kind of laugh: offended on behalf of Mac; amused on his behalf too. "Boy? Boy? Go on, Mr Cambridge, call me 'girl', please. I'd love that – it's been so long."

"I'll call you whatever I want in this room. You're not all sitting round your pathetic campfire reading the *Socialist Worker* now, you know."

Snorts of derision from the SMAC side of the table. Kay tried to intervene. "I think we all need to…" but she was interrupted by a small, polite cough from WPC Stanhope, entirely out of keeping with the temper of the rest of the dialogue in the room.

"If I may, Mr Cambridge," she said, "there are many issues at stake here – not least the Animals Act 1911 – and this case is going to require extensive investigation after we have had a chance to study the video more closely. One thing we do need to consider is whether the gentleman who took this footage was on the premises illegally; in other words, was he trespassing?"

Simultaneously Richard said yes and Stuart said no. Kay and Lee found themselves smiling at each other, inadvertently and unforgivably to Kay's mind. Mac was quickest to the second punch.

"How can you say that? You gave him a bloody job."

"What was his name?" Richard demanded.

"Barry Stevens."

Richard turned to Phillip Blundell. "Phil? Did we hire someone of that name?"

"We did. Not for long, I think, but we did. He was from Manchester if I remember correctly. He claimed he didn't feel settled here in the South, so he left after a couple of months."

Phillip looked pale. His voice sounded hollow, that of a man resigned to his doom. Richard, still standing by the window behind Kay, turned back towards Stuart Mc-Cormack. "Was Barry Stevens his real name? I bet you'd given him a false identity."

The immediate retort was: "Up yours! We've got nothing to hide. You must be getting Stop Maier Animal Cruelty confused with Maier Science. Those bastards are up to their necks in filth."

"Answer the question!"

"We've got nothing to hide. *You* have."

Richard took a step closer to the table. He looked straight at Mac, completely unrepentant in the face of the coup SMAC had just pulled off. "You're a liar," he declared. "This is illegal practice: false identities, undercover filming. I wouldn't be surprised if your man bribed our laboratory staff to act in the way we have just seen. How much did it cost you, eh? How much?"

Kay looked up at her boss and saw a man starting to lose control. Stuart gestured with his hand towards WPC Stanhope, and said to her: "I hope you're making a note of all of these baseless accusations that Richard Cambridge is hurling at us. I trust he's prepared to stand up and defend them in a court of law when necessary.

"Mr Cambridge, we've committed no serious infraction of the law, and our activities in recording and uncovering this despicable practice in your organisation have an undeniable grounding in the public interest. People out there buying the products your research helps to develop, have a right to know that in the process animals have suffered terrible degradations at the hands of the sadists you employ as laboratory staff. The ethics of testing on animals are questionable enough – fuck it, it should just be banned anyway – but to try and draw a veil of secrecy and denial over this disgraceful behaviour when it's presented to you beggars belief. What kind of fucking monster are you, Richard?"

This was too much. Richard lunged towards Mac, even though Kay and then the table was between them both. She took a blow to the back of her head in Richard's initial onslaught. Mac pushed his chair back and got to his feet, ready to defend himself. Richard was too far away to reach him anyway, unless he intended to clamber over the table or run around it. Everyone was now on their feet, apart from Kay who found herself wedged underneath Richard's armpit, as he leaned over her with both hands planted on the table, shaking with anger and shouting ill-advised personal threats at the SMAC leader. Kay removed herself from close proximity to Richard's deodorant and pushed her chair back. She stood up and rubbed gingerly at her head where it had been struck.

WPC Stanhope had now moved forward and placed a hand on Richard's arm, then the other on his shoulder. "Look, everyone, please calm down. I really do think this will have to be dealt with at a later date through interviews and statements at Salisbury Police Station. This kind of heated argument won't further anyone's agenda."

Richard turned on the police officer, still furious. "Agenda? This fucking upstart's sole purpose is to destroy my business and the livelihoods of all my employees by using vicious lies and bully-boy tactics. Then he insults me in the grossest imaginable terms in my own boardroom… and you expect me just to stand back and take it?"

Leaning across the table once more towards Mac, Richard spat another accusation at him. "You didn't come here to engage with us at all, did you? That was never the plan. We believed that with constructive dialogue we could understand each other better – Kay has been working towards this for months – but all you wanted was to strut in here, puff your bloody chests out and smear the name of this company in the shit you pretend to live in over at your ridiculous camp."

Mac, wearing the SMAC smirk like a branded t-shirt, inclined his head in such a way as to say: It's about time you caught up with us, brother. Now, finally, we're on the same page. He hardly needed to speak, but he did so anyway.

"Mr Cambridge, we expect that at the very least you will identify, discipline and/or dismiss the staff members shown to be culpable of malpractice by our evidence, and suspend with immediate effect all research and commercial activities currently underway or planned for Maier Science, until such time as an independent enquiry has taken whatever remedial action needs to be taken against individuals implicated in this breach of the code of practice. We expect that the company and its processes will be transparently reformed in order to ensure that such incidents never take place again. I don't believe that, in all conscience, you have any other choice."

"That's because you're a fool, Mr McCormack," Richard thundered dismissively; impressively, it had to be admitted. "Rest assured, all of you, we will be taking legal advice and will not spare a penny in breaking SMAC apart and exposing it for the pack of charlatans and work-shy corporate terrorists it palpably is…"

Stuart interrupted him: "Oh, now we see who the real bully-boy is! Now we see the money!"

Richard wasn't stopping, though: "Get these people out of here immediately, officer. Get them out of my sight. In fact, no… Kay – get one of our security guards up here to escort them downstairs and off the premises. I wish to speak further to WPC Stanhope."

Kay called down to the front gate and ordered Brian to come upstairs and collect the guests immediately. While they waited for him to arrive, WPC Stanhope told SMAC that she would need a copy of the video that they had showed. Richard then insisted that the SMAC visitors leave the room and wait in the corridor outside. He didn't trust himself, it seemed, to stay in the same room as Stuart McCormack. Kay was ordered to wait with the SMAC people and accompany Brian while he ejected them.

Kay led them out of the room and they stood outside the door, held in abeyance as it were until the security guard arrived. So much had happened during the last fifteen minutes that she had briefly set aside her own concerns. Now, standing in the corridor, just her, two strangers, and the man she had come to loathe, the shock she had suffered came flooding back. Lee was smiling at her and she shuddered. This was grotesque.

"That went well," murmured Mac to his troops. They were cock-a-hoop, laughing and mimicking Richard Cambridge's words, ignoring Kay standing next to them. Lee, however, kept looking at her, unnervingly hard. He joined in the display of high spirits with Mac and Nancy but only occasionally, and evidently reluctantly, did his gaze leave Kay's face. She stared at the wall, swallowing hard, her mouth parched. This might have been a good opportunity to expose Lee for the fraud he was. Her mind was too scrambled, though. Before she could say anything it was too late. Nancy pulled her by the arm, her grin evaporating, and said: "I need to use the toilet. Can you show me where it is?"

"Yes," Mac chipped in, "I need to go too."

"Wait until the security guard gets here. I can't take you both," Kay responded sourly.

"I might have to do it here on your carpet then," Nancy threatened. It wasn't clear if she meant it or not.

Kay wasn't impressed. "Ms Jennings, if you could try and hold on for another minute, it would be most appreciated. Brian will be here very shortly and the toilets are just along the corridor. A little personal class can go a long way."

"What do you know about class? You're just a glorified PR tart. You don't know anything." This was from Stuart McCormack. "Still, you'd do for a one-night stand. I've definitely had worse."

Kay looked at them: Stuart and Nancy glowering at her, challenging her; Lee keeping shtum, tighter-lipped now. They were trying to provoke a reaction. Kay realised that and had no hang-ups about telling them to fuck off; in many ways it would be a pleasure, and she doubted she would have a job to protect at Maier for much longer. To react or not to react... the plusses, the minuses... just then Brian stepped out of the lift down at the other end of the long corridor and came walking towards them. Thank God.

"Everything okay, ladies and gents?" he enquired breezily, in the manner of those who have seen it all and couldn't care less anymore.

"Brian, our guests are leaving, but they need to pay a visit to the toilets first. Can you look after this gentleman – Mr McCormack, and I will go with Ms Jennings."

"Certainly. This way, please," said Brian, and smartly about-turned. They followed him and soon reached the Gents. Stuart went inside and Brian stood in the doorway so he could watch both of the SMAC men at the same time. Kay took Nancy further along the corridor to the Ladies. Taking her cue from Brian, Kay stood in the open doorway, waiting for Nancy to finish in the cubicle while keeping an eye on Lee, who was standing down the corridor near Brian.

Judging his moment though, as Kay had had a hunch he would, Lee suddenly hastened along the corridor towards her, eluding Brian's grasping hand and ignoring his calls to stop. The security guard was now torn between making sure that Stuart behaved himself and having some control over Lee's actions. He couldn't do both. He elected to maintain his position at the lavatory door while keeping an eye on Kay's end of the corridor. When he next looked it was clear that she and the SMAC man were only talking, although he couldn't hear what was being said.

Kay would not have described it as "only talking" however. Lee had rushed towards her and she had feared what was to come next. She was helpless now, vulnerable. He pulled her arm firmly so that she had to step away from the toilet door and it banged shut behind her. They stood facing each other and his grip tightened.

He spoke furtively, desperately: "Kay, we've got to be quick. I've been looking for you for so long. I know I was bad to you, I know we had our problems, but I'm different now. I've changed. And we can try again."

"Let go of my arm, Lee." She shook it vigorously – more vigorously than she needed to, since he immediately loosened his grip.

"Please, Kay, say you'll think about it? Say you'll meet me?" He gave her a piece of paper taken from a pocket of his jeans. "Here's my number. Just call me and we can chat."

Kay couldn't order her thoughts at all, couldn't believe this was happening. It was the nightmare she had feared for more than two years. She couldn't run away. She needed to stop this immediately. But she had taken the piece of paper from him. Why had she done that? Her voice sounded agonised when she heard it. "Lee, no. Don't do this. I can't… I've moved on…"

"Yes, you can, darling. I still love you, we're still married. Please just call me and we'll meet and talk about it. Quickly, before the others are here, say you will."

"Everything all right, Kay?" Brian called from twenty yards away, his voice stern. Lee was looking back and forth between the security man and Kay. He feared that she would summon the guard, but she didn't. She waved at him to say he needn't worry. Lee could have interpreted that as a sign of some favour towards him. Kay moved quickly to puncture that hope.

"Lee, listen to me: I've got a new life, a little boy, a man I love and who loves me. I'm happy now. You've got to let me go. Please, I beg you."

"No, no, no, you're not listening to me, Kay. It's me: your Lee. Remember what we had? We can have that again, and more. I've changed now. Things have changed."

There was a commotion at the other end of the corridor. Brian had hold of Stuart's arm and they were exiting the lavatory. Both Kay and Lee looked anxiously in that direction, each with wildly different hopes. Kay took advantage of the hiatus and pushed open the door to the Ladies again.

She called out: "Ms Jennings – please hurry up. Your colleagues are waiting for you." A muffled reply; she didn't hear the words.

Kay turned back to Lee and was frightened by the desperation she saw in his eyes. My God, he was serious about this.

"Kay, I love you. Please come back." Brian and Stuart were rapidly approaching, only ten yards away now. "Kay, please. This is our last chance. Please, call me on that number."

He looked desperate. Despite herself, Kay felt mingled horror and pity. The two men were close enough to hear now. "No, I'm afraid that won't be possible, Mr… Walcott was it?" Another push of the toilet door: "Ms Jennings, now, please!"

Nancy was washing her hands. Stuart and Brian were standing next to Lee when Kay looked back. Lee regarded her defiantly, but there was no disguising the anguish in his eyes.

She didn't know whether a final twist of the blade was necessary, but she did it anyway: "I said no, Mr Walcott, and that's the end of it."

"What's this all about?" Brian enquired. "Is this person giving you any trouble, Kay?"

"No, I've dealt with it, Brian. Mr Walcott was making a… an unusual request, but we both know where we stand now."

Stuart looked at Lee questioningly. The sound of a hand dryer blowing came from the Ladies. Kay disappeared inside and came out accompanied by a grinning Nancy a few moments later. Kay gave her a hard look as she said quietly: "Get the cleaner up here when we're done, please, Brian. Graffiti."

In silence, they took the three SMAC members down and showed them through to the other side of the security barrier. The sun was hot and high, even at mid-morning, and the road outside Maier was quiet. It seemed a world away from the ructions that had taken place inside the boardroom.

Before crossing the road and heading through the trees on the other side, Mac turned to say a few last words.

"Kay, tell your boss we're prepared to go to the top with this. You're not stupid – you can see what it will do to the company if we get one of the investigative programmes interested. Nobody in your job wants to be on *Panorama*. We've tried to be fair."

"Fair? You call threatening and flour-bombing innocent people fair? Your attitude has been confrontational from the start, Stuart. Please don't start throwing the word fair about as if you own it."

"We bring pressure to bear in any way we can, Kay. We despise what you do here and we want to stop it happening in future, but the very least you guys should do now is to take care of those animals in a humane fashion. It's a fucking disgrace and you know it. I saw your face in there. You were ashamed. Why are you sticking up for these wankers? Unbelievable."

Kay couldn't look at Mac. She looked at Lee instead. She could blow his little game to pieces with one comment right now. He knew it and realised it was on Kay's mind, judging by the worried expression on his face. Something stopped her from doing it, though. There wasn't time to wonder why.

"Well?" Mac demanded. He walked into her eye line to make sure he got her undivided attention.

"I guess you'll be hearing from our lawyers, Mr McCormack." She shrugged. "Until then, goodbye."

She left them by the roadside outside the Maier facility and walked slowly back through the security barrier and towards the office block and the inevitable post-mortem. Behind her, on the grass just beyond the security fence, she let a piece of paper slip from her fingers. On it was printed Lee's phone number.

***

There was a surprise in store for Kay when she got back to the boardroom after escorting the SMAC visitors off the premises. Her head, it turned out, was not on the chopping block. Richard, his rage cooling by slow degrees, in fact asked after the well-being of that head, having been told by WPC Stanhope that he had dealt it a blow in his impassioned charge at Stuart McCormack. So much had happened in the previous hour, so much of it distressing, that Kay had quite forgotten about the whack she had received. She felt it cautiously. There was no lump, no break to the skin. She would live.

Richard was in an agitated, excitable mood though. "For the love of Christ," he gushed when she came back into the room, "have you ever met such a rum lot as those three? We can forget about being friends with those people, Kay. You can strike them off the list. They don't want to listen. They've already made their minds up."

She had been about to apologise for the debacle she had brought upon the company. She didn't expect Richard to see, in the drama of this moment, that she had been carrying out his instructions in reaching out to SMAC, and nor did she expect him to admit that those instructions were and always had been futile.

Ignoring SMAC was easier said than done, though. What about the video? Richard had already put in an urgent call into the company's lawyers; a brief exploratory conversation had raised the possibility of gaining an injunction if the evidence could be shown to have been obtained illegally. WPC Stanhope was not willing to venture an opinion on the likelihood of this; everything would depend upon the particulars of the case, and those particulars had not yet been established. It was obvious that she wanted to get back to her superiors to deliver a report and quite probably hand the case over to someone else.

And the men in the video – the unwitting stars shown to be abusing animals, joking around while they suffered – well, George Levin, Lewis Leathbridge and Micky Biggs had been identified by Phillip Blundell as the guilty men, and he was down there in the laboratory now, taking the first steps towards a disciplinary procedure that might end with them all being dismissed. Somehow Richard was able to joke about it: "Phil will be down there now, emptying the drawers looking for a razor blade so he can end it all."

It seemed bizarre to talk like this after such a meeting, such a challenge to the future of your business. Kay couldn't understand it, unless it was simply a release of stress on Richard's part, or the testosterone was still pumping through his veins. She had far too much on her mind to analyse it at length, though. She only knew that she wanted to get away from these people as quickly as possible. She wanted to call Nick, and tell him that the unthinkable had happened – Lee had found them. She needed to hear Nick's voice.

It was almost lunchtime before Kay finally escaped from the boardroom. She had been hanging on, not saying much, simply counting every second, trying to quell the urgency of the butterflies in her stomach. Richard eventually let her go with a sympathetic smile and another apology for the bash on the head. He must surely have noticed how disengaged she had been from the discussion since returning to the boardroom. She didn't care. She wanted to go home and sit with Davy, surprise him and Jemima by staying for a long lunch. She might even phone back sick and forget about the rest of the day. That would allow her to spend a few hours with Nick at home before she had to come back to this place again.

Outside, the fresh air made her feel a little less queasy. When her car drove beneath the raised security barrier – a wave from Brian – she looked disbelievingly at the spot on the grass where Lee had been standing just an hour or so earlier. Already it didn't seem real, and she wanted to kid herself that it wasn't. Kay drove away knowing that was impossible.

***

Dear Diary

*T*he night before the meeting at Maier Science, we had a get together – me, Mac and Nancy – round at her place in Coombe Bissett. We sat and watched the video again and talked tactics. I had a pretty easy job really. I had to carry the laptop bag, and then set the computer up and get the video rolling when Mac told me to. Even someone as secretly uncommitted to the animal rights cause as me could handle that, ha-ha! Anyway, by now I was getting better at making the right sort of comments at the right times when I was with these people. They were very committed to the cause, which I suppose was admirable. Wish I gave a fuck about anything that much, other than the Arsenal. Oh, and Kay, I suppose.

That evening at Nancy's I felt a lot of pent-up tension. It was hard to believe that I had managed to get this far in such a short space of time. Only a month and a bit before I had been sitting at my desk at work, bored shitless, when the email arrived telling me where Kay was and what she was doing. Now I was bloody petrified!

We all met up again the next morning at the camp site at 9.30. (I've left out a whole lot of stuff there. I suppose it's worth recording for posterity that I turned in at about midnight after coming back from Nancy's, and was still lying there, staring at the ceiling, turning it all over in my head, churning it all over in my guts, five hours later. Then I gave up on sleeping, opened the curtains and watched the sun come up, sitting there on my crappy single bed, in my boxer shorts. I suppose if I was any good at poetry, this would be the moment to get all la-di-da about the sight of the sun breaking out over the top of the buildings, the cathedral spire. Sunny Salisbury eh? You'll think I'm being a prat, but it was kind of a beautiful moment really, full of new hope and all that old rubbish.

It wasn't quite so beautiful an hour or so later when the couple in the next room along started having it off. That wasn't what I really needed to hear at that point. Paper-thin fucking walls.

Anyway, so, other than the two lovebirds going at it next door, it was a peaceful little interlude that morning. I was able to spend some time reflecting on this journey that I'd been through. There had been a lot of bad moments. I know it will be hard for you to credit now, patient reader, but I truly believed – because I'm a dick – that there could be a happy ending to all this. That the old magic would work on Kay somehow.)

Well, on with the story eh? So, I drove down to the camp in the woods. I had the laptop bag, and in my pocket, unbeknown to Mac and Nancy, I had a piece of paper with my mobile number on it. I knew I needed to find a way to speak privately to Kay and pass on the slip of paper. I mean, not even I was fucking stupid enough to imagine that after all this time she'd go "yeah, let's do it, Lee" just like that. I reckoned she'd need to think about it a bit, and maybe we would go out a few times to talk it over as I worked to rekindle the old feelings.

The three of us sat around at the camp until we were late. It was Mac's idea: keep the bastards waiting for a little while. These serious business people hate being kept waiting, he said. I laughed because it seemed the right thing to do. Just agree with everything Mac says. That had been my strategy from Day One, so why stop now? Deep down, I just wanted to get over the road to Maier and see Kay. There's maybe a career as an actor for me, someday.

Nancy intended to graffiti the walls with abuse somehow, and she showed us the marker pen she had stuffed down her sock, and the one she had in her bag. In case those two got found on the way in, she'd put another pen inside her knickers. I must admit that was pretty funny. Those guys!

Finally, when my head was about to burst with the tension of it all, we headed off through the trees, me, Mac and Nancy, to cross the great divide, the little country B-road that separated our woods from the Maier site.

Some old fella on the gate took our names and called up to the offices. Then he searched us all. He quickly riffled through the laptop bag and Nancy's handbag, and asked what the marker pen and various other things were for. He confiscated the whole handbag in the end, and he found the pen stuffed down her sock, said he would leave it all by the trees across the road, awaiting our return. Being the well-mannered old fella that he was, though, he was far too gentlemanly to check Nancy's nether regions, so she got one of her three pens in. Christ knows how comfortable it was, walking around with a fucking marker pen down your drawers!

Before we knew it, we had been taken up to the boardroom, where the famous Mr Richard Cambridge and his attentive acolytes were waiting for us… bloody impatiently, I expect, since we were well late. We walked in and there they were, standing in a line to receive us, like at a wedding: Richard, some other bloke, Kay, and then some tidy young piece in a copper's uniform.

ZIIIIIIINNNGGGG!! Oh my God. Kay Talbot, Kay Campbell – whatever you decide to call yourself, darling, whatever you do in your life, even if I never see you again, and I suppose I never will now – be as perfect as you were that day for whoever the lucky bastard is that gets to be with you (some skinny sod called Nick apparently).

Us blokes will understand this. You look at a bird and you think: she's done something, there's something different. You think maybe it's her hair, she's styled it a bit differently now, but you're not really sure and you don't want to make a tit of yourself. So you just say: "You look nice, girl." And play it by ear after that. I was looking at Kay and one of the feelings I got was that something subtle had changed about her. Nothing massive, you know, but in some way her style had changed – evolved, I suppose. She was tanned and there was this clearness to her complexion that I just didn't remember from before. The features of her face seemed more defined, as if all these years my memories of her had been in early black-and-white film, and now here was the real thing in high-definition TV. She looked good. She looked beautiful. I was almost in tears the very instant I saw her again. Of course, I wanted her badly. She was mine anyway. I wanted her back, totally and completely and immediately. I wanted her to walk out of that room with me. It was only much, much later – sitting here with time to dwell on it, really – that I realised what the difference was between the Kay I remembered and the one I came face to face with that day. She was happy – something I scarcely remember feeling.

Well, we went along the line, shaking hands and introducing ourselves. Kay's face was a picture. She had spotted me pretty much as soon as we walked into the room. Double take! It must have been a real shock for her, and I could see her furiously trying to concentrate as first Mac and then Nancy came before her, while out of the corner of her disbelieving eye she sized me up. It was all I could do not to crack up laughing.

I shook hands with Richard and then Phillip, the second geezer. Then Kay and me were face to face. I'd waited so long for this moment, I suppose it was a shame really that I couldn't just take her in my arms and tell her all the things I felt, but that was obviously a no-go with everyone else standing there watching. I had to introduce myself (as Liam, of course – that caused a flicker, or perhaps we should call it an earthquake, of surprise to shoot across her face). I held my hand out towards her and she just stood there, the silly cow. Get a grip, Kay! I did feel a bit sorry for her. I mean, it's not every day that your husband, who you left in the fucking lurch two years before, suddenly turns up at your place of work bearing a false identity.

It got to the stage where I had to tell her that she had to be Kay, because she seemed frozen by shock. She couldn't shake my hand. Okay, okay, I suppose the warning bells should have been ringing then that she wasn't exactly pleased to see me. With everyone watching her, she finally pulled herself together and shook my hand. The first time I had touched my wife in more than two years!

Those hands... the soft skin of her palm, the smooth, slender fingers, the rich, deep red of her painted, manicured nails. I knew those hands almost as well as I did my own. They were the hands of my nurse and my lover; my cook and my housekeeper. They had soothed my fevered forehead, slapped my arm playfully, run an iron across the creases in my shirts, received the ring that meant we would always be together. I wanted to hold them both in my own hands, and brush them with my lips, like I'd done more than a dozen years before as I knelt at her feet and looked pleadingly up into her eyes, desperate for the yes that came like a dream.

Everything seemed bloody possible at that moment in the boardroom. I thought that once I'd had the chance to explain to her how I had changed, and how things would be different between us, she would realise this was still meant to be; that we could be good again. I held on to her hand and looked into her eyes, and still didn't see what a prat I was making of myself. I did however realise with a jolt that I was now the one who was taking an embarrassingly long time over a handshake, so I reluctantly let go and moved along to introduce myself to the copper they had there.

The meeting then started properly. Jesus H. Christ, what a fucking scene that was! Kay stood up looking nervous as hell and did an introductory talk. At the end of it she said they were going to take us SMAC-ites on a tour of the facility, and that's when Mac teed off. No word of a lie, I thought there was gonna be blood up the walls. Cambridge went abso-fucking-lutely ballistic about all the disrespect coming out of Mac's mouth. Mac read out Ted Chillingworth's newspaper article, throwing some of Cambridge's quotes back at him, and then he asked me to get the laptop running, introducing our little film while I did so.

When the video ended you could tell that Cambridge was ticking. He and Mac went round the houses with it, accusations flying from both of them, Nancy getting stuck in too, the copper trying to bring in the voice of reason. It was all terrific fun from where I was sitting, and Kay seemed to enjoy it as well. There was one moment I will never forget, because it was the last time I ever saw her smile. The copper had raised the question of whether our mole, who had done the videoing, had been on the premises legally or was trespassing, and Mac and Cambridge blurted out exactly opposite replies at exactly the same moment. I looked at Kay and she looked at me and we both smiled, trying not to laugh. That was awesome.

It wasn't long after that, though, that Mac called Cambridge a fucking monster and it really kicked off. Luckily there was a table between the two of them, otherwise Cambridge might have ripped Mac's ears off! Instead, Kay took the brunt of it as her boss went for Mac, eyes blazing. I didn't like seeing my missus getting a whack like that, so I nearly ran round the table and clocked the bastard myself. Again, I think the police girl saved the day, trying to calm everyone down, though there was plenty more abuse flying to and fro.

Anyway, we basically got kicked out of the place. Cambridge did his nut and booted us out and there were all sorts of threats about legal action and what not. Fucking mental it was, very entertaining. I could see that Kay was badly shaken by the way the whole thing ended. They got a security guard up to escort us off the premises and luckily Kay came with us. As we all walked out into the corridor, leaving Cambridge foaming at the mouth behind us, my guts were churning like an old washing machine because my chance to speak to her alone was fast approaching.

As I said before, Nancy had smuggled a marker pen in and planned to find an opportunity to use it on a wall somewhere. After we left the boardroom and were waiting for the security guard to arrive, she asked to be shown to the toilet, and Mac then asked too, leaving Kay in a dilemma because she couldn't keep an eye on both of them. I wasn't too pleased when Mac got a bit leery at my wife and said he reckoned she would do for a bit of rumpy pumpy or something, but I kept my mouth shut. I could hardly blame him for thinking she was a bit of all right anyway, could I?

The security guy got there eventually (we'll call him Bill, shall we? He looked like a Bill) and Kay went off down the corridor with Nancy to the Ladies. This was my chance. Kay was standing alone by the toilet door, waiting for Nancy, while Bill kept an eye on Mac. I went for it. I ran along the corridor and at last me and the missus were alone together.

Kay didn't turn her warmest smile upon me as she saw me coming, I realise that now. I was so anxious at the time, so caught up in thinking about what I had to say and how quickly I needed to say it, that I didn't really notice the look of dread (I recognise it as that now) in her eyes as I arrived in front of her, ignoring Bill's shouts for me to stop. I even grabbed her arm. I remember that too, because it was the last time I ever touched Kay. That seemed to panic her a bit because she shook me off. Perhaps she thought I was going to hurt her. She really seemed to be misunderstanding everything about me.

I remember the conversation was really hard. I can't write it all down word for word. It went quickly, as it had to because I needed to say my piece before the guys had done their abusive graffiti and come back out of the loos. Summing it up, I just said that I had changed, that I loved her and I understood things better now, that I realised I'd been a twat, that I wanted her to think about it and get in touch with me so we could talk about it. I gave her a bit of paper with my number typed on it (my handwriting is shit – didn't want to give her an excuse, I suppose).

She took the bit of paper from me and held it in her hand, and I remember her saying that she had this new bloke and the boy, and that she had moved on, etc. It wasn't what I wanted to hear and I ignored it really. I thought that it was just a line, stuff she had to say *in the circumstances, but that she would think about it really and get in touch with me. She was incredibly brave and looked me straight in the eye as she spoke – I remember that so well – she didn't take a backward step. She begged me to let her go. I remember her saying that. She begged me. These were precious moments for me – to be with Kay again. But even though her words are a scar on my mind now, at the time I wasn't really comprehending the meaning of them. I just had this faith that seeing me again would reignite all the feelings we had once shared. It's a blur really, but one where your senses are so alive, so tuned to the moment, that, like someone in the middle of a car crash, you experience everything in sharp definition, and every second feels like five. It goes too quickly and it seems to last an age. It's a contradiction, I know.*

All too bloody soon, the old bugger and Mac were back with us. Nancy was still writing slogans on the wall as far as I knew. Kay went in and fetched her out, and finally our time together was really done and dusted. Kay had been incredibly polite and even quite formal about it all, calling me Mr Walcott. It had been, to use one of her own favourite phrases, one serious fuck-off performance from my lovely wife. Then they took us down and showed us out of the front gates. Everyone seemed to be bristling! Mac and Nancy had their danders up and Kay was so indignant about everything that her hair was almost standing on end!

There was another not-very-friendly exchange of words by the security barrier between Mac and Kay, and then we crossed the road and disappeared into the cool shade of the trees. I wouldn't be at all surprised if the old bastard Bill and Kay had been able to hear our cackling laughter as we tramped off into the woods. There was no doubting that Mac and Nancy had enjoyed every moment of the confrontation.

We got back to the camp area and Nancy opened a bottle of wine. We each drank a plastic cupful while we went back over the fun and games of the morning. Then Jemima called – yeah, Jemima who was sitting looking after Kay's little boy right at that moment – closely followed by Vince, and the word was put out that a SMAC meeting would take place that evening, round at Nancy's, so we could tell everybody what had happened. I made my excuses and headed back into Salisbury in the car after that, saying I had a few things to sort out with work. Really I needed some space too; space to think through the things on my own agenda. God, I was aching for that woman. Seeing Kay had not satisfied my thirst in any way. I wanted to drown in her.

Looking back, I was in a state of complete distraction that day, and somehow I needed to pull myself together before the SMAC meeting. I could hardly touch my dinner for thinking about everything that Kay had said, persuading myself it all meant something good, but already with the first little cracks starting to appear in my confidence, little chinks here and there that I quickly dismissed. I set off for Nancy's in the car, but took a detour and drove round past the Maier place. Soon after passing the front gates, I got to the end of the road and turned left, and knew I was going to take the next left again and park up behind the camp. I had to go and stand outside the site again, where I had last seen Kay.

I left the car and walked quickly through the trees, ignoring the branches that whipped me in the face, past the tents and all the shit that SMAC kept there, and got to the trees lining the road on the other side. It was still *light, but the car park across the road was pretty empty by then since most of the employees had gone home. Presumably Kay had too. There was a different fella sitting in the security hut, so Bill or whatever his name was had obviously knocked off as well. That was good enough for me.*

I stepped between the trees and crossed the road smartly to stand on the grass on the public side of Maier's big POW camp wire fences, at about the place where Kay had seen us off earlier. I stood looking at the buildings inside, just thinking wistfully about her, and how good it had been to see her. The security guy was watching me now, wondering what the fuck I was doing, I suppose.

I'll never know what it was that made me look down at that moment, but I did, and something caught my eye in the grass there at my feet. It was a piece of paper. Oh, yes – you know exactly which piece of fucking paper I'm talking about, don't you? I didn't need to pick it up and read it to confirm what my reeling brain was already telling me, but I picked it up anyway, unfolded it and stared at it like a blind man. I recognised that series of digits. My series of digits. The bitch had thrown it away. She had thrown my number away just as soon as I had turned my back to walk off.

You might expect to hear that a red mist then descended, that I screamed some kind of blood-curdling scream. You might think that I grabbed hold of the fence and shook it until it and the whole of fucking Jericho came down. You might imagine that the security guy made the very bad call of challenging me at that moment of intense rage, and that he ended up with his limbs rearranged, and that that is why I'm writing this fucking pointless screed from a room that's ten feet by ten feet.

You might think all of that, and you would be wrong. I screwed up the piece of paper in my fist. I turned around and walked, slowly and deliberately, back across the road and through the trees and past the camp to my car. I sat in it for ten minutes, staring straight ahead.

My heart, let me tell you, had never felt harder.

CHAPTER TEN

Any other nanny would have been bewildered by the ferocity of the reaction: Davy had left a couple of small toys on the floor, just inside the front door, but even though Kay didn't actually step on them when she came in from work, she had been angry enough to come at Jemima, sharp-tongued and shouting.

A bad day at work? Jemima had known that Kay was going to have one of those, if Stuart and Nancy and that other guy Liam had done their jobs. That much she had expected. She hadn't expected the level of distress that was apparent in her boss's voice and in her unhappy eyes. She had obviously been crying, and seemed to be on a knife edge. Jemima apologised for leaving the toys out and then tiptoed round Kay until it was time to leave. She did wonder whether Kay had been fired, but that surely would have led to Jemima herself being laid off, she reasoned, and Kay had said nothing to suggest that. She simply sniffed a miserable "Okay" when Jemima said she would see her in the morning, and sat nuzzling her son's hair in quiet contemplation.

Jemima climbed into her VW Beetle outside, thinking it was all a bit odd: super-professional Kay being this emotional about a bad meeting. An hour later, as she was driving to Nancy's for the SMAC meeting, it was still a puzzle to her, but she was mostly looking forward to seeing Stuart again, and hearing what had happened that morning to rattle Kay so badly. She sang along to the car stereo as the Beetle turned into Nancy's road, seeing Stuart's car parked outside, and Vince and Pippa's a little further down.

After parking her own car and walking back to the house, Jemima pressed the doorbell. A few seconds later Mac himself opened the door to her, a glass of red wine in his hand.

"Hey, how's it going?" he greeted her, half smiling, not waiting for an answer as he led the way back into the living room.

Jemima hurried behind him. "Lovely, thanks. Until a certain woman came home from work. Someone has really upset her today."

Mac gave a self-satisfied snort as they walked into the room where Nancy, Vince, Pippa, Anthony and Bhupathi were all sitting. Everyone seemed happy. Had they already started the meeting? Jemima wondered. She wasn't late; she didn't deserve to be left behind. The notion was quickly dismissed, though, as Bhups commented that they were "just waiting for Liam now". Jemima sat down next to Pippa.

They made small talk for a few minutes; killing time, filling glasses. Then Vince said: "Has anyone heard from Liam? How come he's always late?"

A few glances were exchanged, nothing said. Then Nancy spoke: "Mac, let's just get started. Liam was there this morning so he knows everything anyway. He'll get here eventually, I hope."

"Seconded," said Bhupathi, just beating Vince to it. "Thirded," he mumbled sulkily instead.

It took a few minutes for Mac, aided by an occasional reminder from Nancy, to relate the events of that morning.

His memory was excellent, and he recalled the heated exchange between himself and Richard Cambridge practically word perfect. He told the story with relish, enjoying the attention, enjoying revisiting his own best lines. He concluded with the news that Maier was planning legal action against SMAC, and asked Jemima to keep checking their email account for any developments in that regard.

Finally, he sat back in his armchair while his audience reflected on the story. Vince spoke first: "Well, that's got the bastards' attention then. They won't be saying 'SMAC who?' over there anymore."

"I agree," said Mac. "We're in the fucking game, people. Now for Phase Two. Tomorrow I will be putting in a call to a guy called Patrick Bacon at Channel 4, to arrange a meeting where we'll show them this video and negotiate broadcasting rights."

"Awesome," young Anthony blurted out. He didn't say much, but sometimes he just couldn't help himself.

Heads nodded around the room – except for one. Vince was pulling a face.

"Channel 4? Why Channel 4? Does anyone even watch Channel 4?"

Mac didn't look entirely surprised; he swirled his red wine around the glass momentarily. "I know the guy, Vince. He's a contact I made with exactly this kind of thing in mind."

"And you're sure he's going to go for it?"

"Well, no, I'm not totally bloody certain, Vince. He hasn't seen the video yet. Give me a fucking chance, for fuck's sake."

Mac took a swig of his wine.

Nancy spoke. "What are you saying, Vince? That we should aim higher? BBC? Sky News?"

He shook his head. "No, not really." He looked around at his companions – it was clear from their expressions that they thought he was just being contrary for the sake of it once again. He wasn't Mac's yes-man, though, and he had a different idea about how to handle things.

"I know what you all think," he told them. "I know you believe I just disagree with Mac for my own entertainment, but you're wrong. Mac has many good qualities, but his way is not always the only way, and not always, to my mind, the best way. We both believe passionately in the same thing, though. So how about this…"

Vince looked around the room, peering from behind his spectacles as if uncertain that the stage was really his. Everyone was listening attentively. He felt Pippa's hand tighten around his; a silent show of support.

"I want action. That's why I joined the ALF. That's why I joined SMAC. I thought that was why we all did. There's been lots of talking and it has got us to this point. We've got nothing much to show for it except a video that some journalist who we can or can't trust might or might not be interested in; and if they're not interested then we've shown our hand to Maier for no good reason. Oh, yeah, we've also frightened a few irrelevant idiots by throwing flour bombs at them and running off like kids playing Knock-down Ginger. Very fucking clever.

"Does anybody in this room believe – I mean, really believe – that these bastards are going to change by one single jot what they are doing to defenceless animals because of the talking we've done and the so-called pressure we've brought to bear? Anyone? Please, I'd be fascinated to hear."

He looked from face to face. No one said anything. He turned to Mac last of all.

Mac looked down and shrugged. It seemed that might be the sum of his response, but then he looked up again and said firmly: "If you've got a better idea, Vince, spit it out."

"You don't want me to wait for your mate Liam to get here first? I could tell a few jokes while we…"

"Vince, please," Nancy interrupted, "let's just stick to the idea, shall we? No more bickering. I can't bear it."

He gave her an ingratiating smile. "Of course, Nancy. I forgot myself for a moment. Okay, everyone, so let's say that Channel 4, or whoever else we take the footage to, decides to pick up this video. What will happen next? There will be months of talking, researching, seeking legal advice; decisions delayed for months inside their corporate time-wasting executive. They will want more footage, new footage, better footage. They will take it in this direction, and that direction, and make a whole load of editorial choices we very likely won't agree with.

"In short, if it ever does come out, it will take months if not years, and meanwhile we will be left hanging – feeling restricted in our own activities because we won't want to jeopardise the TV programme. And all this time, animals will be continuing to suffer in that place.

"I say we don't need to chase media exposure in that way. We need to take direct, bold, aggressive action – the kind of action that the Maier bastards won't be expecting after the meeting today – and let the media exposure take care of itself.

"The media won't be able to ignore it then, and they will be all over our lovely video as a result. I believe this will also draw new supporters and funding to us. I believe it's what the ALF big chiefs thought and hoped we would do when we set up SMAC. There are animals being tortured while we sit here talking. We're an action group: it's time we acted.

"And finally, one last reason: for what I have in mind, we already have the perfect opportunity, which we know about thanks to Jemima's magnificent espionage work at the house of Kay Campbell. Maier's security is going to be down on the sixteenth of July. Let's break the fucking place open!"

At this several jaws dropped. Jemima was surprised but delighted to have received a mention in dispatches. She wasn't used to her ideas being listened to, let alone acted upon. Mac, however, gave an appalled laugh.

"What in God's name are you talking about, Vince? Just walk in there? Have you lost your mind?"

"Speed, Mac, speed: we will rush the front gate. We know where the labs are, thanks to the map that Barry gave us when he left Maier. If we move quickly, I think we can get in there and give the animals their freedom. Which is what we all want, isn't it?"

"Oh, sure. And are you prepared to do time for this?" Mac challenged him.

"Yes."

"Fine, because that will almost certainly happen."

"That really isn't the point, Mac. The point is that SMAC is supposed to be an action group. We're supposed to do whatever we can to disrupt Maier Science, not sit here on a comfortable sofa and talk and talk and talk. You seem to have lost sight of that fact. You seem to crave some sort of recognition from these people. I want them to recognise that we brought their business to its fucking knees, and I will do anything – absolutely anything – to achieve that. Listen, this isn't just about you, Mac – why don't you ask everybody else what they want to do? Go on – ask them."

"For Christ's sake, Vince… shall we all put our hands up like schoolchildren?" Mac was still mocking him. Vince was defiant.

"Indulge me, Mac, just for a change, eh?"

It had been a while since anyone else had contributed to the conversation. Now Nancy calmly commanded everyone's attention.

"Mac, Vince – can I say something?"

Eyes turned towards her. She didn't wait for any dissent to be voiced. "I know what you're worried about, Mac. You're worried about this being the end of the group, whether we're successful or not, whether we find ourselves being sent to prison or not. But I promise you, if that happens, you and I will pick up the pieces again. And anyone else here who is still committed to the cause. But we *should* do this, Mac. I'm certain of it."

Jemima watched Mac closely while Nancy was speaking. His eyes had widened with first surprise, and then utter confusion. This was Nancy, siding with Vince! They all knew that SMAC had its factions. Mac's leadership was built upon was Nancy's unswerving support for him, and they all knew that too. For the first time Jemima could remember, that foundation of support was absent. The air seemed to be alive with possibilities now. Would there be a coup at the top of the group? Jemima watched Mac. He was red-faced, incredulous, searching the faces of the others. She wanted to express her backing for him, but the mood in the room had turned against him. She held her tongue.

Mac sounded dumbfounded when he managed to speak – as if the most amazing, most improbable thing had just happened in front of his eyes.

"Nance, what… when did you decide all this?"

"I started thinking about it when Jemmy brought us the news about Maier and the security going down. It's too good an opportunity to miss. Surely you can see that, Mac? We might never get a better chance to do this."

He glared at Nancy for an uncomfortable second; then he muttered: "Jesus wept…" He turned to Bhupathi – usually his next most vehement advocate behind Nancy and Jemima.

"Bhups… well, mate, looks like you're my last hope. Let's get talking to this guy at Channel 4 before these crazies get everyone locked up."

Bhups, however, looked suddenly shifty and unhappy to find himself in the limelight. He didn't even speak; simply shook his head, and as he did so he seemed to shrink into himself. It was enough.

"For fuck's sake!" Mac yelled, startling most people in the room. "You've got to be fucking joking me!" His anger brought out his Scots accent, Jemima thought. Her next realisation was that it was a strange time to be thinking that, at what seemed like a pivotal moment for the group. There was an embarrassed pause. Jemima felt compelled to go to Mac, to console him. She stopped herself. Emotions worked across his face. Vince stared at the wall, Pippa squeezing his hand.

Mac looked at Jemima pleadingly. There was no helping the situation, though. Mostly through their silence, the group had spoken, and for the first time that anyone could remember the verdict wasn't in Mac's favour. He necked his wine and pulled a sour face.

"Should I leave?" he said, sounding choked. "Should I fuck off into the sunset? I mean, I had a plan. You guys don't like it. Am I Gordon fucking Brown on fucking election day? Am I the pariah? Yesterday's man? Is this the dreaded fucking vote of confidence?"

His eyes were increasingly wild as he rambled on. Jemima was a little afraid of what might happen next. Nancy was not accepting his descent into self-pity, though.

"Stop talking such poppycock, Mac. No one is saying anything of the sort. We're all behind you, darling. But this time, we think something more is required. This is our big opportunity, Vince is right. Why can't you see that?"

Vince kept quiet. His work was done for the night. It must have been hard for him, after all the reverses he'd suffered at Mac's hands over recent years, to contain his delight, but he was a patient man, and not given to gloating. He contained himself.

Mac, however, was taking it badly. "Bunch of fucking amateurs," he muttered in a low voice that everybody heard.

Nancy was on this straight away. "Oh, for pity's sake, grow up, Mac!"

They glared at each other. Jemima held her breath. Then Mac, in a somewhat flimsy show of petulance, knocked his empty wine glass, which was down by his feet, across the carpet, the glass rolling away towards a handsome pine wall unit that was the prize piece in Nancy's lounge. Anthony happened to be sitting on the floor nearby and stopped it with his hand, but Mac wasn't watching. He rose from the armchair, avoided all eyes, and marched out, heading for the front door. Jemima exhaled. A number of voices rose in his wake, not exactly pleading but suggesting all the same that Mac didn't go, that he stay in their midst.

He was gone though, out through the front door, which he had flung open. Jemima went after him. Outside, he strode down the pathway, his head down, not giving, he continually told himself, a flying fuck about anyone or anything.

The very late arriving Liam was closing the gate behind himself at the other end of the pathway. Seeing Mac coming towards him, he steeled himself for the necessary smile and apology over his lateness. Quickly, he found himself in the way, and Mac brushed him aside in his rampage, but then stopped in his tracks, looking back at him confrontationally.

"What fucking time do you call this?" he snapped. "You were supposed to be here an hour ago. Not that it matters now. Everything is shot to shit. I'm going to get pissed."

Liam stood open-mouthed as Mac turned away and stormed off towards his car. Jemima had come along the garden path now in Mac's wake. Liam could see Nancy and Anthony standing in the open doorway to the house.

"What the fuck's going on?" Liam asked Jemima. She turned a sour look towards him as she walked past, but left the question unanswered. Liam watched as she ran towards Mac's car. He paused momentarily, half in and half out of it, and shouted to her, "Not now Jemmy."

The words brought her to an immediate halt by the side of the road. Seconds later Mac's MG growled into life, and he wasted no time in thumping it into gear and wheel-spinning noisily away. A neighbour peered inquisitively out of an upstairs window. Liam watched the car tear around a corner and disappear from sight. Then he shrugged and continued on up the garden path to where Nancy and Anthony still stood.

"I get the feeling he's upset about something," Liam remarked as he neared the front door.

Nancy eyed him coldly. "He'll be back," she said. "Where have you been?"

"Sorry, I got…"

"Never mind, get inside and we'll tell you what the plan is."

Jemima was coming along the path behind him now. "We're doing this without Mac?" Liam queried, still confused by everything that had just happened.

Impatiently, Nancy turned back to him. "Doing what? He'll be back." She walked through and left him to follow her.

***

For the second evening in succession there were tears in the Campbell/Newman residence, but these tears were not induced by happy thoughts about life and love. These tears were caused by the shock of unexpectedly coming face to face with Lee Talbot.

Kay was trembling, her face tear-streaked, as she paced distractedly in the kitchen; Nick was talking, reaching out to her with hands and words, but it was having little effect on her gut-wrenching hysteria. Davy, thank God, was asleep in bed before Kay felt able to vent her worries. She said she wanted to move away from Hindon, from Wiltshire, from England. She wanted to take off right away, tonight, like fugitives, drive for miles and then find a hotel room for the family. And do the

same again tomorrow, and after that, until she felt safe…
if she could feel safe. There was no knowing what Lee
would do next.

Nick didn't want to tell her she was over-reacting,
knowing that this would most definitely draw an angry
retort from his partner. He tried saying: "Kay, listen to
me. Calm down, nothing bad is going to happen."

In response, she turned on him anyway – perhaps
what he thought had been implicit in the tone of his
voice.

"You think I'm over-reacting? Don't you even dare
think that! You've got no idea what that man is capable
of. You don't know him."

"Okay, that's fair enough," Nick said, aiming for a con-
ciliatory tone this time. "But you're talking about him as
if he's an axe murderer, and he's not really, is he, babe?
I've seen him cowering in an alleyway, remember?"

"You didn't see him today. You didn't see the look
in his eyes." Kay stopped pacing and took a gulp from
her glass of wine. "He looked desperate. He looked deranged. He looked fucking demented, Nick!"

It would have been a bad time to smile at Kay's talent
for the dramatic flourish. Nick knew that he needed to tai-
lor his words and tone to the gravity of the situation, yet
still find some way of soothing Kay's shredded nerves and
assuring her that nothing terrible was going to happen.
Since she had stopped pacing up and down, he took the
chance to take her in his arms and pull her close to him.

"Come on, darling, let's sit down and calm down before we go to bed. We'll talk about it in the morning,
when we've slept on it."

Kay's voice sounded miserable and tear-choked
against his shoulder. "There's no time in the morning.

I've got Jemima coming early to talk about Davy's party and then I've got to get to work. We have to do something now Nick."

"Do something? We can't, darling. It's getting on for eleven o'clock. Davy is asleep. What can we do now?"

She had buried her head against him and it muffled her words. "I don't know. We have to do something. He could be outside. He could be here."

"Lee's not here, Kay. We've got locks and bolts and alarms on all the doors and windows. I will sit up all night in the dark to protect you, if I have to."

"We have to go somewhere, Nick."

"Go where?"

Kay sniffed and fell silent for a second. Then, in a hopeful tone, she said: "We could go to my dad's?"

Oh, shit, Nick thought: of all the things to say. How could he get out of this one without revealing that her dad was in hospital? He patted the back of Kay's head while his mind raced. She was waiting for an answer. The truth, he supposed, might in some way take her mind off the return of Lee.

"Well, no, we can't do that, darling," he said, as gently as he could manage. "That's not really possible." She queried why, as he knew she would. "He's in hospital, Kay."

She looked at him now; studied his face for some seconds. Then she buried her face against his shoulder. "Oh, God… I didn't think today could get any worse."

"It's not like that, babe," Nick consoled her. "He's been ill but he's getting better and he'll be well enough to come and see us for Davy's birthday party. I didn't want to have to tell you this yet, but you've kind of forced my hand."

Nick gave a little chuckle, hoping it might defuse some of this turbulent emotion. Kay was shaking against him, but it wasn't with laughter; she was crying again. He wondered what to say next, what words of comfort might convince her to retire to bed and face this challenge again in the morning. He was at a loss now, he had to admit to himself. All he could do was pull her closer still.

Then he heard the patter of feet behind him, followed by a meekly insistent tugging on his jeans and a soft, pleading voice: "Mummy, Daddy…"

Nick looked down into the imploring eyes of his son, and knew that this scene was at an end.

CHAPTER ELEVEN

Wednesday, 7 July

The stillness of morning… those last precious minutes before the shattering interruption of the alarm clock. Jemima, secretly awake beneath the solitary sheet that was all the bedding she needed in the warmth of summer, cherished these moments. There was a big, bad world out there, and she would have to face up to it at some point, but for now, for these few minutes, however many there were, she embraced the seclusion of her bed.

She thought about Stuart McCormack – thoughts lent greater immediacy by the fact that he was there, asleep next to her, in the bed. The feeling of seclusion was actually illusory, although in the hours he had spent at Jemima's Mac had hardly been good company. He had turned up much the worse for wear after his promised bout of heavy drinking. He was defiant too.

"Did you drive?" Jemima had asked him after opening the door to her unexpected visitor.

"Aye, I did. What of it?"

"Nothing, it's just…"

"What? He was glaring at her with fiery eyes. She backed down.

"Nothing, forget I said anything. Come in."

Mac raided her fridge and made short work of a partly consumed bottle of wine. They sat and talked for a few hours. His mood seesawed from buoyant good humour to scathing rage against Vince, usually via interludes of maudlin self-pity. It hadn't been much fun for Jemima – not even when Mac had told her that after Nancy's betrayal she, Jemima, was the only one he could really trust. It was kind of a nice thing to hear, although she would have preferred it if he had not mentioned Nancy.

Then he had kissed her and gone through to the bedroom, but by the time Jemima had finished tidying up the dirty dishes and wine glasses and had joined him, Mac was lying on the bed snoring, fully clothed. She manoeuvred him under the sheet and soon joined him, reflecting that his performance today had not been his finest hour. Mac's whistling snores indicated that for him the day was over, and she had soon fallen asleep.

Now, six hours later, the sun was rising outside. There was nothing to disturb her as she thought about the events of the day before and waited for the alarm to summon her to another. It was to be an earlier start than usual, because Kay had asked her to get to the house in time for a chat about Davy's fast-approaching birthday party before Kay went to work.

Jemima remembered the meeting at Nancy's, in the wake of Stuart's dramatic exit. There had been some barbed comments to Liam in respect of his lateness. It wasn't the first time and Nancy didn't appreciate it. Jemima didn't feel any sympathy for him, nor did she particularly trust him. He was Stuart's new friend, and that was the best that could be said in his defence.

When the gang had got to discussing some of the finer points of the mission they had set themselves, Jemima had made a confession: she was supposed to be attending Davy's birthday party that same day. It was going to make things difficult if she had to cry off since she had promised that she would help out there. There was some discussion about this, and then Vince and Nancy had agreed that Jemima should go to Davy's party and miss the raid. It would be useful, Vince pointed out, to have someone still on the outside to continue SMAC's work if those taking part in the attack should find themselves in custody.

Jemima found herself feeling relieved and hoped that no one had noticed that fact. She hadn't been particularly enthusiastic about the whole idea in the first place, and didn't see herself as especially suited to that sort of direct action.

There was another reason for her relief, though, one that she was still coming to terms with deep down inside. This little boy had stolen into her heart. In spite of her hatred of his mother's work, Jemima had quickly come to adore young Davy: his cheekiness, his infectious laugh, his wide-eyed wonder at the world he saw around him. Spending time with him was actually the highlight of her day. She wanted to share his birthday. That was the simple fact of it. It wasn't an emotion she felt inclined to share with her SMAC friends.

Jemima lay there for a few minutes, remembering a handful of moments of laughter and happiness with the little boy. Then the clock radio burst into life and she reached out, without looking but with practised precision, to poke the snooze button. That gave her another nine minutes in bed but it soon trickled away and a pop song intruded once more. This time she turned the digital radio off for good, swung her legs off the bed, like a zombie awakening, and sat upright, rubbing her face vigorously with her fingers. She had heard nothing from Stuart throughout all of this and a glance over her shoulder confirmed that he remained oblivious, buried beneath the sheet. Jemima padded barefoot to the bathroom.

When she returned fifteen minutes later Mac was sitting up in bed, the sheet pulled to his chin, his feet still in socks poking out at the other end. He eyed her in a curious way, she thought: with a mixture of sheepishness and accusation, though God only knew how any of this was her fault. Still wrapped in a towel, she stopped in her tracks.

"You're awake."

"Kind of stating the obvious, Jemmy."

She shrugged and walked around to her side of the bed. "Feeling okay?"

"What do you reckon?" he demanded rhetorically. "Is this what time you get up for work? It's only just gone bloody six. My head feels like shite."

She nearly rounded on him and said that, yes, this was the time people got up in the real world, when they couldn't just live off of their mummy's good fortune; but she stopped herself, thinking instead that he looked good beneath the sheets of her bed, and not wanting to discourage the chance of a more meaningful re-run.

"I've got to go and see Kay early today. I told you last night," she contented herself with telling him. Jemima busied herself doing her make up for a few minutes, amused to see Stuart's reflection in the mirror, watching the process. When she had done that she grabbed the hairdryer by her bed, but before she could switch it on he spoke.

"Any chance of a cuppa, Jem?"

She turned and glared at him. "Coffee would be great," he added, giving her a cheeky wink. She called him a piss-taking bastard then smiled despite herself. After a detour into the kitchen to fix him a coffee, which she placed by his side of the bed, she switched the hairdryer on and flicked him a two-fingered salute when he immediately tried to talk to her again. Hair done, she turned back towards him.

"Are you going to get up then? I have to get dressed and go to Kay's."

"Do I have to? Thought I could chill here for a bit and then let myself out at a more civilised hour."

"I suppose so. If you want any breakfast there's some cereals in the corner cupboard," she said, walking round to her wardrobe. She studied the contents for a few seconds before selecting the day's outfit. It was going to be another hot day so she chose a loose-fitting top and a pair of three-quarter-length blue denims. "See you in a minute," she added, and headed back to the bathroom to put the clothes on.

When she came back Mac was still in bed, sitting with his legs drawn up, eyes focused on the coffee cup he held in his hands. He looked a little disconsolate, Jemima thought.

She stood in front of him with her hands on her hips, looking like a fretful mother. "Are you okay, Stuart? You don't seem very happy."

He glanced up at her and she thought his eyes were shadowed by disappointment, though he gave her a valiant grin.

"Just thinking, Jem... thinking about yesterday and all that... wondering what to do with myself, what I should say to Nance. Maybe I should jack all this in, go and do something else."

His answer and the self-pity it betrayed made Jemima want to hit him. She felt compelled to sit on the edge of the bed and argue him out of his defeatism. "Why should you do that? You're still the leader of SMAC."

"I don't know that I am," he replied sharply.

"You are as far as I'm concerned. Vince got his way yesterday but that doesn't make him the group's leader. You're twice the man he is, and you can prove it by accepting what your members decided and making this Maier thing happen in the best possible way."

Mac was staring into space. He didn't speak for several seconds, so she prompted him again: "Stuart? Are you even listening to me?"

"Yeah, lovely words, Jem. Lovely words." He was shaking his head. "What relation they have to reality, God only knows."

"Don't be such a…"

"Such a what, Jemmy? Such a what?" They looked at each other, both of them now irked; then she got up and checked herself briefly in the mirror before turning back to him.

"I haven't time for this now, I've got to get to work. Don't talk to me like you would to Pippa, Stu. I'm on your side. I know SMAC means everything to you. Promise me that you'll talk to Nancy and sort all this out? Text me later. I have to start thinking about party games for a two-year-old."

"Shit, the stuff you have to do for that horrendous bloody woman – Kowtow Kay!"

Jemima wanted to say she really didn't find Kay to be the ogre the SMAC people chose to caricature her as, and that she was actually a reasonable person with a good heart. That wasn't what Mac wanted to hear though, Jemima knew, so she contented herself with saying that she did it for Davy, which was also true but hopefully more palatable to Stuart. His reply was dark, though; darker than expected.

"Don't get too close to these people, Jemmy," he said. "That's not your job."

***

Mac didn't spend too long moping around at Jemima's flat. He had a plan already, and after treating himself to a shower and a leisurely breakfast from Jemima's stores, he headed out to the car and his own flat. It was still not 9 a.m. so he killed some time watching TV. At around 9.30 he switched off the TV and retrieved a business card that he had attached to some papers a few months before.

Then he called the number on the card, and waited a few seconds before a man's voice answered. "Patrick?... Hi, it's Stuart McCormack," he said. "You may remember we met back in February at the anti-vivisection rally." He listened briefly. Then: "Stuart McCormack... from the animal rights group Stop Maier Animal Cruelty. Well, we're part of ALF but we work independently... Okay, never mind, but we did meet in February at the rally, and you gave me your card and said to give you a call when there was a story... What sort of story? Oh, it's a tasty one, involving, between you and me, some fucking outrageous cruelty to animals at a research facility near Salisbury. There's loads of footage. Can we meet up? I'd love to show you."

Mac bit his lip and listened. "You're what, sorry? You're leaving… new job… oh, right. Damn. Where are you moving to? Maybe you'd still be…" More listening. "Ah, okay, I see. Who should I speak to instead then?… Really?… Why do you say that? Why wouldn't they be interested? We can't let these bastards get away with this."

The man on the other end said something that Mac found appalling: they weren't doing these kinds of stories right now; cutbacks, not enough resources, investigative stuff wasn't a priority, sorry. Mac held the phone away from his ear and mouthed a silent obscenity at the man, then brought it back to the side of his head.

"Well, that's really too bad for you guys. Someone else will pick this up and make a real stir with it. Still, I don't suppose you're bothered much if you're leaving the wonderful world of TV journalism anyway."

The man on the phone wished him a less than sincere good luck and Mac hung up. He stared at the wall for several seconds. Maybe Vince had been right about the media after all? No, hang on – this was just one knockback. There were other broadcasting organisations he might be able to get interested, and he would contact them. He didn't have the names of any reporters or editors, though. It would have to be cold calls to find out the names of the right people, and probably long explanations to complete strangers, if he even got a chance to put the case for the SMAC video.

With a laptop computer in front of him and his phone in his hand, he set to work. Three hours later, he tossed the phone to the floor in exasperation. No one was playing ball. People were on holiday, were too busy, had other priorities, or in some cases were honest enough to say right away that they were not interested, for whatever reason. It was mystifying. Animals were being tortured by these bastards in the name of consumer safety and absolutely no one was interested.

Mac got up from the sofa and walked through to the kitchen, where he poured some water into the kettle and tossed a teabag into a mug. He stared at the cooker while the water boiled and his mind ticked over. Perhaps his tactics were wrong somehow. Perhaps there was a right way and a wrong way to approach the media. If that was true, then he had to admit that he didn't know what the right way was. Maybe they needed a media relations expert. Hey, maybe they should give Kay Campbell a fucking job! He shook his head in bemusement and made the tea, then took it through to the front room, still thinking.

Bloody Vince was right, wasn't he? The media didn't give a shite about this because there weren't any people involved, apart from a few Neanderthals at Maier breaking some rules. It needed a big gesture to get their attention; it needed more people. Mac sat bolt upright. Something in his mind had just gone *ping*. It did need more people involved, and in fact so did Vince's plan. There were not enough of them within SMAC to pull this off. They would need to invade a big site like the Maier one from at least two directions simultaneously. A thrust at the entrance barrier probably wouldn't work on its own, but it would help to distract the Maier security people while another group came through the trees on the opposite side of the facility, then through the fences there, which were, after all, actually closer to the laboratories. Yes, indeed. And who could supply more people committed to this cause to bolster the SMAC forces? Why, the ALF of course.

Mac smiled, suddenly excited again. He picked up the phone and dialled another number, this one directly from his memory. His computer screen still showed the contacts page of a media outlet's website. He raised his mug of tea to the screen while he waited for an answer, and saluted it bitterly.

"Thanks for nothing."

***

It was 7.30 a.m. by the time Jemima arrived at Kay's and Nick's house in Hindon. She found Kay looking bleary-eyed and bothered. Davy was already dressed and running around making a great deal of nonsensical noise, which he briefly interrupted to give Jemima a hug. Nick was also there, waiting for his work colleague Jerry to pick him up for another day's hard horticultural graft. Jemima had been with the family often enough now to detect a degree of tension between the two adults – as if she had just walked in on a disagreement between them and they were only keeping tight-lipped with difficulty. Still, Davy seemed blissfully ignorant of the unease in the house, so Jemima guessed that Kay and Nick had not been arguing in front of the boy.

It was still a little puzzling, though, she thought to herself, as she had done the evening before when Kay had returned from work in such obvious distress. It hardly seemed feasible that she could be so upset after a meeting with the SMAC trio – sure, they had stitched up her and her boss, but the look on Kay's face that evening – very much as if she had just seen a ghost – went way beyond what Jemima had expected. And the following morning she was still in a state. Jemima asked if she was okay, but

Kay simply said she was fine, that she just didn't feel very well, it was nothing.

Nick's lift soon arrived and he made his farewells. There were hugs and whispers with Kay in the kitchen while Jemima played with Davy and unsuccessfully tried to hear what was being said. After Nick left, Kay and Jemima finally sat down to discuss the upcoming birthday party.

They decided that there should be a Toy Story theme, since Davy would want to be dressed in his favourite Woody outfit anyway. They could perhaps get a face painter in, and materials for making Toy Story masks; they could devise some simple games around the theme too, and put together party bags containing plastic figures of some of the characters from the film, as well as other goodies. Who wouldn't want a Buzz Lightyear figure, after all? Kay asked Jemima to put some more thought into these things and to start researching the entertainment side of the event.

They would need food and drink, of course: little sandwiches, mini sausages, party rings, cucumber sticks, cherry tomatoes, cheesy biscuits, various flavours of juice. Hindon was a small village – only about ten kids were expected, mostly boys but maybe one or two girls too. Kay, Jemima and one of the other mothers would preside over the fun and games. It would start at 2 p.m. and go on until about 5, which was when the other parents had been asked to come and collect their children.

Kay was still expected to be at work on the morning of the party, but she was hoping to negotiate a few hours off to help Jemima get things ready from lunchtime. Nick apparently had some kind of surprise planned, Jemima learned, and it wasn't clear what time he would get to the house. Again Kay mentioned the maintenance work on the security system at the Maier site, but this time she was more specific about the timings of the planned downtime. It would all happen during daylight hours – starting at 10 a.m., and back on by 3 that afternoon, the employees had been informed. This was news that Jemima knew she needed to report to the planning meeting Vince was due to hold at Nancy's house on Thursday evening.

Anyway, there was still nine days to go before Davy's birthday party, so there was time enough, hopefully, to get everything organised for it. Kay had left Jemima with a list of things to get started on while the child had his naps, and then with evident reluctance she went off to work, leaving her son and his child minder to enjoy a day playing in the garden.

Kay called the house five times from the office that Wednesday, though, allegedly just to remind Jemima about a variety of things about Davy and his care, which Jemima already knew. When the last call came in the mid-afternoon, Nick was home. He spoke to Kay in a low voice in the living room while Jemima watched Davy outside and again tried to catch the gist of their conversation. She was unable to hear much, but there was no doubt at all in her mind that something was troubling them.

Jemima diligently went about ticking things off the party list over the Wednesday and Thursday before the SMAC meeting, but it gave her an odd feeling – she alone was expecting the party to be ruined by the assault on Kay's place of work the same day. There was no other option for her but to proceed according to Kay's plan, though.

All of these things turned over in Jemima's mind as she drove to the meeting at Nancy's on the evening of Thursday the eighth, knowing that she had yet more important information to pass on; information that would be central to the timing of the assault. She was in a state of some excitement, for there was another thing on her mind too. Earlier in the day she had spoken to Mac on the phone. He had called her while she was doing some drawing with Davy, and asked when Vince intended to hold the next planning meeting for "M-Day" – Stuart's not entirely original term for the upcoming mission.

Jemima had told him that the meeting was to be that very evening, starting at 7.30 at Nancy's house. Okay, he had said, and then seemed to weigh up that piece of information for a few seconds. Eventually he said "Have fun", and then hung up. Jemima had smiled to herself. Something in his voice suggested he had some kind of surprise up his sleeve – the vocal equivalent of a glint in his eye. Certainly he sounded more motivated and engaged than the man in a funk she had left in her bed two mornings before. She wondered if he planned to make an appearance at the meeting. If so, it would make for an interesting night.

A summery evening breeze was bucking up its sluggish act as she walked up Nancy's garden path to the front door. By 7.30 everyone was there – everyone apart from Mac that is, but Jemima was the only one who had an inkling that he might show up. She quickly imparted her information: that the site security would be down for maintenance between 10 in the morning and 3 in the afternoon; this was SMAC's window of opportunity.

Thereafter, Vince took charge, with Nancy at his right hand, Pippa at his left. He began with a fairly lengthy motivational type speech, which Jemima soon switched off from. She had done her bit and didn't need to hear this. None of them needed this really. They should be discussing the details of the mission. At length, Bhupathi pointed this out. Jemima wondered whether Vince's new-found authority had gone to his head a little. Even Pippa glanced at her husband with slightly forlorn reproach in her eyes from time to time.

Finally, Vince got into the specifics of his plan. It was getting on for 8.15. He took out a big sheet of paper – a plan of the Maier site that had been put together by Barry Stevens of the ALF after his infiltration of the facility. Vince laid it out on Nancy's dining-room table. Everyone gathered round to study it. The moment felt so serious that Jemima suspected they were all going to synchro-nise watches at any moment. Vince started gesturing towards various parts of the map with a pen, outlining for his audience that this rectangular block here was an admin office, these longer rectangles were the "accom-modation" for the animals, here was the laboratory; this jagged line, the perimeter fence; the security hut at the entrance, manned by a couple of old guys – laughter around the table at this point when Vince called them Mainwaring and Wilson.

"They don't like it up 'em," said Liam obligingly, Cor-poral Jones-style. Everyone laughed again.

The doorbell rang. Nancy went to answer it while Vince carried on talking. In a trice, Mac was there among them, full of purpose – full of beans, it seemed. He looked around the room, smiling. He was beaming so broadly that for a few moments Jemima wondered if he had gone quite mad. She was looking forward to this, though.

"Evening, my lovely people," he began, spreading his arms wide, as if delivering some staggering largesse towards his countrymen. Tension was thick immediately, such was the division in the room. A couple of people muttered "Good evening, Mac" and then contemplated their fingernails. Vince was not one of them. He blinked a few times, folded his arms and watched Mac warily, waiting for more information to act upon before responding to this intrusion on his meeting.

Mac looked around the room. "Everyone got a drink? Yeah, okay, good. Nance, do you mind if I grab a beer? Great. Perfect." He took a tin of beer from Nancy's fridge and cracked it open. He held it up to everyone; they were still watching him, holding their collective breath. "Cheers, guys. What's happening here then?" he asked, affecting innocent puzzlement. "Why the glum faces, people?"

"You know what's happening here, Mac." Inevitably it was Vince who spoke, in an accusing tone. "We're meeting to discuss the Maier break-in. You weren't interested, so this has nothing to do with you."

"Oh, don't mind me, Vince, old pal. Don't mind me. I'll just stand here and listen – if it's okay with you guys?"

The overdone affability of his tone, undercut by sarcasm, was quite something, thought Jemima. He sounded very Scottish again, she thought. She suppressed a smile. Nobody had replied so Mac asked again.

"Nobody minds, do they?" The briefest of pauses. "Cool." Mac moved forward to the edge of the table, put his lager down, and then appraised the map. "Okay, Vince, pal, rock on. What's the plan?"

"If you've come here just to stir up trouble or take the piss, Mac, then forget it," Vince whined. "You can leave now. You're not needed."

Mac kept grinning, giving no indication of being angered or hurt or indeed suffering any reaction engendered by Vince's words. The fool's grin remained on his face, though. "Whoa, steady on, mate. No need for all this aggression. I come in peace, Brother Babcock. I swear to you, no trouble, no taking of piss. Pretend I'm not here, Vincent."

Vince looked agitated. He glanced at Nancy questioningly. It was her house after all – he could hardly order Mac off of the premises himself. She nodded but wagged a schoolmistress-like finger at Mac, as if to say, Don't you dare, young man. Then she instructed: "Let's proceed as we were, Vince, please."

He took a deep breath and resumed his briefing. Mac caught Jemima's eye and winked slyly. A few minutes passed before he spoke again. Vince was getting into an explanation of each SMAC member's role during the mission.

"How many of us are there, Vince?"

He turned and stared at Mac. "What?" he spat.

"Quite simple: how many of us are taking part in this thing?"

"Well… all of us here." Vince looked around the table. "Apart from Jemima, so… six of us. Seven if you deign to join us… if you would be so good as to put your neck on the line, that is."

Mac ignored the implied slur. He sighed and leaned forward, resting his hands upon the table edge, casting his eyes over the map. Then he looked up at everyone with another confident smile.

"Listen, guys, I'm no military expert, but my dad, Major McCormack, he always wanted me to join the army, follow in the family footsteps sort of thing, and before I got old enough to tell him to fuck off, he used to drum into me all this military shite. And one of the things I remember – one of the few things, to be fair – was that if you're going to attack somewhere, something, whatever, you need a lot more blokes charging in than the number of guys sitting there in their holes waiting for you. It stands to reason – you lose guys in the attack, you see, covering ground. So you need overwhelming force."

"Look at the size of this fucking place," Mac continued, gesturing to the map. "You get past the barrier at the entrance and you've still got to run for maybe sixty seconds just to get to the first building. And that's only an office. Where we want to go – where the animals are – well, that's another minute or so of sprinting, even for Usain bloody Bolt. I'm not being funny, but apart from young Anthony here, none of us is exactly in prime condition. I couldn't run that in two minutes, I'd be fucking dead halfway there.

"My point is, very quickly we will be outnumbered before we even get to the rabbit hutch. My point is, it won't fucking work. You're in dreamland if you think it will. I'm not going in there just to have a punch up with Richard fucking Cambridge. We need to get to the animals, and to do that we need more people and a better plan."

He paused to let his words sink in. Liam piped up first. "How then?"

"I'm pleased you asked, Liam." Mac grinned. "It's very simple, and in fact I've already arranged it. We're getting reinforcements from ALF. Ten or twelve of their best activists – and I mean the big guys who can handle themselves – are coming to help out. So, you see, I really am the cavalry on this occasion."

There had been an exclamation of surprise and delight around the table at Mac's news. Nancy in particular clapped her hands together in excitement.

"Mac, that's wonderful. How did you manage it?" she said, gushing a little, causing Vince to raise an eyebrow in her direction. He alone looked unimpressed.

"I just put in a call, Nance, right to the top. There are a few people over there who owe me a favour." Mac smiled around the room, feeling heroic, enjoying the expressions of satisfaction, or perhaps relief, on the faces around him; enjoying the evident discomfort on Vince's. There was a further nasty surprise to come for Vince, however.

"I did have to make one concession, though," Mac warned. Faces turned to him expectantly. "I had to agree to lead the mission personally before they would send us these new friends. Vince, I know…"

His words had caused Vince to slam his palms down angrily on the table top. Mac tried to mollify him, but didn't get far. "Vince…"

"No, you listen to me, Mac. You didn't want any part of this plan. You stormed out like a cry baby when you couldn't get your way. You leave all the hard work to us, sit around feeling sorry for yourself for a few days, then make one phone call and you expect us all to cry 'Hail to the Messiah'? It's out of order. This whole SMAC thing is just about you and your ego, isn't it? For God's sake, you even put your name in the ruddy title…"

Mac burst out in derisive laughter. "Vince, we're called SMAC because we want to Stop a bunch of arseholes called Maier from doing what they fucking do, which is, guess what, Animal Cruelty. It's got less than nothing to do with my name or anybody else's. Now, why don't you let me finish what I have to say, and maybe then you won't feel the need to pummel all our ears with this nonsense, eh?"

Vince glared back at him indignantly; Mac merely waited a few seconds and then took the silence as his cue to finish what he had been about to say before Vince's flash of fury.

"So, as I was saying: I spoke to ALF; in fact, I spoke to Mr ALF himself, Benjamin, and he insisted that I lead the mission, but only because he doesn't really know you, Vince. I said you would be upset – and I obviously wasn't wrong there – and he invited the two of us to go and meet with him face to face to discuss the issues we have here with Maier and for him to get to know you better, Vince. I accepted on behalf of both of us."

There was a stirring of interest at this. "Ben Hunter? The leader of the ALF?" asked Bhupathi, making sure that he and everyone else understood Mac correctly.

"Yep, the very same," he confirmed in some triumph.

"Oh, that's brilliant," Nancy bubbled. "Vince, isn't that brilliant? You can meet the main man!"

Vince's eyes betrayed his quandary: his anger that Mac had out-manoeuvred him; his reluctant admiration of his adversary's ability to get to the man at the top and make a real difference; his own anticipation of the possibility of making himself known to that man, which was a career opportunity he had never really expected to happen. Everyone was looking at him now, no doubt expecting to see a gracious response. Pippa had hold of his hand; she gave it an urgent squeeze.

Vince had to cough to clear his throat. "Yes, I suppose so," he allowed. He still looked completely crestfallen. Mac knew that his victory was by a sufficiently wide margin that he could afford to show some magnanimity. He moved around the table and grasped Vince's hand. His words sounded sincere.

"Vince, you do a great job for us and you are one of the best activists I've ever known. Your passion and commitment are an inspiration to us all. Believe me when I say this: we both want the same thing. We want to turn these Maier filth bags over. Let's do it together, pal." Mac looked around the table at the people he considered his comrades. "Let's all do it together."

CHAPTER TWELVE

Nick leaned down in the blacked-out bedroom and gave his sleeping son a special kiss, a birthday kiss, on the forehead. It was just before 6 a.m. on 16 July 2010 – Davy Newman's second birthday. Nick watched the boy's peaceful features for a few seconds and smiled; listened intently to the soft rise and fall of the child's breathing. Then Nick left the room, closing the door quietly behind him, crept as silently as he could down the stairs to the front door, and gently pulled that shut behind him.

The morning was overcast and cool, but since it was Davy's birthday surely the sun would shine later. Within two minutes Nick was in the car and driving away from the house, with the radio on low and the Satnav giving him instructions that in these local roads he didn't need. He was heading for London and a rendezvous with Les Campbell.

It was about a hundred miles, door-to-door, from the house in Hindon to number two, Birdsall House on the Champion Hill Estate. The journey was supposed to take around two and a half hours, but Nick, not trusting London traffic, had given himself four to make the 10 a.m. pick-up time he had arranged with Les. He also very much hoped not to bump into Drogba the ferocious dog and his confrontational owner on Les's threshold again.

It was less than five minutes before he was on the A303 and motoring towards the capital, into the sun that was fighting, mostly unsuccessfully, to break through the clouds. There were many things to occupy Nick's mind during the journey. There was his son, for instance, who was as sharp and clever as his mother, and as laidback as his father; who would sleep blissfully in his warm bed for a while longer before being woken and spoiled silly by his mum, followed by Jemima, and followed, many hours later, by a new relative – a grandfather he didn't even know that he had.

That grandfather was another thing to think about, his excitement about the meeting to come being almost as palpable as young Davy's when Nick had spoken to him just the day before, to check that everything was okay. Nick couldn't say how proud he was to have found Les Campbell and to be bestowing this gift upon his Kay and Davy – he simply did not have the words to express it. He wondered how the old guy would look now, winning his battle as it seemed with cirrhosis. Would there be the same tiredness etched into his face? Nick hoped that the combination of his hospital treatment and the chance to see his long-lost daughter and grandson would have rejuvenated the man he already thought of as Dad.

And then, of course, there was Kay to think about. Well, there was always Kay to think about, but especially since the nasty shock of Lee turning up ten days before. Her mood had been as changeable as the English weather since then, but during the last few days, with the preparations for Davy's party taking up most of her time, she had seemed less fretful.

Nick had to shake his head when he thought about it – not just the staggering fact of Lee's unwelcome re-emergence in their lives, but his own instinctive belief that all would still be well; an insistence that was born more from the desire to comfort his loved one than from any unshakeable certainty that he was right. He had wondered what Lee's intentions were; had debated in his heart the seriousness of the situation and whether it warranted the family moving – fleeing, in fact – to elsewhere in the country, and the upheaval that would cause; he had even considered contacting Lee through the SMAC organisation, meeting him face to face and talking it out, man to man. So far he had done nothing, though. He had not been able to decide what was best.

The venerable circle of standing stones at Stonehenge loomed into view to Nick's left, but such was his preoccupation that he barely even noticed them. He focused on the road ahead and the car carried on towards London.

***

The birthday boy held his mother's hand and dutifully stumbled along behind her to the bathroom, like a reluctant sleepwalker: dozy in his Buzz Lightyear pyjamas, eyes determinedly closed. Though generally a happy child, Davy was a reluctant riser in the morning, especially when, like today, he was taken from his bed earlier than usual. It was only about thirty minutes earlier, but it made a difference. Kay had to be at the office promptly and she wanted to get him bathed and breakfasted and dressed before Jemima arrived.

Ten minutes in the bathroom, waking up, splashing water around and listening to his mum tell him about the special day she had planned for him, and Davy was a happy little boy again, insisting on his Woody outfit for his big day, and then contentedly eating his porridge as Kay readied herself for work. She was still running around when Jemima arrived, also early as instructed. His nanny accepted the proffered wet kiss on the cheek from Davy and ruffled his hair.

"Happy birthday, my favourite little man," she cooed, hugging him. She had an extra carrier bag in her hand and Davy noticed it straight away. He reached a hand towards it, sensing, as little boys do, that the contents must be intended for him. Kay walked in, still fiddling with her hair.

"Davy, don't grab at things. Be a good boy for Mummy and 'Mima now," she said.

He looked up at her plaintively and then went back to his porridge with a scoop of his spoon. "Ah, bless him," Jemima said. "Is it okay to give him his present now, Kay?"

Kay had picked up a mug of coffee. She turned to regard her son. "In a minute, when he's finished his breakfast," she replied. "Do you want a cuppa? Kettle's just boiled a few minutes ago."

They chatted for a minute about the day ahead, before Davy announced in his unworried way: "All gone." They took him into the front room and sat down. Jemima opened her carrier bag and took out a wrapped box, which she handed to Davy with a smile.

"Happy Birthday, Davy," she said. "Hooray!" She waved her arms in the air, and was joined in the action by Kay. The boy beamed and mimicked the cheering, though waving his arms was harder for him since he was holding his present. He looked down at the box a little uncertainly, then up at his mum.

"Oh, look at that face. Poor love – come on, let Mummy help you, darling," said Kay. He put the box on her lap and together they pulled at the wrapping paper; with his mum's help the present was soon revealed: an eighteen-piece wooden train set.

"Whoo!" Kay exclaimed "Look, what 'Mima has bought for you, Davy – a lovely new choo-choo train set to play with!"

His eyes had lit up and he showed every intention of taking the box away and getting to grips with what was inside immediately, but Kay stayed his hand and reminded him of his manners. "Now, what do you say to 'Mima before you go and play?"

He sheepishly looked towards Jemima and then ran around to her and gave her a smacker on the cheek. "Thank you, 'Mima, thank you, 'Mima!" he shouted. Then he was off with his new toy, taking up position in his usual territory – the middle of the living-room floor – and messily unpacking the new toys.

"Have you given him the 'you-know-what' yet?" Jemima asked. Kay and Nick had bought Davy a rather stylish new push buggy for his birthday, which had been hidden in the shed for more than a week.

"No, not yet," Kay replied. "We'll do it when we're both here later." They watched Davy playing for a few minutes, laughing indulgently at his antics.

"Well, I'd better think about getting off to work," Kay said eventually. She talked through the plans for the day: what food had already been prepared and what needed doing; what was happening with the entertainer; the fact that another one of the local women, Sarah Tideman, would be round mid-morning to help out with preparations. "Everything clear?" she checked. Yes, said Jemima, all clear. It was going to be a fun day, she added.

Kay got her things together for work, and then came to kiss Davy goodbye. "Have a lovely morning, darling, and I will see you later for your party," she said, giving him a motherly squeeze. "'Bye, Mummy," Davy said back, and returned to the serious business of whacking together bits of wood that were supposed to be linked to make a train track. Jemima went to the door with Kay.

"Sorry about having to work today," said Kay, turning back as she opened the front door.

"Don't worry about it, we'll be fine," Jemima assured her.

"I'm sure you will be, but I should be here helping you. Well, never mind – bloody job. I'll get here as soon as I can to finalise everything. I should be leaving work at midday. Okay, see you."

The two women embraced briefly and then Kay headed off down the garden path to her car. Jemima checked over her shoulder that Davy wasn't misbehaving, and waved back to Kay. She shut the door behind her and walked towards the living room to help Davy with his new toy.

You should be leaving work at midday, Kay, thought Jemima, but you won't be.

***

Nick heard the double-beeping sound of the car alarm engaging as he locked his red Alfa Romeo behind him and sauntered off along the winding path that led from Champion Hill around Appleshaw House and towards Birdsall House. He had a spring in his step. It was just before 9.30 a.m. and he had made good progress on the drive up from Wiltshire. He was a little early, but he didn't imagine that Les would mind.

It was now a bright, clear summer morning and the chirping of the birds seemed intended purely for him. Soon the block of flats was in front of him, and he stopped several metres away to appraise the red door of number two, where Les lived. Memories came back of the last time he had been here: nice Mrs Odembe behind her barred door at Number 1, melting at the sight of the picture of Kay and Davy; and, of course, that bloody dog scaring the living bejesus out of him… yes indeed. This time though, there were no dramas. The door to number two opened, and the man himself, Kay's dad, stood in the doorway smiling at Nick.

"Hello, son, you're a bit early. Come on in and have a cuppa."

Nick stepped forward and they shook hands. "Traffic was better than I expected. A cuppa would be great." They shook hands warmly, and studied each other for a long second – barely more than acquaintances but with so much hope invested in this day and what it might mean to both of their futures. Something had come to life in the older man's eyes since they had first met in the hospital, Nick was sure of it.

Les turned to go back into the flat. Nick followed him inside, and the significance of the moment wasn't lost on him: his first steps into the place where Kay had grown up.

They went through to the front room, and Les cleared some things away – a newspaper, a TV remote control, a crumpled and empty crisp packet – so that Nick could sit on the sofa.

"Right, do you fancy tea or coffee then?" he asked, rubbing his hands together.

"I'll have a tea, please, Dad," Nick replied. "One sugar, plenty of milk, thanks."

Les disappeared into the kitchen and Nick had an opportunity to look around the room. It looked like the habitat of a single man who didn't suffer too severely from house pride. The furniture and wallpaper were old and tatty, the carpet stained. There were piles of newspapers and magazines in the corners, some so old they were turning yellow. Nick spied an unwashed plate – worse than unwashed in fact, downright mouldy – on the floor beneath one of the armchairs. He guessed there had probably been a good deal more filthy crockery littering the flat and that Les had attempted a quick clean-up, knowing that he was going to have a visitor. He had missed that one, though.

The whole place shouted out that this man needed help. He had been lonely and cast adrift in life, and then floored by illness. He hadn't been back in the flat very long. Perhaps it was no wonder the place was a tip. Nick had taken just a glimpse into Les's life and it was heart-rending.

Les soon came back into the room, holding two steaming mugs. He hesitated and then gestured with his head. "Do us a favour, son, get a couple of those mats from the side there and put them on this little table here."

Nick did as he was instructed and Les put the mugs down on the mats and then sat opposite him. Nick smiled and appraised the older man's appearance, as he had by the door outside. Les looked far brighter and stronger than he had done in his hospital bed. He was still a little frail, and his skin bore some of the tell-tale yellowing of a cirrhosis sufferer, but the improvement in him seemed considerable to Nick's untrained eye.

"You're looking well, Les. How are you feeling?"

"Compared to a month ago, I feel a million quid," Les asserted. "Thanks mainly to you, Nick."

He laughed: "I'm sure the doctors and the treatment had a lot more to do with it than I did, Dad."

"Maybe…" Les allowed. He glanced away, through the window. There was brightness beyond the heavy condensation. The sound of next-door's TV – crowd applause on some morning chat show – came through the walls. Les looked back at Nick. "God's truth, son, you coming to see me in hospital that day was better than any medicine them old quacks could give me. I mean, to hear from my little girl after all this time, and to find out I was a granddad as well. It was the best day of my life, Nick. Until today, that is…"

Nick was struck dumb. What could he say to such a heartfelt tribute? He found some words; inadequate ones. "Well, it's the least I can do for Kay and Davy, Dad. You know…" Then he remembered something. "Oh, I've got this for you." He took his wallet out and retrieved a copy of the photograph of them that he had showed Les in his hospital bed. He handed it over. "That's for you, Dad. We got another copy done for you."

Les studied the photograph for several seconds. It was as if he was comparing the mental image he had retained from weeks before with the reality now in his hands; as if he was consciously burning that image more vividly into his memory bank. "I will treasure this, like I will treasure today, Nick," he eventually said. "Can't wait to meet the lad… he must be very excited it's his birthday."

"Well, he was asleep when I left home, Dad."

"Oh, bugger, I nearly forgot," Les suddenly exclaimed. "How much time have we?"

"Until we have to leave?" Nick glanced up at a clock on the wall. "About fifteen minutes, I suppose. A few minutes here or there won't matter, though."

"That's good, got something to show you. You're going to love this," said Les, getting up from his chair and sliding a door open on the wooden wall unit. From within he took a small pile of paper-based stuff. Nick guessed what it was going to be immediately: photographs of Kay from when she was a girl. Well, bloody hell, he thought. Kay had none in her possession. She had left everything either with her dad or else with Lee. Nick had therefore never seen a single picture of her as a baby, a toddler, a child, a teenager, or even when she was in her twenties.

Les was chuckling to himself as he got comfortable, sitting cross-legged on the carpet with the pile of old photos in front of him. Nick knew he too would be chuckling very soon – at goofy adolescent grins and shocking fashion faux-pas – and there was nothing that his beloved, one hundred miles away, could do about it.

CHAPTER THIRTEEN

It was a fine morning, thought Mac, but cool beneath the trees; as good a day as any to meet your destiny. Absent-mindedly, he stroked his manicured beard and looked at his companions. All around him was camaraderie and coffee, swagger and sandwiches. You could almost smell the bravado, more strongly than the food and beverages. With this thought, Mac turned to Nancy, close by, helping Pippa by pushing a fresh batch of Linda McCartney bangers around in the pan. Pre-prepared roasted pepper and hummus sandwiches were the cold option.

"Haven't seen Liam yet, Nance. Have you?"

"No. But it's only two minutes past ten, Mac. Don't fret so."

She smiled and Mac laughed. "I'll have another one of those when it's done, Nance," he said, getting up from his stool with his coffee mug and heading over to the throng of people – boisterous SMAC members and their ALF reinforcements – standing round in a ragged circle near the tents, laughing and joking. There was an hour and a half to go. How long before the nerves kicked in and quietened down some of these high spirits?

He clapped a hand on Vince's back. "Hey, pal – today's the day, eh? How long have you waited for this beautiful morning to dawn?"

Vince decided to overlook their past disagreements, just as Mac was doing. His eyes were wide with excitement behind those spectacles of his. "How long, Mac? Too bloody long, that's how long!"

One of the ALF brigade standing nearby was Barry Stevens, who, having secured the undercover film at Maier some months before, had been the catalyst for this day of action. Since he had spent some time working inside the facility, he had the key role of guiding the SMAC members whose task was to break into the laboratory and free the animals inside. They would approach from the trees to the south of Maier Science, close to the laboratory, while eight big lads from ALF stormed the front gate at the eastern end and dealt with the on-site security guards.

Barry called over to Mac. "The bastards enjoyed my video then, did they?"

"Oh, man, you should have seen Cambridge's face! He went from red to purple to green to white and back again. And… poof! There it went: his whole career in fucking shreds. Chew on that one, ya bastard!"

There was laughter around the whole group as they listened to Mac's words. Few of them had ever met Richard Cambridge, but in their minds, especially the SMAC members, he was on a par with Osama bin Laden, Adolf Hitler and Satan himself as an object of hatred and vilification.

Just then Liam came wandering over to the group, chewing on a sausage sandwich, freshly liberated from Nancy. "Everyone sounds very excitable. Something happening today?" he said, with his mouth half full.

"Ah, about bloody time, Liam. That'll be a one pound fine to you for being the last one to get here," Mac answered him. Liam snorted derisively in response.

Bhupathi chipped in: "Looks like the latecomer got to the front of the queue for hot food too. How did you manage that, you bugger?"

"Good timing," Liam defended himself with a shrug. "Bloody good sarnie as well."

This news saw the circle break apart, as half of the activists went and stood in line for one of Nancy's butties. Half an hour later the eating and drinking was mostly done; the boisterousness had calmed a little and Mac called out for everyone to gather around in the centre of the camp. There were too few seats to go around and the women and a few of the men got them, the rest making do with Wiltshire soil beneath their backsides. Mac stood in the middle of them all and watched them settle down. He fancied he could almost see the switch flicking on in their heads – from jocularity to serious intent.

He closed his eyes for a few seconds and composed himself. It was without surprise or alarm that he realised the next two hours would be the most important of his life so far. He was ready for this. Another thought then, of Jemima this time; looking after Kay Campbell's little boy, and missing all the fun. She was the unsung hero in this whole enterprise, and Mac was determined he would recognise her contribution in the words he was about to speak.

Then a third thought: of the maddened black bull, goaded by men with swords, staggering to its end; the lithe, strutting matadors, the sultry heat of the Mexican evening, the cheers and his own tears. Nothing else was required to convince him of the righteousness of his purpose.

He opened his eyes and took in the ranks of expectant faces. He began to speak.

"Only a few of you will know that, many years ago, I had a life-changing experience. We probably all had one in some shape or form. But I was just a bairn – eleven years old – on holiday with my parents and my two sisters in Mexico. At that time, I had no great interest in the welfare and treatment of the animals who share this planet with us. I was interested in football and fighting, like most Scottish lads probably…"

A ripple of laughter caused him to pause briefly.

"One evening my father took us to the Plaza México. Nancy, what's the Plaza México?"

"It's a bullfighting ring, Mac," she replied. She knew the story.

"That's right, it's a bullfighting ring; the biggest in the fucking world. My father took us there. He was an army man, wouldn't take shit from anyone. I suppose he expected me to be excited or impressed or something. He expected a lot of things from me that never happened. He told me that bullfighting was an undertaking of skill and bravery and honour. He neglected to mention the torment and the agony these bastards inflict on the bulls – just defenceless animals.

"I found that out for myself when the so-called entertainment started. It was like football, like the Old Firm. Tens of thousands of crazed lunatics baying for some poor bastard's blood, and not satisfied until they got it. It was disgusting."

Mac paused again and looked around the circle of faces. Not a word from the group. Their attention was avid.

"It was disgusting and immoral. I didn't stay to watch the end. I *couldn't* stay to watch the end. I was sick to the pit of my stomach. I bawled my eyes out…" a smile now "… which is not very cool when you're eleven. I knew as I was running away that I would never forget the horrible things I'd seen that day, and the memory still scars me. Just recalling it again for you people has made it feel like every blow that bull took is falling on me right now. I'm on my knees, coughing blood, just like the bull did.

"I've carried it with me for twenty years and it was that day, when I witnessed a murder, which set me on the path to securing animal rights. Everything that has happened in my life since had its birth in the Plaza México. Maybe in a way that makes it a good thing: the life of one bull in exchange for a lifetime devoted to fighting the atrocities humans inflict on God's creatures? I leave that for you to decide.

"So here we all are. And unlike that outnumbered and outflanked bull, toyed with and butchered for the titillation of twenty or thirty thousand idiots, we can fight back; we will fight back; and today..." Mac, his voice rising to a new pitch, looked very deliberately at Vince "...today, my friends, we do fight back!"

There was a kind of slightly self-conscious outburst of acclaim for this rhetoric, though not exactly a tub-thumping roar. Mac waited and took a mental step back to assess anew the faces before him. People were smiling and nodding, muttering things to the person next to them; they did seem enthused. It was, he guessed, just British reserve that was holding them back from throwing their arms up at the sky and roaring approval.

No matter. He trusted them. It was good enough. He had some more words to add, important words.

"This is the greatest day in the history of SMAC. We stand shoulder to shoulder with our brothers and sisters from the ALF. We welcome them to our ranks and we thank them for swelling our numbers and helping to further our cause. To you guys I say this: it is an honour to have you here. But there is one other person – someone who's not here right now – whom we should all thank; someone who has sacrificed personal glory so that we as a collective can achieve our aims."

Another searching look around their faces.

"I'm talking of course about Jemima Bond, without whose diligence and commitment we would have no idea about today's security lapse at Maier Science. Thank you, Jemima – our constant and unswerving colleague and friend."

There were murmurs of appreciation amongst the SMAC people and a couple of the senior ALF activists, who knew the origin of the intelligence gained. The rest looked a little less moved by that declaration. Mac settled on one last hurrah.

"I can see that everyone is excited. In a short while, those of us who will be making the assault on the laboratory need to head off into the trees to reach our position. The minutes are counting down. So one last thought, friends. Here we all are; we stand together with one objective: dignity for all animals." It seemed appropriate now to raise his eyes to the heavens and punch a single fist upwards, with a final battle cry that soon echoed all around: "Dignity! Liberty! And victory!"

***

There had been a plan, but Davy, with the prerogative of a two-year-old, was having none of it. Sarah Tideman had come round to the house before 11 a.m. to help Jemima get things ready for the party. They had decided to take it in turns: one of them would work on food preparation while the other kept Davy occupied; after a while they would swap over.

That was fine when Sarah, who had a boy and a girl attending the village school at the end of the road, was in the kitchen putting party bags together while Jemima and Davy kicked a football around in the garden and enjoyed the fine weather. When it came to Jemima's turn to work, however, and Sarah replaced her in the garden, the little boy was not happy.

Upon getting into the kitchen, Jemima was supposed to start making some jelly, but the first thoughts she had were of Stuart and her SMAC friends, and their preparations for the raid that was now only about half an hour away. In the event, she had barely more than a minute to herself before Davy ran into the kitchen and clung onto her leg like a limpet, imploring her to come and play. Sarah came in just behind him with a slightly miffed expression on her face.

"I told him that you wouldn't be long and I kicked the football with him, but here we are. You must be David Beckham and me a rubbish substitute."

Jemima laughed. "I'm definitely not David Beckham!" She stroked the boy's hair affectionately. "Davy, be a good boy and play with Sarah for a few minutes. 'Mima has to make some yummy jelly for later."

"No! 'Mima come play! 'Mima come play!" He tugged at her jeans for added emphasis. She looked down at his big brown eyes and his serious little face and melted a bit inside. It was, she could see, the most important thing in the world to him right at that moment. How could she deny him? She looked up apologetically to Sarah.

"Sorry, Sarah. You don't mind, do you?"

Sarah shrugged, waved a hand to signal her acceptance, and Jemima took hold of Davy's hand and led him back out to the garden, where he was soon chasing after his ball without a care in the world. Jemima watched him, and laughed at his antics, cooing with admiration at his dribbling skills. It was almost possible for her to forget what would soon be happening five miles away: the fury that was to hurl itself from the deep forest.

***

Kay stared at her computer screen with a vacant expression on her face, but there was a tumult of thoughts and emotions going on behind her dark eyes. The little black cursor in the top left corner of a blank electronic document winked encouragingly at her, but the right words wouldn't come.

She had thought about this moment probably a dozen times before – the "Dear Richard, please accept this, my resignation" moment – but it was the first time she had got as far as opening a fresh document on her computer to compose the letter. Something, she knew, had died in her on the day SMAC and Lee had come to visit. Before that, she had a project to put together; a test of her professional competence and diplomatic skill, and a well-paid one at that. But now, no matter what platitudes came out of Richard Cambridge's mouth, with her keystone policy of a rapprochement with SMAC in tatters, everything else about her work felt utterly irrelevant. She could see now it had been an impossible hope.

But she didn't care any longer. That much she had discovered. She didn't care, and today, especially, she wanted to be at home with her little boy on his second birthday.

She wanted to hold him and tell him how much he was loved. Nothing that went on at Maier Science was of any interest to her, and some of it, as she had witnessed in the SMAC video, left her in a state of moral disarray. What was she doing, representing these people? How could she ever explain to Davy what Mummy did at work?

Lee had found out where she worked, and for all she knew had found out where she lived too. That was a constant nagging worry. Actually, worry was not the right word. It was terrifying. She and Nick had too much to lose now. The idyll of their lives had been shattered that day her husband had turned up as a member of the SMAC delegation – calling himself Liam, of all the ridiculous names – and Kay needed to run again. It would mean uprooting three lives rather than one, but if the choice was to live with the shadow of Lee across the doorstep, then there was no choice.

So why couldn't she write this damned resignation letter? She had convinced herself that there was every reason to do it, but still... this paralysis every time she was confronted with the blank page. Well, one problem was that she had not discussed this course of action with Nick. They needed her money or they would have to find somewhere smaller to live. The correct thing to do was to talk to him first – he would understand – and then start seeking out new opportunities; line something up and then deliver the news to Richard. She had a great CV. She could quickly find something else.

She wanted to write this letter now, though. If she could just get the words out on screen, even if she then left it for a month, she would feel much better. It would be like the first positive step. She typed: "Richard", and then hit the Return button to start a new line. She stopped. She looked around the office. It was quiet. People had their heads down and were working, with the exception of Alan and Dennis, who were standing by the coffee machine, chatting about the extension that Dennis was having done to the side of his house. Yawn.

Kay checked the time on her computer screen. It was just after 11.15. Only forty-five minutes before she could leave the office and return home for the birthday party. Her fingers rested on the keys of her keyboard again, poised for productivity. She thought about Davy instead, though, and she thought about her dad, who, she was certain, was currently on the way to Wiltshire in Nick's car. It had been so many years… oh, God, what a momentous day, and here she was trying to write a resignation letter! She almost laughed aloud at herself, the relief of black humour momentarily scattering the cloud of her concerns, and sat back in her chair, coolly eyeing the open Microsoft Word document.

A coffee – she would grab a coffee; that would be good actually, Kay decided. She left her desk and walked across the office. Dennis walked past her and gave her a wink as he did so. Alan had disappeared from the room in the other direction. She pressed the button for an espresso and waited. As she was walking back to her desk with it, the facilities manager Derek Atkinson came into the room behind her.

"Everyone…" he called out. Kay hurried to her seat. "Everyone… just a quick update. The engineers have done some work on the security system, and they're going to switch back on soon, to do some live testing. It won't affect you people in here, but we just wanted to keep you informed."

Kay raised her voice: "Does that mean they've finished, Derek?"

"No, not finished, Kay, still things to do. It's a process we're working through. We've got to a certain stage and they want to test some things. I anticipate it will be off and on for the next few hours still."

"Do we need our passes to access the lab yet then?" asked Mickey Mackenzie, one of the product executives.

"Right now? No. In five minutes? Yes. After that, I can't say. It will really depend on lots of things. Just keep your pass with you, Mickey, and you can't really go wrong. Okay, everyone, that's all."

Derek left the room and moved on to break the news at another part of the site. There was a brief murmur of chatter around the office in his wake as the staff settled down again. Kay regarded the fledgling resignation letter on her computer screen, all one word of it, with frustration and impatience. She looked at it for another two minutes, and then closed it without bothering to save it. There was nothing to save anyway.

She walked over to the window with her espresso and sipped it as she gazed out at the sunshine and the trees. Brian was down there, white-shirted, in the control room at the entrance. She saw a couple of the lab technicians strolling along on their break, puffing away.

"You all right, Kay?" The question came from Alan, who had come back into the room. His desk was immediately next to where Kay stood.

"Yes, just thinking, Al," she replied. And it was true – she was thinking. Thinking about the correct order of things: Davy's birthday, hug Dad; discussion with Nick; start job search; put house up for sale; hand in notice; new career, new house, new village.

CHAPTER FOURTEEN

They walked in single file, picking their way between the trees, taking extra care with each step. The snap of a dry twig was unlikely to betray their presence or their intent at this point – they were thirty metres deep in the woods – but Mac had demanded "noise discipline", and no one wanted to draw an over-the-shoulder glare from him at the head of the line.

There was no talking, no joking, no singing – each understood the gravity of the minutes that lay ahead. They followed their leader to the jump-off point for the raid on Maier Science. Two of them – Anthony and Bhupathi – carried heavy wire clippers that they would use to cut a hole in the perimeter fence of the site, through which SMAC would spring into action.

It took them around ten minutes to march from the camp in the woods near the Maier entrance to the starting point for the assault – marked by a belt from a bathrobe that Anthony had tied around a tree trunk the night before. They first had to take a route away from the research site, skirting the treeline along the main road that passed the front gates so that they could cross it unseen further down, and then make their way through the trees that bordered the long side of the site, trees that shielded them from the view of any prying eyes on the other side of the wire.

When they reached the starting point, they gathered round and Mac spoke in a low voice. There were still a few minutes to go before the jump-off time. In truth there wasn't much to say. He had said everything he needed to already. He looked around at his friends, looked each of them in the eye. They were ready. He had no doubts, and he hoped that they also were experiencing the clarity of mind that this moment was inspiring in him. With a few last words of encouragement, they spread out into their starting positions, ten foot soldiers fanning out to Mac's left and right. They crouched and waited. There were two minutes to go.

Two people along from Mac to his right, the one who called himself Liam seemed to stare intently at the treeline thirty metres away, but really he didn't see the trees. The dusty shafts of sunlight that pierced here and there between the leaves scarcely registered in his consciousness either. He didn't visualise the short sprint beyond the trees to the wire fence, nor the fifty metres or so of dead ground that would have to be covered between the fence and the laboratory building. Even so, he waited like the rest, becalmed by tension.

Soon his inattention was broken by movement to his left. Mac had turned his head towards Nancy, who crouched between the two of them. Nothing was said, but she turned her head a little towards Mac, shook it briefly, and when she turned back to face front there was a smile on her face. What the hell was that all about? Liam wondered. Mac was looking at him now. A smile to match Nancy's seemed to be what was required, so he unleashed one that he hoped would suffice. It seemed to do the trick because Mac simply turned to watch the treeline again.

To Liam's right, young Anthony whispered hoarsely to him: "What's everyone laughing at?"

"Fuck knows," Liam whispered back. Anthony burst into a brief laugh, one that was cut short by a quick and decisive "shush" from Nancy. Her face, framed with greying hair, suddenly looked very much like it had never cracked a smile in all of human history. She had her game face on all right. It would tolerate no insubordination and certainly no frivolity. Anthony stared at the ground, lips tight.

The wait went on, but Liam knew it was almost over. He watched Mac now. The Scotsman was toying with some dirt on the ground in front of him. Then he brushed his hands together before casting a look at his wristwatch. Mac quickly surveyed his team, spread out in a V shape with himself at the sharp point. He was looking at Liam again. Their eyes met briefly: the merest of nods was exchanged.

Liam regarded his own fingernails for a few seconds – some kind of subconscious reaction to seeing the dirt on Mac's hands – and when he looked up again, compelled to by a perceptible stirring in the people around him, Mac had one arm in the air. Any second now, then.

A breath… two breaths… Mac's arm came down. The lurch forward, the sudden rustle and stamp of feet quickly on the move. What was that? A small blur of fluttering purple in the air, rising upwards, gone and forgotten as quickly as it had registered. On and on; brushing branches and leaves aside, slaloming past the trunks of trees, towards that intense white glare on the other side of the treeline.

Before Liam got there he was aware that Anthony was already up on his right shoulder and about to overtake him, Nancy was immediately to his left, making good speed for an old girl, and Mac, to Nancy's left, was ploughing through the dangling branches like a souped-up World War Two flail tank, all threshing arms and irresistible intent.

As one, SMAC burst from the treeline into the instant glare and heat of the open air – a line of ten people converging on a single point in the wire fence ahead of them, wire cutters sharpened and ready.

Except that the line no longer numbered ten people, it numbered nine now. As the SMAC team slowed its headlong pelt for the wire to allow the cutters to do their work, the man they all called Liam was sprinting back through the trees in the opposite direction, alone.

***

There didn't seem to be much work getting done in the Maier offices today, Kay reflected, as she idly half-listened to a conversation between Mickey and Dennis – not another one about Dennis's house extension, but instead the goings-on in the Big Brother house. They were over by Dennis's window desk, with Mickey perching on the edge, arms folded, providing his and his wife's considered view that Josie would win the reality TV programme.

Kay didn't care about that or any of the anecdotes the two men were chuckling over. She had been slyly surfing on Asos.com for several minutes now, casting an expert and interested eye over some rather stylish sleeveless shirts and halter neck tops that she reckoned would go very nicely with some other garments from her existing wardrobe. Yes, she was as guilty as anyone for the lack of productivity in the office day.

Should she purchase or not? was the pressing question. It was a choice between a black sleeveless shirt, a sky blue halter neck, or a floral print kimono blouse. Or she could buy all three. That was an option that would make her feel even more guilty, but it was very, very tempting.

Suddenly there was a cry from across the room – "What the fuck?!" – and the startled tone of it made her head snap round towards the source of the sound.

The shout came from Mickey Mackenzie, who was now standing bolt upright, looking out of the window. Dennis was craning his neck to see out as well. Then Mickey called out again, incredulously.

"Shit, we're being attacked!" A second later, with more urgency, more understanding, more panic: "Guys, we're being attacked. They're trying to get in the front."

There was sudden uproar among the fifteen people in the room. Chairs were pushed back carelessly, with too much force in some cases, causing collisions with other office furniture. A chorus of questions rose, and swelled with alarmed exclamations as staff members reached the window and saw the events unfolding down at the entrance barriers.

Kay had enough presence of mind to cancel her internet shopping page, leaving her computer screen showing the inbox of her work email, before dashing over to the window herself. The sight that greeted her eyes seemed like a scene from an action movie, or a re-enactment of some sort, but the lurch in her stomach told her it was all too real. Several balaclava-clad men – ten or a dozen, she guessed – were streaming through the barriers. Down there in the control room Brian was standing up, looking repeatedly from the attackers to the open door at the side of his little hut. Judging by his hesitation, he seemed to be in a quandary as to what he should do first – rush to the door and lock himself in, or pick up the phone and report the intruders. He dallied too long, and the first of the men burst inside, followed by two more. Brian disappeared from view, to Kay's horror, underneath a flurry of swinging arms.

It drew a shout from one of the men near her: "Bastards!"

She watched the unfolding drama, as unforgettable as a slow-motion replay, with one hand covering her mouth. The rest of the attackers, some of them wearing camouflage gear, were making straight for the building: *her* building. Something needed to be done, and done quickly, to prevent them from gaining access. There was a female receptionist downstairs, Rachel, and a couple of small offices and meeting rooms. Most of the manned office space was upstairs, where Kay worked. Someone needed to warn Rachel, in case she hadn't seen what was happening outside. She was usually reading some lifestyle magazine or other, so it was quite likely that she had no idea of the menace bearing down on her.

Dennis reacted quicker than Kay, though, and took charge. He started shouting instructions, his eyes settling on individual colleagues' faces as he did so: "Lucy, ring down to Rachel and tell her to lock the door. Matt, run down there and do it anyway in case she doesn't answer the phone. Pete, go with him. Fiona, call Derek on his mobile and see what's happening with the security systems… see if he can flip the switch immediately. Mickey, get on the Bat Phone to the police."

It was a race against time, and the nominated people each jumped to their task. Kay looked out of the window.

The attackers were led, she noticed, by a tall man with long locks of red hair that escaped from the bottom of his balaclava. They were closing quickly on the front door. She couldn't see any way that their entry to the building could be stopped, unless Rachel was already taking the necessary measures. Dennis appraised the situation outside once again before issuing fresh orders.

"Kay, call Richard and get him and Selina to come through here. We're better off sticking together. Guys, start moving some desks towards the door, but leave enough space for our people to get through while they can."

Lucy called across to Dennis: "No answer yet down at reception." He nodded curtly. Kay picked up a phone and pressed three buttons for Richard Cambridge's extension. His office was along the corridor. His secretary Selina answered after a couple of beeps. Kay explained what was happening, or what they thought was happening, but Selina started asking questions. Dennis evidently guessed this because he grabbed the handset from Kay.

"Selina, there's no time for this. Get Richard in here *now*. Just do it."

He jammed the handset back down, took a deep breath and looked around. Desks were being moved over to the door, and voices were speaking urgently into telephones. Downstairs, the attackers would be reaching the front door. Dennis needed information. Suddenly it came in a rush from several sources. Rachel and some other staff from the ground-level offices came running in, banging the door back against a desk that had been positioned so as to leave just enough room for one person to enter at a time. Matt and Pete were not with them. They had last been seen in a shoulder-pushing competition with the leading attackers at the front door, the newcomers reported. They had not been able to lock it in time, and it would probably only take a few seconds for the weight of numbers against them to prise the door wide open and leave the two men at the mercy of the attackers. How long then before those attackers ran up the stairs and arrived in the upstairs office?

Fiona came off the phone, having spoken to Derek Atkinson, the facilities manager, and she had sensational news. There had been a second attack, targeting the laboratories, but it had been foiled. By pure chance, only a few minutes before, the engineers had activated the security system on those buildings. The would-be SMAC attackers were now milling around outside the laboratory buildings, chanting and pounding their fists on the reinforced windows in their frustration. The police were on their way, alerted by Mickey's call on the hotline, and an alarm signal sent from inside the besieged laboratories.

Richard and Selina burst into the room, looking panicked. "Is it SMAC?" he demanded. "It must be SMAC."

"I assume so, Richard. Guys, push the desks hard against the door now," Dennis ordered. "Hopefully anyone left downstairs can find safety until the police get here."

There was scarcely a moment for those within the room to exchange further worried glances, before the battle cries and stomping footsteps of the attackers reached the corridor outside, and something, perhaps a body, crashed hard into the door. Immediately others followed. The attackers were throwing themselves at it. The desks gave way an inch or two, and then several of the occupants ran forward and put their weight behind the furniture, jamming it back against the door.

Kay watched all of this happening with a deepening sense of disbelief and emotional detachment. Whatever was going on here, it had nothing to do with her. She didn't hurt animals and she didn't want to work for a company that did. She wanted to be with her little boy on his birthday. Kay backed away from the door and the throng of people, her colleagues, who were pressed against and around the hastily constructed barriers, and as she did so she hoped she might be able to simply fade into invisibility behind them, as if by a magic trick. The shouts from both sides of the door, the crashes and bangs of bodies against the wooden frame – it was all real enough, her ears told her that, but somehow it all felt as distant as a dream, ungraspable.

She moved over to the window again and looked down. Brian was there, on the grass beside the security hut, lying face down while one man sat on his back and another held his arms down. In spite of this, it seemed a strangely peaceful scene. The men appeared to be talking to their captive.

As she watched, another figure appeared from below her, from the area of the building's main front doors. It was Pete, she saw, who had gone downstairs with Matt to try and defend the front door. He stalked carefully towards Brian and the two men, but they saw him and the one astride Brian's back rose and walked forward to meet him. The two men stopped and talked. Some kind of entente was being negotiated down there, it seemed to Kay; something very different from the shouting and hellish banging still coming from behind her. It was the most natural thing in the world for her to ignore all that and to think about Davy, and about Nick and her dad instead. She glanced at her watch. When and how she would get out of this place, with all this going on, she didn't know. The thought of her family made her smile all the same.

***

Just a few miles away, the car was full of smiles and laughter as Kay's dad and Nick cruised along the A303 to the north of Salisbury.

It had been an interesting journey for Nick – at times hilarious, and at other times, emotional. Les had been very talkative. He had asked lots of questions about Nick's background and how he and Kay had got together. He had asked lots of questions about Davy, his grandson, whom he was soon to meet for the first time. He had also told stories about Kay as a girl, relating the kind of embarrassing details that only a parent could and would reveal about their child's younger days; the kind of information Kay would never volunteer.

Nick had learned a lot about his partner, and much of it was very funny. Occasionally though, the gravity of what was happening seemed to hit Les. He was soon to see his daughter for the first time in more than a decade. He had got used to the thought that this day would not come, and his personal downward spiral had stripped him of hope. Then Nick had walked into his hospital ward and delivered a matter-of-fact miracle – both Kay and a grandson.

Sometimes during the journey, the twists of fate, the tragedy of Kay's mother's death, his regret for years lost and sense of the staggering deliverance he'd been given, had awed Les to silence. Some tears fell, and Nick reached over with his left hand to console the older man with a sympathetic squeeze of the shoulder. Les didn't care about crying any more. He had a family again. This was the best day of his life since the day Kay had been born, he said.

The Alfa Romeo was now zipping through the sun-kissed countryside, through Hampshire into Wiltshire, and with every mile covered, every roundabout negotiated, Les's beaming face grew brighter, his excitement more obvious. Andover was behind them, and then Amesbury. He was telling a story of paternal pride: his little girl singing in the school concert, amongst a chorus of piratical characters.

He suddenly became aware of the standing pillars of Stonehenge looming out of the ground over to the right of the carriageway ahead. The stones quickly grew in size and definition as they drew closer, and the gaggles of black dots gathered around them took on human form – dozens of people walking around the prehistoric site. Les looked on in silence.

"Stonehenge," Nick announced, glancing at him, unsure if the penny had dropped.

"Do you know, I've never seen that before," Les replied. "Amazing… just standing there all these years in the middle of a field."

"Kay and I went and visited it not long after we moved down here," said Nick. "We didn't spend long there, though, because she already had a bit of a bump with Davy on the way. Pretty cool, though. They reckon some of those big stones came all the way from Wales. Imagine how many blokes it took to drag them along…"

"What's the point of it, though?" Les asked, sounding a little sceptical.

"Good question!" Nick laughed. "I think there's a bunch of theories, but it's kind of like a monument that people used thousands of years ago to help them remember their dead ancestors. I think."

Les seemed to consider that for a few seconds. The traffic around them was slowing as people gawped at the old stone circle, and Nick gently eased off the speed too.

"Is it always that busy?" Les asked.

"You should have seen it a couple of weeks ago, Dad: hippies and druids and all sorts of weirdos turn up for the Summer Solstice every June… thousands of them. It's quite a sight!"

Nick chuckled to himself, while Les gazed across from the passenger seat at the crowds over by the stones. Once past the prehistoric monument, Nick copied the cars ahead in starting to pick up speed again.

"We'll take you over there while you're down, Dad," he said, glancing at his passenger. "It only costs about twelve or thirteen quid."

Les's eyes widened. "Twelve quid? You must be joking. Twelve quid for a few rocks stuck in the ground?"

"Yep, twelve quid for a few rocks stuck in the ground. World-famous rocks though, Dad," Nick corrected him. Les was laughing. He wasn't having any of it.

"You keep your money in your pocket, son. Save it for food and clothing and treating my girl like a princess."

Nick put his foot down as they sped towards Winterbourne Stoke – only twenty minutes or so from home. "Honestly, I ask you," Les chuntered, "twelve quid to wander around some old rocks? I'd want to take one of them home with me for that much."

"You're a philistine, Dad," Nick told him. "You wait until Kay hears about this!" They were both laughing as

they left the brooding stone circle behind, still imposing
its aura, as it did every day, on what Les saw as the gull-
ible multitudes.

CHAPTER FIFTEEN

It was a warm, breezeless July afternoon and the village of Hindon was coming to lunchtime life. Chattering young mothers were heading to the village school to collect their boys and girls; a group of office workers, sleeves rolled up, spirits high, loudly laughing, ducked into the pub; the sandwich brigade, all regulars, began to form a small, friendly queue in the local convenience shop; an elderly couple, she holding onto his arm, walked funereally slowly through the church graveyard before stopping for reflection at one of the stones.

A single motor car – sleek, dark grey metallic bodywork; sunlight glinting off its side mirrors and bonnet – growled a sharp left onto the high street outside the Lamb Inn pub, catching two Smartphone-clutching teenage girls by surprise as they went to cross the road. They hot-footed it sharpish to the safety of the pavement and one of the girls directed an insult her mother would not have been proud of hearing at the rear of the car. It carried on heedless down the high street before taking another left turn and swinging out of their sight.

The car made another two left turns in quick succession, and entered a cul-de-sac, at the end of which it three-point-turned and then parked a few yards behind a white VW Golf. The air quivered around its powerful idling engine for a few seconds before it was silenced, and the entire cul-de-sac relaxed back into its previous repose; just the occasional lazy flap of bird's wings, the continual insect hum, and distant high-pitched playground shouts audible.

The arrival of the car had caused Mrs O'Neill across the road to lever herself up from her sofa and peek through her net curtains. This was a natural thing for her to do: she was well used to being called a nosy parker. She could see that a big grey car had pulled up outside Nick and Kay's house, but she couldn't see who the driver was because the topiary box ball at the front of her house was in the way. There was no movement that she could see from within the car for a couple of minutes, but Mrs O'Neill stayed on her feet anyway, one eye on the daytime chat show on the TV, the other ready for the slightest flicker of activity outside.

There had still been no sign of life from the car, however, when the front door of Nick and Kay's house opened, and a tall, thin, blonde woman stepped out; she called something back inside the house, then pulled the door closed behind her, marched down the garden path and sauntered off to Mrs O'Neill's right, towards the open end of the cul-de-sac. It was Sarah, Mrs O'Neill knew. She was helping the nanny over there to get the birthday party ready for the little boy. She was soon out of view.

Tranquillity returned, but only for a second because just then a man got out of the big grey car, his dark hair and ruddy cheeks suddenly visible above the topiary. He stood looking in the direction Sarah had taken, and then started walking after her. He was of medium height, Mrs O'Neill noted, and was wearing blue jeans and a dark green t-shirt. She didn't recognise him. From behind her curtains, she saw him break into a jog, following in the wake of Kay's friend. Then, as Sarah had done, he disappeared from view at the end of the road.

Mrs O'Neill was about to sit back down to pick up the threads of the chat show when the man reappeared at the end of the road, now walking, but walking fast, and in the direction of the house over the road – the one from which Sarah had just come. He swung open the small gate and went up the path with brisk steps. Mrs O'Neill was late for her midday cup of tea, but she couldn't possibly move away from the window now. She was hooked. Her eyes glowed with interest. The man reached the front door of Nick and Kay's house and stopped. He stood there for a couple of seconds. Then Mrs O'Neill saw him grab hold of the brass knocker and rap it on the door.

***

Jemima rushed to answer the door, thinking that Sarah must have forgotten something when she went out to meet her children at the school gates, but when she turned the latch and opened the door it came at her with such velocity that she took a sharp blow on the forehead. It sent her flying backwards, and as she fell, the wall behind her dealt her another blow, this one to the back of the head.

She fell on her backside and sat there dazed, her mind jarred by the sudden physical assault that had seemed to come from two directions. Her vision was blurred but she was aware that the indistinct shape of a man was approaching her from the now open doorway. She had been about to reach up with her hands to feel her sore head, but the man, if it was a man, pulled her up by her wrists without ceremony and shoved her into the nearby kitchen.

The door closed behind her but Jemima turned and saw that the person was there, on her side of the door. Her stomach did somersaults. Was this the end? Was this what it was like? She had been flung across the kitchen so that her back now rested against the sink unit. The man – she felt sure it was a man now – moved towards her, but her head had started to clear a little, and the appearance of the figure in front of her had started to become more distinct. She knew this man. It was going to be okay; although why he was here when he was supposed to be with Stuart at the Maier place was a mystery.

"Liam?" she said croakily, sounding confused, feeling disoriented. "What..."

She didn't even see the fist and it connected with her jaw with a force that she had never imagined before. She had relaxed momentarily upon recognising him and wasn't ready for it, nor was she conditioned to cope with such things. Jemima collapsed in an instant, out cold before she hit the floor. Lee Talbot stood over her body, looking down at his handiwork, regretting in some way the necessity of it, but marvelling just a little at the haymaker he had thrown.

He crouched down, shook her head gently from side to side a couple of times and checked her pulse. Blood was seeping from one side of her lolling jaw. He looked inside her mouth and saw teeth marks inside her lower lip, caused, he supposed, by the impact of his punch. It didn't look too nasty. He stood up and looked around the kitchen briefly. There were plates of sandwiches and other savouries under cling film on the worktops, as well as boxes of cakes and big family packets of crisps.

The party, of course: the boy...

Lee left Jemima where she lay and opened the kitchen door, shutting it quietly behind him. The door to the front room was just along a short corridor. It felt odd to be here in Kay's house. Lee listened and could hear the little boy singing softly and tunelessly to himself. It didn't drown out the hammering of his own heart, but there was no going back now and no time to lose. That other woman might come back at any moment. So far he had been lucky. He took a deep breath and called back over his shoulder, even though directly behind him was the now closed door to the kitchen, loud enough for the boy to hear: "No problem, Jemima, I'll just go and introduce myself to Davy."

This was pre-planned: Lee didn't want to induce fear or suspicion in the lad if he could help it. After another deep breath he walked into the front room. The boy was sitting on the floor, playing with some toys. Preoccupied as he had been, he looked up at the new person in the room, and the expression behind his eyes changed almost instantly from curiosity to alarm. Lee smiled and saw the boy recoil.

"Hello, Davy..." he started.

"'Mima!" the boy yelled. Lee was taken aback by the power of the lad's lungs. Davy repeated his name for Jemima several more times, each call shriller and louder than the last. Lee bit his lip and pressed on.

"It's okay, Davy, Jemima is just doing something in the kitchen. I'm one of Mummy's friends. We're going to see her now. I've come to pick you up and take you in the car. How about that? A ride in the car to see Mummy!"

He had tried to sound bright and friendly and fun. The boy simply regarded him sullenly. Then he got to his feet and went to walk past Lee, holding onto a cuddly toy bunny like it was his only friend, ignoring the strange man and shouting for Jemima again. Lee felt frustrated; he gritted his teeth.

"Come on, Davy, let's go and see Mummy," he repeated, this time less bright, less friendly, less fun. He put a hand out to stop the boy in his tracks, which Davy stumbled into and recoiled from, fleeing to the corner of the room and breaking into full-throated screams, shaking the cuddly bunny up and down as if he was trying to get money out of it. Lee went towards him. This racket was fucking deafening, he thought. Somebody was going to hear. Dead people buried a hundred miles away were going to fucking hear this. He would have to pacify the boy somehow.

His eyes scanned the room as he inched closer to Davy. Toys everywhere, coloured crayons and books on the floor. And there, over on the table – the boy's dummy! That could be just the thing. Lee moved quickly and grabbed the dummy, then closed the distance between himself and the now plainly terrified little boy. It occurred to Lee at this moment that he had been lucky the boy hadn't taken the opportunity to run out into the garden behind him, where Davy's screeching would definitely attract attention.

As if reading Lee's mind, the child made a sudden bolt for the patio doors, but Lee was too fast and grabbed his wrist and pulled the boy towards him. Davy screamed in his face, and Lee got angry. He shook the boy. More screams. He shook Davy again. Tears and anguished wails now... an improvement... Lee jammed the dummy between the boy's lips as his sobs came in waves, and pulled Davy to him, holding him tight to his chest, thinking to stifle the tears, exhaust them, squeeze the energy out of them. Perhaps if he could soothe the boy as well, show tenderness, he might even make them seem unnecessary. Lee stroked the back of the lad's head, his soft hair.

"Now, now, Davy, be a good boy. Let's go and see Mummy, shall we? What will she say about all this fuss and bother? We'll say goodbye to Jemima first, though. Mummy can't wait to see her little birthday boy."

Davy struggled again and emitted muffled sounds of distress. He wasn't buying it. Lee lost patience. The boy would have to come out like this. He picked him up, still holding the two year old's head to his chest, jamming the dummy in his mouth, drowning out the howling and hollering. The boy's arms were pinned to his sides, one hand still clutching the bunny, and he wriggled and tried to thrash around to free them. Lee wondered how the hell he was going to get Davy into the car and then the baby car seat in the back. He decided to just do it as quickly as he possibly could. There was no knowing how long Jemima would be out cold for.

He ran from the front room, past the closed kitchen door behind which Jemima must still have been lying, through the front door, which in his haste he left ajar, down the garden path, through the gate and over to the BMW, not daring to look around in case he caught an onlooker's eye. Fortunately, he had left the car unlocked. He thrust the boy into the baby seat, taking blows to the head as Davy, now with his arms freed, fought him with soft, futile fists. Lee took the blows with sour acceptance, swearing while he fastened the straps that would keep the child constrained.

That done, he dashed around to the other side of the car and jumped into the driver's seat. He started the engine, glancing back at the boy, who was crying miserably and calling for his mummy, his face wet and messy with tears and snot, the dummy spat out. "It's okay, you'll be with Mummy soon!" Lee shouted, then muttered an exasperated, "For fuck's sake…"

He gunned the engine and then the car jerked forward, heading for the exit of the cul-de-sac and almost hitting an oncoming vehicle as he went to turn right at the end of the road. He swerved the BMW left to avoid the oncoming car, and then right again in its wake, followed the road around to the high street, and turned right onto that, along past the spot where he had startled the teenage girls as they went to cross the road earlier, past the trees that lined the way, past the pub at the top of the road, past the church and its sleepy graveyard, past the village shop with its gossips about the local goings-on, and out beyond the limits of the village, into tight country lanes, driving far too fast.

***

Les Campbell's euphoria at being so close to the grandson he had never met was shaken by the near miss with the big grey car. Nick had stamped on the brakes and thrown the steering wheel to the left to avoid a collision, but Les, with his senses heightened by anticipation, had time to see who the driver of the other car was.

The Alfa Romeo screeched to a halt and Les looked across at Nick, who was staring to his right, where the car had just passed them. Silence crashed down upon the interior of the Alfa. Then Nick shook his head and spoke, betraying his confusion; a question that he aimed at no one in particular.

"How can that be? How…"

"Did you see him too?" Les said sharply. "That was Lee. What's he doing here?"

Nick turned slowly towards him, eyes widening. "Lee?" he repeated. "Lee? Oh, God. Oh, fucking Jesus."

He slammed the gearstick into reverse and the car lurched back out of the cul-de-sac and spun round to face the direction it had come from. Then Nick rammed it into first gear and the car sprang forward again. Les had to reach out one hand towards the glove compartment to steady himself. They quickly reached the high road where Nick slowed and glanced to his right. He saw a dark grey car at the top of the sloping high street, already past the pub and the church, and about to go out of sight as it hit the village outskirts – perhaps 150 metres away. There was no other car in either direction. Nick sent the Alfa skidding up the high road in pursuit of the grey car, flagrantly disregarding the speed limit and not caring at that moment.

Now that the car was travelling in a straight line and Nick was working quickly up through the gears, Les ventured to break the panic-stricken silence of the last few seconds.

"What's happening, Nick?"

He glanced at his passenger and Les saw that the panic was still present. Nick's voice was thick with emotion. "He's got my boy, Dad. He's got your grandson. Davy is in the back of that car."

The words seemed to have the effect of pinning Les back against the passenger door. He looked at Nick in amazement, his mouth sagging. Nick pressed down on

the brake momentarily, out of habit rather than com-
punction, as the car reached an intersection where a second road cut across the high road in front of the pub.
There were no other cars in sleepy Hindon at that moment, though, and they were safely across the intersection in a second with little loss of speed, leaving the pub
behind them, the village shop and the church. The road
bore round to the right and the houses began to thin out,
before the Alfa Romeo suddenly sprang clear of the village altogether and shot into a narrow country lane with
tall hedges to either side.

And there was the dark grey car, directly ahead, about
one hundred metres away. Nick was leaning forward
with total focus, low over the steering wheel, stretching
his seat belt, as if just by doing this he could close the
gap. It was hardly a moment for conversation, but Les
had questions to ask. Though his mind was reeling, he
needed to speak.

"What do you think he wants, son?"

Nick's frown deepened. "I wish I knew."

"Where is he taking Davy? I thought this idiot was
out of Kay's life."

Nick at first could only sigh and shake his head. His
eyes remained focused on the road ahead and the dark
grey BMW whose speed and handling he hoped to match
in the Alfa. His mind raced, and the question from Les
had irritated him because he really had no idea what
was happening. The question hung there, unanswered.
"I don't fucking know, Dad," Nick eventually offered. "I
don't know."

As he watched, the BMW passed some farm buildings
to the right, and then the road bore to the left. After that
it was a pretty straight run all the way up to the A303,

Nick knew. Which way would Lee turn then, though – east towards London, or west towards Exeter? At least he could hope to close up the distance, with any luck, if the BMW had to wait at the intersection for traffic to pass. The Alfa manoeuvred through the gentle left and was again directly behind the BMW, but still around a hundred metres back. Nick pressed down fully on the accelerator now that he was on a straight section of road again, knowing that if any vehicle was coming in the opposite direction, he would see Lee's brake lights go on first and have time to react.

Les was pinching his temples. "This is unbelievable," he began. "I wish there was something I could do." Nick gave a little grimace, but was too busy to answer and there really was nothing the older man could do. He was simply a helpless passenger in what was becoming an increasingly reckless high-speed car chase, the final act of which was right now beyond their control.

They got a little closer – probably eighty metres away now – with the surge of speed. Trees and hedgerows whipped past in a blur, almost close enough to touch had either man been foolish enough to reach an arm out of the car window. Seventy metres behind now, and the A303 intersection was fast approaching. The BMW's brake lights flashed on and off a few times and then showed a constant red, and the Alfa gained ground quickly, but Nick knew he needed to brake hard too. He left it until peril was rearing up in their faces before stamping down on the brake pedal. The BMW had stopped at the intersection ahead but only for a couple of seconds, and when the Alfa was just twenty metres away, Lee's car shot out onto the A-road, across the westbound lane and into the eastbound. Nick had seen its driver turn and gesture to the passenger in the back – his own son, he knew – just before it had accelerated away.

Then the Alfa reached the intersection. Nick looked both ways quickly and appraised the situation instantly: there was a vehicle closing from his right – a lorry – and several were approaching fast from the left; he needed to get ahead of those vehicles on his left, or they would be between him and Lee, who was now picking up speed in the London-bound lane, but the lorry on the right was close, too close, he should wait… he couldn't wait! The Alfa jumped forward; the lorry travelling west was bearing down on them, bigger it seemed than a jumbo jet, and Nick and Les both shouted in terror, in chorus with the blare of the juggernaut's horn, and then they were clear, miraculously, and Nick had the steering wheel on full lock to the right, then straightening up in the London-bound lane, and they were surrounded in their car by fresh, clean air, and not the screeching, roaring, obliterating metal of the westbound vehicle.

Nick and Les looked across at each other, eyes wide in incredulity. Already, just seconds later, that felt like an apocryphal moment.

"Mother of God – I'm never doing that again!" Nick yelled out, pumped with relief. Les looked like he wanted to hug him.

"If you ever do, I'm taking up fucking religion!" Les shouted back. On another day, they might even have laughed at their shared escape, but this was not a moment for levity. There were other, more pressing, things they needed to do, specifically to close down the gap between them and Lee and Davy in the BMW. The car coming up behind was all over their rear bumper, Nick saw in his mirror. In the corner of his eye he also saw Davy's little car seat strapped in, empty, and the sight of it thumped him in the heart. Nick tried to shake his head clear.

"Right, come on, Les. We've got to catch this bastard up."

He squeezed down on the gas once again and the Alfa Romeo responded with a throaty growl. They were probably a hundred and fifty metres behind the grey car now and Nick wanted to be much closer. He thought for the first time about the road they were on. There were roundabouts and junctions the whole length of the A303 where the BMW could exit. As they had only recently experienced, however, there could be slower traffic around Stonehenge, and that could help them catch up.

What was Lee's plan, though? Was he taking Davy all the way to London? Or maybe to Hertford, where he and Kay had once lived together? If so, that was a big problem. Having already driven up to London and back, Nick didn't have enough petrol in the tank to make it that far again. He bit his lower lip and eyed the fuel level indicator: eighty or ninety miles left maybe; a hundred at most, he reckoned. He dismissed the thought. It wasn't worth worrying about until it happened, he decided.

Lee wasn't hanging around, though, that was for sure. Nick had accelerated to 90 m.p.h. but he didn't seem to be making much of a dent in the BMW's lead. Still, the initial panic was beginning to fade. They had turned up in the nick of time and had managed to track Lee through narrow country lanes and onto a major road; had narrowly avoided what would have been a catastrophic smash in doing so. There had been little time for rational thought, but now, on this mostly straight A-road, it felt like there was more time to consider this situation and Davy's predicament. The road stretched out before them and they could see every move that Lee made as they gradually ate up the gap between the two cars.

A rueful thought entered Nick's mind: here he was, chasing Lee Talbot again. Unbelievable...

This felt very different from that first time, more than two years before, though. This time Nick stood to lose the most precious thing in his life. Jesus, there was supposed to be a birthday party for his little boy today, and this bastard Lee Talbot had ruined it now. What had happened to Jemima? She was supposed to be looking after Davy. Nick didn't dwell on that, though. He needed to speak to Kay. She had to know what was happening. How anyone could explain a situation like this to the mother of a child was beyond him, but he had to try.

He pressed some buttons on his mobile phone, which was connected to a hands-free set-up in the car. It was on speaker-phone and the sound of Kay's phone ringing filled the car. Nick felt Les looking at him.

"Kay," he told him, by way of explanation. "Be ready to say hello."

After ringing six or seven times, though, the call diverted to her voicemail. Nick swore as Kay's recorded voice asked the caller to leave a message. Then, after the beep, he said: "Kay, it's me. Call me as soon as you can, please. Something crazy and terrible is happening. I can't explain it on here. Call me urgently, darling. Really urgently."

He pressed another button to hang up and focused once more on the road ahead and the target of the grey BMW. He had definitely reeled it in a little. It was about a hundred metres ahead again, he reckoned. He gripped the steering wheel with renewed purpose and settled again in his seat, to follow Lee... again.

CHAPTER SIXTEEN

There was a good reason why Kay was unable to answer her mobile phone: she was being interviewed by PC Daryl Dexter of the Wiltshire Police, and the phone was out of reach, ten yards away on her desk. PC Dexter was a burly, blond man with a diffident way both of asking questions and receiving the answers to them. He was professional and interested, but not in any way that made you suspect he was about to leap into action.

Around her in the office there were more people – her colleagues – also relating the events of the last hour to police officers, while others sat cradling tea and coffee cups, excitedly swapping anecdotes or impatiently awaiting their turn to be interviewed. Outside on the grass other people were in handcuffs, having very different conversations with officers of the law.

It had been somewhat annoying that Kay had been preoccupied with PC Dexter when her phone had started chiming its ring tone. The whole damn' thing was annoying in fact. She needed to get off home for Davy's party. Just her luck that these lunatics chose today to kick the doors down. It had been quite exciting for a while, though, she supposed, not that those who had dashed downstairs to try and lock out the attackers would necessarily agree with that.

The important thing for Maier Science was that the attack was over and the facility was secure again, and that apart from some frayed nerves – not least those of Richard Cambridge – and a few bumps and bruises, there had been no real harm done to any of the employees.

By a stroke of luck, the security system for the laboratories had been reactivated a matter of minutes before the SMAC assault. Those who had been attempting to storm the labs, neutralise the technicians and free the animals within – Stuart McCormack and his team – had been foiled. Upon finding access blocked, contrary to the information given to them by Jemima Bond, there had been confusion and a heated argument between Mac and Vince. Should they abort the whole mission or stage a demonstration at the front of the site, where the office buildings were?

They had been able to hear the shouts of the other assault group from that direction. It sounded like pandemonium. Surely, as every good general would do, they should march to the sound of the guns, insisted Vince. Son-of-a-soldier Mac disagreed vehemently and he ordered everyone to run back through the hole in the fence, into the woods, and then to make their own way to safety. It was quite simple, he said. The alarm call would now have been received by the police, who would be here in short order. The mission was blown. They must gather themselves together and move on to the next thing. But first they must get away from the Maier facility before the police arrived.

It made sense to most of the group, but Vince refused to go and Pippa felt it was her duty to stay with him. Mac and Vince bristled at each other again but there was no time for a lengthy debate about it. Mac said: "Right, I'm going. Everyone, come with me." And he set off back across the grass, followed by everyone except Vince and his wife and Barry from the ALF who, rather than just melt back into the treeline, wanted to join his comrades in the demonstration at the office blocks.

When the police arrived a few minutes later, there was therefore a much-reduced group of activists for them to deal with. They arrived in cars and riot vans, equipped for big trouble with shields and batons and even a couple of dogs. They found that they easily outnumbered their adversaries and the ensuing struggle was brief and one-sided.

The aftermath of that was now all around Kay: belligerent but beaten activists in handcuffs being led round to the back of police vans; police officers everywhere; and now she saw someone she recognised, down on the grassy area outside the front of the building, talking to a policeman – it was Ted Chillingworth, the reporter from the *Salisbury Journal* who had written the hatchet job article about Maier Science. Next to him was a photographer. It hadn't taken Ted long to get wind of events. Well, he was just doing his job, Kay mused. She could hardly argue that this wasn't a good story for the newspaper.

PC Dexter was speaking to her. She dragged her eyes away from the window to see him looking at her expectantly, pen at the ready.

"Sorry – I was miles away there," Kay admitted. "What was the question?"

A flicker of impatience passed across the officer's face: "I said: was there any indication you can think of from before today that they were planning something like this?"

"Er, no. Nothing specific. We had the meeting with them ten days ago, and you'll find everything you need to know about that in WPC Stanhope's very detailed report. There's been some hassling of our suppliers going on, but there was no real evidence to take action on. Obviously there was the video that we believe they obtained illegally, but you lot haven't done anything about that."

"Us lot?"

"Oh, I just meant... you know... the police force in general, officer. Sorry, I wasn't really thinking."

Kay smiled at him but there was no softening in his expression: he continued to look unimpressed.

"You seem distracted, Ms Campbell," he told her. "Is there something on your mind?"

"Oh, well, yes. All this going on, of course, but it's also my little boy's birthday party this afternoon and I was supposed to have left by now."

PC Dexter looked at her for a second. It was impossible to tell what thoughts were going on behind his impassive blue eyes. Then he gave a small nod.

"Okay, Ms Campbell, no more questions. Please take a seat and hopefully we won't have to detain you too much longer." He turned away from Kay and gestured to another of the employees to come forward.

Kay wandered back to her desk and sank down into her seat. She looked once more at the various documents on her computer screen, the things she should have been doing before the attack started. She had lost interest in them now. She supposed that she should feel angry about all of this but she just felt hollow. Bullshit, the whole lot of it.

Just then her mobile phone started to ring. She had forgotten about the missed call earlier. Hopefully it was Nick. She picked up the handset – no, it was Jemima. Great, she would be able to speak to Davy.

***

Jemima had regained consciousness to find her nostrils burning with an awful stench of bleach. It took a few seconds for her eyes to adjust and focus on what was in front of her. When they did, Jemima saw an elderly woman crouching at her side; grey hair, a wrinkled, concerned face, a burgundy-coloured cardigan. The woman was waving a small bottle under her nose. Everything around her and the bottle was a blur.

Even so, just from what she could see, questions entered Jemima's mind in fast progression: where was she? What was that dreadful smell? Why was she lying on the floor? Who was this strange old woman? What was this bottle in front of her face? To this last question, some potential link between the bottle and the stink seemed to suggest itself. Jemima tried to recoil from it, but felt as if she was pinned down on her back. She tried to lift her head instead, but it hardly moved, and she had cause instantly to regret the attempt as a flash of pain made her squeeze her eyes shut.

When the pain had passed she opened her eyes again. The woman had removed the bottle now but was still looking down at Jemima attentively, deep creases of disquiet on her forehead.

"Can you hear me?" she said. "Are you okay? Is anything broken?"

Jemima had no idea what the answers were to the last two questions, but she could certainly hear them. She tried to move her arms a little, and her feet too, waggling her toes gingerly. It seemed to work. She thought she should answer the woman's questions, but what came out of her mouth was just an agonised, "Yes, I th-ow-ww!". Jemima had not expected to feel that shooting pain in her jaw. Her hand reached up instinctively to feel it.

"Oh, my," the old woman said, covering her lips with her fingers. She regarded the sorry figure before her for a few seconds. The poor girl was obviously still confused and in some pain, but at least the smelling salts had brought her round. It would be good to get her off the floor. There was a kitchen table nearby, with a couple of wooden chairs. That would do for now.

"If you can move your arms and legs at all, dear, perhaps I can help you over to the chair there?"

Jemima looked at her rescuer and muttered yes. It was as much as she trusted herself to be able to say without further pain at the moment. Between the two of them they got Jemima off the floor and, after an initial dizzy stagger, the old woman supported her the few feet over to the chair.

"That's better." The woman smiled, patting Jemima's arm and standing back to admire her achievement. "Now, how about a cup of tea while you tell me all about what happened?"

"Ugh... yes... thanks," Jemima grunted carefully, managing to get her jaw around the words without feeling undue pain. She stared vacantly ahead while the woman clattered about, inspecting cupboards for mugs, pouring water into the kettle. *What has happened?* Jemima was thinking to herself. *This kitchen was vaguely familiar to her but she couldn't recall anything about how she had got here.*

"Where did that man take little Davy?" the woman asked over her shoulder. Jemima sat in silence for a few seconds, thinking through a fog. Davy...

The woman was prattling on about it being lucky that the man had forgotten to shut the front door behind him, otherwise she would never have been able to get into the house and, who knows, Jemima could have been there on the floor for hours. Davy... By the way, the woman was saying now, she should introduce herself. She was Mrs O'Neill from number six, across the road. Davy... and a man...

A man...

A man...

Liam! He had been there, with Jemima in the kitchen, eyes darting furtively around the room then settling on her, coming towards her – the dullness behind those eyes, the determination. Liam. Her fear and confusion turning to relief because it was Liam, someone she knew; he was close enough to touch. Too close, then whack! The barest glimpse of a fist, right in front of her face, just preceding the impact, then nothing. Darkness.

Before that, at the front door... the door had smacked her in the head. She had fallen backwards and hit her head again. Complete bewilderment and shock. A man had dragged her and bundled her into the kitchen. A man... Liam...

Her jaw... Jemima's hand reached up and felt it, stroked it tenderly, pushed it here and there, testing. It felt swollen and sore, and she was suddenly aware that she could taste blood in her mouth. She put a finger inside and it came out red-smeared. She looked at it. The tinkling of a spoon stirring a mug of tea... the woman was still talking over there but Jemima was lost in her own rediscovery. Carefully, she decided, she would try to speak.

"That name. You said a name."

Mrs O'Neill turned towards her, beaming encouragingly, mug of tea in hand. "Sorry, dear?"

"You said a name."

The woman put the mug down on the table next to Jemima. "Yes? Oh, Davy, you mean? It's his birthday today, isn't it? Did the man take him somewhere nice?"

"The man took him?" Suddenly Jemima had forgotten about the soreness in her jaw.

"Yes, he put him in a car and they…"

Jemima jumped to her feet, startling Mrs O'Neill; frightening her even more with the look of panic in her eyes.

She paced up and down muttering the words "Oh my God" over and over. Her body was ice and fire all at once, breaking out simultaneously in goose bumps and hot flushes. Something horrible, she was sure, was crawling up her spine.

It was coming back to her now: she had been looking after Davy for Nick and Kay. Today was the boy's second birthday and Jemima and another girl – what was her name now? – had been preparing for the party. The other girl had gone out to the shops and a few minutes later Liam from the SMAC meetings – Jemima had never quite trusted him – had knocked on the door, barged in and assaulted her. He had left her out cold on the kitchen floor and now the woman from across the road was saying that a strange man had driven off with little Davy.

Jemima was walking quickly but unsteadily back and forth, three steps this way, three steps that, as she pieced it all together in her head. Mrs O'Neill was reaching towards her, as if anticipating another fall. "What is it? What's happened?" she kept repeating, her face starting to crumple at Jemima's distress.

"Where's my phone? I need my phone," said the girl angrily. Mrs O'Neill was about to reply when Jemima ran from the room, knocking her side on the corner of a kitchen worktop on the way, but she didn't even register the pain. She ran through to the front room and found her mobile phone up on the wall unit, out of Davy's reach. Quickly she found Kay's number and pressed the button to call it. She turned to see Mrs O'Neill coming into the front room behind her. Jemima turned away from her, ignored her. She didn't want to look at her, didn't want her there. She wished this could be a very private moment of failure and despair. No merciful hole opened in the ground to swallow her up, though. She could sense the woman still standing there, watching her.

Kay answered her phone. What could Jemima say to her? How could she say it? What words could be sufficient to cushion this? There were none. She blurted it out. She had to. There was no attempt to disguise what she knew, and what she shouldn't have been able to know. She just said everything she knew at that moment, and no amount of throbbing or discomfort in her jaw was going to stop her.

It came out in one long stream: "Kay, Liam from Stop Maier Animal Cruelty has taken Davy away. He came to the house, beat me up, and your neighbour saw him put Davy in a car and drive away. Kay, I'm sorry. I'm so sorry."

She heard a sharp, tremulous intake of breath from the other end of the line, a sound so panic-stricken and fearful that the full impact of this horror and her own collusion with it hit Jemima like a train and she collapsed to the floor, engulfed in tears of shame, unable in her desolation even to hear the urgent questions that were being fired at her down the phone. Jemima's handset tumbled to the floor next to her, but Mrs O'Neill, standing transfixed by the living-room door, could hear the anguished appeals of Kay, her friend and neighbour.

"Jemima…? Jemima…? Jemima! Answer me! Please…"

CHAPTER SEVENTEEN

Quiet, focused determination in one car; pandemonium in the one in front; the boy had fought against his straps long and hard but had now given up on that pointless battle. His tactics now were to emit ear-splitting yells. To Lee it felt like a masterstroke of psychological warfare.

Stonehenge had flashed by on the left, gaggles of visitors wandering around the old stones. Lee had paid no attention to it. He was trying to psych himself up for the next part of his plan. It would require him to make a phone call, but by God... this lad was making such a racket it was just impossible.

The screaming and crying had been more or less incessant since they had left Hindon, quietening down in relative terms only when Davy had set about tussling with his straps for a few seconds. Lee had tried talking kindly to the boy, telling him over and over that they were going to see his mummy, and that she would think he was being a silly boy, making such a fuss over nothing. It was bloody hard and bloody dangerous looking over his shoulder and trying to make persuasive eye contact with the lad while also driving at 80 m.p.h., but Lee had tried repeatedly. His reward was simply a renewed assault upon his eardrums.

Lee put some music on: a heavy metal CD to drown the noise out. He turned the volume up ridiculously high, and for several minutes was almost deafened by Def Leppard accompanied by Davy. Perhaps it was actually Davy accompanied by Def Leppard. It became clear that this ploy wasn't working, so he turned the music off while Davy continued blasting out at top volume.

If only he could stop the car, gag the boy with tape or something, and then make his phone call. Maybe he would do that at the next services. Lee thought about that for a few seconds, trying to block out the noise. No, it was a bad idea. Someone might see him taping the lad's mouth shut, or spot the kid gagged on the back seat as they drove past. It was a sure-fire way to get the police on his tail. Lee shook his head and then grimaced at Davy and shook a fist at him.

He resolved simply to ignore the wailing coming from the back seat. The kid was probably looking for attention, so deprive him of it. Don't give him the satisfaction. Lee gripped the steering wheel tight and focused his attention on the road ahead, but it was like playing a CD on the stereo of a kid bawling its eyes out – a single caterwauling track that never fucking ended. Lee gritted his teeth and concentrated hard, but with every godforsaken second that passed with this din ringing in his ears and smashing through his mental defences, he could feel the temperature beneath his collar rise and rise. The noise went on and on, until the hairs on the back of his neck were standing on end. Keep calm, he told himself; keep cool, calm and collected. On and on it went. Count to ten, Lee. Count to fifty. Count to…

"Will you shut the fuck up!" he roared back at his passenger, whose entire body tried to jump back in fright, only to discover once more that it was trapped. Lee was losing it now, though, his patience all used up. He gave a kind of strangulated cry and pounded his fists on the steering wheel. "Shut the fuck up! You little fucking cry baby, shut up, shut up, SHUT UP!"

The boy looked terrified. "If you don't put a fucking sock in it now," Lee screamed at him, "I'm gonna just leave you by the side of this fucking road!"

The two males, separated by more than thirty years in age, were matching each other for volume. Lee found himself screaming in tandem with the boy, almost as if he were accompanying him in some crazed a cappella or frenzied dervish lament. The ludicrousness of the situation made him howl with laughter, the mirth of a man beginning to unravel.

The effect of this was unexpected, though. The boy ceased his wailing. Lee looked back at Davy again in wonder and saw his shocked, tear-streaked face, his sullen eyes not wavering from his kidnapper's for even a second. The sudden silence was as invigorating as a dive into a swimming pool.

"Oh, thank God," Lee exclaimed. "Thank fucking God." He glanced over his shoulder at Davy a few more times, telling him that he was a good boy, that his mummy would be pleased, that Lee would buy him an ice cream, a chocolate bar, a fizzy drink – anything he wanted. The boy sat sniffling miserably.

It was time to make the call. His exit from the A303 was coming up very soon. Lee punched a few buttons on his mobile phone, which was connected to a hands-free set-up. It rang twice and then a familiar voice answered, somewhat shakily.

"Hello?"

"Hi, Kay, it's me, your beloved."

There was a pause. When Kay replied her voice had hardened distinctly. "Lee? Is that you?"

"Of course it is, Kay. You know that – I gave you my number, didn't I? Oh, yes, that's right, you screwed it up and threw it away the moment my back was turned."

"What have you done with Davy? Don't you dare hurt my son, Lee."

She definitely sounded strung out, he thought. "Listen, I haven't done anything with him. He's here now, sitting in the back of the car, all happy. Well... kind of. Anyway, we're both coming to see you. Hey, Davy, say hello to Mummy."

Lee needed to prompt him again before the boy gave an anguished cry. "There you go, Kay," Lee said. "Right as rain."

"You bastard, Lee. Bring him back to me right now."

"Well, that's exactly what I am doing, darling. I take it you're still at work."

She gave a small laugh, harsh and without humour. "Yes, I am. Surrounded by policemen and watching half of your new gang get bundled into the back of a van. It didn't work, Lee. Whatever idiotic point there was to what you people did today, it didn't work."

"I couldn't give a flying fuck about any of it, Kay. We both know that," he replied indifferently, wanting to get on with his own agenda. "Meet me at the back of the Maier place, out by the trees beyond the wire. And don't bring any coppers with you."

"Why? What do you want?"

"Just meet me, Kay. I want to talk to you. Me and you, and no coppers, yeah? I'll be there in, ooh, about twenty-five minutes, I reckon."

He waited through a few seconds of silence from the other end of the line. Davy's sobs punctuated the quiet. "Kay?" he prompted her.

"Yes. Okay, I'll meet you at the back. Don't hurt my son, Lee."

"I won't, Kay. I won't."

The call ended, and two minutes later the car reached a roundabout. Lee took the right- hand exit and came off the road towards London. They were heading south now. He grinned over his shoulder at the distraught child on the back seat.

"Nearly there, little lad," he said. "Nearly there."

***

After Kay pressed the button to end the call, she turned to the two policemen – a plain-clothes inspector and a uniformed constable – waiting by her side. They looked at her attentively.

"Well… he wants me to meet him," she said flatly.

Inspector Tomalin's brow furrowed. "Where?"

"Round the back of this place, outside the fence and by the trees – he's bringing Davy with him. Lee promised he wasn't going to hurt him."

"I see… do you believe him?"

Kay was looking out of the window, distracted by her thoughts. "What?"

"Do you believe him, Mrs Campbell?"

She hesitated. "Yes… yes, I think so. Lee said he wants to talk to me. He'll be here in twenty-five minutes. I'm going out to meet him, like he said."

"It would be safer for Davy if we picked them up before that. We could put patrol cars and checkpoints on the roads to locate his vehicle and teams in the woods to surprise him. Mrs Campbell, we don't know if he has a weapon of any kind."

Kay looked the inspector in the eye. "He doesn't have a weapon."

"We don't know that, Mrs Campbell. Nor do we know what his mental state is."

"I told you, he wants to talk to me. And he said no policemen, so keep your officers out of sight please, Inspector. This is between me and my husband."

Inspector Tomalin exchanged glances with the police constable. He walked a few paces away and stood looking out of the office window; then he walked back again, rubbing his chin thoughtfully. The young constable, whose name was Attleborough, was watching him. "Guv?" he said.

Inspector Tomalin looked back towards Kay: finally, he was resolved.

"Okay, Mrs Campbell – here's how it's going to be: you go and meet Lee at the back of the facility. Try and get him to step into the clearing between the wire and the trees so he can be seen more clearly. I will have officers begin to infiltrate the wood behind him while you are talking. They will keep at a suitable distance, though. If at any stage you feel Davy is in danger, to whatever degree, I want you to give us a discreet, agreed signal – tug your earlobe like this, for example – and we will intervene immediately. Is that clear? It is more of a risk than I want to take, but you seem sure of yourself."

This all sounded way over the top to Kay. She waved her hand dismissively. "There's really no need for all this trouble, Inspector, this is between my husband and me. I can deal with Lee."

Inspector Tomalin inclined his head slightly towards her and spoke in a low voice. "With all due respect, Mrs Campbell, your husband has assaulted a member of the public and abducted a small child. This is not just between the two of you anymore."

Kay had no answer to that. She retreated to the Ladies to try and steel herself for what was to come.

***

Nick was surprised when he saw the BMW take a right turn off the dual carriageway at the roundabout ahead. Lee was leaving the A303, and was now heading south towards Salisbury. Clearly he was not going to drive all the way up to the M25 and round to Hertford, as Nick had assumed he would.

"He went right at the roundabout, son," Les helpfully told him. Kay's dad had been fretting at his inability to do anything that might bring this situation to a happy resolution.

"Got it, Dad."

Nick flicked the indicator up and moved over to the right-hand lane in readiness for his own right turn. They got to the roundabout more quickly than was legal and he stood on the brakes, watching the oncoming traffic to his right, trying to judge where the best gap might be. He wasn't especially lucky: just as he was about to plough ahead and negotiate the roundabout, another car came shooting round in front of him, itself turning off the opposite carriageway of the A303. Nick shed more speed in some exasperation, and calculated the gap between the back of this unwelcome car and the next one, which he could see was about to circle the roundabout from the road Lee had just turned down. He stamped back on the accelerator and the Alfa shot forward into the gap; he had to yank the steering wheel to the left, then more gently to the right as he went around the roundabout.

Seconds later he was into a single-lane road, and there was another car – a black Peugeot – between his own vehicle and Lee's. Nick swore under his breath. It quickly became obvious that this new road was not as straight and open as the big A-road they had just left. There were going to be occasions when Lee would be out of sight for a couple of seconds. It was unavoidable.

"Well done, son," said Les, patting his arm.

"We should try Kay again," Nick responded. "She must be off the damn' phone by now, surely."

He had been dreading this moment, which had already been put off on several occasions because every time he had called Kay from the car, her number had been engaged. This time it rang, and she answered it immediately.

"Nick, thank God! Listen, something terrible is happening."

"Oh, you know about Lee and Davy already? I've been trying to call you for the last fifteen minutes."

"Jemima called me. He beat her up and took Davy, but it's okay…"

"What do you mean, it's okay? Your husband has given the nanny a kicking and kidnapped our son. It's definitely not okay!"

"I know, I know, but calm down, Nick. I've spoken to Lee. He's…"

"You've spoken to him? What the… how did he…"

"He rang my mobile number a few minutes ago."

"How the hell did he get that?" Nick demanded.

"I really think we should worry about that another time. Now, can you let me just talk for a few seconds, please, so I can explain?"

Their mutual anxiety, unspoken, filled the silence that followed this. Nick, driving as fast as he dared along the winding road, took a few deep breaths.

"Sorry, babe. Go on."

"Thank you. Now, I'm at work and the police are here. There was an attack by the animal rights people and a few got into the building. Don't ask, babe! But anyway, it's all over now. We were sorting things out with the police when Lee rang me. Oh, I'd already spoken to Jemima by then and told the police about it. So Lee rang. He wants to meet me here – out by the trees at the back. He said he's bringing Davy with him, and has promised that he won't hurt him. He says he just wants to talk to me."

Nick and Les exchanged glances.

"You're in the car, aren't you?" Kay said. "I'm on speakerphone, aren't I?"

"Yes, babe. I've got your dad next to me." Nick let that sink in for a second or two. There was an indistinct rustling sound from the other end of the line.

"Hi, Dad," Kay said. Her voice seemed suddenly smaller somehow, as if the little girl she once was had returned.

"Hello, love. This wasn't what I expected," Les called out.

"No… no… well, welcome back to the crazy world of Kay Campbell," she replied. "I can't wait to see you when this is all done, Dad."

"Same here, love."

"All right," Nick broke in. "Kay, what you need to know right now, but don't because I haven't had a chance to tell you yet, is that we are following Lee's car. We're about fifty yards behind him. Like you said, don't ask! He just turned off the A303. I thought he must be going to Salisbury when he did that, but now I know he's heading your way. He's driving like a fucking idiot, which means I'm having to as well. Think I've nearly killed me and your dad twice so far."

"Wow… you're fifty yards behind him? That's incredible," she said. "I… I'm amazed by that. I bet he doesn't even realise."

"Don't think so. We arrived at the house just as he was driving off and we've been on his tail since then."

"One day we'll be able to laugh about your habit of following my soon-to-be-ex-husband."

"Huh! Things were a lot less complicated when I just used to shine the bastard's shoes," Nick sighed.

"Listen, babe, slow down. You don't need to keep up with him now. You know where he's going. Just drive here and head for the gate. I'll tell them you're coming."

"No, I want to keep Lee in my sights, Kay. He's got our little boy, and that's it. Are you going to meet him then?"

"Yes. I think it's the best thing to do. He'll be here in about fifteen minutes. We have to deal with this now, Nick, otherwise it will follow us for the rest of our lives."

That much was clear to him too. Kay told him that the police were going to be watching carefully, but would be out of sight. She just wanted to get her son back, and hug him, and hug his dad and her own. That was what was going to happen. It would be okay, she told them.

Nick said to her: "We will be in the trees behind him, Kay. You can count on it."

As he said it, up ahead he saw the BMW take a left turn – it was a narrow country lane, he knew, and it was exactly the turning that Nick had expected Lee to take. He eased off on the pedal and prepared to go left as well.

323

CHAPTER EIGHTEEN

Overhanging branches whipped Lee harshly in the face as he pushed through the woods towards the Maier Science facility. He paid no attention to the stinging sensation. His mind had room only for a small number of considerations. One was the soft little hand he held in his – Davy, poor defeated Davy, his tears all cried out, his screams and protests now replaced by shocked silence; he stumbled along next to Lee, dragged along by his momentum.

Lee kept looking ahead, to where shafts of light penetrated the treeline, spurring him on, like a worshipper drawn to a glorious stained-glass window. And beyond it, out there in the sunlight, would be his glorious woman: his Kay.

They tramped through the woods in silence, coming ever closer to the sunlight. There were now just a few more yards of woodland to go. Lee looked down at the boy and squeezed his hand. Davy looked up at him, face expressionless. He seemed to take none of the intended encouragement from the squeeze of his hand, just as he had seemed to take none from Lee's repeated statements that they were going to see his mummy. The boy had become mute. After all that noise earlier, Lee could get nothing from him now.

When Lee looked back up again, he saw Kay. She was sitting on the grass, out beyond the treeline, her bare legs folded and tucked to one side. She was looking down and picking at the grass, for all the world like a little girl making a daisy chain. Lee stopped walking just short of the treeline and watched her, struck immediately by familiar yearnings and feelings of regret. Why, oh, why?

Suddenly Davy called out: "Mummy, Mummy!" Kay looked up in their direction. She jumped to her feet and peered through the trees hopefully. Lee knew it was time to step forward and show himself. The brief moments of private appreciation were over. He stood half concealed behind a tree trunk. Davy was pulling on his hand now, wanting to run to his mummy. He had found his voice again. Lee pulled the boy to him tightly, held in front, one arm pinioning his chest, one hand gripping Davy's right arm. Lee looked at Kay. She was beautiful in the afternoon sunshine.

"Hello, Kay. We meet again."

She ignored him, and spoke instead to her son. "Hello, Davy. How's my beautiful boy?"

Lee scanned everything behind and around Kay, as mother and son gazed only at each other. He studied the wire fence that was about thirty or so metres behind her; he studied the buildings of the Maier facility beyond the wire; he scanned the treeline on each side of the facility – there was no sign of any police officers. It looked like it was just the three of them; it felt like it too. Here he was at last, alone with Kay but for the boy. Lee had waited so long for this.

Kay was saying to Davy that she would soon be taking him home. She was fifteen to twenty metres away, but Lee noticed she was edging gradually closer. She hadn't said a word to him yet; hadn't even acknowledged him.

"Okay, enough of that. Don't come any closer now, Kay. That's quite close enough."

She gave him a dark, furious look. "Why – what will you do if I run over there and take Davy from you?"

"Let's not be rash. I've kept all my promises. I came here to talk to you – remember?"

Kay scoffed: "Promises? You've done a very bad thing, Lee. It took me too many years to work out that I was married to an arsehole, but I never expected you to pull this kind of sick stunt."

"You backed me into a corner, I had to get your attention somehow. I gave you my number, Kay, and you just threw it away, as soon as I turned my back. I know you did because I found it. I found the piece of paper screwed up and left on the grass, exactly where we had been standing."

She shook her head in wonder. "Yeah, I did. So what, Lee? Does that really warrant kidnapping my little boy, and scaring the living daylights out of him and me and his dad?"

"It wasn't like that…"

"Have we been punished enough yet for hurting your feelings, or do you still need an apology?"

"No, that's not what I want."

"I'm prepared to apologise, Lee. I'll do anything you want if I can have my son back, and then we can forget all about this. I'll apologise. I'll do handstands. I'll walk around for a week dressed as an inflatable banana if it's what you want. Just tell me what you want me to do, Lee."

Kay noticed that her husband had kept his eyes closed throughout her rant, as if just trying to get to the end of it, and she had taken advantage of this to move a step closer to him and her son; and then another step. When Lee reopened his eyes a couple of seconds later, she was surprised to see they were filled with tears.

"Kay, please listen to me," he insisted, "this isn't what I came here to talk about at all."

His voice was full of woe. He could have been a teenager not getting his own way. Davy stood glum and silent, aware of emotions he didn't understand. Kay felt hot out in the sunshine and could see that Lee was sweating too, even though he was in the shade. Perhaps it was the stress of this conversation, this pivotal moment in their lives. What she knew for certain was that she was perspiring heavily and it was beading on her brow. She wanted to wipe it away, but the instructions of Inspector Tomalin were echoing in her mind: the secret signal she should make to call for assistance from the hidden police officers. It made her keep her arms pinned very firmly by her sides to avoid an accidental alert.

Lee had started speaking again. Unbelievably, Kay realised he was reminiscing; dragging up memories of the early days of their relationship: laughter on holidays; nights on the town; moments of domestic happiness they had shared. These were things Kay had long since forgotten about, buried beneath the negativity and conflict of the later years of their marriage. These were not memories that meant anything to her any longer. She was too busy trying to make new ones with Nick and their son. She became irritated and short on patience as Lee continued to speak.

"What's your point, Lee?" she demanded, feeling no pity for her husband. "I mean, so what? We went on holiday to the Seychelles: so what?"

He hesitated. She could see that he was hurt, but he tried to continue anyway. "The point, Kay, is that we had a great thing going. You know that's true. And we could have it all again. We can find that magic again."

"Oh my God… no, we can't, Lee." It was clear to her that he was about to plead with her.

"We can. Yes, we can. We were perfect together, Kay. What changed? Why can't we get it back to how it was?"

"Everything changed. You changed, I changed. Our love changed and then it died. You know that's true. We were worse than cats and dogs at the end."

A smile of sorts passed across Lee's face, as if he had been waiting for these words to be spoken; as if he knew they would come and had the right response just up his sleeve.

"Yes, I accept we were arguing a lot but that was only because of the baby situation, because you didn't want to have one. And look what happened: I was right all along." Lee gestured to the small boy he still held tightly against his legs. "You turned out to be a great mother, just like I said you would. There was no need to worry after all. That means everything can still be as it should have been."

Kay felt as if she was actually experiencing the process of her eyes glazing over millimetre by millimetre at Lee's astonishing words, his skewed logic. That he could track her down and go to the extreme of forcibly taking her child, and then stand in front of her and plead with her not only to overlook that appalling tactic, but to resume their fractured relationship again… it was staggering; so shocking it made her angry. She wondered whether Nick was close enough in the woods behind Lee to hear any of this deranged, self-deluding nonsense. She had to stamp on it right away. She had been very careful to restrain her language in front of Davy, but now Kay lost control.

"Lee, are you out of your fucking mind? We're finished. It's over between us. I don't love you anymore and I never will. I met someone new and I'm very happy. Together we have something far, far better than you and I ever had. My life is here now, with Nick and Davy. You've got to go back home and forget about me. I'll put the divorce papers through and we'll do it properly. But give me my son back first. There's something better waiting for you out there, I'm sure of that, if you'll just let it happen. Please, listen to me, Lee. Do what I say. You must forget about me and us and all that old stuff you were just talking about. I had a baby with the man I love. I don't love *you* anymore. There's no going back for us now. Please listen to me: give me my son back and we can part as friends."

They looked at each other across the ten metres or so of grass dividing them – Kay desperate for him to accept her will and her argument; Lee visibly upset. In the silence that followed, little murmurs by the breeze and the chatter of insects rushed to fill the vacuum. Kay sighed and cast her eyes from Lee's face down to Davy, and then to the ground at their feet. It felt entirely plausible as she had looked into her son's frightened eyes that her heart might explode. She waited fearfully for Lee to respond or react in some way.

***

Yards away, crouching among the trees behind Lee, Nick was straining to hear every word. He and Les had followed Lee's BMW until it had parked in a layby on the edge of the woods. A strange moment had ensued as they drove past, Nick seeing another man lifting Davy out of the back seat, putting him on his feet and holding his hand as the two of them headed into the trees. It was the first time that Les had really seen his grandson. The two men in the Alfa Romeo had exchanged a glance that was heavy with meaning.

Nick had quickly turned the car around and driven back to the same layby, parking behind the BMW. Then they had ventured into the woods in pursuit of Lee and Davy, picking their way between the trees and remaining a good distance back. When they saw the two figures stop at the edge of the treeline, Nick held up a hand and also halted. He and Les then sank down on their haunches for a whispered conference.

"Why don't we just take him?" Les hissed.

"Because Kay doesn't want us to… and because you just got out of hospital with cirrhosis, Dad."

They exchanged rueful smiles despite the situation. Nick looked around for a few seconds, trying to see if there were police officers hidden in the woods too, as Kay had said there would be; he didn't see any however. At this point they were fifty metres or so behind Lee, and Nick wanted to be nearer. He turned to Les.

"Right, stay here, Dad. I'm going to creep closer so that I can listen to what they're saying."

"I'll come with you…"

"No. Stay here. I'll wave you up if I want you to come, but the less movement back here the better."

So Nick moved from tree trunk to tree trunk, slowly but surely closing the distance to the treeline, until he was about ten metres behind Lee's right shoulder. Nick crouched down once more to weigh up the situation. The memory of a dark alleyway in Luton returned then; he, Nick, hiding in the shadows, while Lee Talbot covered himself with shame. It was a funny old world, indeed. Nick looked back and saw Les watching him. He gave a thumbs-up, and Les started to move. It took several hand gestures for Nick to communicate that this wasn't what he had meant by the signal.

Now here he was, reflecting on the words he had just heard Kay say to Lee. It must have been pretty brutal on the guy, in particular that bit about her having a far better thing now than she had ever had with Lee. In the silence that followed, Nick tried to catch a glimpse of his son, but he knew that Lee was holding the boy close in front of him. Davy was, after all, his only bargaining chip.

Finally, Lee spoke up again, just loud enough for Nick to hear. His question was startling.

"How do you know that Davy isn't my child?"

Davy understood enough of that to try and pull away from the man holding him captive. Lee kept a tight hold though.

"I've done the maths, Kay. If today is his second birthday, then he was conceived while we were still together. How can you be sure he's this other idiot's, and not mine?"

From what Nick could see, which wasn't much, Kay was shaking her head out there in the sunshine. He heard her reply – angry, impatient, flustered.

"Well, for a start, look at him. He looks nothing like you, and a lot like Nick. So there's your first clue. But really, Lee, what clinches it is the fact that we didn't have sex for the last six months before I left you. So try doing the maths again. There's more chance of your mate James being the fath—"

And there her voice tailed off. Nick had been crouching upon the cool earth, momentarily focusing on the ground in front of him. These last words of Kay's brought him to his feet with a jolt, though. Who the hell was James? Kay had never mentioned the name to him. She was still standing there, out beyond the treeline, but she had a frozen look on her face. Nick's guts quailed with unease. He glanced back and saw that Les was definitely a few metres closer than he had been before. Why the hell had Kay said that? The reaction came very quickly, and Nick had no problem hearing this time. Lee was shouting now.

"James? You slept with James? You bitch, Kay. You fucking bitch. All this time… everything that we had… and you were putting it about with my mates like a cheap whore."

"No, I wasn't, Lee! It was just a mistake we made…"

"Fuck you, Kay. You don't deserve to have children. I won't let you have any."

Nick was taut with concentration now, trying to see what was happening to his son, resolved to do something. The desperation in Kay's voice when she next spoke didn't help him hang on to his composure.

"Lee, please… just let me have my little boy back now. You're scaring me and you're scaring him. We can sit down and talk about things. Please, let Davy come over to me…"

Nick saw her walk towards Lee with her arms held out, then she stopped and screamed: "No, Lee, don't! Please!"

This was too much. It had gone on too long and it had taken a very bad turn. Nick was burning with anger. He straightened up and took a deep breath. He saw Kay ham-fistedly fiddling with her ear and fleetingly wondered why. As she did so she screamed: "Come quickly! Come quickly!" And suddenly to Nick's left, about twenty-five metres away, a figure dashed out from behind a tree. It was wearing a yellow high-vis coat. It only managed to run a few metres before it tripped on something and fell into the undergrowth with a crash. Nick saw a policeman, scrabbling to get up. He saw that Lee was now looking back over his left shoulder, in the direction the noise had come from. He was shouting again.

"Kay, I warned you! I said, no coppers! You lied to me!"

He still had his back to Nick, though. There was a general cacophony of shouts and screams from in front now, and it was very much long past the time for thinking. Nick sprang forward, making straight for Lee's back, imagining cross-hairs between his shoulder blades, and was there almost before he knew he had started running. He forgot about the cross-hairs, bent his knees, lowered a shoulder and caught Lee flush in the lower ribs, wrapping his arms around him and pile-driving him into the ground in a tackle that a rugby player would have been proud of. They grappled and flailed viciously for a few desperate seconds, but Nick had the advantage of surprise and momentum, and he was soon joined by other men – three of them in yellow coats – and then Les got there too. Nick was barged away from Lee by the policemen, who then lunged down to restrain the crazed man on the ground as he shouted and screamed wild obscenities and accusations.

Nick rolled away on the grass and looked for Davy: there he was, metres away in the arms of his sobbing mother. Oh, thank God. He started crawling towards them on all fours, too far gone even to get to his feet. Then a hand grabbed his shirt and dragged him upwards and ran with him towards Kay and Davy, and Nick looked up and saw that it was Les, and a moment later the four of them were joined in an embrace, and nothing else mattered anymore.

CHAPTER NINETEEN

I t was 10.45 p.m. The front room was lit by just the flickering TV; the only sound, low but audible, came from the same source. Nick had stood up to turn it off but instead he first stopped to contemplate his sleeping family: his new dad, over there in the armchair, snoring peacefully next to a mug of cold tea; Kay, his beloved Kay, with their precious little boy curled up against her, slumbering soundlessly apart from an occasional snuffle. Watching them, Nick felt a tingle in his fingertips and at the ends of his toes. He couldn't wish for anything more.

He had just finished watching the TV news, which he had recorded for Kay after she dozed off during the national coverage. The story of the SMAC operation against Maier had made a one-minute report on the regional news, featuring interview clips with Richard Cambridge and Inspector Tomalin. There was nothing at all about the kidnapping of a small boy on the occasion of his second birthday, nor of the stand-off at the woods and its eventual dramatic resolution, involving the have-a-go-hero father of the boy tackling the would-be child snatcher. Thank God no one had mentioned any of that, thought Nick.

It had been a watershed day in many ways. Nick remembered those moments in the embrace of his family out in the clearing between the woods and the wire of the Maier facility: the unbridled joy they had all felt.

But was it joy, or was it another emotion that had surged through their veins at that moment? Perhaps it would be more accurate to say it was relief: that Davy was safe, and that their lives could go on as before. Who knew that relief could feel so good?

It had taken some time to deal with the police formalities after Lee had been arrested and led away, strangely becalmed by that point. He had fallen into a zombie-like state of dumb obedience. He looked dazed, beaten. Things were quiet in Nick's car on the way home. Everyone, it seemed, was examining their emotions, picking over the things that had happened that day, trying to comprehend them. Perhaps they were as exhausted and shocked as Nick felt. The magnitude of what had happened – and of what could have happened – was still sinking in.

As he drove home, he had watched Kay for a few seconds in the car's rear-view mirror, their son snuggled tight against her on the back seat, her eyes staring vacantly out of the window. Nick had wondered about what she had said to Lee, out there in the glare of the sun – about a friend of Lee's having more chance of being father to Davy than Lee himself...

What the hell was that all about? Nick knew nothing about anyone called James. His name had never even been mentioned by Kay, as far as Nick could remember. Had she been having an earlier affair before they had got together? Or had the two situations overlapped? Answers to those questions, and another particularly pertinent one, would have to wait, though: this was not the time to force the subject upon her. He caught Les looking at him from the front passenger seat, clocking that Nick was watching Kay and Davy. Nick smiled tightly at him and focused back on the road ahead.

Back home, Davy had brightened up. There was no party, but he had his toys and birthday presents to occupy him. Still, Nick noticed him glance up at the front door from time to time, with a frown. They had invited Mrs O'Neill over for a drink, to thank her for looking after Jemima earlier in the day. Jemima herself had phoned Kay. She had apologised and then resigned from her job with immediate effect. Though she loved Davy, she said that after what had happened she needed to get away for a while, perhaps to her parents back in Oxfordshire. There were, she said, a lot of things she needed to get straight in her head. Kay wondered about that for a few seconds, remembering Jemima had claimed her father had been lost in a car crash, years before. It turned out to be just another part of Jemima's deception. Despite that, Kay let it go without comment. There were more important things on her mind.

They managed to have a warm and happy evening, with Les in good form, telling funny stories about Kay in her youth. Though his face said it all, he repeated it eight or nine times anyway: he was proud of his daughter, she was the apple of his eye, and despite everything that had happened, this was the best day of his life since the day she had been born. There were tears and apologies about the last 10 years from both father and daughter. Les spent several hours playing with his grandson, until the boy had worn him out.

Upon getting home, Kay had needed a couple of stiff drinks, and then she announced that she intended to leave Maier Science. Not wishing to invite debate on the subject, she immediately insisted that they all play games on the Wii. Much hilarity followed. Later in the evening, as they watched TV, Davy fell asleep on the sofa, and Les was not far behind him. Kay toughed it out until a few minutes after 10 p.m. before she too succumbed. Now, Nick thought, looking at them all, it was time to bring this day to a close.

He switched the TV off and then returned to the sofa to shake Kay awake gently. Her eyes opened slowly, drowsily, but she smiled at him. "Come on, darling, time to get these guys to bed," Nick said softly. Kay staggered to her feet and stretched. Les began to stir in his armchair, and then looked around at his daughter and Nick.

"It's bedtime, Dad," said Kay. He nodded and forced himself up and out of the chair.

"Goodnight, girl," he said, giving her a peck. "I'll see you in the morning. Goodnight, Nick."

"Will you be okay, Dad? Don't need anything?" he asked.

"I'm good, son. See you tomorrow." As Les went through to the spare bedroom, he leaned down to kiss his sleeping grandson.

That left just the three of them. They agreed that Nick would take Davy to bed while Kay cleared away the glasses and dishes. He picked up the boy and carried him up to the main bedroom, where he laid him in the middle of the double bed he shared with Kay. Davy woke up as he was being put down and asked for a bedtime story. Nick retrieved a book from Davy's room and read it to him, watching as his son slid gradually back to sleep. He had expected Kay to come to the bedroom after tidying up but there was no sign of her yet.

For the moment, though, Nick's thoughts were concentrated on Davy. He stood and looked down at his son, and wondered what the boy's future held. Would he suffer in the days, weeks, months, even years to come, from the things he had been through today? Nick was no expert on these matters but it seemed inconceivable to him that there would be no psychological fallout from an experience like this. The police had spoken to them about arranging for a trauma specialist to come and visit the family. Well, they would see how that went, he supposed.

What a day it had been. It had taken all of them to the brink of tragedy; an overwhelming experience. Those moments of fear for Davy and Kay remained so vivid in his mind that Nick could still taste the bile that had risen in his throat. The day had proved to him that he loved this woman and the child they had together more than anything in the world, and that he would fight for their safety without a thought for his own.

Where was Kay, though? He couldn't hear her moving about downstairs. Surely she had already tidied up by now. Nick reluctantly left Davy in the bed on his own and went downstairs. He found Kay sitting at the dining table in the kitchen, resting her chin on her folded hands. He stopped in the doorway.

"Sit down a minute," she said. He sat down opposite her. "Is Davy in bed?"

"Yeah, I just read him a story. What's up?"

"Nothing's up. Well… I don't know if it is or not. I need to tell you something. I knew you'd come down eventually if I waited."

The moment was here already. "James," Nick said flatly.

"It was nothing, Nick, honestly. I was lonely and upset about my marriage. This was before I met you. I had a fling with one of Lee's mates. He was attentive to me and made me feel appreciated. We had a thing going for a few weeks. I stopped it when I met you and realised we were going to be involved. I realised we could have something much better."

Nick responded slowly. "Okay. Okay. You stopped it straight away?"

"Yes."

"There was no overlap?"

"No."

They looked at each other for a few long seconds. Neither of them averted their eyes. Then Nick rose, walked around the table and crouched by Kay's side. He spoke urgently.

"Kay, I need to know, one hundred percent, that there is no chance this James could be in the frame. I need to know, once and for all."

She leaned closer and ruffled his hair. Nick watched her eyes, feeling sure he would see the truth there, whatever words came out of her mouth. He didn't see any panic or shiftiness; just happiness and tiredness.

"I promise you, Nick: Davy is your son. You know that already, of course you do. But I understand that you need to hear me say it. Davy is your son, Nick. I give you my word."

"You're sure?"

"Yes, I can show you on a calendar. I remember it all."

He looked away for a number of seconds, deep in thought. Then he turned back to her and spoke in a clear, measured voice.

"Okay. I have to believe you. I have to accept your word."

Kay took a deep breath and then another one, even deeper. "There's something else, Nick…"

He looked surprised, and she gave him no chance to interject.

"I've been thinking – not just today but for a while really, although today has brought it all into focus for me… I mean, today you managed not only to keep our little family together, but by bringing Dad back into my life, you've actually made it bigger.

"And I want us to make it bigger still. I love you and Davy, and I want us to put all this behind us and give him a little brother or sister. It's been a terrible day but I'm hoping that by telling you this tonight, even though it's been on my mind for a few months, it will mean that we remember today as a good day, and not a terrible one. You don't have to agree to anything now. You've had a shock, I know, hearing about James. I will understand if you need to think about it for a while. But this is what I want most."

"I think it's what I want too," he said. He stared at the wall again, turning things over, sifting through words for the right ones. "I've learned a lot about myself today and my feelings for you and Davy. This James thing… I feel I'm satisfied in my own mind. I trust you. I don't ever want to hear his name again."

He stood and pulled her up from the chair. They hugged, checking in little muffled voices that the other was content. Then Nick patted Kay's behind and said: "Come on – our son has a double bed all to himself."

"Just a minute more," she giggled, but instead Nick picked her up in a single swift movement, as if to carry her over the threshold. She giggled again, in surprise. "What are you doing, babe?"

"I'm taking you to bed, my love. Come on." He carried her out of the kitchen towards the stairs and started to climb them, Kay still giggling and beaming at him.

"Mind you don't put your back out, dear," she warned him, laughing.

"It'll be okay. Nearly there now," he groaned. "Good grief, what have you been eating? Never again…"

"No, you should do this every night. I could get quite used to it."

"I'll carry you six nights a week if you carry me on the seventh."

He had reached the top of the stairs now and went along the corridor to the bedroom, where the sight of Davy in his pyjamas, sleeping peacefully in the middle of their bed, greeted them. Nick put Kay down on the mattress, both of them trying to stifle their mirth so as not to wake the boy.

Soon the room was in darkness, and the giggling gradually subsided. In the silence that followed, Nick could hear Kay and Davy breathing and knew that sleep had overtaken them. What a day it had been. It had ended with the prospect of another baby, though. How about that? Nick stretched one arm protectively across Kay and Davy and before long he had joined them in their dreams.